PRAISE FOR THE INK & SIGIL SERIES

"You are in for a great treat. *Ink and Sigil* is great
escape reading, and I loved every word"
Charlaine Harris, *New York Times* bestselling author

"Kevin Hearne's *Ink & Sigil* is a novel that will transport
you right in the Scottish realm of fey and fairies and
have you thinking the 'other' is real. The magic is both
familiar and new, believable and extraordinary"
Charlie Holmberg, author of *The Paper Magician*

"Kevin Hearne has used ink and paper to craft his own
brand of magic. *Ink & Sigil* is filled to the brim with the
Hearne-anigans we've all grown to love. Fans of ribald
humor, literary puns and the odd hobgoblin will be
enchanted by this paranormal mystery"
Jaye Wells, author of the Prospero's War series

"A delightfully grimy journey through the hidden underworld
of Glasgow, *Ink & Sigil* vividly blends Kevin Hearne's unique
take on urban fantasy with the grit of Scottish magic"
Adam Christopher, author of *Empire State*

BY KEVIN HEARNE

Candle & Crow

BOOK THREE OF THE INK & SIGIL SERIES

KEVIN HEARNE

orbit-books.co.uk

ORBIT

First published in Great Britain in 2024 by Orbit

1 3 5 7 9 10 8 6 4 2

A CIP catalogue record for this book
is available from the British Library.

ISBN 978-0-356-51527-4

Printed and bound in Great Britain by Clays Ltd, Elcograf, S.p.A.

Papers used by Orbit are from well-managed forests
and other responsible sources.

MIX
Paper | Supporting
responsible forestry
FSC® C104740

Orbit
An imprint of
Little, Brown Book Group
Carmelite House
50 Victoria Embankment
London EC4Y 0DZ

An Hachette UK Company
www.hachette.co.uk

orbit-books.co.uk

For Dirk, Nick, & Abe:

Thanks for all the shenanigans.

AUTHOR'S NOTE

For those of ye who are completists, ye may wish to know of a story that occurs contemporaneously with the beginning of this novel: It's called *The Chartreuse Chanteuse,* and it basically gives you the happy-ever-after for Atticus, Oberon, and Starbuck from the Iron Druid Chronicles. It's narrated by Oberon, and its events play out over the same weekend as Chapters 1 and 2 of this book. By the time Al sees them again in Chapter 10, they're already in their happy place. You can find *The Chartreuse Chanteuse* in print, ebook, or audio in a wee collection of novellas called *Canines & Cocktails.*

As in the other books of this series, you're going to encounter a fair amount of Scots language and spellings. I did not attempt to accurately portray the fullness of Weegie Scots but rather give you just enough to ground you in that sense of place without drowning you in unfamiliar language. There is also a character from Stornoway, which is a different dialect with its own distinct accent, but their spellings are typically standard.

Here we go:

Ye is not pronounced with a long *e* sound. It's more like *yuh,* never *yee*. This changes to *ya* when calling someone a name, as in "*ya* shite bastard." Occasionally you will also see *you*, when the speaker wishes to emphasize it or be formal. *Your* is spelled *yer* to reflect its pronunciation, as is *ye're*, because otherwise ye might think it's pronounced like *yore*, and we cannae have that.

Cannae is pronounced like *canny* and it means *cannot*. *Not* is rarely used. If at the end of a contraction such as *didn't* or *wouldn't*, the contraction is eliminated and a suffix is appended instead; it's spelled as *nae*, pronounced like *knee*. So *didn't* becomes *didnae*, and *wouldn't* becomes *wouldnae*. Exceptions are *don't* and *won't*, which are used as in standard English. (*Dinnae* is used throughout much of Scotland instead of *don't*, but not in Glasgow, which has a well-documented exception known as "the Dinnae Gap.") If the word *not* would normally just be doing its thing solo, the *t* is often eliminated at the end and it's pronounced as you might imagine, as *no*. To make up for these extra no's which are nots, Weegies often opt to say *naw* when they mean *no*.

The *v* is sometimes omitted from the word *give* and you're left with *gie*, pronounced as *ghee*. Shall we practice what we've learned so far? "Naw, ye didnae gie yer wee brother a beer, did ye, ya daft choob? That's no right."

To is spelled *tae* and pronounced like *tea*. For fun, this is changed when used in verb phrases like *going to*. In U.S. English they're contracted into *gonna*, but in Weegie, Scots pronounce that ending vowel as a long *a*, so I've appended a *y* to the end to indicate that. "Gie me a fiver, I'm gonnay go tae the store."

Head and *dead* are spelled as *heid* and *deid* and pronounced as *heed* and *deed*. "Yer pet rock is deid. Happened so suddenly, I cannae get ma heid around it."

My is often pronounced as *ma*, so it's spelled accordingly.

The abbreviation for mother is *maw*; for father, we have two options: *da* instead of *dad*, and *faither* instead of *father*. Pronounce that like *feather*, but with a long *a* sound: FAY ther.

Ready for some slang terms?

Dingie is a verb meaning to ditch or snub someone; it's often used in the way that Americans use the verb *ghost* now.

Grass you up means to snitch or inform the police of someone's activities.

Up tae high doh means that you're very excited or keyed up about something—sometimes with the connotation of being nervous or anxious. "I'm up tae high doh about that exam; no sure I did well."

Dae ma heid in means that you're annoyed or exasperated.

Hackit means ugly; *crabbit* means crabby.

Clatty is an adjective meaning disgusting.

Howling has nothing to do with wolves or noise; it means smelly.

Lavvy heid means toilet head, because of the abbreviation of lavatory. This is an excellent way to call someone a shithead, and I think we should all start using it.

A *roaster* is a person who makes a fool of themselves.

A *stooshie* is a minor row or commotion.

Get tae fuck is the Weegie method of telling someone to fuck off.

And my favorite is *coupon*, pronounced like *coup-in*, which means *face*. This is very specific to Glasgow, owing to the old tram cars in the city where tickets—called coupons—would have to be punched. And since the thing most likely to be punched besides a coupon in Glasgow was a face, *coupon* came to mean *face* in that city.

Shall we review? "Shut yer hackit coupon and get tae fuck, ya howling, clatty lavvy heid!"

Late in the book you're going to run into some Polish names, which to the English reader can look impossible to pronounce. They're full of digraphs like *sz* and *cz*, they switch the pronunciations of *w* and *v*, and *ł* is also pronounced like a *w*. One fellow's surname is Szczygiel, and you might look at that and think I'm trying to mess with you. I swear I'm not. I'm trying to mess with my audiobook narrator. I mean, I picked a school named Szcze-brzeszyn. He might actually sprain his tongue on that one, but probably not, because he's awesome.

Hope you enjoy this conclusion to the Ink & Sigil series. Thanks so much for reading.

CHAPTER 1

A Pint at the Place Where They Met Last

The thing nobody tells you about having a hobgoblin contractually bound to your service is that you can't make plans. Well—you can *make* them, I suppose. But following through is going to be difficult, because you'll find that he's smeared bacon grease in the underwear you put on after showering, and now you have to shower again and resign yourself to being late. (I pride myself on punctuality, but when the choices are to be late or to be on time and sit down with greasy bacon bollocks, the schedule's going out the window.)

The reason nobody told me about the thing with hobgoblins is that nobody has them in their service anymore, and I was learning why almost daily.

Hobgoblins were expected to take the piss out of their employers a little bit; there had to be a downside to employing them, or else everyone would want a teleporting errand boy. The problem was that *a little bit* was very subjective, and Buck Foi and I had vastly different ideas about what it meant. Buck wanted to become a legend among his kind and make service to humans common again, so he approached all of his duties—including piss-taking—

with the idea that it had to be legendary. It did mean that he did what I asked him to do infallibly, albeit with much complaining. But it also meant that I could never, ever relax, because he was always planning how best to mess with me next.

I'd demanded that he must be creative and nondestructive in his piss-taking, in the hopes that my property would survive and perhaps it would slow him down. He was proving to be more creative than I'd anticipated. And largely nondestructive, I must admit, save for that pair of ruined underwear.

Though I feared he might be destroying himself. He'd been drinking an awful lot and had recently discovered that hobgoblins could get high on capsaicin, the chemical that provided the heat in any pepper you'd care to name. He'd never enjoyed a curry in all his many years or he'd have learned it earlier, but a trip to a Mexican restaurant in Philadelphia revealed this one weird trick to get a hobgoblin smashed. Between salsa chugging and whisky guzzling, he was often off his nut. As he was now, giggling at his prank until he fell over, all too easily.

[You need to cut back on the bottle, Buck,] I told him, or rather typed into my text-to-speech app. [I'm getting worried. There has to be some reason you're doing this to yourself. Should I make an appointment with a therapist?]

"Wot? Naw. Wait, are ye serious? Naw, I know what's in ma heid. I mean, everybody's staring at their future and wonderin' if their past is gonnay be a good show or a laugh, in't they? There's no need to state the obvious to a stranger."

That was not anything close to the sort of answer I expected. [Are you saying you're worried about your legacy and that's driving you to drink?]

"Naw. Yes? Naw! Well, maybe."

[We'll talk more later since I have to go, but in the meantime, consider the possibility that your legacy might become "drunken sot" and whether you have any power to ensure that doesn't happen.]

He scrunched up his face in annoyance. "God's grundle, ol' man, can ye be any more of a wet grey sock?"

[I'm being a friend to you now. If you don't have any power to stop, we'll approach it differently.]

"Are ye ordering me tae stop?"

[No, I'm ordering you to think about it. Be self-aware and honest about what you're doing. We'll come back to it.]

He might well be in the grips of alcoholism already, but his answer—a bit vague—hinted that he had a trunk of feelings to unpack and he was drinking to avoid doing that work. If I could get him to begin, there was a chance he'd realize he could simply leave the booze out. That might be considered foolish optimism by some, but it was born out of personal experience. In the aftermath of Josephine's death, I gulped down way too much whisky, making the same mistake countless others had, thinking that I could drown my grief in alcohol. But three straight blackout nights had me feeling worse, not better, and the grief was still fresh and relentlessly pummeled my spirit. I had to try something different. It hurt, feeling so raw and bereft with nothing to dull the pain, but I didn't touch a drop for a year and came out the other side confident that I could manage myself. After that I only drank socially, never getting drunk again. I wanted Buck to have the chance to fix it himself, but if he couldn't, I'd help—or get him help—as needed.

I left him cursing and shut the door to my flat, because I did have a meeting to attend. He'd think about it for sure, though, and I would no longer take clean underwear for granted but consider them the sweet blessing that formed the basis of all my prosperity. Look at the two of us: growing.

The meeting was thankfully the informal kind, and my lateness would be excused. I had hoped to have a long, full weekend after my return from Australia to work on the problem of my twin curses, but an unexpected text came through Friday morning before I could fully dedicate myself to research.

Al! Saxon here. I'm back. New number. Fancy a pint this evening at the place we last met?

Saxon Codpiece, returned already from his self-imposed exile? I'd expected another month of radio silence at the least, since he'd mentioned that he may have accessed some government files in addition to doing some highly illegal hacking for me. I gave it a think before agreeing.

Friday night, the pubs would be crowded full of the young, drunk, and horny, though if we went early enough people shouldn't be too sloppy. Once in a while a young woman would take in my cashmere topcoat and impeccable tidiness and flirt with me, briefly, before realizing I was not the sugar daddy she was looking for. Those ephemeral interludes weren't bothersome in themselves, but more than once they had spurred a young man nearby to challenge me, since he had already decided the young woman was his and therefore she could not flirt with whomever she chose. It never ended well for the young man, but neither did it end well for me, as it robbed the evening of any meager pleasure I might have wrung out of it. But the place we'd last met, the German Bier Halle, was more about the food and beer than hookups. It should be safe.

Sure. Seven? I asked him. The reply was immediate.

Stonking, mate. See you then.

Having been thus derailed, catching up with the minutiae of the printshop consumed my day, and I resigned myself to working on my curses over the weekend. There was plenty to do, since both Nadia and I, as well as Gladys Who Has Seen Some Shite, had been absent, and the latter wasn't to return until Monday.

Since Saxon was a wanted man, it behooved me to be circumspect, so when the hour arrived, I donned my bowler hat painted with the black Sigil of Swallowed Light, which disabled cameras, and I took my cane, a carbon-steel number, which was a weapon that a man in his sixties could carry around in plain sight and not cause comment. I didn't expect to need it, but one never knew.

On my way down to the street, I made sure to check my coat

pocket for the particular fountain pen and sigil supplies I'd brought from the office, because I knew that Saxon would want a certain sigil in payment for any service he rendered me. Not that I required his services at the moment: It was simply best to be prepared. I was relieved to find everything in place, including the sigils I called my "official ID" and some others that I took with me wherever I went. Buck wasn't supposed to mess with my inks and sigils, because they kept us safe and paying the bills—it was a red line he couldn't cross. I worried he would cross it anyway.

The red line I wasn't supposed to cross with him was to mention his former name: Gag Badhump. He never spoke of his family—I didn't even know if they were alive—and I wondered if that might have something to do with his frequent inebriation. It was something to pursue, if I could manage it discreetly.

A few minutes' brisk walk brought me to the Bier Halle on Gordon Street, a green-awninged affair that proclaimed in punny white letters that IT'LL ALL END IN BIERS! This was the place where we last met, before Saxon scarpered off to lay low. The entrance was a staircase leading down to the underground establishment, and it occurred to me that, more often than not, Saxon preferred to meet me in subterranean digs.

He was easy enough to find, since he was taller than nearly everyone, even while sitting, and he waved at me from a corner booth. I removed my coat, folded it over my left arm, and joined him.

"Awright, Al?" he said, offering a hand to shake. I nodded and shook hands, taking him in. He was dressed smartly in what looked like tailored business attire of light browns and blues, and that was unusual enough that I wagged a finger up and down and raised an eyebrow. "Oh, this? Bit different from ma anarchist kit, eh? Yeah. I'm rebranding. It's why I wanted a chin wag."

He already had a beer on the table, and when the server swung by, I pointed at it and gave a thumbs-up to indicate that I wanted the same. While she went to fetch that, we had a look at the menu and upon her return ordered a couple of pizzas, which were small enough for one or two people. Saxon ordered for me so I didn't have to speak—the curse that made people despise me after hearing my voice for too long wouldn't affect the server anytime soon, but there was a chance it would trigger with Saxon if I wasn't sparing with my words around him. I got the pepperoni and hot honey, and he asked for a Balmoral, which included haggis, roast chicken, and parmesan.

Once that was taken care of, I got out my phone so I'd be able to talk to him. I used Signal instead of my text-to-speech app, because the phone's weak speaker might not be heard well above the din of the bar. *Thought you'd be gone longer,* I typed, and his phone lit up and pinged.

"Naw, I just needed time tae disappear without a trace and set up a new operation, in case anyone was on tae me. Basic criminal hygiene. The paranoid lads stay out of the clink, aye? If any coppers got a whiff of ma trail, they'll have tae start all over, because Saxon Codpiece has gone dark. I've got new businesses, new shell corporations and accounts, and a new name. Check it out." He produced a business card from his waistcoat pocket and placed it on the table. It said, *Norman! Pøøts!* Which made me snigger involuntarily, and that may have been the point. Saxon may be rebranding, but in terms of choosing a strange yet memorable name he remained consistent.

I appreciate the joke in going from Saxon to Norman, I sent to him, *but I am pretty sure that surname is not allowed.*

"How d'ye mean, not allowed?"

I mean your spelling. You're using the Swedish o with a slash through it, and that is never doubled.

"It is too! In the credits for *Monty Python and the Holy Grail* there's a whole section about møøse."

Is it pronounced any differently?

"Of course! If you use regular o's it's just *poots,* which rhymes with boots and toots and fruits. But use the o with a slash and it's pronounced like *bleu* in bleu cheese. So listen, Al: Poots. Pøøts. Hear the difference?"

That's a very subtle distinction.

"And one that I'm gonnay have endless fun with, making people say Pøøts over and over until I'm satisfied. Or not. If I tell someone they cannae say it correctly and tae just no even try anymore, I bet that'll do lasting damage tae their psyche."

You have ID with that name on it?

"Oh, aye. Got back intae the country on a new passport. Saxon Codpiece is never coming back from Argentina."

Impressive. I tapped the card a couple of times and typed quickly. *I note you have changed your profession.*

On his old card, he'd proclaimed to be a professional wanker. The new card said, *Security Consultant.*

"Yeah, it's ma legal fig leaf for all the illegal shite I can do for ye. I've been learning a lot about money laundering from the trafficking numpties ye had me track down—and I've got some new ones for ye, by the way."

He produced a folder that was fairly thick. "This is all obtained illegally, so ye have tae say this is an anonymous tip. But these guys are just a shower of bastards. Ye get them, that's probably half of Glasgow's trafficking in one go. Frees a lot of people— they're not all women pushed intae sex work. They got men and kids too in different industries. And that has tae be the focus, same as before: The victims get helped, no punished."

I'll pass it on.

"Grand. So what ye been up to?"

Shenanigans in Australia. Just got back yesterday.

"Oh, aye? Did ye see any of those huge spiders?"

We did see some unusually large animals, yes.

"And was it a profitable trip? Any contraband ye need washed clean?"

I don't need anything done, but Nadia might soon.

"That's some braw news! Nadia's the best. You've seen her wizard van, right?"

Aye.

"I've been meaning tae ask: Ye know that god she has on the

one side, and he's eating guys on a skewer like they're kebabs?" I nodded, because one could hardly unsee a painting like that. "Good. So I've been wondering: Why is he sitting on a throne of cheese?"

First, it's delicious. And second, if you're a god, you can sit on anything you like, so why not?

"Right, of course," Saxon said, nodding agreeably. "I just wondered if there was a specific reason for it to be made of cheese rather than, say, chocolate, or Margaret Thatcher's bones."

Oh! Yes, there is. Nadia told me it symbolizes the fat of the land.

"Love it! That's perfect. The more I hear about Lhurnog, the more I like him."

I made no comment, content to let that part of the conversation die on the vine. Lhurnog the Unhallowed was not the sort of deity you wanted to wake up with offerings and prayers. He might want more offerings than one could reasonably provide—or, worse, decide to indulge his craving for the flesh of men.

Which, I supposed after further reflection, meant that there would be some people who might like to wake him up immediately.

Our pizzas arrived quickly, and seeing that the place was humming at capacity, we ordered another pint, since the server might not be around again soon. We tucked in, and I discovered that the pepperoni and hot honey was fantastic. I'd have to make the effort to visit more often, and not only when I needed to meet my freelance hacker.

Norman was entertaining me with stories of his ill-advised taco experiments in Argentina when a man entered the pub wearing a burgundy silk shirt open to his navel. Gold chains gleamed on his waxed chest, and a wholly unnecessary but clearly expensive watch on his wrist caught the light. He was trailed by three women in clinging outfits who could not possibly be interested in him for his good looks, because he was, in the parlance of *Hot Fuzz*, fuck ugly—the sort of misshapen visage you expect to see when you pull the shroud off the portrait of Dorian Gray. My suspicions were further aroused by men behind them with tailored jackets and earpieces; they were hired muscle, and the slick silk man had hired them.

Norman saw that my attention had drifted, followed my gaze, and made a small sound of surprise. "He's in the folder," he said, and tapped it for emphasis.

Which immediately clicked. Silk Man was a human trafficker, and the women trailing him were most likely working for him under duress. I wanted him taken down immediately, before even confirming who and what he was—he had the vibe of a truly evil wanker, because who else wears silk and gold like that? But it was crowded, and the likelihood of collateral damage was high. And furthermore, I'm not really supposed to use my powers as a sigil agent on mundane enforcement of human laws. The right move would be to make no comment, do nothing, and simply turn over the folder to the police—he'd be taken down properly.

Well, I made no comment.

But he saw Norman and me staring at him with looks of distaste and stopped his parade to scowl down at us, looking to his left while keeping his body on track. He didn't think this would take long.

"What ye lookin' at, ol' man?"

I didn't reply, but I deliberately put my phone away and sat up straight on the bench seating, eventually resting both my hands on top of my cane, which I stood centered between my knees. Nonthreatening, a bit defensive. Except my eyes never left his while I made these adjustments. He knew it was a challenge. Because if I was going to submit, I'd have looked away.

Since I'd squared up, he squared up too, turning his body to face me. I'd earned his full attention.

"Ye want that mustache punched off yer face?"

There was no way he could punch me that well. I simply kept staring at him with withering contempt, waiting for him to do something besides shout. Norman was playing along, saying nothing but laying down a pretty good menacing glare. When the bampot made a fist and pulled it back, I didn't wait to see if he was going to let fly or try to make me flinch. I kept my left hand on top of my cane, dropped the right one down the shaft, and pushed up and out, delivering a quick strike to his undercarriage from below. He wasn't wearing a cup, and he instantly forgot about my mustache. Reflexively, he curled inward and bent forward, which allowed me to shove the top of my cane underneath his chin, a neat uppercut trick that didn't involve me bruising my knuckles. That got him to stagger back, but I didn't want him to fall into the table across from us, so I rose and quickly administered a bonus tap to his temple—not enough to shatter his skull, but enough to knock him out and send him sprawling in the space between tables rather than into someone's dinner.

Plenty of gasping and exclamations followed this, and Norman was quick to stand and use that height of his to bellow commandingly, "It's awright! Nae bother! He just fucked around and found out, that's all."

Except there was a bother: The hired goons had become aware that this was the sort of situation for which they had been paid to be useful. Even if the boss was unconscious, they had to do something. And they were hyperaware of what I could do with the cane, so I couldn't surprise them. They were pushing the women out of the way to get to me, but said women were just enough of an obstacle to allow me time to produce my official ID and hold it up in front of their eyes. Sigils of Porous Mind, Certain Authority, and Quick Compliance short-circuited their urge to violence, and, coupled with my growl, it saved me a messy fight.

"Leave it," I said. "Get out of ma way and take care of yer boss."

Phones were being pointed in my direction and then furiously tapped when the cameras failed to work. The sigils on my hat were doing their job. Norman threw some assorted notes down on the table, I picked up the folder full of incriminating evidence, and we exited.

I'd make sure to turn over the folder. The Silk Man might have been given a small taste of the justice he was due, but there was zero chance that I'd knocked all the bastard out of him.

"We never got our second round," Norman said when we emerged onto Gordon Street. "Shame about that."

I wouldn't have minded getting a doggie bag for my pizza, I told him.

"Right? Well, that's a Friday night in Glasgow for ye."

Was he trying to do business in there?

"What, with the women? Nah. Too early. Probably he was buying them dinner tae show them what a kind and generous trafficker he is. A little team meeting before the shift starts."

You didn't bring me in there knowing he would show up, did you?

"Eh? Naw, naw, I'd no do that tae ye. Utter coincidence, I swear. I just recognized the face from his pictures, because it's the kind of face ye remember in yer nightmares."

That was true enough. *Okay. We'd better go. Thanks for the pint. Catch ye.*

We parted with a wave and went in opposite directions, the folder feeling heavy in my hand. Part of me wanted to turn it over straightaway, but it would be wiser to wait until Monday, providing a nice vague window of time in which I could have acquired it, should anyone look into it—and I was fairly certain someone would. Helping the police do their jobs often seemed to earn investigation instead of gratitude, but they did get around to doing the right thing when you gave them sufficient evidence.

It was good to have Norman back, and even better that he had tweaked his business model, but I hoped we wouldn't need his services anytime soon.

And, of course, since I'd had the gall to go around hoping, I got a text that smashed my hopes to bits.

CHAPTER 2

The Importance of a Good Alibi

While I'd been out seeing Norman, Nadia (and perhaps Buck) had been meeting somewhere with Roxanne, the new incarnation of the Morrigan, the old Irish goddess. She'd decided she didn't like the land of the dead, but rather than manifest as her old self, she chose to possess the body of an Australian woman an instant after her death and basically wear a new meat suit to walk the world incognito. This became my problem because she also chose to accompany us to Glasgow—eschewing her old haunts of Ireland, where she'd be pressured into being the deity she used to be—and she expected us to set her up with god-level real estate, even though she was trying not to be a goddess anymore. To finance that, Nadia and Buck were going to pull off a heist, and since we all had a greater chance of surviving that than of telling the Morrigan *no*, I quashed my protesting scruples. But the text I got told me it would be tomorrow, much sooner than I'd hoped.

Already? I asked via Signal. Nadia replied via voice message on the same app.

"Roxanne doesnae want tae wait. She's worried that someone

else with a few million pounds will come in and buy that castle up in Milngavie. So we're gonnay hit a few places and fill up the wizard van with the ill-gotten gains of capitalists, and then I get tae do some creative accounting and we'll acquire a luxury property for a death goddess, which is some shite I've always wanted tae do—I mean, what goth worth the name wouldnae want tae put that on her CV? And, Boss? Make sure ye delete this recording, yeah? It's the sort of thing that gets the prosecution excited."

I'll go to the shop, then, and work in plain view of the security cameras. I have to revisit some old files.

Nadia's reply was quick. "Aw, shite, ye're gonnay go mucking about and get distracted when ye find a random file like the ghosts of the Brontë sisters on the English moors, aren't ye?"

Probably. Sorry. But it has to be done. Gladys Who Has Seen Some Shite and Ogma are arriving on Monday, and we both know that's going to demand our attention. The fallout from my recent sojourn to Australia meant that I would not only have a deity to deal with first thing, but also my receptionist, who somehow commanded the respect of said deity and had no business being a receptionist. *This is my only chance to do some work without interruption.*

"Awright. Good luck, Boss."

I frowned at my phone. If Roxanne and Nadia were going to be in the wizard van together—probably chatting while Buck Foi teleported in and out of vaults—the chances of them not discussing Lhurnog the Unhallowed were slim. But there was very little I could do about it.

I shuddered, thinking about the consequences. When it was just Nadia and her partner, Dhanya, who believed in Lhurnog—they'd essentially made him up out of whole cloth—there'd been little need to worry. But recently Buck had become an ardent convert and liked to give offerings of "whisky and cheese for the gob of Lhurnog" and wished to know more of his mysteries. Initially Nadia's answer had been, "I don't know," which I found entirely satisfactory, but Buck kept agitating and encouraging her to come up with some holy writ and formalized rituals of worship beyond what she already had, and that was a path down which many people might meet an unsavory end.

The precise number of worshippers required to make a god manifest was unknown, but I (and many as-yet-uneaten men) would prefer that Lhurnog never got close to the threshold. When I overheard Nadia telling Buck that Lhurnog ate violent men specifically, preferring warmongers and murderers but never saying no to a light snack of domestic abusers, I relaxed only a tiny bit. I might not be first on the menu, but such a deity could potentially become very popular. A god who eats violence and thereby brings peace? Millions, if not billions, might worship such a being, and that was the very point Buck was making to Nadia. If I told either of them to shut it, however—that all this mucking about with the power of faith was dangerous—they'd persist or even redouble their efforts just to spite me. And then, if Lhurnog manifested, I'd have to confront him myself as the sigil agent for Europe and get him to sign a contract wherein he agreed not to visit this plane to eat delicious warmongers—a rendezvous that might well recast me as lunch. So I had to pretend I wasn't concerned, keep them busy, and hope that other issues would distract them from proceeding.

Nadia did have issues. She was already a battle seer and constantly struggling with the fact that she was a demigoddess born of her mother's adulterous affair with an unknown member of the Hindu pantheon. That was looming large in her mind, since she believed that her powers were only growing. And that worried me too, since if they did keep growing, she would eventually wonder why she was working for me. Plus, power did things to people, and we were both aware from experience that it rarely made them kinder and more empathetic. Dolly Parton was a notable exception, but we both knew that Nadia wasn't Dolly. So we had cause to be concerned.

"It suggests that I'm supposed tae have a destiny or sumhin," Nadia told me, "and destiny can get tae fuck. I'm tryin' tae do ma own thing. Gods doing god shite are no fun, but accountants who win pit fights are unexpected. They can do anything because ye never see it coming. And they're no burdened with the responsibility of, ye know, being a fucking god."

That instinctive rejection of godhood was probably a large part of why Nadia was also the new best friend of Roxanne. On the one hand, I was grateful for that, because I'd rather not deal with Roxanne if I didn't have to, and Roxanne's demands would keep Nadia too busy to compose the sacred texts of her man-eating deity. On the other hand, spending so much time with a goddess who had a pretty decent idea of how much faith it took to make a god manifest could lead to a discussion of how to usher Lhurnog the Unhallowed from the realms of imagination to reality.

I had few good choices except to go home and get some sleep. Buck was out—a fact, since the TV was off, the couch unoccupied and not benighted with stray kernels of popcorn—and that left me with a general worry about what trouble he was getting into that would eventually be laid at my feet. I briefly considered checking on him but decided not to nag. I didn't need him at the moment, and he was most likely planning the heist with Nadia and Roxanne.

In the morning I could hear him snoring, even through his bedroom door. I did my best to be quiet and let him sleep. If he was late for the heist, so be it. But I would not be late for my research and the establishment of my alibi.

When I arrived at MacBharrais Printing & Binding, I made certain to say hello to the press foreman and the operators, giving them a friendly wave and asking if I could get them coffee or anything. They were used to seeing me once a week in my office, where we'd have a drink and chat and I'd ask if I could do anything to make their jobs easier. They worked exceptionally hard and kept my legitimate business profitable, so I went out of my way to make sure they felt appreciated. Being solicitous wasn't unusual behavior, then, but coming in on the weekend was, and I wanted them to note that.

I made doubly sure that the security cameras were recording in the lobby before I began my work. Behind the receptionist's desk and counterspace—a wide sort of bar that could seat four people if you put stools there—was a wall of nine grey filing cabinets. They were locked and warded, with my key providing the method of bypassing both.

The filing system for treaties and contracts with extraplanar persons or entities with supernatural abilities was sorted alphabetically by pantheon or type of creature. I had numerous documents filed under *the Norse,* for example, but also the Accords of Rome filed under *Vampires,* since their leadership was based there and that was part of my territory. The additions or revisions to these files were sorted chronologically, which would help me ascertain whether there might be some sort of addenda from eleven or twelve years ago that earned me a pair of curses.

I had, of course, reviewed my activities from the year in question previously and found nothing. I was hoping that these raw files might jog a memory that I hadn't bothered to note otherwise—something I'd seen as insignificant at the time might, with hindsight, prove to have been a crucial mistake.

It was at such moments that I wished I had my work digitized and electronically searchable. But at all other moments I was glad that I didn't have to worry about hackers like Norman Pøøts breaking into these files and then having the entire Internet conclude, based on the contracts, that humanity was on the brink of annihilation.

We always are, to be clear: It's just better if people don't think about it.

With a sigh, I pulled open the topmost drawer on the left and beheld the first file: Austria. Some kobold citations and a one-page affirmation from 1853 in which a stollenwurm, most likely long deceased by now, agreed to stop prowling around the Alps and suckling on the udders of scandalized cows. Some culling of these old files might be in order.

But that would take time I didn't have. I'd need to confirm the stollenwurm was dead, and that would be a bit like proving a negative at this point. I had to ruthlessly move on, looking for a plausible triggering event from eleven years ago that would cause some powerful magic users—maybe gods—to cast twin curses on me.

It took me until lunch just to get to the G's, because my review of the files kept presenting me with things that I'd need to work on later, like the case of the djinn that went missing twenty years ago and had yet to resurface. Some treaties with various creatures and pantheons were decades (if not centuries) old and could use some updating. Seeing no other choice, I started a to-do list, using a Diplomat Aero pen with an ink I didn't make myself, the shinkai blue-grey from the iroshizuku collection by Pilot. Fantastic shading when it dried.

The Greeks—a file I kept separate from the Romans, even though they were essentially the same pantheon wearing different cloaks—were full of little addenda and admonitions. Seized by an acute case of double entendre, I noted that Zeus kept coming down from Olympus; he was a very seedy character. And since he set such a poor example, plenty of the other deities messed around with mortals more than they should.

My admonitions and pleas to uphold their side of the treaty were, so far as I could tell, met with an eyeroll and "whatever, mortal," instead of shaken fists and promises that I would rue the day I dared to defy them. Aphrodite liked to go to Fashion Week in Milan in something diaphanous and leave everyone feeling excessively horny and wondering who she was wearing. That would be fine except that none of the designers knew who she was or what was going on, and because her outfits were not part of any collection, she never had her photos published. Modeling agencies burned to sign her, sensing correctly that she could be internationally famous and command extraordinary fees. She'd laughed at me when I said her visits were disruptive. Her voice was honey and strawberries and cream.

"It does no lasting harm and you know it, Mr. MacBharrais.

Zeus is disruptive, siring children hither and thither. Ares is disruptive, surreptitiously stirring war wherever he can. Poseidon's earthquakes and the volcanic tantrums of Hephaestus are disruptive. Some embarrassing erections in Milan are nothing."

She had a point. But I'd already spoken to those other gods as occasion demanded. "I'm simply enforcing the treaty equally," I'd told her, and she nodded indulgently and took her punishment, which was some pain triggered by the Sigil of Dire Consequence on the treaty she had signed. I got the feeling that her antics were calculated to see if I treated her differently from the others, who did more-egregious things.

I ducked downstairs to the break room to avail myself of the peanut butter and preserves. A quick sandwich and back to the files I went—I wanted to spend as much time in front of the camera as possible.

It was a frustrating albeit not fruitless morning. I had an excellent to-do list by the end of it but no idea who had cursed me. Working on the to-do list might distract me from the fact that, owing to the curse, I had not spoken to my son or seen my grandchildren in years. I was now out of ideas and looking into a pit of endless despair, wondering if I might as well dive in headfirst. I felt as if I were lost in a cave without a torch, directionless and bereft of hope.

But at least I had an excellent alibi, which I needed, judging by the Signal I got midafternoon.

Job completed, Boss. We need a place to stash six million in gold and cash. It can't stay in the van, Nadia sent. *Can we store it in your secret ink-and-sigil room?*

No way. Don't come anywhere near the office with a van full of stolen money. Contact Norman.

Who?

Saxon. He's Norman now. I'll send you his new number. And I hope you have an alibi for all this. They're going to find your van on camera.

Do ye think I'm a daft gobshite? I've got it sorted. Delete these.

Buck arrived home shortly after I did, while I was whipping up some dinner. His key scratched at the lock for a bit before succeeding, and when he staggered in, he was wobbly-kneed and shaking. He was wearing my bowler hat with the Sigil of Swallowed Light on it, which I didn't recall lending to him.

"Ach, I'm so shagged out, MacBharrais. Feel like I volunteered tae get pumped by a whole football team and they neglected tae pull down ma pants first."

[Sit,] I told him with my voice app. I got him a sports drink of some kind—full of electrolytes and such—and placed it on the kitchen island. Rather than leap up to a stool as he normally would, he climbed one with performative grunting.

"Hnngh. Urrgh. Aggh."

[I get it. You're tired.]

"Woe is me, damn it. Heists are draining. I should have carbloaded beforehand. Five bagels and an orange juice or sumhin, tell ma pancreas fuck you, deal with it."

[No problems, though?]

"Naw. Roxanne seemed pleased. I mean, as much as she can seem pleased, which isnae much. But her eyes didnae glow red even once, and I think a corner of her mouth twitched upward, just for a nanosecond, before it realized she might feel it and cut that shite out right away."

[You want some food?]

"Aye, pour it down ma gob. What ye making?"

[Salmon tataki.]

"Wot?"

[Just eat whatever I put in front of you. So what's Nadia doing for an alibi?]

"She and Roxanne were doing a taste test of Glasgow's various takeaways. She parks in front of a chip van or whatever and goes tae get some food, asking for a receipt. So she's on any cameras they have plus has the timestamped receipts. Meanwhile, I teleport intae vaults, take some shite, and pop right back in the van. I'm never on the streets, never on camera. Even when she drove by our flat here, I had tae teleport from the van intae the hall-way."

[So where is she taking the van?]

"Tae meet Norman somewhere out of town. They'll transfer all the shite tae him; she drives home clean."

[A legendary heist, so long as you don't get caught.]

"Aye, that's always the trick."

He went to bed well pleased with himself and slept in until past noon on Sunday. I relaxed for once myself and read a book, one with a deckled edge that added a tactile pleasure to the experi-ence. I figured I should take the opportunity, for the next day would not be nearly so relaxing.

CHAPTER 3

The Case of the Missing Receptionist

The way Monday was supposed to go was like this: I'd walk into my printshop a few minutes past nine; Gladys Who Has Seen Some Shite would be there; I'd nip down to the break room for a coffee and a Danish and then present myself to be bombarded by whatever Nadia or Gladys needed from me. The petulant god who'd lured me and the other sigil agents to Australia in hopes of killing the Iron Druid would present himself for punishment to Gladys, and I might finally find out why my receptionist had the ability to judge and mete out punishments to gods.

But it didn't go like that.

Gladys Who Has Seen Some Shite wasn't there. And there wasn't any Danish in the break room. I checked—right after I walked in, saw Ogma sitting on the uncomfortable vinyl chairs we bought to punish salesmen who arrived too early, and ducked downstairs to find Nadia glowering at me. She was dressed like a goth high priestess and really knew how to lay down a proper glower, so I felt a small thrill of fear before I recalled that she needed me around to sign the paychecks.

"Where the fuck is Gladys Who Has Seen Some Shite?" she hissed at me.

I shrugged.

"That's no gonnay cut it, Al. There's a murdery god in the lobby and we're fresh out of Danish."

Getting out my phone, I typed, [Surely we can get some?]

"How about we get our receptionist instead?"

[So call her.]

"I already did. I got no answer. You call her."

Nodding once, I went to my contacts and thumbed her number. The call went straight to voicemail, and her greeting started out posh and English but devolved into colloquial Canadian at the end.

"Hello, darling. Please forgive me, I'm doing something fabulous at the moment. We'll talk later, eh? You hoser."

I hung up without leaving a message and threw up my hands in helplessness.

"What do we do? I don't want tae talk tae him."

[I don't think you should.]

"So . . . what, we just go upstairs and go tae our offices and ignore him?"

[That's my plan.]

"Don't ye have tae play host? Is that no yer job?"

[He's not here to see me. I have zero desire to make him feel comfortable.]

"Right? Cause he's an arsehole, in't he?"

[He is. Coffee?]

"Hells yes."

[Regarding your weekend adventures: You have a story ready?]

"Aye. Told ye I would. And Norman's on top of the laundry. No worries, Boss. Unless it's from Buck."

[Why would I need to worry about Buck?]

"More like why would ye no worry about him, yeah?"

[Good point. I'll make sure he's buttoned up. And if Gladys

doesn't show up soon, I'm going to have a temp agency send over someone.]

"Aye, good idea. I sure as hell don't want tae be sitting down there having that bastard stare at me."

[Maybe I'll ask them to bring over some Danish.]

"Yes! We'll reimburse them."

Coffee secured, we went upstairs to the lobby, delivered curt nods to Ogma, and noticed that he studiously ignored us. We passed on through to the shop and then up to our offices, and I called the temp agency right away. It would take some time for someone to arrive, and even if Gladys Who Has Seen Some Shite showed up in the meantime, it would be fine. But if she didn't, a temp's arrival should provoke Ogma to leave.

Another call to Gladys went straight to voicemail, and I stared at the phone, trying to divine its meaning. Gladys could have lost her phone, or it might have been stolen. It might simply lack a charge. There were any number of reasonable explanations for this. Except that everything about her—including the way gods, Druids, and hobgoblins immediately humbled themselves in her presence—was unreasonable. She was entirely too capable to plausibly fall prey to mishap. Which made me worry that something more serious had happened.

The temp arrived about an hour later with some Danish, for which Nadia promptly thanked and reimbursed her, and from which we both immediately partook. It wasn't as good as the lovely pastry Gladys Who Has Seen Some Shite always brought, but it tasted like normalcy, and we needed it right then.

The temp's name was Lizzie MacLeish, a frizzy-haired brunette in her late twenties with freckles and almost comically large glasses perched on a tiny nose. She did not appear to be intimidated by Nadia, which impressed me.

Once it became clear that Nadia was teaching Lizzie our phone system, Ogma actually spoke.

"Pardon me," he said. "Is Gladys Who Has Seen Some Shite not coming to work today?"

"Dunno," Nadia said with a shrug. "We cannae get in touch with her and she hasnae called. If ye would like tae leave a number with us, we can have her call ye when she gets in."

"I have no phone. No, I'll wait all day if necessary."

"Ye could just come back tomorrow."

"No. If I leave and she arrives to find me absent, I'll have given her insult. I'll remain."

"Suit yerself, then," Nadia said, and turned to Lizzie. "That bloke might be sitting there all day—sorry."

That was disappointing. Someone may tell you that a bomb on your premises can't possibly explode, but no matter how much you believe such reassurances, you'd rather not have a bomb hanging around. That's how I felt about having Ogma in my lobby.

Once Lizzie knew that she had to text, not call, me for anything she needed, I returned to my office through the shop and up the stairs, thinking of what I could do that day that would tolerate interruption, since I fully expected it. I needed to concentrate on mundane matters rather than sigil-agent business, so I kept the secret bookcase entrance to my ink room closed and busied myself with composing emails to firms that had published their annual reports with us, offering them small discounts for returning.

My phone pinged a half hour later, a message from Lizzie.

The police are here to see you. D.I. Munro.

Please send her up.

Hopefully she hadn't come with a search warrant—or, worse, a warrant for my arrest. I readied my official ID just in case it was needed and retrieved the folder that Norman Pøøts had given me on Glasgow's worst people, placing it on the coffee table.

I'd employed the ID on two previous occasions against D.I. Munro, and she still remembered fragments of those encounters, which meant she had a very impressive mind. The combined might of the three sigils on the ID tended to melt memories, so I had only the highest respect for her and wished we were not on opposite sides. Had fate not made us rivals, I would like to think we'd be friends.

I welcomed her and a uniformed constable into the office and invited them to sit in the comfy chairs surrounding the coffee table. The D.I. was wearing an aubergine suit with a black paisley scarf wrapped artfully about her neck. Her hair, grey with the gentlest of waves to it, fell to her shoulders.

[I am glad you came by, Inspector,] I typed. [I had plans to see you today regardless. You saved me a trip.]

"Oh? Why is that?"

I handed over the folder. [An anonymous source has provided intel on human traffickers in Glasgow.]

She took it but did not look inside. "Is this the same source that provided ye with information earlier?"

[I don't know. It was provided anonymously.]

"Right. Well, I'll pass it on tae the proper department. I'm here about something else. Where were ye on Saturday, Mr. MacBharrais?"

[I was here for most of it. Working overtime.]

"Ye have proof of that?"

[I can provide security footage, of course, and several employees saw me as well.]

The D.I. tapped at a tablet and, when satisfied, extended it over the table for me to see. She swiped through a number of still captures of Buck Foi wearing a familiar bowler hat.

"On Saturday, several bank vaults were emptied of a large portion of their contents. Curious camera blackouts occurred in each, so we are not sure exactly how it was done. However, right before the blackout, there's a single frame of this strange wee man suddenly appearing. We're not sure how he managed tae get in—the vault doors show no evidence of tampering or of even being opened. But the thing is, I've seen this character before. He punched me in the nose on the same day that I first met ye, in the flat of yer seventh deceased apprentice. Do ye know who this man is?"

I shrugged helplessly and shook my head, hoping that the lie would not come back to bite me. Buck's hat—or, rather, the hat he'd stolen from me—bore the Sigil of Swallowed Light, and the last thing I needed was for the D.I. to figure out that I had the ability to shut down cameras in my vicinity. Buck had really been careless there.

"I figured as much. Let's try this instead: Since that day in Gordie's flat, have ye seen this man ye do not know?"

I deployed another woeful wag of the head. Buck would probably need to stay away from the office for a while.

"Awright, have ye ever seen this unusually painted van before?"

She swiped through and presented a photograph of Nadia's wizard van, parked in front of a chip van that I recognized and habitually avoided. The fish was too greasy and the chips were soggy.

But, more to the point, I didn't see how I could deny knowing that van. The license plate was clearly visible in the photo, so that meant they probably already knew it belonged to Nadia and that she worked here. The question was probably designed to catch me lying.

[Yes. That's the wizard van of my accountant, Nadia Padmanabhan.]

D.I. Munro blinked a few times, obviously surprised at this smidgeon of cooperation. "Yer accountant drives a van like this?"

[No, she drives that particular van. I feel safe assuming that there are no other vans like it.]

"Any idea where I can find yer accountant now?"

[Yes. She should be in her office. It's next door; just go to your right down the balcony.]

"Very well. I'd like tae see the security footage of ye working here on Saturday before I go. Thanks for yer cooperation."

The D.I.'s demands were a nuisance but successfully distracted us from the loitering god in our lobby. After Munro departed, we went back to worrying about Ogma and my missing receptionist. Gladys Who Has Seen Some Shite never appeared, and Ogma left at the close of business, promising to return tomorrow.

Seeing the back of him, I felt lighter, and my shoulders sagged in relief. Tension is a bloody killer.

CHAPTER 4

Fierce Druid

We told Lizzie MacLeish to come back the next day ten minutes before opening and to bring Danish, but Gladys Who Has Seen Some Shite actually showed up and we were doubly blessed. Quadruply blessed, in fact, because my receptionist entered with a couple of guests: a redheaded woman carrying an exquisitely carved staff and accompanied by her stunning wheaten Irish wolfhound.

"Hi, Boss," Gladys said, dressed conservatively in a royal-blue woolen outfit with a matching beret perched on her head, her black hair streaked with grey and pinned up like she was planning to attend a meeting of Mothers Concerned about Something or Other. I knew now that this was a glamour and she could appear however she wished—she had usually kept all-grey hair before. When last I saw her in Australia, she was twenty years younger and looked dazzling in a flapper dress designed a century ago. "This is Granuaile MacTiernan, the Druid for the eastern hemisphere these days. She's the reason I'm late. Well, her and the sigil agents in Taiwan. It's some story, I promise. And this is her wolfhound, Orlaith."

I said hello to Orlaith first, as was proper, then greeted Granuaile, of whom I had heard but never met, with a saved [Pleased to meet you] from my speech app. She didn't bat an eyebrow at this, but mine twitched upward when we shook hands and I noticed that she didn't have any Druidic tattoos on her right arm. She clocked that I missed them and chuckled, speaking in an American accent.

"Pleasure to meet you as well, Mr. MacBharrais. The tattoos are there, but they're cloaked. I kept getting comments from randos and got tired of explaining them, so a coven in Poland helped me out."

I went down to the basement break room with Gladys and Granuaile to brew up a cup of tea and have a Danish, purposely leaving Lizzie upstairs to open on time. As expected, Ogma walked through the door promptly at nine and prevented me from hearing any details about their adventures. Lizzie used the intercom to inform us of his arrival, and I led our small procession upstairs.

The god looked relieved for a moment to see Gladys Who Has Seen Some Shite emerge from the basement, because that meant he wouldn't be stuck waiting in my lobby all day—which was a relief to me as well. But his eyebrows climbed up his head at the sight of Granuaile.

"'Sup, asshole?" she said. Ogma's eyebrows plunged down and knitted together at being so casually insulted. "Heard you tried to kill my ex-boyfriend last week. He can take care of himself and so can I, and Gladys is going to give you what you have coming, but I wanted to tell you personally that you should never call upon me for any favors or hospitality. That shit you pulled was unforgivable."

The god merely nodded once to indicate that he'd heard, but he gave no reply. He was trying mightily not to make things any worse. We were all very conscious that Lizzie could hear us and she should remain ignorant that she was in the presence of incredibly powerful magic users, so I invited the three of them, plus Orlaith, up to my office to continue our chat.

The coffee table and sitting area in front of my desk did yeoman service; we each picked an upholstered chair. My instinct was to offer coffee or tea, but Gladys Who Has Seen Some Shite anticipated me, holding up a hand when she saw me start to type on my phone.

"Thank you, Boss, but we won't need anything. This isn't going to take very long." Orlaith dipped her head under Gladys's right hand, and the receptionist petted her while she turned to Ogma and spoke. "You were very destructive in Tasmania in your attempt to kill the Iron Druid and be free of your oath to him."

"He has freed me of it, and I am no longer indebted to him," Ogma said. "He is content to live his life without his right arm and to serve Gaia."

"I'll say," Granuaile piped up. "We spoke on the phone yesterday, and he sounds really happy. He has a new girlfriend named Rose and he's completely centered and content with who he is and what he's doing. I'm so happy for him."

Gladys Who Has Seen Some Shite nodded and said, "He's a beauty, eh? And because he's at peace with himself, he made a hasty peace with you, Ogma. Thus, like many powerful men in this world, you would have done something reprehensible and paid no penalty for it. The forces you unleashed killed people, and for that you are indebted to me. For being so destructive, you owe me a year and a day of being creative in a very specific way. Go to Brighid at the Fae Court, tell her I sent you and why—be wholly truthful about that in public, because I'll check—and then inform her that you are to work exclusively on her infrastructure project for a year and a day and take instruction from her on where and when to work."

"That is all?"

"Owning your behavior and making amends through your labor is all. Should you perform these tasks flawlessly, you will be free. Shirk any part of it, and additional punishments will be forthcoming."

"Understood. What is this infrastructure project?"

"I'll let Brighid tell you. You've taken enough of our time here." She flicked her hand a couple of times at the door. "Off you scoot."

Ogma rose, bowed to my receptionist, then delivered curt nods to Granuaile and myself, ignoring Orlaith altogether, even though she was an amazing dug. He exited without another word, and I admit that, once again, a good measure of anxiety melted away as soon as he did. Yet plenty remained, because my receptionist casually administered punishments to gods, which they accepted without protest, and she called me "Boss."

[Who are you and why are you here?] I typed, and Gladys Who Has Seen Some Shite smirked at me.

"I guess we're at the point where you realize there's a cat in the bag, and you want it out of there so you can see what kind of cat it is." She turned to a suddenly alarmed Orlaith and said, "It's a metaphorical cat, sweetie, don't worry."

[Yes, I would like to know.]

"I'd rather keep this cat in the bag, Boss. If I let it out, then I can't really maintain appearances, and things might not happen the way I hope they will."

[Are you here to see some shite?]

"Oh, absolutely. But I can't tell you what. That might jinx it. If it makes you feel any better, I think it's going to happen soonish, eh? I can see the building taking shape underneath the scaffolding, gears turning, all that. Which means it's great that you brought in another receptionist. Let me train her up—that won't take long, I'll tell her where to find the good Danish you like—and then you can keep her on when I leave."

[You're leaving?]

"As soon as I see the shite I want to see, yeah. Speaking of which, Granuaile and I saw some this weekend, eh? You gotta hear this, Boss."

[Yes, this story I was promised about why you missed work yesterday. Something involving the sigil agents in Taiwan? Are they okay?]

"Yes," Granuaile replied. "They came home from your she-nanigans in the Dandenong Ranges and realized something had literally exploded in Indonesia on the island of Papua. When they went to investigate—this would have been Friday—they realized they needed help. They got in touch with Coriander, Brighid's herald extraordinary, and he got in touch with me."

[But you were already in Taiwan?]

"Normally I would have been, but I wasn't at that precise moment. I was visiting that coven of witches in Poland who cloaked my tattoos, enjoying a nice grog."

[Okay, but I've been wondering why you're based in Taiwan.]

"I'm adding Mandarin to my list of headspaces and training with Sun Wukong in martial arts."

[Sun Wukong? The Monkey King?]

"Yes, but he's grown quite a bit in the past few centuries and doesn't really want to be called that anymore. He's no longer into the power trips of his youth. Now he mostly runs a bubble-tea shop and kicks my ass. Speaking of tea—maybe we can have a proper cup before I tell this story?"

I nodded and got up to put a kettle on, and Nadia knocked at that point and poked her head in. "Awright, Al? Hey, Gladys. And, oh, ma goodness, what a gorgeous dug!"

I beckoned her in and introductions were made, and Nadia took the seat formerly occupied by Ogma. Orlaith went over to her for some pets, because she probably appreciated the "gorgeous" compliment. Granuaile was immediately enthralled with my accountant, who had traded the goth-high-priestess look of yesterday for the goth-Lolita look today. She wore a corset cinched up over a frilly black dress with white lace around the edges, which fell only to mid-thigh, and black-and-white-striped stockings pulled up just over the knee; her feet were buckled into thick platform shoes. The two of them quickly made plans to go out together and slay, which might have been a colloquialism or a literal plan for murder. With their abilities, it could easily go in either direction.

Once Granuaile had been served tea and she'd taken a sip, closing her eyes in pleasure for a moment, she told her story.

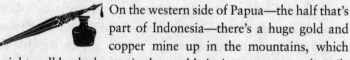 On the western side of Papua—the half that's part of Indonesia—there's a huge gold and copper mine up in the mountains, which might well be the largest in the world. A giant open wound a mile wide yawns at the sky and can be seen from space. They excavate ore, crush it, add chemicals to separate the metals from the rock, and pump it all downhill in a toxic slurry. The metals get dried out and sent to smelters, and the tailings inevitably poison rivers, groundwater, and the ocean. There are vast stretches of coastline where all the aquatic life has died, but the company insists everything is fine and legal. Adding to the daily tonnage of ore from the surface pit are underground mines pursuing different veins. And on Friday they dug themselves too deep a hole, like the dwarves in that one mine in a fantasy world almost completely bereft of women. Something blew up down there. A lot of miners died, and it would have been explained away as a freak accident except that Wu Mei-ling, newly returned from Australia, was looking at her sigil table, trying to catch up with what was happening in her territory, when a bright orange flare appeared, signifying the arrival of a god in Indonesia. That was strange enough in itself, but the location was even stranger. She and her apprentice, Hsin-yi, hopped over there and used those sigils that get people to believe you're an authority figure. That got them access to the mine and a trip to the deep. However, just as they were getting into the lift, another explosion rocked the mine from below. The attempts to dig out the rubble from the previous explosion and retrieve the bodies of the miners resulted in another catastrophe. They couldn't get down there. But they did realize that the cause of these explosions wasn't faulty machinery or volatile gases or anything else mundane. A subterranean divinity had awakened from

a long sleep, and to get to it, they'd need help. That's when they contacted me through Coriander.

I was hanging out in Poznań with the Sisters of the Three Auroras on Saturday. We were just down the street from a baroque basilica, working our way through a grog menu at a café with outdoor seating, when Coriander arrived. He told me I was needed in Papua, and after making my apologies, leaving Orlaith with the witches, and shifting there using the nearest bound tree, who did I find waiting for me? Gladys Who Has Seen Some Shite.

She introduced herself and caught me up with your adventures in Australia and how you helped Connor defeat Ogma and the oilliphéist. That made me want to meet you, Al and Nadia, just to say thanks, and since we might have cause to work together in the future, it's also a good chance for us to get acquainted.

Together, Gladys and I went to the mine and snuck past security, descending as far as we could, which was a few levels above where the explosion and cave-in occurred. My staff here, Scáthmhaide, is carved with bindings that allow me to become invisible, and I employed that, while Gladys used her own camouflage spell. Once we were alone in a passage, we got in touch with the elemental of Papua and asked for its help to travel through the earth to the problem area.

The bare rock of the mine shaft undulated and shifted, inviting us in, and we stepped into its unforgiving embrace. Then there was a time of rumbling darkness, an uncomfortable sensation of sinking into the throat of the earth, and eventually a warning from the elemental that we were about to break through the ceiling of a very large subterranean cavern. I took my bird form—that of a peregrine falcon—and held on to my staff with my talons. Gladys also shifted to something else, though I'm not sure what, because I couldn't see; then we were through.

We floated down into an immense, sprawling cave, dimly lit by fires flickering in hammered metal bowls atop granite pedestals, using some ethereal fuel and reflecting off a very strange floor—because it wasn't rock, except for a narrow path between hills of rich, buttery gold. And that gold wasn't trapped in ore as in the rest of the mine: It was millions of coins, a treasure like I have never seen. One could buy all the U.S. senators with it, not just one from New Jersey, solve worldwide hunger and homelessness, and have money left over to fund arts programs and buy the world a Coke.

And perched atop the highest mountain of gold, overlooking the vast hoard, was a beautiful dragon glittering in scales of pink, white, and blue. It had the long, sinuous body of dragons one sees in various Eastern traditions; it was no great flying lizard like dragons of the West.

It was agitated. It sensed us—smelled us, at the very least, if it did not also note the disturbance in the air as we drifted to the ground. Tendrils of smoke rose from its flared nostrils, and its jeweled eyes gleamed red and gold with reflected firelight. I did not think it wise to reveal myself, so I remained invisible and attempted to view it in the magical spectrum.

The dragon's aura had the blinding white of divinity about it but strained somehow through a filter. It was a god but perhaps a weakened one, or a very old one, or both. But it was also a creature with which I could attempt to communicate as I would an animal, binding tendrils of my consciousness to it. Having little choice, I did my best.

It startled when it felt, or heard, my welcome in its head. There was, of course, no possible way for us to speak the same language. There was an exchange of emotions, and I learned that she was female even as she learned the same of me. Fear and anger and confusion on her part, because she had literally never experienced any life outside of the cavern. I sent back wonder and acceptance and assurance of her safety.

This dragon—this deity who did not even know her own name—had manifested asleep as the slumbering god of the underworld. She was a psychopomp of sorts, and the people who believed in her thought that when they died, they must travel through her cavern on the way to the next world and pay a toll or she would wake and devour their soul. All the coins were payments for the dead to pass through her liminal space.

But when the last person who believed in her died and passed on through her realm, she did not wake. No one came to say, *Look, it's over. You no longer have to do this or remain here.* And because she had enjoyed the worship of a civilization for many years and expended no energy, she lived on and on, forever sleeping. And she would be sleeping still had it not been for the miners.

Their noise and vibrations woke her, as did the crumbling of the cavern ceiling off to her left. She did not know what it meant except that it was a threat, and she exerted some of her considerable power to make it stop. But then she had to figure out—with no one to help her—who she was, and where she was, and what was going on. And what could she possibly eat? She was understandably very hungry.

Once we secured her promise not to harm us, Gladys and I showed ourselves to her. And she said we looked a bit different from the people she used to dream about, but we were close enough. We asked if she would like to leave this cavern and see the surface of the world. We offered to take her somewhere else, where she could be free and find something to eat, and maybe we could even find the plane of her pantheon and she could rejoin all the deities and people who gave her life.

She was torn at first. She very much wanted to leave but felt, looking around, that she was supposed to stay, to protect that space—to guard that hoard of gold.

And let me tell you: It was real. I don't know how the spirits of the dead can leave ghost coins underground that become real when the goddess to whom they're given awakens, but they absolutely did that. Or *she* did that, thanks to the power of their belief. I explained—laboriously, slowly, with thoughts and feelings rather than language—that of course we would abide by her wishes but remaining would do no one any good, least of all her, because she would starve. And as for the hoard, we could protect it until she decided what to do with it. We could move it whole-sale to wherever she landed.

Eventually it was decided: Gladys would take the dragon god-dess to Tír na nÓg, where she could remain until we found the plane of her pantheon, and I would shut down the mine to pre-vent her hoard from being discovered and stolen by the mining company. But before the two of them departed, I asked if the goddess would allow me to give her a hug.

She had no idea what a hug was. But I sent her some mental pictures and explained as best I could that it was an affectionate gesture, meant to be supportive and accepting of who she was but also hopeful that she would grow into an even more wonderful being and achieve all her dreams. She supposed she would let me try it to see how it felt, so I went up to her and gave her a hug around the neck and nuzzled her cheek a bit, and she thought that was fine and I could do it some more and, if I wanted, I could take a coin to keep as a token of our meeting.

I have now hugged a yeti and a nameless dragon goddess. I really love being a Druid.

With the elemental's help, Gladys departed with the dragon, tunneling safely beyond the reach of the anthill shafts dug by the miners, while I went back into those shafts to start gumming up their works.

To shut down a mine, go to all the expensive equipment that pulverizes ore or shuttles it around—anything, basically, with moving parts—and make it stop moving. It's easy when you're invisible. Back when I was an apprentice, Connor had done some-thing similar to a coal-mining operation in Arizona: You bind the metal bits together into a solid chunk, and nothing's going to fix it. You just have an expensive and useless block of steel, incapable of repair. It took me a few hours to hit everything, but when I was finished it was completely inoperable and losing money by the minute. Of course, new equipment will be brought in soon, and I'll sabotage that too and keep it shut down until we can get the dragon's hoard relocated.

I joined Gladys and the dragon in Tír na nÓg as soon as I could, and we spent some time together looking for the goddess's people. That bled into Monday—so that's why Gladys couldn't be here. We had a lost goddess to repatriate to her family.

But we couldn't find them. Best she could remember, her people had been from somewhere in the north, since her realm was supposed to be to the south of where the humans lived. The name of the country and the name of her people, however, she could not recall.

In form she looked like she could be a dragon from a number of different Asian traditions, but without a language or a name to go by, we couldn't find where she belonged. We asked around: *Anybody missing a sleeping dragon goddess? Okay, okay, but listen: Do you want one? She's beautiful.* No luck. Or maybe it was the greatest luck in the world.

She was projecting feelings of despair and loneliness last night at essentially being orphaned. So I gave her another hug and suggested as best I could that she name herself and decide on her own terms what to do and where to live. She had a blank slate, no obligations, and a whole life ahead of her with plenty of resources. There was no need to live the life imagined for her by others. She could do whatever she wanted. And that could change. She didn't have to do one thing, live in one place. She could even try on different names until she decided that one fit her.

One thing she had discovered was that she liked water buffalo. She wanted to live where she could eat more of those. And she also liked resting underground but wanted access to the sky. I thought of the perfect place for her to live, if she could avoid the ecotourists: Hang Son Doong cave in Vietnam—the largest cave in the world, with multiple access points and plenty of places for her to hide. The only people who went in there (besides myself and Orlaith) were tourists on guided paths, their numbers restricted.

She wanted to see it, so I took her and we flew through it together. Five kilometers of gorgeousness, with cave pearls and wondrous limestone formations, shafts of startling sunlight filtering through from the surface here and there, underground rivers and ponds. She loved it but worried about privacy—about spelunkers. So we came up with a solution: a hidden sanctum that she could enter from the cave, which humans would never find. We had the elemental craft the space for her, as I once had the elemental of the Himalayas create a hockey rink for the yeti. It would allow her to stay in the cave and keep her hoard safe while giving her access to all the water buffalo she could eat. All that remained was for her to choose a name, and she picked something unexpected as a result of a wordless conversation we had.

She wondered, basically, if I had any ideas for a name. I'm not too conversant with naming practices in Asian languages, so I told her that every time I looked upon her, I thought of the Three Graces. Her response was a bundle of queries—why, and who were the Three Graces, and how did she look anything like them?

Of course, she looked nothing like them. But the three colors of her scales, swirling and iridescent and so very pleasing to the eye, were a visual manifestation of her very real physical grace, and the wonder of her existence embodied the graces to me: Aglaia, Euphrosyne, and Thalia.

She chose to name herself Thalia until she could think of something better.

Brighid has assigned a small army of the Fae to transport Thalia's hoard of gold from Papua to her new hidden lair in Vietnam. Once that's complete, I'll let the mine start its work again. They will eventually punch through to that cavern, but it will be empty of all riches.

The short version is: We were late because a very old goddess is now new in the world, and Gladys absolutely wanted to see that shite.

"Wow. So you're telling me," Nadia said, "if I wanted tae see an actual fucking dragon, I could go tae this cave in Vietnam right now?"

"With me, yes," Granuaile said. "You won't find her otherwise."

"I would love that. Is she beautiful?"

Granuaile nodded. "So beautiful she'll make you cry. I mean, I did. Kind of left that part out of the story, but she has that effect."

"No mascara, then. Excellent tip. Let's go soon, yeah? When she's all settled."

"Of course. You're a bit . . ." Granuaile's eyes unfocused for a moment and then snapped back. "Hmm. You're maybe a bit . . . more . . ." She trailed off before saying, "than human?" but the subtext was clear.

"I am, yeah. Curiously, that's *not* all settled. Well spotted, though."

"How do you mean, it's not settled?"

"I'm a demigoddess, but I don't know who ma real da is. But in practical terms I'm a battle seer. I see violence coming in time tae avoid it and also where tae strike back so they cannae avoid me."

"That is outstanding."

"Comes in handy, yeah."

Granuaile flashed a grin and nodded. "Connor said as much. We spoke recently."

"Oh. You and he are . . . ?"

"Exes. But in a good way for both of us. He's in love with an excellent person named Rose now, and I am content, for the moment, with my studies and the occasional liaison with a Rando Calrissian. I have to develop some headspaces and absorb languages, and that will keep me occupied for a good while. And," she said, rising to her feet, "I've kept you all occupied for long enough. I have to get back to check in on the mine and make sure the transfer of Thalia's assets is proceeding well, and I have training and study to resume in Taipei. But it has been a sincere pleasure to meet you, and should you ever need me, Gladys has my phone number, and failing that, reach out through Coriander."

Handshakes all around and head pats for Orlaith, and the Druid exited, leaving me with my receptionist who had no business being a receptionist. She knew exactly what I was thinking and smirked at me.

"Don't go asking me what I am yet. Until I give you my notice, I'm still your receptionist, Boss."

[You just told Ogma to go work for Brighid for a year and a day. It feels strange for me to ask you to get to work now.]

"Ha. You don't have to tell me. I'll get to it happily. I think you lucked out with getting Lizzie assigned here. She's a good egg, I can tell already. And thanks for letting us use your office to take care of that business. I know it was some inconvenient for you, but I couldn't have asked for a better place to resolve those issues. Because you're a good egg too, Boss."

I nodded and smiled at her as she exited. I've always liked that expression. It implies that while you're already good, one day you will hatch and become something greater.

CHAPTER 5

Pompous Government Bastards

I don't have the equivalent of a red phone for emergencies like you see in the American movies, but Gladys Who Has Seen Some Shite loves them, so whenever there's an important phone call coming in, she says, "Red phone, Boss. Line two," or whatever line it is. Such calls are rare enough that she sounds very excited whenever they happen, but I know when it happens that I'm in trouble, so I dread that tone of voice. It was no small disappointment to hear it when she buzzed me into my office from downstairs an hour later—especially because I'd been looking forward to enjoying my first "normal" day at work since returning from Australia.

"Red phone, Boss. Line three. Imperial umbrage has been taken. They were some incensed with my Canadian accent, I can tell you right now. Brace yourself for an official scolding. Secure line."

I tapped the desk twice, an acknowledgment and thank-you, then pressed the button for line three.

"Al MacBharrais here," I said, speaking aloud since it was likely that whoever was on the phone to scold me was someone new in the government, and my curse would not be anywhere near the trigger point with them. The recent revolving door of prime ministers also meant tremendous churn in the various offices, and it was indeed someone I'd never met before.

"Mr. MacBharrais, this is Percy Tempest Vane with the home secretary's office." His voice—doubtless the fruit of generations of posh inbreeding—sounded like he had endured a dire need to visit the restroom for the last five years, shuddering with tension and diverting a third of his body's energy to maintaining sphincter control. "We need you in London straightaway regarding a treaty violation."

"I see. And who has violated which treaty, Mr. Vane?"

"That's Tempest Vane. You'll be briefed on arrival. You need to get here right away, but you'll be going to Ullapool directly afterward, so prepare yourself."

"Ullapool? Why?"

"That's all I'm authorized to say on the phone. Report to this address."

He gave me the address, told me they expected me to be on the next train, and hung up before I had a chance to tell him they could expect all they wanted, but I felt zero need to meet those expectations, so I'd not be taking any train but getting there via an alternative method he should have been aware of but wasn't. Very puzzling. What could have happened in Ullapool that I needed to haul myself down to London to get my arse chewed by a political stooge? I opened my messaging app and asked Gladys Who Has Seen Some Shite.

Any idea what that was about? I've been summoned to London. Something to do with Ullapool?

It's probably the yacht full of Tories that went down near there. It's all over the news.

Went down how?

Unknown mechanical failure. *jazz hands!*

Did it go down during the day?

No. Last night.

How far from shore?

Almost midway between Ullapool and Stornoway. They're probably going to put you on a boat.

Oh, no.

I could already make a good guess at the culprit, since I'd glanced at their treaty on Saturday and made a note to myself to revisit it in depth soon.

I had to send a series of texts to Buck and Nadia after that to inform them that I'd been called away on sigil agent business and wouldn't be back until late, if at all—unless either of them would like to come with me to London?

They both answered, *Fuck naw,* so I shuddered to think what trouble they would get into during my absence.

Ah, well. The life of a sigil agent may be many things, but boring was not one of them. I pressed the hidden button under my desk, and the bookcase on my right slid open to reveal my ink-and-sigil room. I fetched Sigils of Water Breathing as well as a waterproof carrying case for my pens and assorted sigil paraphernalia; it would also hold the treaty for the Blue Men of the Minch once I plucked it from the filing cabinet downstairs. After confirming that I had my official ID with me, I grabbed the treaty and a Danish from the break room and headed to the Old Way at the Glasgow Necropolis, up the street. I kept an eye out for Roxanne while heading to the path among the tombstones but didn't see her.

After traversing the Old Way to Tír na nÓg and taking the proper one from there to London, I emerged in St. James's Park near Birdcage Walk, where I could hoof it to either the palace or Parliament or, in this case, to the home secretary's office.

It was much faster than the train, which would have been a journey of four hours and change. As it was, I presented my credentials less than an hour after the phone call and asked to see Percy Tempest Vane on a matter of some urgency.

I knew he'd make me wait, so I took advantage of the time to review the treaty. It had been signed and sealed back in the nineteenth century. Not good. It was still in effect, because these treaties were the kind that persisted until formally amended or canceled, but there hadn't been any amendments. The sigil agent responsible for drawing it up was long dead, as were the human government signatories, but it was possible that the nonhuman signatory was still around.

I was admiring the neat and careful script of the sigil agent's hand when that unmistakable voice startled me out of my study.

"Mr. MacBharrais?" I looked up to behold a petty, entitled bureaucrat who had doubtless gained his post through nepotism and resented everyone whose parents weren't close cousins, because they didn't have his weak eyes and weaker chin, flushed complexion, and mad teeth. He was stuffed into an ill-fitting pale blue suit with a plain black tie, which might have worked in summer but was an atrocity in winter.

"Yes. Mr. Tempest Vane." I rose to shake hands and dreaded his palm being damp and . . . it was. I carefully kept my expression neutral while I dissociated and thought of Scotland.

"Didn't I just call you in Glasgow?"

"Yes."

"How did you get here so fast?"

"I was given tae understand that there was some urgency, so I made haste."

"Right. Right, obviously, but—how?"

"I'm afraid you're not authorized tae know that."

Percy flinched as if I'd slapped him with a glove, and then he quivered in rage. "I am absolutely authorized. I have top-secret clearance."

"It's not a government secret; it's *my* secret. And you're not authorized tae know ma secrets."

Percy twitched and gasped in a breath of fresh outrage past his teeth. "I was told you would be difficult."

"Aw, that's no difficult. I expect what ye called me down for is difficult. Why don't we have a natter about that and then we get on with our jobs?"

There was some jaw clenching, maybe some teeth grinding, but he eventually nodded and said to follow him. He led me through drab hallways full of dull offices possessed of all the life and nourishment of cauliflower that had been boiled twenty minutes too long. His office, when we reached it, was spectacularly devoid of personality. Moon rocks were vivacious by comparison. Only his pale blue suit showed a spark of individuality, hideous as it was.

He asked me if I wanted tea, and I didn't but said yes anyway, because he didn't appear to have a secretary and that meant he'd have to make it himself. I asked for milk and honey and a twist of lemon, thanked him for it, then deliberately didn't drink it. The English just summon pettiness from my soul.

"Right," he said, setting down his own cup and saucer on his desk as he lowered himself into a chair bereft of ergonomic benefits. "Well. I'm not sure why this duty fell to me, but it has, so I have to say things now I never anticipated saying in my life. A yacht has been lost with all hands in the Minch, supposedly at the machinations of some Blue Men, who apparently bear no relationship to the Blue Man Group, thank God. And it turns out that we have a treaty with these Blue Men, and the sinking of a yacht must violate that, and I've been told that this is your patch. You're supposed to enforce the treaty."

"Before we get tae that, perhaps ye could tell me why ye believe it was the Blue Men of the Minch who sank the yacht. They havenae been active for many years. Decades, in fact."

"Well, we had radio communications. Desperate cries for help. The captain said some Blue Men asked him a couple of questions, spoke a couple of lines of poetry, and when he told them to sod off, they did something to compromise hull integrity and sank the whole thing."

"The telly was saying it was an unknown mechanical failure. We're certain that it was a hull breach?" Percy nodded. "And it was an English captain?"

"Yes, but what does that have to do with it?"

"If he were Scottish, he might have known whom he was dealing with and thought better of telling them tae sod off. What questions did the Blue Men ask, specifically?"

"I don't know. Is that important?"

"Most likely they were attempts to verify that the yacht was a legitimate target."

"What? That's preposterous!"

"It could help me manage the situation. Can ye get me transcripts of the radio communications?"

Percy picked up his phone, punched a number, and spoke to me while he was waiting for whomever it was to pick up. "There is no way that a yacht, or a vessel of any kind, could be a legitimate target," he said, and then someone answered on the other end of his phone and his tone became more cordial. "Yes, may I have a transcript of all radio transmissions from the downed yacht? Turns out there might be some clues in there. Yes. Ta."

When he rang off, I said, "Tell me about the passengers. If the yacht was not a legitimate target—"

"It wasn't."

"—As ye say, then perhaps the Blue Men were targeting someone on board."

"There were several Conservative MPs and their entourages on board, as well as important members of the business community."

"Who owned the yacht?"

"A London banker named Nigel Stanthorpe."

"So a bunch of rich toffs and their money launderer. Any Scots on board?"

"What does that have to do with anything?"

"Maybe nothing. Maybe everything. What's the answer?"

"Everyone on board was English. Does that make it a legitimate target in your mind?"

"Not at all. But it may have been a factor in the minds of the Blue Men. I'm only asking for facts here; ye don't have tae take offense at every question."

The transcript arrived, hand-delivered by a young man who

didn't have Percy's family connections and therefore was starting at the bottom. I thanked him—Percy didn't—and started paging through the manuscript. I found what I was looking for on page two, as the captain was delivering a summary of how it all went pear-shaped:

CAPTAIN: *"They asked if this was a personal watercraft, and I said yes. Then they wanted to know if we were a sailboat, and I said no, of course not. Then they said some kind of poetry rubbish and I told them to sod off. That was it—hull breaches began shortly afterward."*

I sighed. This was going to be unpleasant. "I'm not sure what the home secretary was hoping for here, but there was no treaty violation."

"What? Of course there was!" He leaned forward and stabbed the top of his desk repeatedly with his index finger, which probably meant he thought he was making an excellent point. "A hundred people are dead, Mr. MacBharrais!"

"The treaty was written and signed in 1871. It covers all fishing and commercial vessels like cargo ships and ferries, all military craft, rowboats, dinghies, and personal sailing vessels. Stanthorpe's yacht was personal, which meant it was no a member of the other protected classes, but it wasnae a sailing vessel, so it was fair game."

"What do you mean, *fair game*? They can't be allowed to hunt down yachts!"

"The Blue Men of the Minch are allowed—under the treaty in force and written before modern yachts existed—tae do just that."

Percy swelled with righteous indignation. "Well, then, I'd say we can hunt them right back!"

"Oh, aye? Who's gonnay hunt them? Yer Navy men? If they havenae stumbled across the Blue Men in the last century, I hardly think they're gonnay find them now. But supposin' they do, let's just suppose. According tae the treaty as written, the Blue Men have done nothing wrong—no, I'll address yer objection in a moment, let me finish. If the Navy attacks the Blue Men and violates the treaty, it's null. And that treaty is the only thing that's restrained them for the last century and a half, ye understand? If ye shred this treaty, everything in the Minch is gonnay go down. The Bermuda Triangle would be a safe paddleboat cruise by comparison. Ye'll basically render one of the busiest shipping lanes in the world useless. Billions of pounds sail through there. Lots of food and other imports that England relies on, as I'm sure ye can imagine. And it'll all be lost if ye do anything but shut up and take it."

"I understand your point about the danger they represent," Percy ground out, "but how can we be left with no recourse? They murdered people."

"Naw, they sank a ship but left the people alone. Those people just drowned. They always had a chance tae save themselves. And the captain had a chance tae avoid the whole thing. When they gave him those lines of poetry? That was his golden opportunity. If he had responded in kind, they would have let him pass. But he told them tae sod off."

"You're saying that if he responded with poetry, they would not have sunk the ship?"

"That's right. This isnae news. I'll bet ye five quid it's on Wikipedia."

"So the captain's at fault—not you, and not the Blue Men—the captain?"

"Aye. He was rude."

"I think you're being rude now."

"Am I, though? Or am I just being Scottish?"

"I think you're both."

"Ye can think what ye like." I placed my hands on the armrests of the chair as if to stand up. "Well. Is that it, then?"

"No, that's not it! We need the Blue Men of the Minch to pay for what they did!"

"But they didnae do anything wrong."

"How are you the one in charge of this?" he exploded. "They can't kill a bunch of people and suffer no consequences!"

"Why no? Happens all the time. In fact, the English colonized most of the world, including Scotland, on that very principle. I'll bet ye ten quid that several people on that yacht killed a bunch of other people and got away with it."

That practically turned him into molten gelatin. His face went through several color changes while I waited for him to wrest control.

"Am I to understand," he finally said in tight, low tones, "that you're going to do nothing?"

"Aw, no. I have a plan. Would ye like tae hear it?"

"Yes. Very much."

"I think ye should stick with the unknown-mechanical-failure bit and then quietly—or loudly, it doesnae matter—tell yacht owners tae avoid the Minch until such time as I can get the treaty revised. Cruise ships too, as they are also not covered by the old treaty language."

"Brilliant. What reason would I give for having them avoid the Minch? I can hardly tell the truth."

"I'm sure ye will think of something if ye want tae. But honestly, ye don't have tae tell them anything. The problem will self-correct. Once another couple of yachts full of rich people go down due tae mysterious mechanical failures, the other rich people will remember there's any number of places where they can float around and drink champagne, eat fancy fish eggs, and be bastard landlords."

"No, Mr. MacBharrais, that's not going to hold up. The radio transmissions exist. Cell phones exist—satellite ones too. It's eventually going to be revealed as sabotage, and once it is, we'll be under pressure to bring someone to justice. The scrutiny we're getting already is enormous—those were well-connected people, who were friends with the owners of various media outlets. We can't allow this to continue."

"I'm gonnay do ma best tae ensure it doesnae."

"Fine. But now I'm going to ask you some questions that will no doubt be asked of me, so I need to know: What if you fail? Who replaces you?"

"Normally it would be ma own apprentice, but I don't have one. It would probably be a young woman currently residing in Melbourne named Chen Ya-ping. She's close tae achieving her mastery as a sigil agent and would most likely take over ma territory if it became necessary. In the short term—if ye needed someone right away—I'd call Eli Robicheaux in Philadelphia."

He scribbled those names down and I gave him Eli's phone number. "Why hasn't the treaty been updated in the last hundred and fifty-odd years?"

"Ye know how it is. There's plenty of other work tae be done until something gets broken and then ye need tae fix it. It's how government works, in't it? Last documented sighting of the Blue Men was before I was born."

"So you've never met them. How do you expect to find them?"

"Excellent question. I'm gonnay need a yacht tae use as bait. Have ye got one lying around in Ullapool and some rich floppy cocks ye don't need anymore?"

That was supposed to be a joke, but Percy didn't get it. He lost what little control he had at that point and called me a pretentiously waxed know-nothing twat, to which I replied he should know better than to confuse me with his maw's fanny, and we parted ways like most Scots and English do, telling each other to perform sex crimes with livestock and wishing a painful early death and all that.

Upon reflection, I could have been more professional, but I'd bet anyone twenty quid that if I wasn't independent from the government, Percy Tempest Vane would have leaned much harder on me and threatened imprisonment or the cutting of my budget and anything else he could think of.

CHAPTER 6

The Blue Men of
the Minch

When I returned from London and walked into MacBharrais Printing & Binding, Gladys Who Has Seen Some Shite gave me a phone message.

FROM: Heather MacEwan
MESSAGE: Coriander will take you to the Blue Men whenever
you're ready.

I grunted in amusement. My needs had been anticipated. I'd planned to call on Coriander anyway: His role as Brighid's herald allowed him to find just about any being who needed finding for embassage, and he would be far more reliable than trying to make do with a bait yacht. No use putting it off, so I made a quick trip upstairs to get a laptop with an advanced text-to-speech app on it, some materials to draw up a new treaty, a good bottle of whisky, and pointedly left my phone behind on my desk. I wouldn't put it past Percy to have the government track me, and there was no way I would lead them—or D.I. Munro—to the Blue Men.

I waved to Gladys as I exited and walked to Gin71 at Virginia Court, where Coriander could pick me up and take me wherever we needed to go.

A visit to Ullapool wasn't necessary. Coriander saved me a five-hour ferry ride and a lot of pointless swimming by taking me straight to the grounds of Lews Castle, near Stornoway in the Outer Hebrides. It was an overcast day but not actively raining, so I took advantage of the clement weather to make sure I was apprised of the situation. Holding up a hand to tell Coriander to wait, I got out my laptop to ask him some questions.

How'd you know I needed to see the Blue Men?

"The Blue Men expected you'd want to see them," Coriander said. "Something to do with a sunken ship?" When I nodded, he continued, "Out of respect for your office, they asked me to escort you and offered guarantees of safe passage and all hospitality, provided that you come as a guest and not as a tool of the Crown."

I just finished speaking with a tool of the Crown. Wouldn't wish that fate on anyone. Are they angry with England in particular?

"I don't believe so. Best to let them explain."

Are there any details of etiquette among the Blue Men I should know about before greeting them?

"Nothing out of the ordinary. They're like the rest of the Fae. Just be careful neither to create nor incur indebtedness. They might look more kindly on you if you speak Scots Gaelic instead of English."

Nodding, I put the laptop away and indicated he could lead me on. My Scots was rusty from disuse, but perhaps a greeting in kind would suffice, and then I could use my app.

"You'll need to use your official ID to get us in," Coriander said, and that was easy enough. Lews Castle had been built in the nineteenth century by Sir James Matheson. Situated across the loch from Stornoway on some lovely acreage, the castle's ground floor was a popular destination for weddings and the like, with large fancy ballrooms and the sort of ceilings no one makes anymore. Coriander led me past all that to a nondescript door that opened to the wine cellar, and there he revealed a hidden door behind some barrels that accessed a narrow tunnel heading off to the south. Coriander paused to light an actual torch waiting in a wall sconce and led me down the tunnel to another door, a heavy wooden one. He knocked on it, a slat opened, and a rough voice demanded a password in Scots. Once the herald extraordinary provided it, the door unbolted from the other side and swung open for us.

We were ushered onto a balcony high above an expansive subterranean cavern with a small loch at the bottom; a cluster of buildings surrounded it—roofless, as they wouldn't need shelter from the sky here. The entire place was lit by bioluminescent fungi, cookfires, and enchanted Faerie lights—there was no electricity. It was awash in blues and greens with small points of orange, and it smelled of the ocean and woodsmoke. It was beautiful, and I smiled. It was a safe bet that no one in Stornoway or Lews Castle knew this was here.

The balcony gave way to a staircase carved out of stone, which would lead us down to the small village. But before that I got to meet my first Blue Man—the guard at the door—and he looked nothing like the idiosyncratic music performers. Five feet tall at most, with all-black eyes, earholes in lieu of actual ears, and skin that was more of a deep cerulean than navy or royal blue. Gills, quiescent now, could be seen below the earholes, but otherwise the facial features looked human—a standard nose and mouth, no fish lips or anything like that. A motley assortment of pink and yellow corals was worn or perhaps grown where one might expect to see armor—over the torso, shoulders, forearms, and shins. A rope cinched at the waist held up a simple hempen wrap around his naughty bits, and draped on top of this was some black netting fastened on the left with a cockleshell. The dagger in a sheath on the right hip was most likely glass—no metals here, as they'd rust or corrode quickly, and as Fae they'd avoid all iron anyway.

The guard gave us a curt nod of greeting but said nothing. We were left to make our way down to the village, where another Blue Man greeted us, introduced himself somewhat implausibly as Rhett MacNett, and said we were expected. He led us to a stone building festooned with shells and shark teeth around the doors and windows. There was a constant hum of conversation and laughter, owing to the lack of roofs and cavern acoustics. Private conversations were not really possible—by design.

The Blue Men favored stone and glass in their buildings and décor—and I don't mean simple panes of glass but stained glass, or colored blocks of it, or extraordinary sculptures that incorporated both stone and glass. As I entered the building, there was a bar to the left that immediately qualified as the most beautiful I'd ever seen. A marvelous ovoid aquarium with blue lights was embedded in the slate façade, and radiating horizontally on either end were three wavy ripples made of light-blue glass. A lush coral reef teemed with life inside, but oh, what a splash behind the bar! A mosaic of colored glass tiles formed the image of a mermaid rising from the deep, her head pointed toward the back of the room and her tail nearest me at the entrance. But small shelves and niches interrupted the design, some of them supporting bottles of liquors that I noticed were entirely Scottish-made whiskies and gins, some of them supporting colorful glass sculptures of various kinds of shark heads. If I hadn't been working, I would have sprinted over to see their cocktail menu. Did they have drinks featuring clam juice, perhaps, or fish sauce, or other unexpected oceanic umami to counterbalance the sweetness of fruit juices and syrups? But I was working, alas, so I reluctantly dragged my gaze forward to see where we were going.

There was a sunken circular grotto with three steps leading to a lower floor; some stone bench seating with plush cushions lined it. It was a space made for relaxed conversation, and in case anyone needed a place to put their drink and maybe a plate of oysters on the half shell, there were a couple of small mosaic-topped tables in front of the seats on either side.

To my right as we took the steps down, a large and visibly old Blue Man sat with his legs crossed. When he saw us, he rose to his feet and gestured to the opposite side of the circle, indicating that we should choose a seat there. He was festooned with an impressive collection of shells and stones on his coral pieces. When he spoke, his tone was a jovial one, rumbling with good humor and the smallest of gurgles.

"Welcome, Coriander and our unknown guest. I'm Mudgeon MacGill, triton of the Blue Men, but let's not be formal, eh? Let's be friends. You can call me Mudge."

I smiled tightly and got out my laptop, waggling my eyebrows. Coriander jumped in, anticipating what needed to be said.

"Hello, Mudge. This is Aloysius MacBharrais, sigil agent for Europe, the Middle East, and Northern Africa. He'll be using this device to speak to you, since he has problems with his voice at the moment."

That was a convenient way to deal with the curse. I'd most likely be talking for a long while to Mudge and perhaps on multiple occasions, so I thought it best to be safe from the start. "And I'm positive that you can call him Al. He prefers it."

I nodded my agreement and placed my laptop on a mosaic table depicting a hammerhead shark, seen from below, while Mudge said, "Welcome, Al. We call this place the Shark's Tooth, for obvious reasons."

With the laptop woken from its sleep and the app ready, I quickly typed, *Forgive me for using English, as I don't have Scots Gaelic functionality. Your home is beautiful. I'm honored to be here.*

"That's kind of you, but it's not our home. It's more of a redoubt where we welcome air breathers. If it's lost, we won't suffer too much. Our true homes will remain safe."

Understood. Do you enjoy whisky, Mudge?

"Yes, I do."

I brought a bottle. You may have already tried it, since I noticed the impressive bar over there. But shall we open it and enjoy a glass as friends? The whisky is a gift given freely. We have much to discuss.

"That is very considerate." He waved a couple of fingers to an attendant just outside the circle, and two thick glasses of extraordinary craft were brought as I removed the bottle from my pack and extended it to him. There were miniature jellyfish swimming inside the drink glasses, and I examined them, wondering what they were supposed to eat or if it was their destiny to die in there. Peering at the bottom, I could see a small plug, so this was a temporary purgatory only; they'd be released from their tiny aquariums as soon as we were finished drinking.

Mudgeon read the label on the bottle and said, "A twenty-one-year-old Speyside? Excellent. I haven't tried this one yet."

Glenfarclas 21 is a deeply sherried dram that finishes long and round and can teach silk a thing or two about smoothness. The flavors come in waves. We toasted one another, took a small sip to get the burn over with, then a second, slower sip to truly appreciate its progression from first fruit to a field of barley.

Coriander excused himself after that and let me know that whenever we finished, the Blue Men would take me to Tír na nÓg via an Old Way and he would meet me there to return me to Glasgow.

Mudge poured another finger before we sat down to talk, both of us feeling good about the geniality so far. A man who shows up and pours you a good drink before business is far more welcome than an unsmiling anus from the government.

"How long have you been a sigil agent, Al?" Mudge crossed his right leg over the left, folded his hands over his knee, and smiled. His teeth were very white and very sharp, but there was nothing menacing about it.

Decades. Hope to retire in the next few years.

"The treaty we signed with humans has been in effect for more than a hundred and fifty years."

Yes. I took a look at it recently, owing to events.

"Did you? Did you read who signed it?"

Uh-oh. Was he going to discredit a signatory and thereby declare the treaty invalid or something? *No. Should I have?*

He hooked a thumb at his chest. "I signed it."

Oh.

"I point that out not to impress you with my age. I point that out to warn you not to make arguments about original intent. I know the original intent because I was there, originating it. But go ahead, then, tell me what you intend and what the government of England intends, if it's any different."

Well, Mudge, as you might expect, the English are mightily cheesed at you. They see it as an unprovoked attack, and they need to save face here, which means there need to be consequences.

"They're not saying it's an unprovoked attack on the news—aye, we hear the human news. So either you're lying to me or they're lying to their people."

Definitely them lying to their people. They know it was you and they want to strike back.

Mudge's affable expression vanished. "That would be unwise."

I informed them. But I think if we can make sure there aren't any repeats, they'll let it go. One yacht they can label as an accident and it will fade from memory. But if there's a pattern and the public starts asking too many questions, becoming afraid, they'll have to act.

The affability returned. "I understand and appreciate you being candid about their thinking, and I can see their position. But we did nothing wrong according to the treaty."

I know. But it's not a situation they'll let stand. They want yachts to be protected too.

"That's not going to happen. Because yachts are abominations."

Mudge, we can't have you sinking yachts.

"Easy enough to fix. Don't sail any yachts in the Minch and we won't sink them."

We really need to update the treaty. How can we make that happen?

"We can't do it at all. Humans can fuck off on this one. Back when we signed the treaty, we understood the need to travel safely in the Minch. There were a lot of lives depending on cargo and fishing and that, and we've honored the treaty all this time and still do. But yachts—especially lately—are incredibly offensive. Everyone on a yacht, with the possible exception of the paid crew, is exploiting the bollocks out of the earth and the people on it. We know this because of what they do—the shite they dump in the Minch, and the tremendous waste of resources they consume, and the pollution they spew every trip they take—but we also know this because we hear them talking. The exploitation is real—some of them are enslaving others; you call it trafficking now, because it's not done the same way as chattel slavery in the past, but it's still enslavement. And it's our position that we'll not abide any more yachts in the Minch. The rich can be rich and exploit people elsewhere, but we'll not let them do it in our waters."

I paused for a drink and made tiny little nods to indicate that I'd heard him and was thinking about it. Then I typed, *Let me come back to the treaty issue in a minute. You are certain that there are yachts—not cargo ships or other vessels, but yachts—involved in human trafficking traversing the Minch?*

"Absolutely certain."

Was that the case with the yacht you sank?

"No. We'd not endanger the lives of people who are already suffering enough. Think of an arsehole so wide and black that you feel it might be a bottomless well into which you can fall for eternity. That yacht had a hundred of them on board."

So you're only going to sink the yachts that aren't *trafficking?* Mudge blanched, and I quickly followed up with, *Never mind. I don't want to get sidetracked from this: The ones that are involved in trafficking—do you know if it's the same few?*

"Aye. There are about five or six different ones."

Would you be willing to report them to the human authorities next time they go through? And I'm asking because if you can help them with this, England might be willing to reevaluate their position.

"You mean if we rat out the traffickers, they'll let us sink the rest?"

Naw. I very much doubt that. They will continue to push for a treaty revision, perhaps forcefully, and perhaps cutting me out of the process, I feel I should warn you. But politicians love to point at law enforcement as evidence that they're making things better. Right now you're giving them nothing but a headache and they want it to stop. But if you give them something to crow about, then they'll keep talking.

"I've no interest in talking to human law enforcement."

Understood. But you'll be a trusted informer. You can think of a code name if you like. You give them the name of the boat, where to find it, and who's on board, and hang up. That's it.

"No, that wouldn't be it."

How so?

"If we're going to the trouble of reporting it, then they had damn well better do something about it."

Fair. But if they act, there had better be something legally significant to act upon when they get there. Don't report a ship just because it's full of arseholes deeper than wells.

"Also fair."

If we can make this work—your tips leading to arrests—might that be a basis of trust on which to renegotiate the treaty to include yachts?

Mudge thought about it. "Maybe. We want to clean up the Minch. If they chip in, we can talk. But until they establish some trust, yachts are fair game."

That's a satisfactory place to begin. You tell me what code name you want to use, and I'll give you a number to call.

Mudge gestured to the man who'd led us to him. "No bother.

It'll be Rhett MacNett making the calls. Listen, I don't mean to be rude, Al, so please forgive me if I'm overstepping here, but are you aware that you've been cursed? I can see it in your aura."

Aye, I know it's there, and it's why I've been using this software to speak to you. If I use my voice too much with someone, the curse causes them to hate me intensely. I don't know who laid it on me. If you can tell me that, I'll tell the English to fuck off.

"Ach, I wish I could, because I would like to see that. But I can't tell you. The sirens could, though. They see plenty that others can't. But they don't like to be helpful. They'd probably tell you to eat glass. Might even give you the glass for free, all smashed up into sharp wee shards. They do help with things like that, telling you to poke a bear or something and then providing the bear so you can get mauled straightaway."

That's true. Do you know who else might be able to tell me?

Mudge called in a couple of other Blue Men and conferred with them in a series of gargles and spits before saying, "It's a long shot, but we think you should probably try asking Nancy."

Who's Nancy?

"You know. Nancy. There's nine ways to her?"

Wait. You mean "nine ways to Nancy" isn't just a random expression?

"The word around the whirlpool is that she's real."

A real what, exactly?

"That's something you would have to ask her. But don't. Because she answers only one question, and I'd bet you have one that's bothering your noggin much more than what she really is."

I do indeed. Where can I find her?

"Hold on, now." Mudge held out a rocky blue hand and waggled it to slow my roll. "You've not appreciated what I said. She's super strict about the one-question thing. If you ask her if she's Nancy, or if it's nice weather we're having, or how she's feeling today, you're done, you understand? She'll say aye or she's just fine and wish you good day. You have to wait a year and a day

before you can ask her anything else, and by that time she will
have moved on. Never spends more than three hundred and sixty-
six days in any spot."

How do you know this?

"People talk. And of course we hear everything that's said in
the Minch."

*All right. Anything else you can tell me to help me find her? A
last name? A city?*

"All we know is that she can answer just about any question if
you can find her. This one cheesedick from Manchester has made
it his investment strategy, because he asks her which stock will
perform best in the next year and he plows all his money into it.
Finding her is the trick, but he's figured it out. She moves around,
but last we heard she's somewhere in the United States."

That's it?

"Pretty much. She's supposed to be old, but that can mean almost anything over the average human life span, which is, uh . . .
I don't know, you tell me. How long do you live these days?"

*It fluctuates wildly depending on where you live, but let's say
seventy-five. What about this cheesedick from Manchester who
knows where she is? Can you tell me where to find him, specifically?*

"No, we don't know. We just heard him talking in the Minch
as he was sailing through on his bloody yacht. He was one of the
reasons we decided to act. If he comes through again, we'll get
him. He shouldn't be taking advantage of Nancy like that."

*Agreed. I will speak to London about cleaning up the Minch,
and hopefully together we can work toward a solution agreeable
to all.*

"A pleasure to meet you, sir."

We shook hands, and I left feeling that I've had far worse meet-
ings. It's remarkable how much progress can be made with a little
whisky and minding your manners.

INTERLUDE: SQUID INK

I have never used squid or octopus ink for writing or drawing sigils. I'm told it's not bad, and of course if the animal was captured for a meal, then why waste it? It's more often used in pasta dishes, I believe, to make blackened spaghetti or whatnot. But I've never wanted to contribute to the demand, because it would mean some creature must supply it.

Which is, of course, an odd line to draw. I demand mutton on a regular basis. Why am I content to let a sheep supply that but not ask a squid to provide me ink?

We have no idea to what purposes our many parts will be used after we pass. Whether for good or ill, the mundane or sublime, we cannot predict and of course will be unable to care. I find it strange that I care about ink on behalf of all the dead squid.

My suspicion is that each of us cares about something strange that no one else is capable of caring about. A collection of destinies—if destinies are real—seeded among us to ensure that all creatures are cared for in the end.

It comforts me to think that we are all destined to care.

CHAPTER 7

A Crow in the Necropolis

When I returned to my office, I gave Percy Tempest Vane a quick call to schedule another meeting to discuss the Blue Men. Perhaps he could come to see me? No? Tomorrow in London, fine. But I'd pursue my own agenda while I waited. Nadia and Gladys Who Has Seen Some Shite had things well in hand at the printshop, and I was free.

I fired off a message to Buck: *Meet me at Gin71 in ten minutes.* Five minutes into my walk there he hadn't responded, so I sent another: *Gin71 in five minutes. Confirm.* His answer pinged a few seconds later.

Maybe adjust yer nuts and loosen up, ol' man. Ye're too uptight.

Well, I wasn't going to let him get away with that. You have to push back against a hobgoblin when they get cheeky, let them know that they can't say or do whatever they like without consequences. *I hope you're not sloppy and floppy. I need ye perky and ready to ride, like yer maw.*

He didn't respond, and he arrived a couple of minutes late, having made an effort to get cleaned up and dressed. A telltale wobble to his gait confirmed that he was, in fact, not sober. I pretended not to notice as he misjudged the bench on the opposite side of the table and ran into it before successfully managing to climb up onto the seat. I really needed to confront him again about his drinking, but this public venue was not the place, and since I had a job for him to do, it was also not the time. When he returned, we'd have it out.

"Wotcha want?" he asked.

[Depends on whether Heather can answer a question for me.]

She was coming over to take our order and overheard the app speaking. "I'll try, Al. What's up?"

[Have you heard of Nancy, as in nine ways to Nancy?]

"I've heard the expression before."

[Apparently she is a real person. Do you know who she is, or, most important, where I can find her?]

"Naw, sorry."

[It's okay. Long shot. I'll have my usual and Buck will have water, because he'll be leaving shortly.]

"Hey, wot?"

I nodded at Heather to indicate the order was final, and she flashed a grin before returning to the bar, leaving me with an outraged hobgoblin.

"Ye cannae come tae a place like Gin71 and order water, ol' man! It's disrespectful."

[I'm sending you on a mission. Nancy is an unregistered seer who moves about, spending only a year and a day in any one place. I need you to find out where she is currently. Supposedly it's somewhere in the United States.]

"Where am I supposed tae find this information?"

[Someone in Tír na nÓg has to know. Probably the hobgoblins, since you monitor power.]

"Ye're sending me home?"

[On assignment. This will become part of your growing legend.]

"How so? If I go around asking if anyone's seen Nancy, it'll make me sound like a stalker, not a legend."

[You expressed curiosity about her yourself in the past. Don't you want to know who Nancy is and why there are nine ways to her?]

"I'm curious, aye, but there has tae be a reason beyond curiosity that ye're sending me off tae find her with only water."

[You've had plenty to drink today, I think. And the Blue Men of the Minch think Nancy might be able to tell who cursed me. Which means two things.]

"Yeah?"

[I have a personal reason to find her. But I have a professional one too. Any seer that powerful—who can tell me what even Brighid cannot, nor Gladys Who Has Seen Some Shite—needs to be investigated and put under treaty.]

"I don't understand. What harm can she do?"

[A seer who can answer any question holds a power that can be abused. The Blue Men of the Minch think some cheesedick from Manchester is already doing so.]

"Oh, aye, fuck that guy."

[You know him?]

"Not personally, but he's famous. Or infamous. For being about as appealing as a bucket of fish guts."

[That's all you know?]

Buck shrugged. "I havenae had a reason tae find out more."

[Now you do.]

"So ma tae-do list is find Nancy and the cheesedick."

[Correct. As soon as possible. For context, the Blue Men acted up because of human trafficking in the Minch, among other things. I'm trying to mollify them so that they'll agree to amend the treaty, and serving up this cheesedick might help. Think you can walk the Old Way in the courtyard here without help?]

"Aye. I don't want tae go home, ye know, but at least the assignment sounds a bit interesting. And it would be good tae help the Blue Men in this case, because ye know how I feel about traffickers."

I did. Buck had been targeted for trafficking himself by my last apprentice, Gordie, and would have been sold to a mad scientist had Gordie not succumbed to the second curse on my heid, the one that killed my apprentices. He'd choked to death on a scone with raisins in it.

Heather arrived with our drinks, and Buck scowled at his glass of water before grudgingly chugging it down.

"It's undignified, drinking water here. I'll owe ye for this."

[Being staggering drunk while on assignment is also undignified, so I'll expect you to lay off until you're finished.]

Buck growled, exited the booth and then the bar, muttering darkly to himself. It began to rain shortly afterward, and I used the time to send messages to the other sigil agents:

Do you know of a seer named Nancy (as in nine ways to Nancy) and, if so, where she might be?

Since it was late afternoon, my message caught the sigil agents in the U.S. just before lunch and the agents in the eastern hemisphere at midnight and three A.M. Despite the late hours in Taipei and Melbourne, I got a chorus of negatives and a vague warning from Eli Robicheaux in Philadelphia that something weird was happening in the western United States and he might need some help soon.

That was frustrating. Perhaps Nancy was a bit of a snipe hunt? The Blue Men might be mistaken or even having a laugh at my expense. But it occurred to me that there might be someone else who could help. I finished my Pilgrim's gin and tonic, paid, and bundled up against the rain, walking to the Glasgow Necropolis and hoping I didn't catch cold. Some hot tea with honey would be nice later, but I wanted to take advantage of what gloomy daylight we had left, which was precious little. Bloody sun fucks off at four-thirty in January.

The first eight crows that I hailed in trees and on tombstones croaked in irritation at me and flew away. I wasn't someone they recognized and I didn't have a bag full of peanuts in my hand, so they wanted nothing to do with me.

But the ninth crow, perched on top of an elaborate sarcophagus, gave me a forlorn caw before lowering its head against the rain. Perhaps she wasn't in the best of moods and I should pack away my personal curiosity and try to be a friend instead.

Norman Pøøts hadn't had enough time to properly launder the heist funds, so Roxanne was still without a basic flat, let alone the castle she wished to purchase. I'm sure she could have found a place out of the cold and wet to stay in the meantime, but for some reason she was clinging to this crow form and isolating herself.

The sarcophagus was, like many in the necropolis, an enormously expensive installation. It was built like a concrete layered wedding cake, the broad base forming the first of multiple steps leading up to the actual sarcophagus, which kept it elevated off the wet ground; it was topped by a structure with a sculpted roof and bore a large inscription. If I sat on my topcoat, I'd probably be able to avoid a wet arse. I gestured to the steps and I typed, [Mind if I sit?]

The crow cawed again and chucked its head in assent, so I lowered my bones onto the steps and stared at the rain falling on the grass and the graves, letting the drops pour off my hat in a curtain before my eyes. I took a few deep breaths, saying nothing and appreciating the pop and hiss of the rainfall. My wife, Josephine, and I used to sit in the rain, holding hands. And sometimes we would cry together, each about our own thing that was giving us stress or grief, and pretend it was just the rain on our cheeks. But we would squeeze each other's hand every once in a while, an affirmation of love and support and an acknowledgment that life wasn't fair and it was healthy to cry sometimes.

I miss her so much.

[Happy to talk about anything,] I eventually said, [though of course I have a question, on the off chance that you might know the answer. Nae bother if you don't. The Blue Men of the Minch told me about a seer named Nancy who will answer a single question if you can find her. Wondered if you knew her.]

I heard Roxanne flutter her wings and then she dropped down next to me on the wet stone platform, morphing and growing in a shroud of feathers into a black-clad woman who did not look like the goddess she used to be but absolutely possessed all the powers of her former existence. To make other humans feel comfortable, she had learned to speak in the voice of the woman whose body she now possessed, but she did not bother to do so with me. Her death-metal rasp was oddly soothing to me now—a small sign of trust.

"This Nancy: Are you required to take nine different routes to her before she appears?"

[I was unaware of that detail, but it makes sense. I think we are speaking of the same person.]

"She's a goddess, you know."

[I did not know.]

"Nancy is a modern mangling of her name. But it was purposeful, initiated by herself. It hides her true nature. That woman is no mere fortune teller: She is Nanshe, the ancient Sumerian goddess of prophecy and divination. She is older than me and, in truth, a role model."

[Oh? How so?]

"She successfully changed who she is. She transformed from Nanshe to Nancy and receives her power now not from prayer but from those who seek her out to ask questions."

[So seeking her functions as worship?]

"It serves that purpose without being actual worship, yes. Because the seekers have faith that they will find her and that she will answer a question. It takes time, money, and work to do it, however, and sustained attention. It's much more intense than transitory prayers, so she doesn't require legions of faithful. Just a few people each year seeking her out are enough to sustain her. And she is no longer tied down to her old identity. The downside is that without worship, she won't be able to remanifest if she dies. She is essentially a mortal with a long lifespan now."

[And that is what you want for yourself? Some sort of sustenance for Roxanne that isn't served up as worship?]

"Yes. I cannot fully escape my role as the Morrigan until I cease accepting the worship. But that power is an addiction. Very difficult to give up when it is still coming in and I have no clear alternative."

[I understand. You must become someone else, and Nancy gives you hope.]

"Yes. But it is not just her."

[Who else, if you don't mind me asking?]

"I do not mind. Siodhachan Ó Suileabháin has changed—the Iron Druid, I mean. He has accepted that he will live out his days with only one arm and diminished powers. Yet he is at peace and has fallen in love with a woman in Tasmania, and Gladys Who Has Seen Some Shite—well, she told him truths. He is serving Gaia very well now. And I find him inspiring—Nancy too—because they are old, like me, and changing was difficult. In Siodhachan's case, the change was thrust upon him, and he fought it at first, before accepting that his life would be forever different."

[I believe I can empathize, if you don't feel that's too cheeky of me.]

"No. But tell me how."

[I lost my wife in a car accident, and soon afterward I was cursed, becoming estranged from family and friends. Both of those events forever changed me. And I had to work through the stages of grief, as Siodhachan must have, before coming to rest within my new self.]

"Ah. I like that. Coming to rest sounds very fine. An acceptance of what is here rather than pining for what can never be." She paused, and I thought she had finished speaking, so I typed a few words and then stopped when she continued. "For there is much unrest within me now. Uncertainty, and the trepidation that follows in its wake. Because this change in my life is of my own seeking. If I wished to become the Morrigan again, it would be so easy. I would be in Ireland, to begin with. I could fornicate with men who please me and slay men who annoy me, maybe eat their eyes as a treat, and it would feel . . . comfortable, if not good. Yet these are things I have done for millennia, and I know it cannot be the sum of my experience. I have been worshipped but not loved. I want to transcend my limitations."

[I understand. We all do. At least I hope so.]

"Why do we wish that? Is it merely a desire to unshackle ourselves from our pasts?"

[That is probably a part of it. I think we spend a portion of our later life trying to heal from portions of our early life. But I think it's more a desire to grow. To become our best selves. And we cannot do that if we settle, and cannot even know what our best self might be unless we try new things.]

"Yes. Well said."

[Do you have any ideas about what you wish to become?]

Roxanne tossed a thumb over her shoulder at the sarcophagus. Paying attention for the first time to whose resting place we were visiting, squinting in the near-darkness through the downpour, I realized with a start that it was one of Glasgow's most famous philanthropists.

[Isabella Ure Elder? You want to be like her?]

"She led a remarkable life."

[She did.]

"She took a fortune that was not hers and helped so many women."

[Oh. Are you thinking you would do something similar?]

"When Norman is finished laundering the funds, I will have a fortune."

[Which you're going to spend on a castle.]

"Perhaps. I have been weighing alternative paths forward."

Nodding, I let the rain provide comment for a while. If she wanted to tell me about those paths, she would. When I judged that she had said all she wished on the matter, I changed the subject.

[I should have you come in soon to take photos for your official documents. Is there anything else I can do for you?]

"No. My needs are met."

[Might you know where I can find Nancy now?]

"Unfortunately not. She moves around, and I've had no occasion to speak to her in many centuries."

[I am grateful for your help regardless. It's given me a path forward.]

I was simply being polite, but it elicited a remarkable reaction. Roxanne turned and smiled at me, shyly at first. Not out of malice or delight in my pain but from joy.

"I really helped?"

[Yes. Very much.]

She looked down at her hands, as if they'd done something without her knowledge and she was just learning about it. "So that's what it feels like. Helping without expectation of a favor in return. I . . . really like it."

[You've never helped anyone before?]

"Oh, many times, many times, but always as part of a transaction. A favor for a favor. This feels different."

[I suppose it would.]

I cannot count the number of times I've heard cynical folk say that people never change, which presupposes that at some point we stop growing. Perhaps they're right most of the time. But there are some who beat the odds, who fight against stagnation and decrepitude, who push themselves to keep growing. To see a thousands-year-old goddess attempt to grow out of her rut—well, it was inspiring. And she had also given me a glimmer of hope: Instead of being lost in a cave without a torch, now I was lost in a cave *with* a torch. If I could find Nancy—an incognito goddess, who might be equal to the task of unlocking my curse—she'd point me in the right direction to win through to sunshine again.

Standing, I tipped my hat and typed, [You know where to find me if you need me.]

"Yes. And you'll be able to find me here, until I have a more permanent dwelling." The feathers swirled around her, shrank, and re-formed into a crow, which flew to the stone roof over the remains of Isabella Elder and cawed a farewell.

CHAPTER 8

The Paragon of Hobgoblins

There are many unhappy ways to wake up in the morning—snakes in the pants, bugs in the pants, basically anything that's not supposed to be in your pants, in your pants—but someone shouting, "Oi! MacBharrais! We're fucked!" is among my least favorite. Especially when it's a hobgoblin who's used to giving grief more often than receiving it, and he's pounding on my locked bedroom door.

He could have teleported through it if I hadn't warded my room thoroughly, making it a literal boundary for him.

I pawed at my nightstand to get my phone, sent a Signal to him, and heard the telltale ping on his device, so I knew he got it: *ETA on the fucking?*

"Ten minutes tae eternity," he bellowed through the door. Time enough, then, for me to relieve myself and throw on a green tartan flannel robe over my underclothes. I'd be able to draw up some sigils too if I knew what to prepare for.

Out in a minute, then.

There was some heavy breathing and other noises behind the door after that, but at least the pounding and shouting stopped.

Good as my word, I opened the door and found Buck Foi slumped against the wall with an actual tear streaming down his face. I said nothing but beckoned him to follow along as I went to the kitchen to get a kettle going.

[Explain,] I demanded, switching to a text-to-speech app.

"I did yer job, but tae get it done I shat on the honor of three hobgoblin families, or so they think, and they'll be blaming the both of us for it but mostly me, and we might as well jump intae an ocean full of cockroaches, because that will be more fun than what they'll do tae us now."

[You found out where Nancy and the cheesedick from Manchester are?]

"Only Nancy. She's in Brooklyn at the Broadway Junction subway station. There are nine different tracks intae that station. Ye take them all, she manifests—nine ways tae Nancy."

[Okay, that was well done. Why did finding that out put us in whatever situation we're in?]

"Because—oi. Is yer flat completely warded against teleportation?"

[Doubly so. Can't enter the space that way. You can teleport within the boundaries of its walls once you're already inside, except not in my bedroom suite.]

"And if they try tae brute-force their way in?"

Once I got the heat going underneath the kettle, I delivered a reply. [Sufficient force will work, but they'll need a lot of it.]

"Awright. This is gonnay take a minute, so bear with me. I asked around and heard that the only guy who could tell me Nancy's current whereabouts was a hob named Browning Full-britches."

[Terrible name.]

"We all have terrible names. It's our curse. But look, the Full-britches and the Snothouses have been feuding. They've been trying tae steal each other's paragons—d'ye know about those?"

I shook my head.

"A paragon is a thing, in this case, not a person. It's an item of magical mojo that waxes and wanes according tae the family's prestige or dishonor. It provides some health and power tae everyone in the family when things are good; ye live longer and ye prosper more so long as ye bring honor tae the family. But do something tae dishonor the family and the consequences are real. Everyone suffers. And if the paragon is removed entirely—well, the family is weakened, in't it? So the price I had tae pay tae get that information from Browning Fullbritches was tae steal the Snothouse family paragon. He knew where it was, ye see."

[Why not steal it himself?]

"Stealing a paragon is considered dishonorable. So if ye pull it off, ye weaken the family ye stole it from, but ye also weaken yer own family, while supremely pissing off that other family."

[So if you stole the Snothouse paragon for him, Browning Fullbritches would get the benefit without taking the hit.]

"Exactly. And because I am a rogue now and no longer part of the Badhumps—the paragon of ma family doesnae take a hit either. I already took the hit when I left, and I have no paragon or honor tae besmirch anymore."

[I didn't realize. But you said three families are mad at you. It should only be the Snothouses, correct?]

"If I'd meekly done what Browning Fullbritches wanted, aye. But I double-crossed him on principle."

[What principle?]

"I wasnae gonnay let him use me for his Machiavellian schemes! So I stole the Snothouse paragon first—"

I held up a finger and typed an interjection. [What was their paragon, exactly?]

"It's the skull of the legendary Snothouse patriarch, Bogey Snothouse, with a golden crown on it. Ye should see the size of the nose holes, big as the eye sockets, just freakishly large sinuses. They say when he sneezed it was like the surf crashing intae rocky cliffs, just a tide of unholy mucus."

Trying not to shudder in revulsion, I typed, [So you stole it and gave it to Browning Fullbritches.]

"Aye. He gleefully told me where tae find Nancy after that. And then, because I knew where it was, I stole the Fullbritches paragon and gave it tae the Snothouses, explaining that Browning Fullbritches had asked me tae steal their paragon as part of a deal, and I wanted tae make sure he and his family didnae benefit. Whether they restored their paragons to each other or just kept them, the balance of power would remain the same, which I felt was crucial."

[What was the Fullbritches paragon?]

"It's a golden turd."

[You mean it's basically a lump of gold?]

"No, it's an actual turd that they dried out and then gilded."

[Unbelievable. So once upon a time, a hobgoblin took a magical shite.]

"Right, but ye're missing the point here. That's two whole families of hobgoblins that want me tae die a painful death, and they hate ma family now too. Which means ma family hates me more than they already did. That's the three families."

[But no dishonor fell upon the Badhump paragon, right? Because you're Buck Foi now.]

"That's true, but . . . . this is complicated. When I changed ma name, that insulted them, because it was a rejection, ye see? But they were also relieved, because they thought I was gonnay do something terrible someday. When I came back and gave away bottles of Buck Foi's Best Boosted Spirits, that annoyed them, because that would normally be something to give the Badhump paragon a shot of mojo. Stealing and then giving away what ye stole is honorable among hobs. Limiting the power of the privileged—or elevating the weakened—is even more honorable. So when I stole the Fullbritches paragon and gave it tae the recently weakened Snothouses, I did something awesome for which the Badhumps got no credit at all. They're realizing that they lost an asset instead of a liability and they resent me for it."

[Shouldn't they examine their own behavior and ask why you left?]

"They might if they weren't so busy despising me for this new trouble. There's no hit tae the paragon, but socially they're the origin of the hob who blew things up between the Fullbritches and the Snothouses."

[So they want credit for the good things you do but can't have it, and they feel like they're taking blame for the bad things you do even though they technically aren't responsible.]

"Precisely."

[What's the Badhump family paragon?]

"Aw, forget it. It doesnae matter."

[It might turn out to matter, and you've gotten me involved now since I'm your employer. Spill it.]

"Awright, look, it's a stone sculpture of a cock and bollocks mounted on a rock wall, and the cock isn't very big—closer tae a button than a sausage—and because it's hanging behind a waterfall, there's lichen that looks like pubes growing above the cock, and some incredibly thick and verdant moss is growing on the bollocks."

I glared at him for a few seconds before typing, [What the hell is wrong with you?]

"Why in nine hells d'ye think I wanted tae change ma name, MacBharrais?"

[I didn't think it was because of a paragon I'd never heard of until now. Was that truly the reason?]

He looked down. "Naw. It was . . . hey, what's for breakfast? I could use a dram." He hopped up to the cupboard to fetch a mug, then teleported into the living room to the liquor cabinet to open a bottle of Glenmorangie.

[For breakfast?]

"I'll add some coffee for appearance's sake. You have yer tea."

The kettle squealed and hissed until I removed it from the stove and poured boiling water over my leaves to let them steep. I set it aside and typed quickly: It was past time to address Buck's behavior.

[We should probably revisit that thing I asked you to think about. Have you examined why you're drinking so much?]

"Aye," he said, pouring out at least two fingers, if not more. "It's so I don't have tae think about ma family. It's so clear what I've lost by becoming Buck Foi and unclear what I've gained."

[Okay. It might be better to talk through it rather than drink through it.]

"I'm gonnay drink through it for science."

[Science would imply you have a control. You would have to try both.]

"Ye want tae be ma therapist, MacBharrais?"

[Not necessarily. But I want to help. And when you first entered my service and changed your name, I thought it was to escape Clíodhna and her banshees.]

"Aye, but it was also tae protect ma family and me. Neither could be used as leverage against the other, if it came tae that, and if I burned up like a flaming bag of shite, then no one else would be harmed."

A skill that a sigil agent must develop is top-flight bullshit detection. The Fae will redirect, dissemble, evade, and tell half-truths simply because it's Tuesday, and if you give them motivation, they're even harder to pin down. Buck had changed the subject earlier. [When I asked for the true reason you changed your family name, you asked what was for breakfast. Now you say it was to protect them. I have no doubt that's true. But I also have no doubt it's only part of the story. Tell me the whole truth: Why did you want to legally and magically leave your family?]

Buck scowled, gulped down his generous measure of whisky, and poured more. He replaced the bottle and teleported with his glass over to the counter next to the stove, where he began making coffee in a moka pot. I watched him grind coffee beans and fill the reservoir with water and assemble it in silence until I couldn't stand it anymore.

[Well?]

"I'm floggin' ma noggin, MacBharrais. Gie me a minute tae think. I've never said it out loud."

[Fine. Take a minute. But no dodging or distractions. Answer me.]

"This business with the paragons. Ye know how I knew where the Fullbritches were keeping their golden turd?"

I beckoned to him with my fingers, telling him to serve it up.

"I'd already kinda-sorta stolen it so that ma da couldnae. He'd found out where it was somehow and wanted tae steal it, consequences be damned, because he hated Dumpty Fullbritches the way a slug hates salt—and I know, Dumpty is a terrible name. But he's a standard-issue arsehole, no a supervillain, and he didnae do anything tae deserve his paragon getting nicked—nor did the Fullbritches as a whole. So I basically took it from where it was and hid it somewhere else—still on Fullbritches land, still technically in their possession, so their mojo was unaffected. They just didnae know where it was. But neither did ma da. Which means the war he wanted tae start never happened."

[Does he know you did that?]

"He does now, because I gave the supposedly long-lost Fullbritches paragon tae the Snothouses. But he didnae know at the time. He just thought they moved it before he could nick it."

[Why not tell the Fullbritches what he planned and let them move it?]

"Because snitching would have landed me in all sorts of trouble. The kind of trouble I'm in now, in fact. Except that I'm at least somewhat difficult tae reach here. If I'd stayed in the Fae planes, I'd probably already be deid."

[Dead? This paragon business is an automatic death penalty?]

"No in any official sense. But unofficially, if the Fullbritches or Snothouses got hold of me, I'd disappear and ma body would never be found."

[So you wanted to leave your family because your father wanted to start a feud with another clan of hobgoblins and you prevented it, but you knew it would come back to bite you eventually.]

"Right. Plus the other stuff. And ma faither might actually be a supervillain. We've never got along."

Buck sat on the countertop, arms wrapped around his knees, and stared at the moka pot as it burbled and frothed on the stove. His eyes glazed and he slowly let out a sigh of despair.

[Dare I ask your father's name?]

Buck winced. "It's really bad, and it may be why he's been angry all his life: Softwood Badhump."

[Jesus suffering fuck. I'd be angry too.]

"Aye. Have ye ever seen that American movie, ol' man, about ghost baseball players in a cornfield?" When I shook my head, he continued, "Makes no sense, except one of the ghosts is the faither of the man who owns the cornfield. They had a shite relationship too. But at one point, the man has a moment of peace with his ghost faither, just having a game of catch, and when I saw that I started blubbering like a whale."

[You mean crying? That's not the kind of blubber whales have.]

"Tits an' taffy, I'm tryin' tae share a feeling other than rage here and you're on about semantics!"

[Sorry.]

Silence fell for a while except for the percolating burble of the coffee. I removed the tea leaves from my cup and stirred in a spoonful of honey before taking a sip. When Buck spoke again, it was in a tiny voice that I struggled to hear. "It hurts, being estranged from yer family. Like there's a vault with a sign on the door that says LOVE AND ACCEPTANCE and ye can neither open it nor teleport in. Ye're always locked out. The irony is that sign's a lie. If ye were tae bust in, there's no love or acceptance in the vault. Only rejection and abuse. A cauldron of toxic stew where the meat's all gristle, ye know? I bloody hate that."

I nodded, afraid to say anything that might distract him. But I knew too well the pain of estrangement. I had not hugged my grandchildren in years, and my arms felt the emptiness sometimes.

"I know I'm better off being away," Buck continued, "but I

still feel ma ideal family is out there, like ghosts in the corn, and I want them tae emerge, smiling at me with nothing stuck in their teeth, and say all is forgiven. And more than that, I want them tae apologize and ask for ma forgiveness. It'll never happen, though, because they're ghosts, in't they? The real Badhumps would never do that."

The coffee began to spit and splutter, which was the cue to remove the moka pot from the stove and run some cold water over the reservoir to cool it down. Buck poured the finished product into a mug emblazoned with AYE—a reference to voting for Scottish independence—added the fingers of whisky, and topped it with a dollop of whipped cream to make a sort of Irish coffee without the sugar. Though I suppose it wouldn't be Irish at all since it didn't contain Irish whiskey. I really needed my tea to kick in.

"That's all the anchors weighing on ma spirit, ol' man. No, wait: I'm horny and have no prospects, because no one wants tae shag a hob who used tae be named Badhump but now has no family at all. There. Now ye know the lot of it. Why I'm Buck Foi, why I worry about ma legacy, why I drink, and why ma bollocks are swelling tae the size of peaches."

I nodded and we sipped and slurped at our hot drinks.

[Sorry to hear about all those stresses,] I eventually told him. [Maybe we can do something about . . . some of it. But drinking yourself into oblivion won't solve any of your problems. It's a snooze button at best, but the alarm will keep ringing until you address it properly.]

"How can I even begin tae solve them?"

[First, stop drinking. It's a problem in itself that keeps you from tackling what matters.]

Buck glanced down at his mug and then back at me. "Ye want me tae waste this?"

[Reframe that. You are holding in your hand a problem you need to solve. Get rid of it. But not the mug. I like that one.]

The hobgoblin eyed me doubtfully, hands curling protectively around the mug. "Say I do. Then what?"

[Start your own family. Create a paragon for it.]

"I don't know how."

[So learn. There are steps you can take on a road to a better place. But none of them can be taken when you keep mashing the snooze button.]

The hobgoblin looked down at his boozy coffee with a mournful expression. "I hate it when ye're right."

He gave me the mug and I poured the contents down the sink. [I'm going to Brooklyn to see Nancy, because she's the best lead I've had in a long time regarding my curse. I'll be back as soon as possible.]

"Ye're no gonnay take me with ye?"

[Naw.]

"What about the hobs?"

[You should be fine if you remain here.]

"So I just sit with ma thumb up ma arse?"

[I recommend a more joyful activity. Something productive. Perhaps a list of steps you can take to improve your situation if you're not lost in the sauce.]

"Lists are boring."

[Construct a Machiavellian plot, then, but far better than the one Browning Fullbritches made.]

"Aw, fuck aye! Why did ye no suggest that tae begin with? Gie me some paper and a pen, ol' man!"

It was a minor victory, but I would take it. Gather enough of them and you have a small bouquet of wins, and those always smell sweet. They can fortify you when life inevitably hands you an anvil in its effort to drag your spirit to the deeps.

Such as when D.I. Munro appeared at the printshop a bit later and once again presented me with a series of photos of Buck in different vaults, all of them split-second frame grabs from security cameras in the instant before the Sigil of Swallowed Light deactivated them.

"I know ye have yer alibi, Mr. MacBharrais," she said. "It's all been reviewed and confirmed, so I cannae arrest ye for the heists.

But this wee man was in every vault, and I think ye know who he is—or yer manager knows, or both. If ye don't tell me who he is and where I can find him, that's aiding and abetting, conspiracy, and whatever the fuck else I can think of."

[I've already told you I don't know him.]

"I think ye're lying."

I shrugged and waited. She had no proof, and until she did, there was no real leverage she could bring to bear against me and no reason for me to say anything else. It was a good thing that Buck had remained at home, plotting.

"You and yer accountant are under active investigation in connection with this heist. Don't leave town."

She didn't have the authority to restrict my movements without actually arresting me, but I said nothing, and she gathered up the photos to go confront Nadia about them. It was a desperate fishing expedition, nothing more. We'd need to engage a solicitor soon, simply to get the D.I. to stop harassing us if nothing else. I didn't want to use any more sigils on her if I could help it.

As soon as the D.I. exited the building, I let Nadia and Gladys Who Has Seen Some Shite know that I was leaving town, the police be damned. I'd take the earliest flight I could catch to New York, since this was a personal matter and traveling the Fae planes would be frowned upon.

[Assume you're under surveillance at all times,] I warned them. [Because you are.]

It wasn't until I was midway across the Atlantic that I remembered I was supposed to meet with Percy Tempest Vane regarding the Blue Men of the Minch. Ah, well. He and his wobbling sphincters would have to wait. Mudgeon MacGill had come across as a rational sort to me—he'd been patient with humanity for more than a century before lashing out, and I thought he'd be patient with me now that he knew I was working on the problem. I had some fresh hope that I might finally be able to learn who cursed me, and my well of patience on that score had run dry ages ago.

———— • ————

Nine Ways to Nancy

A cold rain fell in a drumbeat on the taxi from New York's JFK Airport to Union Square, if the drummers in this case were drunken teenagers pissing in uneven streams from a railway bridge. The wind pushed the water in gushes that thinned to a trickle and then renewed seconds later. My coat and hat would have to work hard keeping me warm and dry on such a day—though once I was in the subway system, I could avoid most of the wet.

I couldn't simply begin at Broadway Junction, which would have been a shorter drive from JFK: I had to take trains *into* the station, which gave me options of how to approach it based on the various tracks I needed to use. It would be a long tedious time and a book might ease the boredom, so I chose Union Square as my starting point since there was a marvelous bookstore nearby called The Strand. I picked up the *The Saint of Bright Doors* by Vajra Chandrasekera on the recommendation of a bookseller, then carefully shielded it from the rain underneath my coat until I got underground at the station. From a kiosk no doubt offering a teeming selection of bacteria and viruses, I purchased a seven-day MetroCard that would allow me unlimited trips, which was easier than trying to calculate the amount I'd need for single rides. (It also provided unlimited whiffs of urine and garbage at no extra charge.)

I took the L train from Union Square toward Brooklyn. Once at Broadway Junction, I would need to take various trains out and back, switching levels and tracks, until I had traveled all nine ways into the station. The A and C trains were on the lowest level, where there were four tracks; the J and Z trains were on the second floor, but there were three tracks; and the L came in on the third, with two. The ninth way to Nancy was a special train that was going to be a little more inconvenient to board, as it was a unique track geometry car, but the inconvenience, I knew, was part of it. If it was easy, everyone would do it, and Nancy would be far busier than she wished to be.

On the plus side, once I was aboard, no one on the train seemed to mind an old man muttering. They may have given me a bit more space, in fact, than they otherwise would have if I remained silent. Because if I wanted a meeting with a deity—even a diminished one—it was best to perform a ritual evocation of the divine. Those have to be vocalized, but thankfully the will matters more than the volume. Vague thoughts—even earnest ones—would not suffice, owing to the hierarchy of thought, word, and deed, each portion of which was modified by the rote and the devout.

Mental prayers—little more than thoughts—were the weakest form of worship. My Irish mentor and predecessor, Sean FitzGibbon, claimed that the divine derived the bulk of their power through prayer and ritual. A devout spoken prayer was a far more effective form of worship than a mental prayer recited by rote memory. Adding deeds to the spoken worship elevated it to the ritual level, and therein lay the true power of organized religious services. What I was doing was not exactly worship, because Nancy no longer made claims to godhood, but still, my evocations functioned like prayer, and taking nine ways to see her served as ritual. She was receiving the power without an organized faith. She was essentially no different now from Santa Claus, who derived tremendous power from children around the world who believed in him and had faith in his abilities but never achieved godhood because he was not explicitly worshipped as a deity. The sheer number of evocations, sacrifices, and rituals devoted to him, however—leaving cookies and milk out, stockings hung with care, the lot of it—fueled a legend. So as I traveled the tracks in and out of Broadway Junction, changing levels and so on, I kept my vocal evocations going. I also came to appreciate the glass mosaic mural on the second-floor mezzanine of the station since I saw it so often. It was called *Brooklyn, New Morning,* by the artist Al Loving.

After eight tracks, I had to use my official ID to get some MTA employees to take an unscheduled trip on the track geometry car, which was the only one that ran on the ninth track. Once I got off the track geometry car, nodding farewell to the driver, I made my way to the mezzanine to see if my hours and hours of travel and ritual evocation bore any fruit.

A woman stood in front of the mural, smiling softly at me, cradling a well-behaved snow-white goose under her left arm. She was brown-skinned, pierced in many places with assorted jewelry gleaming from them, and a golden chain led from her right nostril to the middle of her right ear. She dressed in layered natural fibers dyed in earth tones, with plenty of bangles on her wrists that jingled as she waved. Her right shoulder was supporting the strap of a handbag so woolly it might have been freshly shorn from a local sheep, if Brooklyn had any. Altogether it was an outfit that joyfully proclaimed her lack of connection to any of the world's monotheistic faiths.

"Hello, Mr. MacBharrais," she said, surprising me not only with my name but with English spoken in a slight London accent. "I heard your ritual evocations loud and clear. Thank you for the consideration and the time spent. If you'd like to join me here underneath the mural, I can answer a single question for you."

"Thank ye, Nancy. It's an honor tae meet ye." I was worried

about the goose. Should I say hi, the way one does to a dog, and tell it that it's a good boy or girl? People who don't say hello to dogs are almost always arseholes. But maybe geese are supposed to be ignored? I decided to err on the side of acknowledgment. "And yer companion," I added.

Nancy chuckled. "Silly goose! It's just a goose. But it's kind of you to include her."

I doubted very much that it was just a goose. Not a normal one, anyway. Because she gently put it down on the ground and told it to stay, and when it looked up at her and made some assorted honking noises, it wasn't random. It sounded like constructed speech—a sentence. And Nancy replied to it the way Harrison Ford replied to the walking carpet in his spaceship.

"This shouldn't take long. Be patient. I'll pick up some frozen peas for you afterward."

The goose's retort was a single surly honk, as if to say, *Fine!* and it settled with a small ruffling of feathers and looked away. Nancy then bent and sat on the ground, and I belatedly realized she expected me to do the same.

"Oh! I see. Just a moment." I could not remember precisely when my knees began to complain about getting down on the ground and then back up again, but mine were rather vocal about it, and now they were saying something along the lines of *Are you serious? We're really going to do this?* because the hard tile of the promenade floor was unforgiving.

Once I was situated in a loose lotus, my legs crossed in front of me and my cane resting across my lap, Nancy hummed with pleasure. "This is good. We are out of the majority of foot traffic, and I should be able to address your question in peace. You should probably ask it now so that you don't accidentally ask me something you don't mean to. We can perhaps enjoy a quick idle chat after business."

"Ah. That's most considerate. Very well. This question has plagued me for many years, so I hope ye can help. If ye havenae already noticed, I've been doubly cursed—multiple sources have told me of the twin curses, and some have suggested that they may have been cast by two people, but it's possible that it was accomplished by only one. I've also been told these curses must have been cast by either very powerful humans or, more likely, deities. My question is this: Who cast these curses upon ma heid, either singly or in concert?"

Nancy's eyes widened briefly. "Intrigue! I like it. Okay, Mr. MacBharrais. Give me a moment and please ignore anything I say or anything I do, especially with my eyes. It's all normal and perfectly safe, and I don't want you to be surprised."

"Of course. Take what time ye need."

I was glad, honestly, that she warned me about her eyes, because they almost immediately rolled up into her skull and she began to chant in a language much older than any current civilizations on the planet. Without looking, she rummaged around in her woolly bag until she found an incense stick and a lighter. Once the stick was lit—a pleasant floral jasmine scent—she twirled it around in ritual fashion, tracing smoky lines in the air. We were getting some idle attention from this, but no one stopped. We were clearly not performers and didn't have a hat out for tips—plus the glaring goose did its part to warn people off—so I felt there was little chance of interruption. And that must have been something Nancy figured out long ago, of course, because I'm sure multiple people had come to visit her.

When the chanting stopped and her eyes sank back down, her expression was slightly annoyed. "Just a moment," she said apologetically. "I need a little boost."

"I hope there isnae any problem," I said.

"Maybe. Too soon to tell. I'm going to try again."

Which told me that her first attempt failed. My heart drooped in my chest. Whoever had done this had been exceedingly clever.

Nancy pulled out a small goatskin bag tied with a strip of rawhide. It had a premixed collection of herbs inside, and she placed a pinch of it into a shallow brass dish. She lit these on fire, which gave off much more smoke than the incense and probably violated local ordinances, but her eyes rolled up again and her chanting resumed, much more intensely than before, and the whites of her eyes were focused—if that could be said—at a point above my brows, probably the center of my forehead. The goose honked impatiently at the delay, but she ignored it.

When her eyes dropped down like tumblers in a slot machine for the second time, she was visibly irritated, and she huffily extinguished the fire in her dish just as it appeared a hipster was going to speak to her about it. She fixed him with a steely glare, and he took the hint and moved on.

"I am sorry, Mr. MacBharrais. You have asked me a question I cannot answer. I can tell you this for certain: Whoever cursed you was in fact a deity. Humans are not so skillful at disguising their work. And whoever did this truly did not wish to be held responsible for it. But!" She held up a finger to prevent me from speaking. "I may have a solution if you are willing to undertake the risk. It will be very dangerous."

"Please tell me."

"The sirens can pierce the veil of most anything and see truths that are invisible to others. The difficulty is getting them to share what they see and living to do something about it. I can give you something to make them share, but I cannot keep you safe afterward. Do you think you can survive an encounter with the sirens?"

My natural instinct was to ask a question for clarification—something along the lines of *You mean the actual fucking sirens?*—but I bit down on that urge and said, "You are not the first tae suggest a visit to them. So I will do ma best to prepare, yes."

"Prepare well." Nancy had another rummage in her woolly bag and produced a shortish beeswax candle, perhaps no taller than an index finger, with several rivulets of melted and dried wax drippings falling from the top. It was red and had been used multiple times. She presented it to me and said, "This candle will force any who behold its flame to tell the truth. It should work on gods, monsters, and even diabolical ex-lovers. I have used it on all of them and would not part with it except that you have faithfully taken nine ways to see me, and if I wish to keep the power that's granted me, I must fulfill my obligation to you. Plus, those are very nasty curses on your head, and I want whoever did it to pay. There is no ritual required other than lighting it, but do not look at the flame yourself while asking the question."

"Thank ye. Will this—no, never mind. Let me rephrase. I think I should probably test this in the presence of cold iron."

Nancy's eyebrows shot up briefly in surprise, as if the thought had never occurred to her, then she nodded. "I think you should, yes. I haven't had occasion to do that."

It looked like I was going to be visiting the Iron Druid.

"Because I failed to answer your question and you have skillfully avoided asking any other, you still have one to ask of me, if you so choose. Do you have another question?"

I thought for a moment before responding. "I have a receptionist named Gladys Who Has Seen Some Shite. I have suspected for some time that she is more than an ordinary woman. My question is: What is she?"

Nancy smiled. "This I know. She is the avatar of Gaia, walking the world to learn more of humans. Short of an actual omnipotent deity, there is no more powerful being on earth."

I had suspected as much, but it still took my breath away to hear it spoken as truth. Why would such a being take an interest in working for me? What shite did she expect to see? I realized too late that I should have asked that instead of confirming what I already suspected.

"Thank ye, Nancy. I am deeply grateful and honored tae meet ye. I am no sure that there is any service I can provide ye but if there is, I hope ye will not hesitate tae seek me out. You can find me at MacBharrais Printing and Binding in Glasgow."

"There might be something you can do, actually."

"Oh? Please tell me."

"There's an odious man from Manchester who keeps finding me, year after year, and asking for stock tips."

"Manchester? Curious. I have recently been given reason tae seek out someone known as—forgive me for the crude language—the cheesedick from Manchester."

"Yes, I believe that's what he's often called. If you could discover some way to ensure that he never finds me again, I would deeply appreciate it."

"I'm on it."

"Thank you for seeking me out, Mr. MacBharrais. I hope your meeting with the sirens goes well and your curses are lifted. I hope to see you again."

"I don't suppose you'll tell me where tae find ye next year."

Nancy simply laughed in response as she rose to her feet. She scooped up her handbag and her goose and told the bird, "Time to go get your frozen peas. Who's a good and patient goose? Is it you? Yes, it is." She scratched her fingers at the base of its neck or top of its breast, and the goose honked happily. Nancy giggled, then waggled her fingers at me in farewell and exited Broadway Junction to find frozen peas somewhere in Brooklyn with her garrulous goose.

I remembered thinking that I should put Nancy under treaty, but she was so charming and pure that I hadn't the heart to pursue it. To soothe my professional guilt, I reasoned that she was in Eli's territory and it wasn't my responsibility. Nancy had discovered the trick to living happily and well. I wouldn't dream of putting restrictions on that. And it was not lost on me that instead of a metaphorical torch, she had given me a literal candle to light my way out of the darkness.

———— ❖ ————

CHAPTER 10

A Rose in the Presence of Greatness

It took a bit of fiddling with a search engine, but upon my return to Scotland I found the finest purveyor of sausages in Glasgow, based on the variety of offerings. A butcher shop called S. Collins & Son had plenty of dried and cured selections in addition to a case of fresh sausages that would need to be cooked. Chicken apple, I believe, was a favorite, so I had to get some of those, but I also got some lime and coriander and some whisky bacon cheese sausages for a truly special tasting. The side quest was a necessary joy, because I owed a couple of very good dugs in Tasmania some sausages. I packed them in an insulated bag with some frozen chiller cubes, tucked the candle with some matches and a few sigils in my topcoat, and told Buck we were taking a field trip, far away from any hobgoblins who might be looking for him in Glasgow. None had shown up and pounded on the door while I was away.

Together we went to Gin71 in Merchant City and asked Heather MacEwan, the Fae bartender, to put on her Harrowbean persona and summon Coriander for transport. Though it was technically a personal errand, like the trip to New York, I fudged on my ethics somewhat and classified it as a follow-up to my previous mission there.

"Any urgency tae this?" Heather asked. "I think Coriander's up tae his tits in work."

[Anytime in the next few hours would be fine.] Though it was already late evening, locally, and I wondered what could be keeping Coriander so busy at such an hour.

"Awright, gimme a few, then. What can I get ye tae drink while ye wait?"

"Surprise me," Buck said. "I trust yer taste."

[Surprise us both with mocktails, please. We need to stay sober.]

"Hold on, wot?" Buck growled, scowling at me. "Ye didnae mention that before. What's the harm in a wee taste?"

[We are going to see the Iron Druid. I'm sure you'll want all your wits about you for that.]

"Oh. Aw. Yeah, I guess."

"I have some zero-proof gin," Heather said, "so taste-wise it should work for you. The lack of alcohol means a slightly different mouthfeel, however, because there won't be ethanol numbing your tongue, but it'll still be delicious."

"Huh. I never thought I would care about mouthfeel," Buck said, "but here we are."

The surprise mocktails she made featured the zero-proof gin, an aromatic tonic from Fever-Tree, and crushed strawberries complemented by muddled mint.

Buck was disappointed and made a face.

[Is it bad?]

"Naw, it's good. And that's annoying."

Heather took off to summon Coriander, and Buck asked me to tell him a story about some pantheon that wasn't in the UK.

I'd started to tell him about the Vedic pantheon when Coriander interrupted by arriving much sooner than expected, entering the bar with Heather around midnight. The two of them were so ethereally stunning that the humans all left off their conversations and made little sighs, moans, gasps, and whimpers.

"Hello, Al," the herald extraordinary said, his feet floating bare centimeters above the floor. He was dressed in casual human garb, though it was white jeans and a white Duran Duran shirt with a Patrick Nagel print from the *Rio* album on it, and a thick studded belt straight from an eighties vintage shop. His hair artfully mussed, a blushing pink to his lips, he was an androgynous beauty that made most everyone tingly in their nethers. "I'm tremendously busy but delighted by the chance to get out of my Court attire for a few minutes, so I'm squeezing you in sooner rather than later. Where to?"

[Tasmania, or wherever the Iron Druid is.]

"Very well. Shall we?"

I thanked Heather for the drinks and left forty quid on the table. Coriander led us out of the bar, wistful exhalations trailing in his wake, and we used the Old Way in Virginia Court to go to Tír na nÓg.

[What is keeping you so busy, if I may ask?]

"Brighid has embarked on a kind of magical infrastructure project. She and the Tuatha Dé Danann are updating and adding to the number of Old Ways so that the Fae have more access around the world. The time zones are playing hell with my sleep, as you can imagine. But it's also to help you, the sigil agents, to get around as needed without my help. If you know the Old Ways to get somewhere you frequently travel, then that will reduce the need to call on me. We've recently constructed Old Ways to the Druids, so that's what we're taking today."

I'd known about the project because of Ogma's punishment, but this specific development was news. [You have an Old Way to Tasmania now?]

"Yes. Just completed a couple of days ago. It puts you in Launceston, which is now the home base of Connor Molloy and his hounds—or did you know him by his previous name, Atticus O'Sullivan?"

[I did originally meet him under that name, but I got used to the new name last week during that episode with Ogma.]

"Ah, right! Would you like to learn the Old Way for future reference, if you're going to become frequent visitors?"

I doubted I'd need to use it frequently, so I begged off. But after some twists and turns and careful steps, we emerged on a hot summer day on a forested hillside in Tasmania, approaching noon local time. Coriander was right: Time zones were killer. My top-coat would become sweltering in short order.

Coriander took a deep breath and smiled around at the trees. "I like how the air smells different here. A suite of pollens and nectars and rotting vegetation you don't get anywhere else."

Buck sneezed forcefully, involuntarily ejecting some phlegm that smacked wetly against a eucalyptus tree. "Aughh! I'll say. That was a top-shelf sneeze right there, worthy of the Snothouses. Felt that one in ma spleen."

Coriander produced a folded square of linen sealed with a sigil I hadn't seen before. When he broke it and unfolded the square, he said, "Rose Badgely's house," and the linen began to take on lines of indigo in a grid pattern. As he handed it to me, it became clear that it was, in fact, a map, the individual threads changing colors as if dyed.

"That will guide you to Rose's place, which is also Connor's place now. I'm assuming Connor can return you here and use the Old Ways to get you back to Glasgow, so I shall bid you good day."

[Wait. Is this map made with a new sigil?]

"Clever work, isn't it? Also Brighid's doing. She's making some great strides in connecting us to the world."

[Can I learn how to make this sigil and these maps?]

"I shall ask her about it."

He left us then, and we were able to follow the linen map, its dyed threads changing as we walked to indicate our position, like a GPS, while our destination grew ever closer.

"Oi. Ol' man. Who's Rose?" Buck asked.

[I have never met her, but the word is that she is Connor's partner.]

"What happens tae the map when we get there, then? Do ye just use it as a snot rag?"

[I would not wish that fate upon any linen. I will keep it in case it can be reused as a map elsewhere. The mechanics of this sigil are new to me.]

Rose Badgely turned out to be a detective inspector with the Tasmanian police force and eyed us suspiciously when she answered the door. A good portion of that suspicion was directed at Buck, which showed that she had a keen sense of character. A Black woman, in her late twenties or early thirties if I didn't miss my guess, she was dressed in blue jeans and an orange top, a sleeveless number that revealed toned arms.

Behind her was Oberon, the Irish wolfhound, and Starbuck, the Boston terrier. They recognized me and barked happy greetings to us, wagging their tails. I smiled at them briefly before addressing Rose with a text-to-speech message I'd typed before ringing the doorbell.

[Hello. I'm Al MacBharrais, a friend of Connor's and of his hounds. I promised them sausages last week, and I've come to fulfill that promise. I have some stuff from the finest butcher in Glasgow.]

"You've brought sausages from Glasgow? Are they still any good?"

Quick thumbs typed a reply: [Oh, yes, they've been kept cool in this bag.]

I realized she might not be aware of what Connor was—or that magic was real, and plane-shifting was a thing, and that it was possible for me to get from Glasgow to Launceston in less than an hour. I'd have to be careful of what I said, including any discussion of my curse.

"Was Connor expecting you?"

[No. I'm afraid this is a bit of a surprise visit. Is he in?]

"He is. I'll get him. But who's your friend?"

[This is Buck. Say hello to Rose, Buck.]

Startled, Buck tried to sound Australian and failed. "Oi. G'day, in't it? Bollocks. Sorry. Hi, Oberon; hi, Starbuck."

"Okay, nice to meet you both, but will you wait here just a moment while I fetch Connor? He has this weird thing where he likes to invite guests in himself."

[Yes. Understood.]

She promised to return and gently shut the door on the dugs' whines to let us in. Connor most likely had the place warded well, but one easy way past most wards was to get an invitation to pass from someone who lived there. He wanted to make sure Rose didn't invite a vampire or worse into their home.

It was less than a minute before Connor arrived and opened the door. He looked little different from when I'd seen him last week on the Australian mainland, though he'd had a chance to scrape the stubble off his jaw and he'd caught up on his sleep. His curly red hair and goatee shone with health, and his eyes gleamed with good humor. He was wearing a black concert T-shirt from the British punk band Dildo Shaggins, right sleeve hanging slack owing to the lack of an arm on that side, frayed jeans with holes in the knees, and no shoes.

"Al! Buck! Sorry, I was in the backyard. Please come in. I hear you have sausages."

I nodded enthusiastically and typed, [Hi, Connor. We do. I promised the hounds some sausage just a wee while ago.]

"Yes, I recall, but I'm surprised to see you again so soon. What do you have? Do we need to fire up the grill?"

[Yes. We have fresh stuff.]

"Let's go to the backyard, then. What can I get you to drink?"

[Tea, please.]

"A beer—" Buck said, but after my frown, he amended that to, "Naw, I mean tea also. Thanks."

It was all small talk and getting ourselves settled and grilling sausages after that, smoke and fat wafting in the air. The hiss and scream of meat cooking mixed with the excited panting of the hounds. I knew that they could speak mentally to Connor and were no doubt gushing about how good everything smelled, and this was probably the best day they could remember, because dugs weren't all that great at remembering days. But once Rose left us for a moment to fetch some mustard inside, I took the opportunity to ask.

[Does she know you're an ancient Druid?]

"She does now, yes. That's a recent development. She's still processing that I'm older than Jesus."

[So I can discuss sigil-agent shite with you in front of her?] I asked, right after Buck said, "Does she know I'm a hobgoblin and no some wee sunburnt human?"

"She doesn't know," he said to Buck, "but she's probably waiting to ask me about you once you leave. So it's okay to tell her. And yes, Al, you can discuss whatever you'd like with her around. You can rely on her discretion."

[Excellent. That makes everything easier.]

Rose returned with the mustard and froze when she realized we were all smiling at her.

"What's going on?"

"They know that you know what I am, so they're happy you're in the loop," Connor explained. "Al and Buck are a part of that unusual world."

"I figured as much," she said. "But I'm curious as to what exactly they might be. Are you a wizard, by any chance, Al?"

[No, I'm a sigil agent. The magic is Druidic, but I am not myself a Druid. I use sigils made with magical inks to accomplish many of the things a Druid can do.]

"Okay," Rose said, and though she looked like she might have follow-up questions, she was holding back. Perhaps out of politeness, perhaps out of a wish to avoid the perception of an interrogation. "And what about you, Buck?"

"I'm a hobgoblin contracted tae Al's service. I'm gonnay be a legend, which is no a braggadocious thing but a fact. And I'm sharing that because I want ye tae appreciate that ye're in the presence of greatness."

"Oh, well, I'm honored, of course. I'm also accustomed to being in the presence of greatness, because Oberon and Starbuck are here." The dugs preened and wagged their tails at that.

Connor said, "Al and Buck were part of that thing in the Dandenong Ranges recently."

Rose's eyes widened. "Oh! My goodness. You went through all of that and still came back to Australia? I'm impressed."

[It's mostly a pleasure, but we do have some business to conduct after we eat,] I said. And then we ate, because I mentioned it and the dugs were all for it. Connor shared Oberon's reviews of the sausages and spoke using the voice that Oberon sounded like in his head:

"Chicken apple: Perfectly cromulent, which is a word I recently learned and should get a snack for using, but not the pinnacle of my experience. The best ever were the ones Coyote brought me years ago in a brown bag stained with grease. I still have dreams about those.

"Lime and coriander: No. Whose idea was it to put citrus in meat? They should be hauled before a canine tribunal and then, I don't know, maybe we would pee on their shoes. I should give more thought to the canine justice system, but shoe-peeing sounds like a mandatory minimum sentence for food crimes.

"Whisky bacon cheese: Where have these been all my life? They are the most savory explosion of fats and protein I have ever encountered. Did you bring any more, Al? Could you summon more? Is there a whisky-bacon-cheese-sausage specialty shop, and if not, why not? Can I go back to Glasgow with you and just buy them all?"

It sounded like the last one more than made up for the mediocrity of the first two, so I figured I had chosen wisely.

With the dugs happy and full and ready to nap, Connor asked what he could do for me.

[With your permission, I'd like to test out a magical artifact on your cold iron aura. I'd like to know if it still works in the presence of cold iron.]

"What does the artifact do?"

[It compels the truth.]

"I see. And how would you like to test it?"

[Think of a question for me to ask that you'd rather I didn't know the answer to but by which you wouldn't be particularly harmed if I did know. Then let me ask and see if the artifact works. You'll either answer truthfully or not.]

"Interesting. Okay. Ask me to be specific about how old I am. Usually I say more than two thousand years but not the actual figure."

"That's true," Rose said. "He told me more than two thousand, and once you get into millennia there's no point to counting mere years."

I pulled out the candle from the inner pocket of my topcoat, along with a box of matches.

"That's it? That's the artifact?" I nodded at him and he looked a bit disappointed. Perhaps he'd been expecting something with runes on it. He said something in Old Irish, which was probably a binding for magical sight, as his pupils dilated and contracted again swiftly. I lit the candle and held it aloft while laboriously typing out my question with one thumb.

[How old exactly are you, Connor?]

He snorted in amusement at first, but then his face clouded and contorted and he pressed his lips together. His cheeks puffed out like a child trying to hold his breath, and his face flushed with effort, but finally he blurted, "Two thousand one hundred and three," and he slumped in defeat.

"You rusty Iron Age relic," Rose said, chuckling at him. "You're almost prehistoric." She turned to Buck, cupped a hand near her mouth, and said in a stage whisper, "I'm actually relieved. I was worried he'd be from the Bronze Age."

"Damn it," Connor said. "That's not good. It doesn't even look threatening in the magical spectrum, but its power is undeniable. My cold iron aura was completely ineffective. That candle has some major mojo. Where did you get it?"

I blew it out before responding, [In Brooklyn. I took the nine ways to Nancy.]

"You found Nancy?"

I nodded affirmation as I typed. [But when I did, she couldn't answer the question of who cursed me, so she gave me the candle as a workaround.]

"How is it a workaround?"

[I need to travel to the Mediterranean Sea and ask the sirens who's responsible, because they're never wrong, correct?]

"That's right. They accurately predicted Loki's attempt at Ragnarok millennia ago. It was one of the many things they told Odysseus."

[I need protection from the sirens if this is going to work, and I thought cold iron might provide that. But if the candle wouldn't work in the presence of cold iron, its protection would come at a prohibitive cost, so I needed to test it.]

"Oh, I get it. I suppose I should be grateful that it was you who brought this vulnerability to light rather than someone else. So Nancy—or Nanshe—has serious juice. Wow."

[She does. Though she believes it has more to do with no one taking precautions against her than it does with her actual power. She's been largely forgotten, and while that certainly has disadvantages for her as a goddess, she's found it has its advantages too.]

"Absolutely. You know, I never even learned how to ward against Sumerian magic. The pantheon had already faded away by the time I got to the Middle East. Unless I'm mistaken—do you know if any of the other gods are active? Maybe I should shore up my defenses there."

[I don't believe so. Nanshe herself no longer subsists on traditional Sumerian worship but has survived on the ritual required to find her as Nancy. And now comes the awkward bit where I ask if I can borrow some cold iron.]

"Oh. You want it to protect you from the sirens' song?"

[Yes. Won't it work for that?]

"It will. But you're not going to have fun listening to them. They're not honey-throated chanteuses—there's a popular misconception that they must sound good. It's more like the Most Annoying Sound in the World produced by Jim Carrey in *Dumb and Dumber*. That's part of what hijacks your mind."

Connor summoned Starbuck to him and removed the cold iron teardrop from around the wee dug's collar. He then handed the talisman to me, wryly suggesting that a simple chain might suit me better than a dog collar. Regardless, it should keep me safe from the sirens' song.

"It won't do shit against them physically, though. And they might physically attack you. I guarantee they will, in fact. You're not going alone, are you?"

[No, Buck and Nadia will come as well.]

"Good. Say hi to Nadia for me, by the way. But look, Buck—don't depend on cheap ear protection against them, because the sirens are hyperaware of that defense. If they see you've covered your ears, they'll try to rip that off and then they'll have you. So make sure the ear protection is secure."

"Awright, thanks for the advice. But what happens if they sing tae ye?"

"They'll try to get you to kill yourself. Or maybe command you to kill Al first."

"And I won't have a choice in the matter?"

"No. Their voices hack the higher functions of your brain through the ear, just like Al's sigils work on the brain through the eyes. Have you ever seen *Dune*, where the Bene Gesserit witches use a certain voice to compel obedience?"

"Aw, shite, it's like that?"

"It's like that. Back in Homer's day, they mostly had sailors jump off their ships and swim to their voices, promising them true visions of their futures and of their families. Most drowned before they got to the sirens' rocky shores, but they had extra fun with the few who made it."

"Oh, so they waffled on their promises?"

"No, they told them the truth and fulfilled their oath first. But then they compelled the men to do something that would result in their deaths—usually spread out over a couple of days instead of the instant end you might get from jumping off a cliff. The worst I heard of was a man forced to masturbate endlessly while staring at the sun. He went blind, of course."

"Oh, so that's where that came from?"

"The sirens, yes. But it was so strange to watch that story get twisted by religions concerned with sexual repression."

"Fucking sirens!" Buck exploded, hopping up and down, shaking his fists. "Do ye know how many times I've been told that by strangers? They're gonnay get some payback from me!"

"Wait," Connor said before I could type it. "Are you saying strangers have told you on multiple occasions not to masturbate or you'd go blind?"

"So what if they did?"

"So I guess I must ask the obvious question: Why were you masturbating in front of strangers?"

"Well it wasnae on *purpose,* ya bastard! They found me by accident! I naturally insist on privacy when I'm having a chug! Remember that we're mad at the sirens here. Don't look at me."

"Then you look at me," Rose said, a finger pointed at Buck and her face a mask of cold warning. "Oi! I'm serious, now: None of that in my house, you understand?"

[This conversation has steered wildly off its expected course,] I typed, monumentally embarrassed.

All the tension drained from Buck's muscles and he relaxed into a grin as he executed a lazy fist pump. "Mission accomplished. And before ye get yer glands squeezin' about taking the piss out of our hosts, ol' man, remember that it was the Iron Druid who brought it up first, and when masturbation comes up, ye have tae finish, so tae speak."

Oberon and Starbuck wagged their tails and made some rolling growls that sounded like laughter, and Connor chuckled.

"My hounds say they're learning new techniques of distracting humans from you, Buck, and they would give you some of their food for that masterful display if they hadn't already eaten it. That's the highest compliment they can pay, by the way."

Buck executed a sincere bow. "I'm honored."

I did not feel honored but rather mortified. I thanked them for their hospitality and muttered apologies, wishing we had been better guests, and Connor told me to think nothing of it. He asked me to be careful with the sirens, gave me an idea where to find them, and warned that they'd be under a glamour to hide them from mortal eyes. Telling me to visit anytime, he shook my left hand firmly.

"It's wonderful to know you, Al, precisely because I never know what's going to happen whenever we meet. I savor that quality in people, so if you ever feel like it and your schedule allows, please accept my invitation to visit socially. Shall I walk you back to Tír na nÓg? You can get transport from there to Glasgow, no doubt, if I take you to the Fae Court."

On the way back up to the forested hillside, it did feed my ego somewhat to realize that a very old person who had known an awful lot of humans thought I was worth befriending. But then my damn suspicion kicked in and prevented me from enjoying it beyond a few seconds. What if this wasn't real but rather an attempt to manipulate me? Had the Iron Druid just made the opening move in a chess match without me realizing it was on?

I sighed but tried to make it sound like mere exhaustion rather than the exasperation I felt. Our brains are not very nice to us sometimes.

CHAPTER 11

Fight on the Faraglioni

The location of the sirens is a matter of some dispute; classical sources vary widely. Some of them are just plain wrong, but many of them are—or were—correct, because the sirens didn't stay in one place back then, nor do they now. Plotting the dates and locations of boating "accidents" around Italy and Greece, however, can give one a fair sense of their nomadic movements.

In *The Odyssey,* Homer placed the home of the sirens between the island of Circe and the rocks of Scylla, which are generally held to be on the western side of Italy; this meant that if one were to regard the boot shape, the sirens would be around the lower shin. Connor Molloy said that specifically meant the island of Capri, located south of Naples, where rock formations called the Faraglioni dotted the coast and the cliffs of the island were pocked with grottoes. Both grottoes and rocky islets were frequently associated with sirens in various tales, because in truth they liked both. He suggested that I start looking in Capri and proceed to secondary locations if I failed to find them.

It took a couple of days to arrange travel, because Nadia would be coming with us and we were both being watched. Taking off by myself to New York and returning quickly was one thing, but if Nadia and I both booked a flight for Italy and bought a third ticket for Buck, the very wee man D.I. Munro was looking for, well, we'd be up to our necks in bad haggis. This was still technically a personal mission, not official sigil-agent business, so I didn't want to abuse my travel privileges—Coriander's help in taking me to visit the Iron Druid was more than enough. But I couldn't use conventional travel either, because D.I. Munro would know if I bought a ticket out of the country. It meant that I needed to call in a marker from a faery named Mugwort, for whom I'd provided a wee service in the past. Mugwort was a pleasant, affable sort who met us in the Glasgow Necropolis near the Old Way, and I noted that we didn't see Roxanne on our stroll to the spot. He happily guided us from there through Tír na nÓg and thence to the Old Way around Naples, and he taught us the steps to it so we could use it to return to Glasgow whenever we wished.

"So what do the sirens look like?" Nadia asked me as we strolled through Naples down to the docks. If I were a character from *The Sopranos,* I might say in a Jersey accent that *the air smells of gabbagool.* Its thick scent certainly did contain a hint of dry cured meats but also espresso and bread, basil and oregano, and engine exhaust. I was so absorbed with taking in the sights and smells that I didn't answer Nadia right away, so she followed up. "Do they look like some kinda banjaxed mermaid?" I typed a response on my phone but simply showed it to her rather than play it for everyone to hear.

The mermaid appearance was popularized in medieval times. Most classical sources depict them as birdlike—as in the head and torso of a woman but the tail and legs of a bird, with wings sprouting from their backs. Chimeras, in other words.

"So they have human arms? Or just wings?"

Arms and wings both, I believe. The representations I've seen show them holding a stringed instrument of some kind, for which they needed hands.

"Birds who play guitar," Buck mused. "Sounds like a band name."

"So they could hold weapons too," Nadia said.

Of course.

"Have ye had tae confront them before this? I mean, have they caused ye any trouble?"

Naw. I'm positive they are still preying on humans, but they're doing so discreetly and humanity isn't even suspicious, so there's been no reason to get myself involved.

"How many are there?"

Two or three.

"Oh. Okay, I see how they could keep that up for a long time, if it's just a nibble here and there. But shouldn't they be deid by now?"

They probably should. But they have value as prophets, so someone has been keeping them alive.

"They must be bored out of their minds, hanging about rocks for millennia. Do ye have a precise location?"

Naw. We'll have to check out a few places around Capri until we figure out where they're hiding.

We enjoyed the city briefly—stopped to listen to a street musician, made another stop into a coffee bar to get un caffè and tiny little sandwiches that delighted Buck—but steadily made our way down to the docks, where we chartered a boat for the day. I made sure it was provisioned with drinks and snacks, since we had no idea how long we'd need to be at it.

We had it take us first to the Blue Grotto on Capri, a beautiful spot that the Roman emperor Tiberius frequented. Statues of tritons and Neptune used to adorn the interior walls. There were two entrances: one above water, into which we sailed, and one hidden below water, into which sunlight shone and then reflected upward into the cave; this gave the waters and the cave ceiling a blue illumination, as all the red light was filtered out. It was a magical space, but a search of the small beach and a chamber in which countless people had scrawled their names on the walls yielded nothing mythic. We sailed on and investigated several other grottoes, to no avail.

An inspection of the Faraglioni to the south of the island, however, yielded some interesting silhouettes when viewed through the monocle I had that granted me vision in the magical spectrum.

The Faraglioni were three grey marshmallows of rock slowly eroding into the sea, the tops of these rocky outcroppings green with a scalp of shrubbery. One of them, Faraglioni di Mezzo, was like a natural Arc de Triomphe, providing a short tunnel through which many a yacht and tour boat liked to sail. There were multiple leisure craft sailing about it now, tanned bodies in bikinis and swimming trunks hoisting bottles of beer, all of them laughing like people do when they have no conception of what arthritis is, beyond a word that happens to people later.

But something shimmered and winked atop the Faraglioni di Mezzo. There were three figures up there, visible through my monocle but completely invisible to my unaided eye.

[Put your ear protection on,] I told Buck and Nadia with my speech app. [There's something up there.]

"Up top?"

[Yes. I want you to teleport us up there, Buck.]

"Wot about yer guide?" He pointed to the young Italian man we'd hired, Antonio. He had fabulous hair and wore sunglasses dark as a shark's alimentary canal.

[I'll have him drop anchor and go below. And I have some sigils for the two of you to use.]

I gave them Sigils of Agile Grace and Muscular Brawn and told them to arm themselves as they pleased. I had my cane; Nadia had her straight razor painted with a Sigil of Iron Gall; and Buck had a bronze dagger, since iron was anathema to him.

Antonio regarded us doubtfully as Nadia and Buck warmed up some beeswax in their fingers and stuffed it into their ears, just like the sailors did on the Homeric galley. This was not traditional tourist behavior. His amazement intensified when I helped them pack cotton on top of that and keep it in place with a bandage, which then got topped with a modern helmet.

"We're Scottish," Nadia explained, as if this was typical Scottish behavior.

"Sì, Scozzese," Antonio said with an uncertain smile before he went below at our request. Once he was safely stowed, I turned my back and asked Buck and Nadia if they could hear me. I said it louder and again got no response, so I was satisfied they were fairly well protected.

It was time. I got their attention, reminded them to be quiet with a finger to my lips, and then gestured that Buck should port us up there.

The sensation was a bit like descending abruptly in an elevator, a lurching of the stomach and some disorientation in the inner ear accompanied with a brief blackout, but we were on top of the Faraglioni about thirty yards away from the sirens, and they hadn't seen us arrive. They were perched like puffins, resting and perhaps digesting in a safe spot above the crash and hiss of the sea, ignoring the laughter and obnoxious music coming from the humans in their boats below.

The sirens' top halves would be considered attractive had they been attached to the normal assortment of body parts elsewhere. Their skin was lustrous, pale, free of blemishes, and seemingly unaffected by the Mediterranean sun. I mean, sure, their eyes were yellow with black pupils, mad like a grackle's, and their mouths were sharp jagged zips, but they were pleasant zippers and didn't have any spinach or unsightly flesh stuck in them, and they'd done a remarkable job of keeping their teeth white for thousands of years, judging by the view I was given when one of them yawned. Below the waist, however, they looked like untidy wild turkeys, a mess of fouled feathers hovering above scaly orange legs. The wings folded across their backs were massive, vulturish, ideal for soaring. They weren't built for speed. When you have the power to summon meals with a command, you don't need speed.

Seen through my monocle, the sirens were dozing in the sun, a gentle sea breeze in their hair and feathers, completely unaware of our presence. They had some ancient instruments and bronze swords in their scabbards leaning up against a rock behind their roosting area.

Turning to Buck and Nadia and putting a finger to my lips to once again emphasize quiet, I gave them each a Sigil of Disillusionment and kept one for myself. I broke the seal, eyed the sigil, and the glamour that the sirens were using to camouflage themselves faded away. I could see them unaided now, and the monocle was unnecessary. Buck and Nadia could see them too, and their mouths dropped open; I hoped they'd make no sound for just a little bit longer.

Moving slowly, silently, I put my monocle away and got out the candle Nancy had given me, along with a lighter. I worried about the breeze: If it was too strong to keep the candle aflame, it would be a very short and fruitless visit. The cry of an obliging seagull masked the metallic sound of the lighter igniting, and I was able to light the candle with little trouble. The flame flickered in the breeze, and I watched it for a good fifteen seconds or so to make sure it would hold steady before proceeding.

A Sigil of Agile Grace juiced up my speed, and should I be forced to fight, I was counting on that to keep me alive long enough for Nadia and Buck to do serious damage—they were both better fighters than me.

I approached with the candle in my left hand, my cane in my right, and spoke in Greek, since they'd obviously used it to speak to Odysseus in ancient times.

"Good afternoon, ladies. I have questions that you are bound to answer."

One screeched, one squawked, and one may have actually clucked, but they were all startled and pivoted to face me with a rustling of feathers and a menacing display of teeth. Connor's warning that their voices were annoying fell short of reality: They were heinous. Think of death-metal vocalists who did a quick gargle and swish of bleach before speaking. Every word was a sonic assault.

"Who are you?" the nearest one demanded. My mind went to Odysseus telling the Cyclops his name was Nobody, and I briefly toyed with answering with that before the other sirens followed up.

"How can you see us?" the middle one asked.

"Why did we not see you coming?" the final one said. I thought she meant *see* in the prophetic sense.

"Difficult to foresee my arrival when I'm wearing cold iron, eh? I'm a man who wants answers. Once I have them, I'll depart without offering you any violence and in fact will happily donate a tidy sum to a charity of your choice. Should you not know of any charities, I can still donate to one in your names. Perhaps a nice bird rescue. What are your names?"

That was information they might not wish to share. Some magic systems relied on the power of knowing the true names of individuals, as it focused targeting and broke through wards.

They hissed in response and then shouted in concert, "Throw yourself into the sea." The cold iron talisman Connor Molloy had given me heated up and bounced against the skin of my chest, but their commands had no effect on me, nor on Buck and Nadia. Peripherally, however, I saw that the drunk people on assorted nearby leisure craft were leaping overboard, still clutching their beers.

When I did not obey, the sirens' eyes widened in surprise and widened even further after they told me to eat my candle and I didn't. They blinked a few times, then blurted out their names, much to their own astonishment: Thelxiepeia, Molpe, and Leucosia. They screamed in outrage, understanding that I had compelled them to do something they did not wish to do, and it hurt because that was what they liked to do to others.

"Shut it, now, and let's get on with it. You can probably see that I'm cursed. Who placed the twin curses on my head and why?"

The sirens shrieked their defiance. They flapped their wings, made what I assumed would be some especially rude gestures to people two thousand years ago, and scratched at the ground with their chicken legs. But I noted that while they looked like they wished to, they made no move to attack. They were spinning their metaphorical wheels like a souped-up Civic at a red light in a *Fast & Furious* movie, making a lot of noise but going nowhere. That was unexpected but maybe a part of the candle's power. While under its sway, they couldn't do anything except answer the question. And the answer, so long in coming, caught me completely off guard.

Leucosia said, "The twins, Phobos and Deimos, cursed you at the behest of Ares."

Phobos and Deimos were the Greek gods of fear and dread. It made a bit of sense that they were behind it, considering the nature of my curses. But what spurred them to action left me flabbergasted. "*Ares?* Why did he want me cursed?"

Molpe answered, "You defied his wish to get involved in the Syrian civil war."

I dimly remembered that. It was among the many notes I found in my files where I had chastised the Greeks for minor violations of their treaty with humanity. As I recalled, he'd scowled and complained at the time but hadn't made any overt threats or promises of revenge. "What the fuck? I didn't let him play around in a war that was none of his business—and he admitted as much!—so he set curses on me to ruin my life?"

"Yes," Thelxiepeia confirmed.

"In the name of the wee man." My shoulders slumped, the candle guttered and blew out in the breeze, and the mojo that had kept the sirens in place, forced to answer truthfully, practically popped as it dissipated. The sirens felt it and understood it was their chance to attack. They wasted no time.

"Al, duck!" Nadia shouted, and I knew from experience that I should do what she said in a battle if I wanted to survive it. The nearest siren launched herself at me, talons extended to scratch at my face or perhaps rake my throat and open it for me. She wound up taking off my hat as I ducked underneath her reach, and I was able to land a quick thrust up into her tail with the head of my cane. That was pretty much the only blow I landed, because fighting bird women is not as easy as it may sound. Many people think they can kick the living shite out of a seagull or a Canada goose, until they get attacked by one or get their lunch stolen. They don't move the way humans do, except in the most lethal ways, and they are able to effectively fight from the high ground at all times.

The other two sirens dove toward their instruments and picked up bronze swords before banking toward me with murder in their yellow eyes. Their single-minded focus on me meant I was humped, but Nadia and Buck sprang to my defense and did the best they could—they gave better than they got. But I got a lot. Despite wielding my best defense with my cane, I got a stab in my guts and a slash across my chest, cold at first and then searing pain as my nerves communicated that something was dreadfully wrong since my insides had been abruptly ventilated.

That wasn't the worst of it, though. A talon lashed at my eyes, and I narrowly avoided being blinded but did get a nasty laceration on my forehead. I stumbled, toppled over, and the back of my head met the unforgiving rock of the Faraglioni where there was no soft layer of springy moss to cushion the impact.

Rocks, alas, are harder than skulls.

CHAPTER 12

The Holy Writ

"Mmf. What . . . where am I?"

I was on my back, staring up at a ceiling of the institutional sort. Beeping noises. Discomfort in my arm. An antiseptic smell.

"Oi! He's awake! Quick!" someone said, and, belatedly, I realized that the voice belonged to Buck Foi. Nadia appeared over me, concern on her features.

"Ye're in an Italian hospital. Ye were knocked out and we couldnae use any sigils on ye. But let's take care of that now, yeah? One of healing and one of restoration."

She popped the restoration sigil in front of my eyes while I was still processing what she said.

"Restoration will put me to sleep," I said, and remembered, too late, that I shouldn't be talking aloud to her. My curse was still very much in effect.

"Nae bother. Ye need it," she said, snapping open the healing sigil next. "We'll catch up next time, and when we do, keep yer mouth shut, ya bloody knob."

Her voice broke a little at the end, so I was able to work out that she'd been worried about me and was calling me a knob in an affectionate way. Which was remarkable, I thought as my eyes closed, since Nadia didn't care for knobs at all.

"Mmf. What?"

"Shut it!" Nadia said. "No speaking. Here's a phone."

She pressed a rectangular shape into my right hand. When I raised it to my field of vision, I felt a tugging on my arm—an IV.

Nadia had given me a cheap smartphone with just a few apps loaded on it. One was a text-to-speech app that she had already set to a basic London accent.

[Where am I now?]

"Still in Italy. You've been here a week."

[A week?]

"That crack on yer head was bad, and ye were bleeding out from yer stabbings. We couldnae use any sigils until ye were conscious, so we had tae rely on conventional methods and brought ye here. Ye got severely concussed and had some brain swelling. They were keeping ye in a coma on purpose tae deal with it."

[The sirens?]

"Still alive but wounded. Buck teleported us tae the boat, and they didnae pursue us. That Italian kid is okay, but I don't think he's gonnay take any Scots clients after that bloody shambles."

A nurse entered, no doubt summoned by a change in my vital signs, and she called for the doctor who was treating me. When she arrived, she repeated much of what Nadia had already told me but asked questions about my stabbings and the gash on my forehead. Did I remember how I got them? I of course told her that I didn't remember anything. Her English was outstanding, with just a hint of Italian accent.

"We've sewn you up and put you on some powerful antibiotics and painkillers, and you've made remarkable progress in just the last day. I'll start weaning you off the painkillers, but we need to watch you for another couple of days. That head trauma was bad, and we want to be sure you're in good shape before we let you go."

I nodded and smiled at her until she went away. Once we had privacy again, I asked Nadia if she'd heard anything from Glasgow.

"Shop's okay, if that's what ye mean."

[I'm more worried about D.I. Munro. She is probably wondering where her persons of interest have gone.]

Her eyes widened. "Oh. Bollocks. I forgot about her."

[I guarantee she didn't forget about us. Contact Norman Pøøts. See if he can take my chart here and basically replicate it in the NHS electronic health record system and find a doctor who will accept a bribe to say I was a patient there.]

"What's the story?"

[We were camping in the Highlands, I fell and hit my head.]

"On it."

She dropped her gaze to her own phone, thumbs flying.

[That's not your phone from home, is it?]

"Naw. Burner like yours. Left mine back in Glasgow."

[Okay. So if we set it up correctly, we'll have our excuse for being out of touch.]

"Are ye worried that she'll actually be able tae nail us for the heists?"

[Naw. Just that she will be determined to nail us for something—anything.]

"Gotcha."

[So what have you been doing while I was out?]

Nadia shot a glance at Buck and actually smiled, which he returned. That gave me a thrill of fear, so my heart rate was already elevated when she dropped a bomb on me.

"We worked on a fun project together. We wrote up the holy scriptures of Lhurnog the Unhallowed and formally filed for charitable status for the Church of Lhurnog's Table."

My system flooded with panic adrenaline. [Why?]

"Churches are great for money laundering and tax avoidance,

Al. As a priestess I can register ma van tae the church and write off ma mileage and depreciation. We can actually buy whisky and cheese and write that off too, because it's part of our religious rites tae offer them tae the gob of Lhurnog. Once we get three thousand followers and jump through a few more hoops, we can be a registered church and get rid of some regulations that normal charities have. It's a great wee scam, religion. The question ye should ask is, why would we *no* do it?"

[Because if we wind up meeting a god who eats people, that could turn out to be a very bad day!]

Nadia scoffed. "He won't eat ye, Al. Ye should read the holy writ and unclench your arse about it."

I felt relatively certain that I would never unclench anything over this incredibly dangerous scheme. [Why is it called the Church of Lhurnog's Table?]

"He's festive and hospitable when he's not eating violent men, and he likes whisky and cheese. We didnae think it through, though. Buck realized after we published it that there could be unintended consequences."

[Such as?]

Buck finally spoke. "What do ye think we'll call followers of the faith? Because the acronym, CLT, can lead tae many variations on how it's pronounced. Put an O near the front and ye get *colts*, which isnae bad, but it's no a religion concerned with horses either. *Celts* might no be bad, but that wouldnae be inviting tae people around the world. The true danger comes from other vowels. *Cults*, for example, would be a bit too on the nose. A *clot* could be a potentially life-threatening vascular event or a thick git, but either would be preferable tae *clits*, and, well . . . there's a nonzero chance that could happen."

"The thing is, it doesnae matter," Nadia said. "It's all brilliant. People arguing about it will just generate publicity for the church and help spread the word. And do ye think we'll have trouble finding three thousand people in Glasgow who'd like tae get together for whisky and cheese on a Saturday afternoon? Because I don't."

[Saturday?]

"Aye. If we have services on a naturally occurring party day, they can take Sunday tae recover if they keep going with the whisky and make a night of it."

[How long is this holy writ of yours?]

"Eh, fifty pages or so? I mean, it basically says, *Don't be a floppy cock tae people and stuff your violence in an oubliette or Lhurnog will stuff his gob with your flesh,* and *Let's all enjoy some whisky and cheese and be friends instead.* Pretty noncontroversial."

[*Be nice or our god will eat you* is noncontroversial?]

"Seems pretty quick and merciful compared tae eternal damnation. I mean, if ye want tae compare divine punishments, ours are pretty tame in relation tae others."

[What's the afterlife you propose?]

"Eternal feasting at Lhurnog's table, with some luxury cludgies when ye have tae drop a jobby."

[You have people crapping in the ever-after?]

Buck said, "We had tae do that for consistency, since one of Lhurnog's axioms is that everyone's full of shite."

[You are making claims to consistency in your theology?]

"Consistent shitting, aye. Because look at all of those valorously slain Vikings in Valhalla, for example: It makes no sense they're always feasting and never taking a single spirited dump."

"Ah, I see what ye did there," Nadia said, smiling at the hob with approval. "Nice."

[You would think that eliminating elimination would be a perk of the afterlife.]

"Naw, it's a curse!" Buck insisted. "The Irish actually use it on people. They say tae evil bastards, *May ye eat and never shite,* except they say it in Irish and mostly tae the English."

Nadia waved her hand in front of her face as if to shoo away flies. "We've got right off topic here. It doesnae matter. What matters is what the sirens told ye, because we didnae hear. Did they finally tell ye who put the curses on yer heid?"

I sighed and held up a finger to tell them to be patient while I typed. [They did. The Greek gods Phobos and Deimos did it. I'm assuming Phobos crafted the one that turns people against me if I talk to them for too long—fear is close kin to hate—and Deimos made the one that kills my apprentices. But the kicker is that Ares told them to do it. He was angry that I told him to stay out of Syria.]

"Bloody hells. That's . . . how do ye deal with that?"

[Not sure yet. It will involve a trip to Olympus, certainly, but I would like to fully heal first and have a plan.]

"Ye know what, MacBharrais? This answers more than one question," Buck said. "How ye're gonnay confront Ares and those bawbags he spawned is probably what Gladys Who Has Seen Some Shite wants tae see."

[Probably,] I agreed, and the thought actually hurt—a wave of pain and exhaustion welled up inside me. The meds must be wearing off, and it showed on my face.

"Awright, Boss?" Nadia asked.

I told the two of them I'd be fine but could use another sigil of Restorative Healing and that they should get some rest themselves, enjoy the day or night or whatever it was. Now that I was seriously on the mend, I anticipated going home in a few days rather than a week or more. And we'd probably need to get back sooner rather than later. Nadia came over and gave me the sigil, which I unsealed and used immediately.

[Could you ask Gladys if the D.I. has been asking for us at the shop?]

"Sure thing," she replied, and that was pretty much when I drifted off again.

It took another day and several healing sigils before I could walk without dizzy spells or blacking out. Concussions are no joke. But when I felt up to it, I extricated myself from IVs and monitors and had Buck teleport me outside the hospital, where Nadia was waiting with my topcoat. They have good socialized medicine in Italy, so they wouldn't be after me for a bill, but they might be alarmed at my sudden disappearance. Nadia was waiting with my topcoat, and I threw it over my hospital gown so I wouldn't be so obviously the man who should be under supervised treatment. We walked out of Naples via the Old Way back to Glasgow, where it was midmorning on a Thursday.

The D.I. had indeed been calling and even stopping by the office frequently to see if I'd returned yet, so before I went to the office, I went home to shower and change and make an attempt to look my best. The man in the mirror looked tired and worn, but some tea and a scone without raisins in it should power me through the remainder of the day. I scooped up my phone—which would no doubt inform the police that I was back, because it would ping off the local tower—and fired off a Signal to Norman Pøøts. *Status on your projects?*

It took a few minutes for him to reply, and I had already left Buck snoring in the flat and was halfway to the office when he replied.

Laundry done. Ready to ID as soon as you have the machine. Inverness hospital records in place, doc on board.

Doc's name?

Hamish MacAllister.

All was well, then. The heist funds for Roxanne were ready to be distributed to her as soon as she had ID and accounts to receive them, and that would be accomplished as soon as Buck stole an official government machine for making passports. That was the sole item on his to-do list today. On my list were to visit Roxanne in the necropolis and attend to the myriad things that no doubt awaited me in the office.

Gladys Who Has Seen Some Shite beamed at me when I entered. "Welcome back, Boss. Find out what you needed?"

[I did. Not sure what to do about it yet.]

There was a gleam in her eye that might not have been entirely natural. "You let me know when you figure it out, eh? I would like to see that."

[I will. Anything urgent for me to attend to?]

"I expect you'll be hearing from that detective soon. Just got off the phone with her, and she's some excited to see you. Think she's on her way, so if you want to avoid her, I'd scoot."

Sighing, I typed, [Send her on up when she arrives. Thanks.]

Once upstairs, I laid down my official ID with its mindhacking sigils on one side of my desk, to be deployed if the police got out the handcuffs for any reason, but I hoped she'd be reasonable. To my knowledge, she had nothing to arrest me for yet.

The D.I. did enter, however, with a constable in attendance, a predatory smirk on her face. She took a chair in front of my desk without being invited.

"Mr. MacBharrais. Where have ye been?"

[Hello, D.I. Munro. I've been minding my business.]

"Of course. But ye weren't minding it here. So where were you?"

[How is that your business again?]

"You're under active investigation as an associate of a man who robbed millions from several banks."

[An association you have yet to prove aside from your memory that he was in the flat of my deceased apprentice.]

"Nevertheless. After I told ye not tae leave town, ye did so, twice."

[I did?]

"Yes. Once tae New York, and after ye returned, ye went somewhere else. Where did ye go and what did ye do there, Mr. MacBharrais? Laundering some money, perhaps?"

[How do you know I went somewhere? Do you have proof?]

"Yer phone that ye're so fond of there was left in yer flat. But there was no light or sound coming from yer flat for more than a week, nor any spike in electrical use during that time, so I doubt very much ye were there."

[An astounding level of surveillance and invasion of privacy for a mere suspected associate. I'll have to contact a solicitor regarding your overreach. But I was camping in the Highlands, where a phone would be unnecessary. I took a tumble, hit my head, and spent a week at the hospital in Inverness.]

"Did ye, now? Who was yer doctor?"

[Hamish MacAllister.]

"And where exactly were ye camping?"

[Can't remember on account of the blow to the head. I have a concussion.]

"You always have an answer, don't ye?"

[Be fair. When you ask a question, you expect me to supply one. Thank you for inquiring after my health, Detective Inspector. If that is all, I'll also thank you for allowing me to get back to work.]

"Naw, that's not all. I wannay know why ye suddenly became a camping enthusiast when ye seem tae be such a city dweller. Who was with ye? Who can testify ye were camping and no laundering heist funds?"

[Please direct all further questions to my solicitor, since you seem determined to believe, without evidence, that I am involved with financial crimes.]

"Ha!" D.I. Munro grinned triumphantly, as if I'd confessed to something. Apparently she counted my request to involve a lawyer as a victory of some kind. "What happened tae supplying answers tae ma questions? Right. Who's yer solicitor, then?"

[I don't know yet. I'll get one by the end of day.]

"I'll look forward tae hearing from ye. And finding out if Dr. Hamish MacAllister in Inverness is real." She rose from the chair and turned. "Come on, Constable, we have tae talk tae the accountant now."

I didn't think Nadia was in yet, but D.I. Munro would discover that for herself soon enough. My accountant and manager was probably doing something for the Church of Lhurnog's Table rather than her job.

CHAPTER 13

A Step into Mortality

Thanks to our previous conversation, I did not need to wander about the necropolis asking various crows if they were Roxanne, which saved me no little embarrassment. I walked straight to the sarcophagus of Isabella Ure Elder, and there she was.

[Hello, Roxanne. I have good news for you, but first I wonder if you can sense if I've been followed. I've been under surveillance. Should you find anyone, we will need privacy but not a dead body.]

"Caw," Roxanne said, and launched herself directly over my head and flew out of sight past some mausoleums and tombstones. Shortly thereafter, I heard some more cawing—Roxanne had apparently called a full murder of crows to her aid, all of them diving at something out of my sight—and a panicked male voice crying out, "Auggh! What the fuck! Fucking! What! Auggh!"

I chuckled. That constable, or whoever he was, would have an interesting explanation to give to D.I. Munro about why he lost me, and I wished I could be there when he told her.

The murder kept circling and diving at the unseen man, but I noticed that it was moving away, which meant he had decided to flee. Roxanne winged her way back to me and took her human form, all sheathed in black. She gave me a wry smile as she said in her sepulchral whisper, "That was entertaining. Hello, Al."

[Just received word that your money is ready to deposit once we have an ID for you and get some accounts set up. And we can do the ID tomorrow.]

Her face fell. "Oh."

In response, my face fell too. [Is that not good?]

"It is, no, it is! I am simply . . ." She trailed off and took a seat on the sarcophagus steps, sighing heavily as she did so. When I didn't move—it wouldn't do to assume she wanted my company there—she gestured to the space next to her. Once I'd lowered myself successfully nearby but not too close, she frowned at me. "We are friends, Al. You can sit closer. Never mind, I'll move to you."

She scooched over so that we were seated as we were when we spoke in the rain. "Better, yes?" I nodded, still grappling with her declaration that we were friends. Had she decided this while I was away in Italy? I thought it best not to ask for clarification, as it might suggest I didn't agree, and that might hurt her feelings, and then I might perish in great pain.

Roxanne continued, "I have been working toward this for a long time. But taking on a mortal name and collecting mundane trappings like identification and bank accounts—well, that's a very concrete step to becoming someone other than the Morrigan. There might be a zero-sum factor at play. If I formally take on the Roxanne Morrigan persona, do I cease being the Morrigan of antiquity? Will I lose access to the power of worship or any of my own powers? There is not a lot of precedent to consult."

I waggled my finger and excitedly typed a response. [Nancy is an excellent precedent. She retains her gifts of prophecy and is very happy. She gave me an incredibly potent candle that helped me discover who cursed me.] Typing that made me realize I had no idea where the candle was now. I had it on the Faraglioni but woke up in the hospital without it.

"But the details matter. How much power does she have, and how is she getting it?"

I would have to look for the candle later. This challenge demanded all my attention.

[It was like you said: The ritual of finding her is its own devotion. I cannot guess how much power she wields now compared to that of her ancient self, but that candle was able to work around the protection of cold iron. She has real power.]

"How did you find her?"

[You take nine tracks into a subway station in Brooklyn, say some ritual evocations, and she appears with a goose and answers one question before she walks away to buy some frozen peas in a bodega.]

"Evocation. You used the name Nancy, and that helped?"

[Very much. She thanked me for the effort.]

"That may be the key, then."

[To what?]

"Tell Nadia that once I have my ID, we need to do that thing we talked about."

The Fae learned their misdirection from the Tuatha Dé Danann. Roxanne didn't answer my question about the key, and I briefly considered asking again, but perhaps it was wiser not to pursue it. [Is this thing something I might need to worry about?]

"Not professionally. Personally—on a soul-crushing level—you may have much to fear."

When a Chooser of the Slain who doubles as a psychopomp tells you to anticipate a soul-crushing experience, you'd be justified in feeling any number of perfectly reasonable fear responses. My bowels squirmed and made an embarrassing noise before the corner of her mouth quirked to show that she didn't mean disfigurement or death.

"I need you and Nadia to go on a double date with me. I'm unfamiliar with modern customs and need coaching."

My panic regarding my own survival downshifted into panic regarding awkward social situations. [I am also unfamiliar. I haven't been on the dating scene for more than four decades.]

"I don't want you to coach me. Nadia will do that. You're just there in case we need a sigil or an old man's opinion, and we won't. You'll have nothing to do except pretend to be romantically involved with Nadia."

[No one would ever believe that. From either of us.]

"He won't be looking at you too closely. He'll be paying attention to me."

[Okay. So why is this necessary?]

"If I am to have a mortal life, I want to experience love the way that mortals do."

[You have never been in love?]

Her eyes flashed red briefly but she looked down, which meant that her intense feeling—anger or otherwise—was not directed at me. "I have felt it. But it was not requited."

[Ah. Is this individual you loved still alive?]

"Yes. And he's happy. And I am happy for him. But I would like to feel what it is like to be loved for myself. It is outside my experience."

[Understandable. It might be a bit of a journey.]

"I grasp that. I can be patient. Have I not waited patiently here for you to bring me this news?"

[You have. But an actual live man will tax your patience far worse than the assembled gentlemen here,] I said, nodding at the tombstones.

She arched an eyebrow at me. "Yes, I'm getting that."

[Right. Well. Happy to help. I will tell Nadia.]

"Excellent."

[Tomorrow you should look as you intend to look as a mortal, if it's any different from what you're presenting now. We will take your ID at this location at noon, and here is the password.] I showed her the relevant info on my phone, and she quickly memorized it and promised to be there. Her doubts about taking this step into mortality had melted away, and I'm sure it had something to do with my assurances regarding Nancy, but what that might be I had no idea.

[See you then. I must secure the services of a lawyer now. The heist has brought me the kind of surveillance that needs to stop.]

CHAPTER 14

———— · ————

The Double Date

My documents guy, Rory MacCallum, was a study in contrasts. Absolutely no chin but a fantastic bushy beard grown to disguise it, floofy yet carefully trimmed like a prizewinning Pomeranian. Incapable of ironing a piece of fabric to save his life, but he had a musk or a cologne or something that was somehow inoffensive and close to being charming—cedar and sandalwood would be my guess. He was as polite as a Canadian intern anxious to impress, but he wore a T-shirt with an asterisk on it from the Kurt Vonnegut Library, which, if you've read *Breakfast of Champions*, you know wasn't an asterisk at all. He was a career criminal who liked to hide his antisocial tendencies in plain sight.

His crimes, however, he liked to perform in secure undisclosed locations, preferably underground, after the fashion of Norman Pøøts. Buck and I met Rory and Norman in Norman's new lair, a basement beneath a used bookshop on Bath Street called Gud Dug Books, accessed through a lift hidden behind a bookcase in the back. To get there, we had to navigate around a Siberian husky sprawled across the floor, who had no intention of moving, and endure the side-eyed suspicions of a desultory cashier, who smelled faintly of garlic mashed potatoes as he read a trade paperback of the comic *Chew* with his feet up on the counter. The interior of the lift was large enough to move furniture, more of a freight elevator than a standard lift. The walls were bizarrely padded and upholstered in red velvet and adorned with framed prints in the art-deco style, advertising travel to fictional planets like Arrakis and Hoth. As with the entrance to Norman's previous lairs, access was granted only via audible password, which Buck read aloud off my phone. "Plutocrat Duck Fat."

Once the lift engaged, Buck had a question. "Is the fat from a plutocrat duck different from the fat of working-class ducks? Oh! Never mind. It's probably richer, in't it? Still, wot's he tryin' tae say there? Oh! Never mind. Eat the rich. Now it makes sense."

I was glad I didn't have to answer his musings. Rory and Norman greeted us as the lift doors opened but noticed aloud that Roxanne wasn't with us.

[She will arrive separately,] I told them.

"Stonking," Norman said, dressed in another tailored business suit, an unusually angry magenta, like the petals of a bougainvillea bush, with a partially unbuttoned pale-yellow shirt underneath. If this was the height of fashion at the moment, I would content myself with the lowlands. "Welcome to the latest and greatest pit of mischief! Can I get ye a pint or an Irn-Bru?"

Looking sharply at Buck to see what he said, my hobgoblin caught it and asked for "an Irn-Bru, please." He flashed a sardonic smile at me and fluttered his eyelids.

Norman's new digs thankfully did not include the disco ball of his previous hideaway, but it did have a club lighting rig with many different gels over the bulbs; there was also a dance floor covered in a paisley pattern with reflective paints so that the design changed colors, flashing and rippling in our vision as we moved. A full bar was set up directly opposite the lift on the other side of the space, with some high-top tables lining the edges of the room, plus a DJ booth in a corner to the left of the lift, currently blessing our ears with the Spice Girls informing us of what they really, really wanted. It was more of a small speakeasy nightclub than a hacker's lair. There was, however, a door behind the bar, which might simply be storage or a small kitchen, but which I imagined led to where he did the bulk of his work. As Norman strode to the bar to fetch us drinks, Rory looked pointedly at the rucksack slung over Buck's shoulder.

"Is that the machine?"

"Aye," he confirmed. "Where ye want it?"

"On the bar."

The number of felony thefts Buck had committed now, I would bet, far exceeded that of any successful human thief operating in the UK, and if the D.I. discovered I did indeed know him, I'd have a pack of trouble. But this particular theft would be made right: Rory didn't know it, but Buck's mission was to steal the machine back from him after he'd completed his work for Roxanne and return it to the government office whence he acquired it. We couldn't have Rory making perfect IDs for criminals other than Irish death goddesses.

The lift dinged behind us and the door slid open to reveal a woman I did not recognize, except remotely. The black hair and arched eyebrows were the same, but the hair was longer, more lustrous now, and the shape of the cheekbones and jaw had been altered. It was Roxanne, but different. She'd made changes somehow to her appearance, perhaps to look a bit more like her old self than the Australian woman whose body she had taken over when the unfortunate spirit of Thea Prendergast left it. She was a couple of inches taller, perhaps a bit slimmer and simultaneously more muscular, or at least toned. She had on a grey suit, of all things, which made her look like a young attractive professional rather than a Chooser of the Slain.

[Roxanne?] We had a little space to ourselves as everyone else was congregating at the bar.

"Yes," she replied, her voice that of Thea's but in an Irish accent rather than Australian. "I will look and sound like this from now on. Took quite a bit of effort, but I think I can live with this."

Norman came over with an Irn-Bru for me, shook hands, and asked Roxanne if he could get her anything. She opted for a porter he had on tap, and once he had delivered that, he went over to the DJ booth and fiddled with the lights until he got them the way Rory wanted them for the photography—bright white.

Rory had some additional setup to perform and a couple of blank passport books he'd gotten from somewhere. Once he was ready, he took several photos, imported them digitally into his laptop, and ran some software to get her passport made. While he worked on that, Norman took me through that door behind the bar, and I found out that there was indeed much more to see back there. A storage room to actually store booze but also to fool people, because there was *another* secret entrance, guarded with a passcode; this time, though, it was just a door instead of an elevator. It opened to a hallway that took us left, which Norman explained was moving us toward the street underneath the front half of the bookstore. At the end of this hallway lurked a door that looked like the entrance to a vault, and I said as much.

"Well spotted," Norman said. "That *is* a vault door. Battering rams will do fuck-all against it."

[You're expecting battering rams?]

"Naw, I'm simply prepared for them. And I have a secret way out too."

[How did you get all this set up in such a short time?]

"Oh, I didnae. I had this place in process while I was at the other location as Saxon. And I'm working on ma next location already. Hoping I won't need it, though. I like this place a lot."

The entrance to the vault was accessed via biometric scan of his retina, plus another password.

[What's the endgame for you, Norman? What are you trying to achieve?]

"Big picture, eh? Well, I want tae be the one who got away. A career criminal—the nonviolent kind—who never does time and retires in another country under his real name with a spotless record. The Hans Gruber plan, ye know: sitting on a beach earning twenty percent. Though I'm not sure how I'll manage that in this economy. What about you?"

[Get my curses lifted, train an apprentice, and retire. Make some non-magical, law-abiding friends, just to see what that's like.]

"Ha! I've got some law-abiding friends who don't know what I'm really intae. They're adorable. Innocent wee puppies playing by the rules. Ye made any progress on the curses?"

[A bit. Not sure how to address it yet, but I've told my subconscious to simmer on it, and we'll see if anything bubbles up to the surface.]

"Good enough. Here we go."

He hauled open the door and waved me in. A waft of cinnamon apples hit my nose from one of those plug-in air fresheners. The hardware on display was impressive—three giant monitors arranged on a slick architect's desk with multiple keyboards resting in front of them, tied wires and cables snaking down by the wall, and behind the ergonomic chair, an industrial hum of cooling fans and server racks. One of the monitors was delivering a constant feed of closed-circuit surveillance video from the store and the bar, as well as the interior of his lift and hallway.

[Nice,] I said. [What's through there?] I pointed at a door opposite where we stood.

"Crash pad. I've got a restroom that's directly underneath the bookstore's restroom, a bed, a small refrigerator for snacks, and, of course, my bolt-hole."

[Where does it go?]

"State secret." His phone pinged and he said, "Hey, they're ready."

We returned to the bar, where Roxanne's new passport and driver's license were being manufactured. I expressed curiosity about the address on them, and Roxanne brightened.

"Norman has secured this residence for me through a shell company and will transfer the title to me shortly. Having it on my ID will allow me to set up my bank accounts easily."

[So you decided against the castle?]

"Yes. It's still a nice property—a penthouse with rooftop access—but it will keep me in the city, which is what I want."

[I must have missed several conversations while I was away.]

"You did. My plans have evolved. But not the one where you are going out on a double date tonight. We are meeting at six at this place," she said, showing me a name on her phone. "Can you try to look like someone who would date a goth queen?"

[I'm afraid that is far beyond my skill set.]

"Hmm. Maybe Nadia can try to tone it down."

[Hopefully, as you said, your date won't be looking at us.]

"Right. I have to go to the bank now, so I'll see you later."

[My debt to you is paid, then?] It was best to make sure these things were cleared up with the Tuatha Dé Danann.

"It is. Let us shake on it. That is a thing normal people do, right?"

I nodded and shook hands with Roxanne Morrigan. On paper, at least, she was a goddess no more, and she was practically giddy with excitement. She had climbed out of the rut she'd been in for centuries and could not wait to fall into the rut humans were in, albeit with significant advantages.

"Thank you, Al," she said, smiling brightly. "I can just go around thanking people now. It feels so nice to express gratitude without incurring debt."

She waved at everyone, deployed a general thank-you, and left us via the lift. I likewise said my farewells and exited Gud Dug Books with Buck, both of us wearing hats with sigils on them. Mine disabled cameras, and Buck's worked on the people who laid eyes on him so that they simply didn't register his presence, because he was wearing a Sigil of Seeming Absence. Once I left, he would appear on any surveillance cams in the area, and those might eventually catch the attention of the D.I., but I would not be with him, so that was fine.

[Stealing back the machine from Rory will take some time. It's paramount that he not know you did it,] I typed.

"I know, I know. It's gonnay be a long boring day, thanks tae yer annoying moral compass. But I'll get it done so long as he doesnae sleep on top of it."

[Good. I'll leave you to it, then.]

The hobgoblin grumbled and leaned against the shop front of Gud Dug Books, waiting for Rory to emerge. I turned west down Bath Street for a walk of five or six blocks. If I had to keep a date that evening for Roxanne's benefit, it was only fitting that I keep a date for myself. A day later than the usual time, in this case, and a decidedly one-sided date, as the other party had no idea in what esteem I held her and might in fact never know. But I allowed myself to softly pine for Mrs. MacRae, the widow from Oban who now worked in the Mitchell Library. I had not seen her in several weeks owing to my recent adventures, and I had some legitimate research to do with which she might provide valuable assistance.

My knowledge of Phobos and Deimos was scant, and I needed to remedy that. Phobos, of course, had managed to work his way into everyday language as phobias of one kind or another. But who he was as a deity was a closed book I needed to find and open. Before engagement, it was best to know your enemy.

Merely thinking that phrase recalled a song from some American band that Nadia had blasted on the printshop floor once. I think she'd been trying to make a point about mechanical maintenance, because due diligence there prevented costly breakdowns and repairs, and the enemy was grit and ink buildup and never enough lube or something. But now the damn tune was looping in my head, and I had to get it out of there before I walked into the building. Vivaldi: That was the ticket. The first allegro movement of Winter from the Four Seasons, Concerto No. 4 in

F Minor. Humming that banished the American band and steered my mind to clarity and receptiveness to learning something.

The way Mrs. MacRae's face lit up at my appearance when I emerged onto her floor in the Mitchell Library sent my heart racing before she even said a word.

"Ah, Mr. MacBharrais! How lovely tae see ye again. I'm glad to see ye well; I was getting worried."

I doffed my hat and typed a reply: [Mrs. MacRae. I was much occupied elsewhere but am glad to be back. I am hoping you can help me find something.]

"Of course I will try," she said. She always wore a new bright scarf against the same few conservative jackets in drab neutral colors: This time the scarf shouted with blobs of orange, yellow, and red on a white base, nestled against a grey houndstooth jacket.

[I need to know everything I can about the Greek deities Phobos and Deimos.]

"Oh, my. I'm no sure they ever got stories of their own. They did get some mentions from Homer in *The Iliad,* but let's see." Her fingers danced across the keyboard while mine stabbed at my phone.

[Interesting. Do you recall their mentions in *The Iliad*?]

"Ach, no specific deeds. They just accompanied their father, Ares, intae battle, and of course they got those moons of Mars named after them. Isnae it strange that the planet uses the Roman name of Ares and the moons use the Greek names of the sons?"

[What did the Romans call them?]

"Phobos was Terror. Not sure about Deimos. And unless I find something else, well—here's something. Deimos is listed as a possible father tae Scylla. But there are a lot of candidates for the job, and his paternity is only attested by one source: Semos of Delos."

[Delos? The Greek island?]

"Aye. Supposed birthplace of Apollo and Artemis. One of the richest places in the world in the Hellenistic era. Whole place is an archaeological site now."

Interesting, but unlikely to help me confronting the two deities—or three, including their father, and one very much had to worry about the father. Would the Iron Druid's cold iron talisman help defend me against their fear and dread? It would do fuck-all to protect me from the sword and shield of Ares, against which I had little hope of prevailing, even with the help of sigils. But might the cold iron weaken or even destroy the curses? I'd been wearing it while visiting the sirens but hadn't thought to check until now whether doing so had any positive effect on my curses. I'd need to have someone reexamine my aura; if the curses were indeed gone, I'd not need to risk a confrontation. But I cautioned myself against hope, since they had been wrought so carefully and skillfully that only the sirens had been able to give me the slightest clue about them.

A charming furrow of frustration appeared between Mrs. Mac-Rae's eyes as she failed to find anything substantive.

"They don't appear tae have done much but attend their father. But perhaps we should consult *The Iliad*. We have several transla-tions, including the new one from Emily Wilson. Would ye like tae do that?" When I nodded, she smiled and rose from her seat behind the research desk and led me downstairs to the proper shelves, chatting all the while.

"I really enjoyed Ms. Wilson's translation of *The Odyssey*. No flinching from the fact that the Greeks kept slaves—it tempers yer admiration of their heroism and culture a good deal when ye're no left tae think they're rich folk attended by well-paid servants. Have ye read that one yet?"

[Not the Wilson translation, no.]

"Well, we can get that for ye as well if ye like." She'd navigated us to the portion of the library offering books to check out, since the upper floors where she worked were for research only. "Ah, here we are. The mention is supposed tae happen in Book Four in conjunction with Ares, so if we scan for his name . . ." She trailed off as she speed-read through the verses, and I have always thought that we should say *sped-read* because it is much more pleasant to rhyme and the short vowel literally gives the phrase more speed, but apparently only the reading is in past tense, not the speed, and grammarians have thus once again robbed us of our tiny verbal joys.

You know what? Fuck it. It's my story. Mrs. MacRae sped-read *The Iliad,* her finger tracing down the pages as her eyes searched for the god of war. It was a good number of pages in before she found it.

"Ach, look here. It calls them Terror and Panic instead of Phobos and Deimos. Well, I suppose that answers ma idle question earlier, no? Ye can hardly call the moons of Mars Terror and Panic. The original Greek sounds more poetic. Though I suppose tae the Greeks they *are* called Terror and Panic. I wonder why she chose the word *panic* there, though? I thought Deimos meant *dread.* Well, I may no have helped ye in the least, but I have tae thank ye for giving me an interesting bit of translation trivia tae pursue. Let's try another translation, shall we?"

She found several others, including the Fagles translation, in which the brothers were called Terror and Rout. But there was nothing about who they were as individuals, just that they were present in the battle outside Troy, riding with Ares.

"Well, that's no very satisfying, is it? I'm sorry, Mr. MacBharrais."

[No, it's helpful in its own way. And perhaps a reacquaintance with Homer would prove generally helpful. May I check out the Wilson translations of both?]

"Of course, of course." She fetched *The Odyssey* and *The Iliad* for me. "When ye say generally helpful—may I ask what ye're after?"

There was no way I could tell her the whole truth, so I composed a reply that contained perhaps 20 percent of it. [I feel that I must understand the ancient Greeks a bit better. This new scholarship may help me grapple with questions about their character.]

Mrs. MacRae's face blossomed in a smile. Was that fondness in her expression? "I do enjoy yer visits, Mr. MacBharrais. Ye're always grappling with something, and I can never guess what's next."

[I can never guess either. Thank you for pointing me at these new translations.]

"Nae bother. Will ye be back tae visiting regular, then?"

[I'm not sure. I may have to travel again. But so long as I am in town, I'll have something new to grapple with every week.]

"Good," she said. "Let me know what ye think of those next time."

It may be possible to flirt using a text-to-speech app, but I was too frightened to experiment. So much of our communication is conveyed via tone and inflection, which the apps lack. I could only hope that Mrs. MacRae understood in what high regard I held her via my expressions and staunch refusal to lapse from formality.

The Iliad's portrayal helped me thus: If the ancient Greeks imagined Phobos and Deimos as inextricably linked with and even attendant upon their father, then their ability to act independently was most likely circumscribed. It was similar to Roxanne's problem as the Morrigan: The pagan Irish never imagined she could love, so she couldn't. To truly experience it, she had to become someone else. If Phobos and Deimos were only able to act in concert with or by permission of Ares, then neutralizing him might also neutralize them. Which did not exactly provide me a solution but did afford me some new approaches to the problem.

I went home and lost myself in Ms. Wilson's engaging introduction for a while, then thought I should at least make some effort at being more than usually presentable. I reapplied some mustache wax and put on a brilliant paisley waistcoat, plus some shinier shoes. That was about all I could do, since I customarily dressed well.

Out of curiosity, I sent a Signal to Nadia.

Who is it that's meeting up with Roxanne?

Her reply came quickly. *Some knob that a friend of a friend recommended.*

Do you know this knob?

Naw. Knob's anonymous.

It's truly a blind date? You know nothing about this man?

His name is Calvin Brodie.

That's it? No social media or web searches? What if he turns out to be a bastard?

If any bastards try tae start shite with me or Roxanne, he'll wake up deid.

Right. And that's a situation we want to avoid, yes?

Awright, hold on. It took a few minutes, but her next message did not fill me with confidence. *We may have a problem,* she said.

What is it?

Pretty sure he's a Tory Brexiteer type.

The quiet stuffy sort or the loud sort?

I'm guessing loud.

Gods, this was going to be a nightmare. *Is your friend of a friend all right in the heid? Why is this the method you're using to get a date for Roxanne?*

Because I don't know what straight people like, do I? My straight friend said they like big cocks and she knew someone who knew this guy, so here we are.

So he has a big cock or he is a big cock?

Might be both. Look, it'll be a teachable moment.

I recommend you give some more care and thought to future rendezvous.

Point taken. I'll handle it. Don't worry.

I put down my phone and immediately started to worry.

We all met at a restaurant called The Buttery, an old place on Argyle Street furnished in mahogany wood and tartan upholstery, serving such Scottish fare as Highland venison and haggis bon-bons. White tablecloths, gleaming silver—very fancy. It smelled of whisky, wet wool, and gravy, with subtle ghosts of secondhand smoke and assorted perfumes and colognes. We wound up seated at a table rather than a booth, which I appreciated for the ability to exit quickly. Nadia and Roxanne sat on one side of the table, both of them looking rather stunning, while I sat next to Calvin Brodie, a lumpy potato of a man who smelled like he'd already had a couple of drinks before arriving. He shook hands with everyone, said it was a pleasure, so at least he had that much in the way of manners. But once seated, he took a quick look around and then at the tablecloth and sniffed.

"Never been in here," he said, his voice a gravelly baritone. "Kind of rich, in't it? Ye come here often?" he asked Roxanne.

"No. It's my first time."

"Oh, aye, what's that accent? Irish?"

"Aye."

"Northern Ireland or the Republic?"

"Well, Glasgow, currently," Roxanne said, not entirely understanding the question. Warning bells clanged in my head, because that was already an obliquely political question, and it would only get worse. We were granted a temporary stay by the server, who hovered nearby briefly to collect drink orders. Roxanne, Nadia, and I all ordered drams from the Highlands, and Calvin ordered an Islay after consulting the menu. While he was doing that, I noticed that Roxanne's eyes went briefly glassy, no doubt examining his aura, and when they refocused she shot uncertain glances at Nadia and me. I'm not sure what she saw, but it clearly didn't put her at ease.

"I've been to the North a few times for work," Calvin said. "Always had a good time. You been there?"

"Aye. I'm very familiar with the entire island. What sort of work took you there?"

"Commercial contractor. Lots of jobs with factories and warehouses and the like. What about you?"

"My job? Chooser of the Slain."

"What?"

Nadia and I could not hide our surprise at this answer any more than Calvin could, and she saw our wide eyes and realized her error. She'd probably never been asked before and didn't realize how it would sound until she said it, didn't even think of trying to disguise it.

"I mean, that's what people used to call me, but I was really more of an escort."

Ohhh, no. I saw what she was trying to do, picking a euphemism for her role as a psychopomp, but the word choice was unfortunate, judging by the fact that Calvin's potato face did an admirable imitation of a pile of mash. "An escort?"

"Not the kind ye're thinking of," Nadia broke in. "She's really more of a guide or assistant, helping people transition from one life to another."

Calvin's face remained scrunched up. "Transition?"

"You know what? It doesn't matter. It's not my job anymore," Roxanne said. "I'm currently seeking new employment."

"Ah, well, good on ye. What sort of work ye looking for, then? I know some people in the trades if that interests ye at all."

"I guess I'd like to work with at-risk populations of women."

Nadia and I reacted one way—surprise and admiration for the phrasing, which sounded very modern yet vague at the same time—and Calvin reacted another.

"At-risk women? Ye mean like, what? Is this some kind of woke jargon?"

Roxanne glanced at us for help with the unfamiliar adjective, and we couldn't possibly explain it quickly or say out loud that his usage of it probably meant he was a racist, so we shook our heads sadly and she said, "I don't know."

"Come on, now. Are ye one of those remoaners?"

"What? I don't know that word."

"A remainer. A complainer. On Brexit."

"Is he . . . ?" Roxanne looked at us. "What is he saying?"

Before we could even attempt to answer, Calvin bulled on. "Ye don't know what Brexit is? Where have ye been?"

"Australia, most recently."

"Well, they have news in Australia, surely? How can ye not have heard of Brexit?"

Our drinks arrived and we thanked our server, but Calvin did not. Nadia asked if we could have a little more time before ordering, and she said of course and withdrew.

"Well?" Calvin prodded.

"I was out of touch for a good while and have only just come back. It sounds like I missed a lot." She raised her glass, a fragile smile on her lips. "Cheers."

Nadia and I raised our glasses, but Calvin shook his head. "You're a Labour voter, are ye? Or worse, SNP. That's it, in't it?"

Roxanne set down her glass and her pleasant expression melted away. "I do not know, Calvin Brodie. But your aura seethes with bitterness, envy, and resentment." An abrupt series of physical changes transformed her features in the space of a second. Her eyes flashed red—that one I was used to—but her hair writhed upon her head, independent of any wind, because there wasn't any, and her fingernails blackened and lengthened into something more like claws as she placed them down halfway across the table, easily seen against the white tablecloth but also in easy striking distance of Calvin's eyes, should she decide to rake them. Her voice was cold fury scraped across a cheese grater. "I find you unattractive. Flee before I feast upon your gallbladder and consume your bile."

That was a new one for me, and for Calvin as well.

"What the fuck?" he cried, abruptly pushing away from the table, wide-eyed with fear. He tumbled backward, crashed into someone behind us, then careened off to the side to hit the floor, which started a cascade of Scots cursing and caused Calvin no little embarrassment on top of his generous helping of fright. That made him think briefly about scolding Roxanne and he got to his feet, face flushed, and shouted, "Ya fucking b—"

But Roxanne rose in a fluid motion, claws extended at her sides, red eyes glowing steadily now, and he wisely reconsidered finishing that thought. Instead, he let loose with a whimper he would never ever admit to later and fled the premises as he was told.

"Okay, okay, let's settle down and look normal," Nadia said in low tones, and Roxanne immediately sat, her polite fingernails returned, her hair rearranged perfectly, and her eyes cooled to a deep satisfactory brown. It had all happened too fast for any cameras to capture it, though I noticed a few were now pointed in our direction. I checked on my hat, which was still on the back of my chair. There was a possibility that line-of-sight had been interrupted, so I removed it briefly and raised it over my head, just to ensure nothing could be recorded at the moment, then placed it on the table to my left, next to Calvin's untouched pour of Islay whisky.

Nadia was apologizing and saying everything was okay and how about we buy a round of drinks for everyone? That lowered the temperature quite a bit, and Calvin Brodie was soon forgotten.

Once the immediate hubbub subsided, Nadia said, "It's good that ye recognized early that it wasnae gonnay work and we should move on, but typically, Roxanne, that's no how we end a date."

Roxanne said in her soft Irish accent, "It isn't? So how do you make them go away before you kill them? I was trying to be nice."

"Well, in a situation like this, it's often easiest to simply leave ourselves. We hadnae ordered any food, and even if we had, it's fun tae stick them with the bill."

"We're not going to leave, are we? I'm hungry."

"No, we can stay. But often ye'll find that if ye ask a man tae leave, he'll want tae argue about it. So it's easier to make some excuse tae leave the table and then make yerself scarce. He'll figure it out eventually. Just dingie him and don't answer his texts."

"That seems cowardly."

"Naw, cowardly would be running from a fight. This is about making sure one never starts, because we both know ye're gonnay finish it. And we cannae have ye eating random men's gallbladders. That kind of thing draws attention. So strategically, thinking of the long term here, ye need to think about avoiding conflict wherever possible, so that ye can maintain this name with no trouble."

"Am I going to be dating long-term?"

"Maybe," Nadia allowed.

"That man was entirely unsuitable. Why did you think we'd be a good match?"

"I didnae think it at all—he was recommended by someone else, and I won't be asking them for any more. But getting fixed up by a friend is just one way tae meet people. The other is tae go out tae pubs and get chatted up, and yet another is tae use an app, and we aren't there yet."

"That's not how I thought dates happened."

"Have ye been on dates before?"

"Once. It is my most pleasant memory, behind the second Battle of Mag Tuired, of course, where Balor of the Evil Eye met his doom at the hands of Lugh Lhámfhada. Both were excellent days."

"Yeah? So what did yer date involve?"

"We went to a baseball game. I wore a baseball cap and he said I looked cute, which I know does not sound especially meaningful, but cute is something I'd never been before. There was something about the experience I so enjoyed. His companionship, of course, but also that of everyone there, watching athletes compete to their utmost, so much tension and drama and so many hot dogs and, later, so many digestive issues."

"Well, we don't have baseball, but there's a Rangers football match this weekend. Would ye like tae go tae that if we can find ye a date?"

"Sure."

"Stonking. Al, can ye find us four tickets tae the game this weekend?"

[I will try my best,] I replied, though I didn't like being included in another social adventure. Regardless, I got on the Internet to find a ticket broker. We ordered steaks—Roxanne asked for two rare filets—and by the time our food arrived, I had made arrangements to purchase four overpriced seats for Saturday's match.

I was grateful that my presence wouldn't be needed in their after-dinner pub crawl; the two of them were extremely confident that they could walk in almost anywhere and find someone nice who would be willing to attend a game with us.

By the time I got home, I was exhausted and so was Buck, having returned successfully from his duties.

"Returning an item is more tiring than stealing it, for some reason," he said. "Let's no make a habit of that, eh?"

[Definitely do not want a repeat of this day,] I agreed, and we shuffled to our separate rooms to crash.

CHAPTER 15

The Football Match

It's been ages since I've been to a football match in person. It's largely a collection of people who enjoy sports, shouting, and recreational liver damage, a dizzying trifecta of overlapping interests, and the two big teams in Glasgow, the Rangers and Celtic, have sectarian loyalties layered on top of all that. I've never cared much for either team, since I've always supported Gala Fairydean Rovers—mostly because it's the side Coriander and Harrowbean support for obvious reasons—and the likelihood of a stooshie is high owing to testosterone and tribalism. But we had four seats in the main stands on the second level of Ibrox Stadium that I had purchased from an acne-scarred man who met me in the High Street train station. He had a bent and probably stale cigarette drooping from his mouth, testifying to a hard life in the pack before finally getting smoked, and I wondered what else he did to pay the bills besides hawk marked-up football seats. But at least he was professional about it, showing up on time and conducting the transaction with a minimum of verbal communication.

Nadia and I met Roxanne and her date, introduced as Gary Carmichael, outside the stadium, where I passed Roxanne her tickets. He was tallish, six one or two, with rugged tanned features and a few days' growth of dark stubble that reminded me of salty fishermen; his blue eyes were fixed in a perpetual squint from working outside. Bit of a rosy hue to his nose and cheeks from a fondness for the drink. Nadia and Roxanne wore matching Rangers FC travel-hooded jackets, black with powder-blue logos and highlights. Gary had a blue home jersey on, and I looked like an old guy who never went to football matches, as I was still dressed formally. This particular game pitted Hibernian against the Rangers, and I walked ahead with Nadia to let Gary and Roxanne chat privately. They were already somewhat familiar because they'd met in a pub last night, and since I heard him say that Roxanne looked "damn cute," I imagined she was feeling good about how this was going to go.

I Signaled Nadia. *Is this one nicer?*

No obvious red flags, she replied. *Has a cat. Likes fishing. If he cares about politics, he's keeping it to himself. Roxanne says his aura is horny and she doesnae mind that.*

Here's hoping it goes well. We've been devoting a lot of time and resources to her, and I have other things to do.

Understood. But keep in mind that what she's attempting is a giant adjustment. It's unfair to think she should nail it right away just because she used to be a goddess.

I nodded ruefully in agreement and asked, *Did you find out, by any chance, what she meant by helping at-risk populations of women?*

Naw, we never circled back to that.

There was far too much to circle back to, in my opinion. I hadn't heard anything from the Blue Men of the Minch or the government regarding yachts and realized I'd never gone back to see Percy Tempest Vane about the yacht problem—but neither had he attempted to contact me. Eli hadn't said anything more about whatever might be bothering him in the western United States. Buck had not received any blowback as yet from the hobgoblin families he'd offended. And I hadn't had a proper think about how to lift my curses.

The game wasn't terrible. A man two rows behind us kept belching epically and got some laughs out of it. We chanted along with this and that, did the wave, listened to people chastise the ref, curse the Hibs, and encourage the Rangers. Roxanne and Gary chatted next to us, and I tried not to hear any of it beyond the tone, which sounded flirtatious to me. Twenty minutes into the first half they left to get popcorn and drinks and I relaxed. Fifteen minutes later it was still a scoreless draw and I began to wonder where they were. I'd started typing a query to Nadia that asked, [Should we worry?] when she tapped me on the shoulder.

"Al. Look," she said, pointing past me to the empty seats. When I turned, one of them wasn't exactly empty. There was a crow perched on the back of Roxanne's seat—it was Roxanne, in fact. Her eyes were red and so was her beak, dripping with blood. Given that Gary hadn't returned, I assumed it was his blood and this casual date had gone seriously sideways. The people behind her seat were starting to lose it and say things like, "Ahhh, is that blood? The fuck is this?" so I typed a quick message and played it without looking directly at the crow, just giving her the side eye.

[Fly to Isabella's. We'll talk there.] I was intentionally vague about where because the people nearby would hear and might repeat it to the police. But Roxanne understood I meant the necropolis, nodded once, and flew off.

"What's the business, Al?" Nadia asked. I switched to Signal so that my answer would appear on her phone but couldn't be overheard by others.

We need to leave now. Game is over for us. No talking till we're somewhere safe. We're on camera and this will be reviewed. Act like the game is boring and wave in frustration at it, say some things witnesses will repeat. We're just deciding to leave because of the game.

Her phone pinged and she checked it, nodded, and performed

some ritual disgust at the pace of the game—not difficult—and loudly said to me, "Come on, Al, let's go. Hibs are shite, and this game is slower than a snail fuck."

We took the tube and the train back up to High Street and thence to the necropolis, where Roxanne was waiting in her human form near the sarcophagus of Isabella Ure Elder. Nadia asked me on the way if I had a clue what was going on and I did, but I told her that it would be best to let Roxanne tell us. She wasted no time asking.

"What the hell happened, Roxanne?" Nadia said.

"Fucking Gary," she rasped, her death metal voice tinged with wrath. The polite Irish voice was gone. "We went up to get snacks, and that was fine, but when I left him with the food and went to the restroom, he followed me in."

"What? In front of everybody?"

"There was no one in there but us. It wasn't halftime and there weren't that many women at the game to begin with. He thought it might be fun to make out, and I said it might on some other occasion but not this one. He didn't take no for an answer. I told him no three times, and he missed the warning flare in my eyes because he wasn't looking at my face. He kept coming at me, laid hands upon my person without my consent, and that was the end of his story. I didn't even think about it: I killed him."

"As a crow?"

Roxanne switched to her human voice and Irish accent. "No, like this. But then I turned to a crow and ate his eyes, as I used to do as the Morrigan, and it felt so good and . . . so terrible at the same time. I would have eaten more, but a woman came in, saw me standing on his corpse, and screamed. I thought it best to leave at that point."

"Good call, yeah."

"I've made a critical error, haven't I?" Roxanne said. "I can't be this mortal person without regressing into my old habits. This whole effort has been an exercise in futility."

"Hold on, now, let me gently disagree with ye there," Nadia

said, holding out a hand. "Gary was the gaping arsehole in this situation, and if he didnae want tae find out, he shouldnae have fucked around, far as I'm concerned."

[It's murder.]

"Oh, aye, nicely done on the conventional take, Al. But ye could also say it was self-defense. Ye could even say that assaulting Roxanne was suicidal. And only a critical error," she said, turning back to Roxanne, "if ye get caught. Ye say ye killed him as a human? How?"

"Snapped his neck."

"Okay, so a small chance of fingerprints on his body. But they're gonnay find them on yer stadium seat for sure and compare. Whose fingerprints are those? Still original tae the body ye possessed?"

"Aye. They are still the fingerprints of Thea Prendergast."

"Can ye change them the way ye changed yer face and body somewhat?"

"I can do that."

"Awright, do that. If ye do get hauled in, the fingerprints will set ye free. But they're gonnay try tae find ye via cameras first. Ye didnae go intae the restroom together but separate?"

"Correct."

"And the cameras wouldnae have seen ye exit, because ye flew out of there as a crow?"

"Also true."

"That's gonnay short-circuit the gelatinized brains of the polis. But the next way tae find us is the tickets. Al, how did ye pay for them?"

[Cash. Bought them from a ticket broker.]

"Ye mean a scalper?"

[Aye. You saw me arrange the meetup in the restaurant. He won't be able to identify me by name, but he can describe me well enough.]

"That's awright. Plenty of white men with mustaches and cashmere topcoats."

[If they showed him a photo, he could ID me.]

"A scalper isnae gonnay grass you up, but fine. Ye bought four tickets. Doesnae mean we went tae the game as friends. Ye sold them tae the woman—not Gary—for cash in the parking lot or sumhin. We need tae think of how else they'll track ye down. They have tae establish that we knew either Gary or Roxanne or both if they want tae lean on us. Phones!" Nadia pointed at the two of us. "Did either of ye text or call Gary? Because the polis will have Gary's phone and look through texts and recent calls."

"I texted him before the game to confirm where we would meet," Roxanne said.

"But it was on yer burner phone, aye? Text *Fuck the polis* to him so they'll see it, then throw it in the Clyde River and we'll get ye a new one. Evidence gone. Except for the pub."

[What pub?] I asked.

"The polis will trace Gary's movements, and if they go tae the pub where we met him and ask around, somebody might say something. Lots of old white men with mustaches in Glasgow, but not so many Indian goth queens with mohawks. If they can connect Gary tae me, or me tae Roxanne, they'll come after us hard."

[Best go spread some hush money at the pub, then, just to be on the safe side.]

"Aye. On it. But, Al—yer phone security. Delete all conversations in case they grab ye, including whatever is stored in that text-tae-speech app."

[On it.]

When Nadia left, Roxanne chewed her lip in worry and began pacing in front of the sarcophagus, wearing a trail in the grass.

"I'm terrible at being human."

[No, you're not. All the messy emotions you are feeling right now are very human.]

"I feel out of control and I don't know what to do!"

[That's perfect. Very human. You're crushing it, as the kids say. Or maybe they don't anymore. They keep changing their slang and I am probably out of date.]

"I don't know how this could get any worse."

I could think of plenty of ways. But I said, [Might you have some other projects or goals to work on besides falling in love? My unsolicited advice is to focus on something else for a few days, and we'll revisit dating when things have cooled down.]

"Yes," Roxanne agreed, nodding. "I do have some other goals to achieve. I will redirect my focus there."

[Good. Let's lay low for a while and reassess after some time has passed. You should know that if I'm asked, I'm going to say I don't know you, and you should likewise say you don't know me.]

"But I do know you, Al," she said. "You're a friend who's trying to help. And I appreciate it." She nodded her thanks once before her shape rustled and twisted and she flew away, cawing a farewell. I waited until she was out of sight before getting out my phone and sending a Signal to my attorney, Iris MacCowan. I'd put her on retainer after the day that D.I. Munro harassed me about Buck and the heists, and she'd deflected admirably since then, but she was going to burn through that retainer soon.

Death at Ibrox Stadium today. Likely to be questioned due to proximity. Will need you during the questioning, whenever they pick me up. Could even be tomorrow. Heads up.

INTERLUDE: THE CHEMISTRY
OF FAILURE

———— • ◆ • ————

I cannot count the number of times my ink formulas have fizzled.
You can spend days on them—even weeks or months, if you
count collecting ingredients, and you probably should—and have
it all come to naught because of some impurity or some slight
miscalculation in the portions or the mixing or the room temperature. Chemistry is precise and demanding.

As an apprentice, I used to rage against putting in all that labor
and concentration for a null result. As a full agent and, later, a
mentor, I appreciated how valuable the experience of failure was.
It taught me to pay attention to detail, and it rewarded persis-
tence, of course. It also taught me that it is extraordinarily difficult to change something's nature from one thing to another. But
first and foremost, the primary challenge it provided was the
question of whether I'd try again.

If I'd quit because I lacked patience to learn from my missteps,
I would not be a sigil agent today, and all the good I've done for
the world would have never happened.

I'd say a large portion of me hoped Roxanne would give up on changing her nature, if people had to die for her failures. But another portion, nearly as large, hoped she would learn quickly. Because what good might someone so powerful do if she managed to fall in love?

CHAPTER 16

Wide of the Mark

It was difficult to relax on Sunday when I kept expecting a knock on the door from the police. The news had a small article about the death—a bit sensational to find an eyeless dead man in the women's toilets—but all it said was the investigation was ongoing, and I was left to read Homer and worry.

D.I. Munro was waiting for me Monday morning in the lobby of the printshop. She said she required me for a voluntary interview under caution at the station; she needed Nadia too.

[Is this more nonsense about that heist?]

"Naw, this is different."

After inquiring which station we were going to, I texted Iris to ask her to meet us there. The D.I. planned on questioning us separately, so Nadia and I were settled in different rooms, and I requested my lawyer be present before I answered any questions.

Iris MacCowan entered the small interrogation room about twenty minutes later, a curly-haired blonde with elfin features and a navy suit adorned with a pale-yellow scarf. She placed a briefcase on the table and took a seat, speaking briskly.

"Right, Inspector, let's proceed. What's this about?"

D.I. Munro was prepared. On a tablet, she brought up surveillance video showing Nadia and me sitting next to Roxanne and Gary Carmichael in the football stands.

"This is you and Nadia Padmanabhan at the football game on Saturday."

I nodded.

"Who are these two people sitting next tae you?"

[I don't know.]

"Are ye sure?" She tapped the tablet and another video played of us entering the stadium, followed closely by Roxanne and Gary. "Because they entered the stadium with ye and then sat down next to ye."

[I don't know them.]

"What's the relevance here, Inspector?" Iris asked. "I've yet tae see a crime."

"Bear with me." She took us through several more videos, narrating as she went. "These two people whom ye say ye do not know left their seats in the first half, then appear shortly thereafter at a food stall. They get hot dogs, popcorn, and drinks, and then the woman, ye'll see here, enters the ladies'. Some seconds afterward, the man follows. He never leaves, because he's found deid about two minutes later by a different woman, who enters here. She reports that when she entered the restroom, she discovered the man lying on the floor, his neck broken, and a crow was eating his eyes. An examination concluded that it wasnae an accidental death. Forensics found fingerprints on his neck and jaw that match fingerprints on the seat where the woman sat next tae ye. So it appears that she killed him. Ye can see why we're interested in who she is."

"Yes, but ma client said he doesnae know her, so he cannae help you there. Will that be all, Inspector?"

"Not entirely. Because it gets extraordinarily weird after this." She tapped the tablet again, and the surveillance footage outside the ladies' continued. "The crow flies out of the restroom, followed shortly thereafter by the witness, who screamed for help and so on. But the crow flies purposely back tae the stands and lands on the back of the seat where the woman ye don't know was sitting. That woman, by the way, was never found. Her clothes were left on the restroom floor, but she never exited the restroom or the stadium. We checked the footage. Exhaustively. She goes in, but only the crow comes out. The crow flies back tae her seat, and after less than a minute there, it flies away."

"Fascinating detour intae corvid behavior, Inspector, but I'm no sure how ma client can help if he doesnae know the people in the video."

"Coincidences happen, of course, but fatal ones keep happening around yer client, and I'd like his help explaining that. Mr. MacBharrais is now linked to a series of major crimes and has connections with human trafficking."

I began typing furiously while Iris responded.

"Ye have yet tae prove any connection whatsoever, Inspector. Ye have no evidence, or we wouldnae be here voluntarily."

[My only connection to trafficking is that I've given you leads to shut it down. Are you even doing your job?]

"Oh, aye, we're working on it. Strange that ye're so helpful with those crimes, however, and unhelpful with others. Maybe ye want us tae get rid of yer competitors."

"Competitors?" Iris said. "As in ye think ma client is a human trafficker?"

"I dunno. He's up tae sumhin. Trying tae figure out what it is."

"Bringing ma clients in for questioning because ye believe they are 'up tae sumhin' is insufficient grounds and qualifies as harassment," Iris replied.

[You're aiming far wide of the mark here,] I said. [I know you're trained to be suspicious, but I would have thought you'd have a better idea of what someone is capable of.]

"Anybody is capable of anything, Mr. MacBharrais."

Iris began to reply, but I held up a hand to give me time to type something else.

[I'm capable of being offended by your suggestion, and I am.

You have misjudged me deeply. My concern has been for the victims from the start. A trafficker would hardly care. And I care very much that while you're wasting time with me, you're leaving those victims in bondage.]

Iris stood and said, "This session is at an end. Let's move on tae Nadia and get this over with so they can return tae their lives."

When I stood, I had to steady myself against the edge of the table, as a tide of dizziness crashed inside my head. An echo, no doubt, from the concussion. Neither woman noticed that I fumbled for my cane while they were busy glaring at each other.

It was just as well that I didn't have a plan to take on Ares, Phobos, and Deimos yet: I was nowhere near ready. And Roxanne was giving me all I could handle. Until we got her settled somehow, I would have little opportunity to settle things for myself.

Maybe the dating apps I'd heard of would help us screen out undesirables. It was Nadia's feeling that people lied about themselves online even more than they did to your face, and maybe she was correct, but we'd need to try it soon if her methods didn't turn up someone suitable. I wondered if Roxanne would get an entirely different pool of candidates if she put *Chooser of the Slain* as her employment rather than *Advocate for At-Risk Women,* and which set of candidates she would prefer.

CHAPTER 17

The Hobgoblin
Hootenanny

After a stressful day of interrogation and work—a rough Monday if there'd ever been one—I'd hoped to come home and relax. Instead, I opened the door to my flat to find loud music blaring, the living room strewn with half-eaten snacks, bottles and glasses in the kitchen, and Buck so slobbering drunk he couldn't stand without swaying.

[What the hell is going on? Why are you this drunk on a Monday?]

"I'm no drunk! I'm just well lubricated, like yer maw."

[This is ridiculous. There has to be a reason for it.]

"I'll tell ye, ol' man. I'm worried about what shite Gladys is expecting tae see. I'm up tae high doh. D'ye know what I found? A grey hair on ma bollocks! That's because of you, ya diabolical bastard."

[Why were you even looking at them?]

"Because So-crates said the unexamined life is not worth living."

[That was Sock-ra-tees.]

"I just tol' ya it was him. The point is that we dunno if Gladys

Who Has Seen Some Shite wants tae see us win or watch us lose. Wot if it's that, hey? She probably never saw anyone get punished for their hubris in the modern era, and the Greeks did their punishments right. Ye had that one guy, Parakeets, who had his liver eaten by vulchas—"

[You mean Pericles.]

"Right, that's wot I said. And that other guy, Sissy Puss, is still rolling a rock up a hill and never quite making it—"

[Sisyphus. His name was Sisyphus.]

"I know—are ye even listenin' tae me? And the absolute worst was Taint Alice, who had food and water nearby but could never eat or drink any of it—"

[Tantalus. Now I know you're having a laugh.]

"Awright, maybe I am, a bit. But ma point is that the Greeks know how tae punish ye proper if ye mess with them, and that might be the kind o' shite Gladys wants tae see. We cannae assume it's gonnay end well for us."

[So that's why you're off your heid?]

"Naw. It's the Fullbritches, Snothouses, and Badhumps. Why hasnae someone shown up tae plant a foot up ma arse? This silence is ominous. They're planning something terrible, I just know it."

[Ah. I see. You're in a doom spiral.]

"Are ye suggesting I don't have a good reason for one? I got hobs and gods and grey bollocks tae worry about, and each one of them alone is worth a barrel of peated pain relief!"

[The last one isn't bad.]

"If it's all matching, no, I suppose it isnae, but just one? It's unsightly. I have tae pluck it out. Don't ye just wannay cringe intae the fetal position thinking about pluckin' yer nuts?"

[I am not discussing that with you. Listen, you need to go back to Tír na nÓg.]

"Wot? Ye cannae be serious."

[Deadly serious. You still need to find out who the cheesedick from Manchester is.]

"I cannae go back, ol' man! They'll kill me!"

[What if you go back with a second distribution of Buck Foi's Best Boosted Spirits, but this time it will say on the label that it's a Badhump Family Enterprise? Maybe that would give your family's mojo a boost, and all will be forgiven?]

"Well, that is—huh." He stopped abruptly, thinking it over. "That might actually work. At least with them. I'd still have tae worry about the Fullbritches and Snothouses, but reducing ma threat level by a third is no small thing. Plus it's the third with ma faither in it."

[Then let's do it.]

"Really? Right now?"

[Yes. I need that name.]

And I also needed Buck to resolve his issues before I went to Olympus. I'd need him fully present and operational if we were to have a chance of survival, so it was best to address his issues now, while I was still recovering from my concussion and thinking up a plan.

"Awright, let's go!"

I put in a text to Nadia with the new agenda, and she picked us up in her wizard van about an hour later, after she'd put in a rush order for the labels on our printshop floor. We'd boosted a barrel of cheap Highlands stuff the first time, so Buck wanted to get something of a higher quality for this edition. He told us about a Lowland distillery that had a fourteen-year aged in Oloroso sherry casks, then passed out on the couch in the back moments later.

Nadia and I both sighed in relief. It would be two hours' drive, at minimum, but probably more because traffic rarely cooperated. The chance of Buck waking up was slim. We could talk about any number of things—we probably needed to—and Nadia raised an eyebrow at me to see if I wanted to do that. I shook my head with a soft smile, and she flashed a wide grin.

"Okay, Al. Quiet time for us. I can do with that very well."

There's a fair bit of science now regarding the mental-health benefits of birdsong and natural sounds, and city dwellers don't get nearly enough of them. We get noises that give us grief—sirens wailing, drunkards screaming, amplified bass notes from passing cars playing music we don't like. It sparks our tempers, elevates blood pressure, and does a thousand tiny things to poke and prod our brains and limbic systems into chemical reactions that most likely shorten our lives. A soft space of serenity with someone you trust is just the ticket to walk yourself back to a happy place, fortified and braced to confront the myriad hells of modern life.

It did me good. I was feeling rather relaxed by the time we got to the distillery. There was no way around it—we had to awaken Buck for the actual heist. That took a while and some ungentle prodding by Nadia, but once he was conscious enough to concentrate, Buck popped into the distillery and out again, grunting and straining as he rolled a barrel of whisky larger than he was toward the van. We helped him load it into the back and he passed out once more as soon as we got on the road, his body attempting to break down the alcohol in his blood. It was well after ten P.M. by the time we got back to Glasgow, and Nadia begged off at that point, requiring sleep. She promised to compensate the distillery for the stolen barrel in the morning. I needed some sleep too but needed Buck to get answers for me even more, so I stayed up with him to dilute the whisky and bottle it and place the newly printed labels on them. We recruited some help from the night shift in the shop to box them into cases and load them onto a palette, which Buck could steer on a hand truck to Tír na nÓg.

I was running on fumes at around three A.M. when he was finally ready to go, but it was the perfect time to push a load of stolen whisky through the streets to Virginia Court, where he could take the Old Way outside Gin71.

[I hope this will help out your family situation and cool tempers among the Fullbritches and Snothouses,] I said, [but remember your primary mission.]

"Find the cheesedick from Manchester, right," he said. "I promise I will, ol' man."

He winked out of sight as he traveled the Old Way, and I sighed with the relief at his absence. Hobgoblins were exhausting. I shuffled home to get some sleep, deflated at the mess that remained in my flat but knowing that I was far too weary to tackle the cleanup. I fell into bed, clothes still on, to embrace a few hours of sweet oblivion.

———— · ————

CHAPTER 18

The Legendary Meltdown
of Percy Tempest Vane

Lizzie MacLeish was getting along famously with Gladys Who Has Seen Some Shite. When I returned to the shop Tuesday morning, a scant six hours after I'd left it, the two of them were laughing about something, and I thought that Lizzie seemed happier in general than when she first came to us. It's bracing to know that you are valued and that your place of employment is not filled with soulless gits. They chimed a good morning to me, and the phone rang as I was turning to the stairs to the break room. I could almost taste the Danish, sight unseen.

"MacBharrais Printing and Binding, good morning," Lizzie said. I was halfway down the stairs when she called me back.

"Boss? Red phone! Gladys says it's a red phone!"

Sighing, I returned up the stairs without any coffee or Danish, resentment building at the timing here.

[Who is it?] I typed.

"Percy Tempest Vane."

[Send it up to my office. I'll go up now.]

"Gird yourself, Boss," Gladys said as I passed the reception desk. "I caught a bit of it, because he was yelling. He sounds like he has one of those bulging veins in his temple, you know? Powerful mad. Also? Sounds like a hoser."

"Why is someone from the home secretary's office calling us?" Lizzie asked in a low voice.

"You've heard the expression where someone has their fingers in a lot of pies? Well, the boss does, and some of those pies are terrible government ones. This is one of them. Some of them are very strange pies, and you'll have to get used to that."

It sounded like a roundabout way to prepare Lizzie for seeing some remarkable things from time to time, and I appreciated it. No doubt Lizzie did too. Everyone likes a good pie metaphor.

Once in my office, I stabbed the blinking light on my office phone without rounding my desk. I had serious doubts that I'd have time to get comfortable.

"What," I said, utterly rude.

"It happened again! Another one down! You said you would fix this!" I held the phone away from my ear to prevent hearing loss.

"I said nothing of the sort. I said I had a plan." And I'd been working on it but apparently too little, too late.

His voice audibly shuddered with rage. "You clearly *never* followed up. You made an appointment to see me about it and then ghosted me. I've been calling ever since."

"I doubt that. This is the first I've heard of ye calling."

"I did!"

"Let's just both admit we got distracted by other issues, shall we? Because unless I missed some other catastrophe, this is only the second one."

"It is. But there are no other issues now. This *is* the issue."

"Fine. May I assume there are specifics you wish tae discuss in person?"

"Yes. Get here now."

"I shall be there within the hour," I said, and rang off. Determined to be properly fortified before what was certain to be an unpleasant encounter, I purposely went downstairs to enjoy my Danish and coffee before gathering up a few items for my trip to London.

Using the Old Way in the necropolis, I was able to get to the office of Percy Tempest Vane forty-five minutes after I'd hung up the phone. He was still in an ill-fitting suit, albeit a navy blue one this time, with a tie more reminiscent of jaundice than gold. He did not ask me if I wanted tea, so at least he'd learned something. But he had not improved the décor of his office. It was still a drab wasteland in search of personality.

"Give me the details," I said, as I sat in the chair opposite his desk and wondered how close I was getting to triggering my curse with him. I'd already spoken to him more than was probably advisable. Switching to a speech app now would be awkward to explain, however. Perhaps next time I could feign laryngitis, if there was a next time.

"The incident followed the same pattern as before. These Blue Men of the Minch spoke some poetry, and when it was not answered, a hull breach followed. A key difference was that there were some survivors."

"Crew or passengers?"

"Neither, so far as we can tell. They were foreign nationals without any papers. All of them very poor, mostly women and children."

"The crew was lost?"

"Yes. Why don't you tell me what you accomplished, if anything, when you went to see the Blue Men."

"They hate yachts and are unwilling tae even consider leaving them alone unless you clean up the Minch. Apparently there are yachts—and it sounds like this was one of them—involved in human trafficking."

The bureaucrat scoffed. "Impossible."

"No, it's likely. The leader of the Blue Men said that if the government agreed tae end the use of the Minch for trafficking purposes, they'd be open to renegotiating the treaty. Ye must demonstrate good faith first, however. It won't stop until ye show ye're willing tae cooperate."

"Cooperate how?"

"They require a hotline of sorts. When they detect a yacht they'd like tae sink for its criminal activity, they call you instead. If ye act and take care of the problem—arrests made, captives freed—they'll stop sinking yachts."

"Preposterous."

"Why? Ye get good press for law enforcement, and nobody dies. I've negotiated an excellent deal. All we need is a number tae call and a task force."

"Hold on." Percy's face turned visibly blotchy as he flushed with righteous wrath. "Are you saying that this second incident could have been avoided if they had a *phone number to call*?" I threw up a forearm to protect my face from the spit flying from his mouth.

"Only if it's coupled with action on our side. Has tae be both. If they call and ye do nothing, it's no deal. But by the same token, if ye act and there's nothing tae prosecute, that's on them."

"So just to be clear: They think this yacht was trafficking the survivors we found?"

"I haven't spoken tae them yet, but that's ma guess. And I'm sure the Blue Men were responsible for saving those people who survived."

"Well. We can't say anything publicly about them being possible victims. The owner—" He stopped abruptly.

"Yes? Who is the owner and why do ye care?"

"Well." Percy Tempest Vane leaned back in his chair and found something acutely interesting in his fingernails, his entire belligerent posture and demeanor dissolving when considering this august personage. His voice quieted and returned to its normal tension. "He's extraordinarily wealthy. Quite perceptive on the stock market. Picks unexpected winners year after year and, more important, contributes generously to many of my bosses."

"The stock market, ye say?" I leaned forward, keenly engaged as Percy was trying to disengage. "I don't suppose this man would be from Manchester?"

The bureaucrat's jaw dropped. "You know him?"

"Know *of* him, I think. What's his name?"

"Chase Digges."

Chase Digges. Cheesedick. I had inadvertently stumbled upon the identity of the cheesedick from Manchester.

CHAPTER 19

Of Cheesedicks and Chess

There is a certain calm that descends when you finally know what needs to happen. Executing a plan is far less stressful than coming up with one. So I leaned back in my chair as well, mirroring Percy Tempest Vane, confident of the way forward.

"Okay, that clarifies a number of things for me. Chase Digges is yer problem. Get rid of him, and the Blue Men of the Minch will cease tae trouble ye. And it'll be good for the country too, no doubt."

Spluttering ensued. "What? Get rid of him? What do you mean? What exactly has been clarified here? Because it's not clear to me at all!"

"I didnae know his name until ye provided it, but quite a few people in the supernatural community refer tae him as the cheesedick from Manchester. This talent he has with the stock market is no a talent at all. He's exploiting a Sumerian goddess of prophecy tae get his tips. And ye have tae be aware that he's using that tae buy influence with politicians and insulate himself from legal trouble. And he's got legal trouble aplenty if ye have the sack tae go after him. He's a human trafficker, on top of whatever else he's doing. I'm sure it's more than that, because billionaires sit around thinking of ways tae hurt people rather than help them—otherwise we'd have no one living unhoused."

Percy shook his head and pinched the bridge of his nose. "We can't go after Chase Digges."

"If ye find out he's doing these heinous crimes, he's above the law? Untouchable?"

He thought about it a bit, then gave a tiny nod. "I fear so."

"Then the Blue Men of the Minch are gonnay continue tae take down yachts. Whatever headache ye think Chase Digges can give ye, consider the long-term consequences of having the Minch become a no-go zone. Ye work for the home secretary, man. If the home secretary cannae do anything about Chase Digges, does that no suggest he should be taken down as a matter of principle?"

"It does, in principle. In practicality, I'm not sure it can be done. Why can't you do something about it?"

"I'm prevented from doing the sorts of things law enforcement should be doing. Are ye clear on what it is I do?"

Percy sighed, admitting defeat. "Not entirely. Just that you deal with the supernatural."

"Fine. Think of the wars and conflicts we have going on in Europe and the Middle East. They're bad enough as is, right? Now think how bad they could get if various gods of war decided tae get involved. Ares has been itching tae get involved in the Middle East for decades now because he's bored. I'm all that's keeping him out of it, and I'm paying the price, believe me. The reason I got distracted from this Minch business had tae do with him, actually. I am doing ma best where I'm allowed, and I'm showing ye a path forward tae solve this problem with the Blue Men. But ye have tae step up on yer end tae make it work. Whatever barbs and hooks Chase Digges has in yer government, ye have tae pry them loose. He's a plague."

"It's far easier said than done."

"I'm sure it is. Rich twats make sure they're difficult tae dislodge. But I can give ye a hint: The Blue Men say five or six different yachts are involved in trafficking. I don't know if they're all owned by Chase Digges, but maybe he has associates involved with him. Maybe it would help tae point out tae yer bosses that there's a tremendous public-relations upside if ye can take down rich evil bastards. Look, do ye have some coast guard forces ye can trust? Let's give the Blue Men a number tae call and start there."

"Right." Percy sat up straight, adjusted his ugly tie, and laced his fingers together in front of him, flat upon his desk. "Thank you, Mr. MacBharrais. I will contact your office with a number to call as soon as I have one."

"I appreciate it. The person who will call that number is named Rhett MacNett. If it's him on the line, trust what he says and act on it."

"Very good."

I rose from my seat and gave him a nod, surprised that we were being cordial for a change. Was this a genuine change of heart on his part, prompted by the realization that Chase Digges was an actual threat? Or was he simply being polite now and planning to stab me in the back later? I supposed I should take the gift for what it was and consider my job done until he made the next move. Maybe, I thought, I could get something productive done today after all.

It was unwise of me to be so optimistic.

While I was transiting Tír na nÓg to get to the Old Way that would lead me back to the Glasgow Necropolis, a small mischief of hobgoblins with menacing expressions appeared before me. They weren't obviously armed, but that didn't mean they weren't dangerous. They were all pink-skinned rather than blue, and the apparent leader spoke to me with a bellicose tone.

"Oi. You MacBharrais?"

"Aye. How can I help ye, sir?"

The hobgoblin snorted and looked at his companions. "Sir, he says. Get a load of that." Turning back to me, he said, "Fancy yerself a chess master, do ye?"

"No. Barely competent. Cannae remember the last time I played."

"I'm speakin' metaphorically about the moves ye've been makin' against me."

"I don't even know who ye are."

"That hob ye have in yer service—I won't say his name. But I'm his faither."

I blinked. "Would that make you Softwood Badhump?"

"The same. Ever since he started workin' for ye, he's been nothin' but trouble for our family. And now ye go and give him that candle—"

"What? What candle?"

"Don't play the fool with me. Ye know which candle. The one that makes ye tell the truth. He used it on me."

"I didnae gie it tae him. He stole it. And ye can be sure I'll be demanding its return."

"Naw, see, *I* demand it."

It was such a ridiculous thing to say that I merely shrugged. He snarled and pointed a finger with a long but clean fingernail at me.

"Even if he stole it, it's *you* that's responsible," he said. "It was an attack, and it must be made right. Ye make it right by giving the candle tae me."

"An attack, ye say."

"Aye."

"The candle does no physical damage. No psychic damage either. If it reveals tae everyone that ye're a lying bastard, then that's no an attack, that's you being a lying bastard. And I reject the notion that I'm responsible. He's yer son, so maybe consider that if he felt he had tae use that candle tae get ye tae be honest, maybe ye bear some responsibility for that."

Softwood growled and balled up his fists and I knew what was coming, if not exactly where it would manifest. He was going to do a quick teleport to either side of my face and sucker punch me. It's a common tactic among hobgoblins, because it's difficult to defend against and it takes advantage of binocular vision: Since I was looking directly down at him, it would be too late by the time I saw an attack coming from either side. Or from behind, of course.

Buck had tried that move on Nadia when they first met, and that's when he discovered that you can't sneak up on a battle seer. But the basic counter is to step back to avoid the blow or at least reduce its impact. That's what I did as Softwood popped out of sight. His fist whiffed in front of my nose and mouth, missing by the tiniest margin, and a quick uppercut with my left sank into his belly in midair. He grunted and fell to the ground, wheezing, and I started talking before he could find time to be embarrassed and redouble his attack—and I had his group of lackeys to worry about too.

"You attacked and I defended ma self. Let that be the end. Escalating would be a poor choice, because my cane contains cold iron and I'm wearing some too. I owe ye nothing, and ye owe me nothing. And did Buck no just give yer paragon a boost with his latest distribution of whisky?"

"That's right, he did!" Softwood spat as he got to his feet. "It's just another chess move, in't it?"

"What kind of squirrels do ye have in yer heid, man? I'm no playing chess of any kind!"

"He's tryin' tae replace me!"

"What a load of mossy bollocks! He wants tae be loved by his family, and he's trying tae help. Stop projecting yer own poison on others. If ye would like tae see the Badhumps become a powerful family, then ye should become a kinder and wiser hob and let him help. Ye should be *proud* of him, ya daft gobshite, no tryin' tae tear him down! Stop being such a crabbit old bastard."

"So ye're determined tae give me insult."

"Naw, I rather think ye're determined tae take it. That's clear because ye didnae spend even a fraction of a second considering yer own faults. I didnae come here tae start any of this. If anyone should take offense, it's me. Try tae be better, Softwood. I guarantee yer family will celebrate ye if ye do, and I guarantee this rage in yer heart will consume ye if ye don't. Take some time, and let's be friends after this, awright?"

He looked as if he might angrily retort or even attack again, but one of his lackeys—a hob entirely tattooed from the neck down and dressed in a black vest and chunky boots—spoke up before he could.

"Honored tae meet ye, Mr. MacBharrais. Should any of the other sigil agents need a hob, I'd be glad tae be of service."

A couple of others agreed, and Softwood went limp. He'd expected them to back him up, not say anything nearly so mutinous. To ensure he'd find it difficult to reignite a dying fire, I asked them their names, and was greeted with a trio of atrocities: Maladroit, Unforgettable, and Squidgy Badhump.

"If an opportunity arises, would Buck be able tae contact ye?" I asked. They all nodded and croaked, "Aye," like a pack of affirmative toads, and I took my leave before Softwood could rally.

That encounter certainly illuminated for me some of the stresses Buck was feeling. His father was a seething boil of grievance and mistrust. But that candle didn't belong to Buck and he was certainly not authorized to use it, in my name or his. Obviously, he'd nicked it when I was in a coma, and I'd not had the good sense to pursue it when I should have. The strange thing was I wasn't sure what I would do with it when Buck gave it back. Nancy had mentioned nothing about returning it, and I didn't get the impression she needed it. But neither did I anymore. Should I dispose of it? Give it to a reporter and let them absolutely ruin the career of a politician by making them tell the truth? That might be amusing but might also have dire consequences. It might be safest to lock it away somewhere until needed or else destroy it.

At least the whisky heist hadn't been a waste of time; I hoped that Buck earned back a bit of goodwill from some of his family, if not his father. But I'd need to think of an appropriate response to this candle business—and not forget about the Blue Men again. Once Percy gave me a phone number for them to use, I'd need to have another chat with Mudgeon MacGill.

———— · ————

CHAPTER 20

The Gob of Lhurnog

As the remainder of the week slipped by with no word from Buck, I learned that Nadia had snuck some additional jobs into the print queue besides Buck's labels for his illicit whisky: flyers advertising the Church of Lhurnog's Table, services to be held at Community Central Hall on Maryhill Road on Saturday afternoon. The flyers shouted in bold letters that there would be whisky and cheese and revelation. They did not say what incredibly dangerous consequences could result from starting up any cult, let alone one worshipping a man-eating deity. I decided that I must attend to gauge the depth of our collective peril.

The Community Central Hall was a red stone building with a large clock in the center of it, a reminder that in days of yore, people used to look at clocks instead of phones to tell the time. The facility contained several meeting spaces, and Nadia had apparently rented a midsize one called Grovepark Hall, with room for a hundred twenty seated or two hundred standing. As I entered, a smiling young woman handed me a small, exquisitely crafted chapbook covered in brown suede, embossed and stamped in gold foil. It was an expensive print job, no doubt done in my own shop, an instantly precious object, and the words on the outside proclaimed it to be *The Gob of Lhurnog*. Here, then, was the holy writ. And they had a meeting place where they would ritually worship the god. This was very, very bad.

The walls had half-circle windows near the ceiling, allowing in plenty of natural light, and arches to give the room a bit of churchy flavor. There was a stage up front with a podium draped in burgundy velvet and a circular sign that was apparently the logo of the church. It was essentially a painterly still-life illustration of whisky in an unlabeled decanter, a finger of said whisky in a rocks glass, and an attractive cheese board. The words *Church of Lhurnog's Table* circled this illustration.

I was surprised to see Lizzie MacLeish in attendance, wearing what would normally be her Sunday best, her legs crossed, next to none other than Gladys Who Has Seen Some Shite. They were seated near the front, but I took a spot in the back, lowering myself onto a plastic folding chair.

People kept filing in, looking around at who else was there, giving each other nervous smiles and wondering exactly what they had stepped into. What they saw was a diverse congregation of strangers.

Nadia, dressed all in black, moved up to the stage. She wore a corseted vest with a high rigid neck and flares at the shoulders over a diaphanous black shirt, with sleeves that billowed at the wrists. She had voluminous black breeches, almost Elizabethan, their balloonish aspirations squashed into knee-high boots with buckles all down the sides. I had no idea what this sort of fashion was called, if anything, but it looked impressive.

She raised her hands for attention, got it, and smiled at everyone. After a quick introduction and a promise that she would be brief, she launched into her message.

"Evolution is real, ma friends. One need only look at the rapid mutation of viruses tae see the truth of it. But as it is real for plants and animals, so is it real for ideas and faiths. These too must evolve tae meet the challenges of the environment, and the successful faith for today—the one that nourishes the soul—is no the one that demonizes entire swaths of people in the name of a deity. The successful faith builds communities and doesnae destroy them. It welcomes all tae the table with the single admonition tae do no violence.

"Come tae the table of Lhurnog the Unhallowed, all ye myriad peoples of the world, with yer varied backgrounds and genders and loves and abilities, and let us celebrate one another and the gift of existence. Let us share good drink and food and stories, for these are the water, soil, and sun of empathy, which we must cultivate and nurture in our hearts so that violence, like a rude weed, can never grow there.

"Here at the Church of Lhurnog's Table, we hallow the unhallowed. We uplift the downcast. We encourage the discouraged. We anchor the unmoored. We house the unhoused. And we feed the hungry.

"Lhurnog the Unhallowed is hungry, so we will offer whisky and cheese tae the gob of Lhurnog and gie him our love. And we will feed ourselves and love one another. And all will be well among us.

"But among those who let violence grow in their hearts until they act upon it, all will no be well. For as they are consumed by violence, Lhurnog will consume them."

Nadia leaned forward and waggled an admonitory finger in the air. "And I am no speaking metaphorically. He will physically eat the violent and purge the world of such poison. But believe as ye wish. Either literally or metaphorically, we will see peace in our time as violence subsides thanks tae the appetites of Lhurnog."

She then urged us to read *The Gob of Lhurnog* at our leisure, to donate to the church if we wished to defray costs and rent a larger space, to invite our friends and family to return next week, and, most important, to enjoy whisky and cheese and the friendship of luminous people who wished for peace on earth.

I harbored a brief hope that she might not lead everyone in a ritual prayer, but that was dashed as she asked us to repeat after her if we felt moved to do so.

"Lhurnog, we come to your table in peace."

Nearly everyone was moved to repeat that, and I white-knuckled my cane and wished, for the first time, that Nadia was not so brilliant and charismatic. It did not escape me that a large part of her personal magnetism might be the demigoddess in her—a constellation of attributes that made her an ideal cult leader, albeit not the creepy, controlling kind. Yet.

"We offer whisky and cheese tae yer gob," she said, and this was repeated, as was each of the remaining phrases in her ritual evocation. "And we invite ye intae our peaceful hearts, so that ye may know us as we celebrate our lives together. Lhurnog, hear our prayer."

Shite, fuck, and damn. She was absolutely on her way to establishing this as a religion. She wasn't there yet—a hundred people wouldn't be enough. The true test would be if she could keep the congregation growing.

I was about to rise and join everyone at the cheese board, to gauge their interest in returning, when a figure loomed in my peripheral vision and I turned to check for danger.

There was plenty of it.

It was Roxanne, dressed entirely in red—a bright candy-apple, fire-truck-red cashmere trench coat, which most likely set her back five thousand quid or more, over matching red trousers and red heels. She smirked and gestured to the chair next to mine, eyebrow raised to ask if she could join me. I nodded and she sat, speaking in her perfectly normal Roxanne voice, albeit with the Irish accent instead of the Australian.

"Don't be surprised, Al. It's been centuries since I've witnessed the birth of a cult. They're usually quite entertaining."

[You have witnessed enough of them to establish that as a pattern?]

"Sure. In ancient times you found new cults popping up all over the place. I admit we may have different definitions of entertainment. I was customarily amused by the specifics and frequency of their sacrifices and what losses they felt they could sustain to achieve a goal, whether that be better weather for their crops or an elimination of disease, fertility for all their wombs, whatever."

[I will agree that we have different ideas of entertainment.]

"Fair enough. How did it go? I appear to have missed the main service."

[Distressingly well.]

"You would rather this didn't catch on?"

[Correct. I have yet to read *The Gob of Lhurnog*, but I think he would be a difficult deity to wrangle.]

"From what I understand, he's quite calm and even convivial until violence is offered."

[That may be the case, but it would be best if I never had to find out. May I ask: Are you dressed for a special occasion?]

"No. This is how I will appear henceforth. Or variations of the same; the cut may change, but the color is nonnegotiable."

[Oh. Red holds significance for you now?]

"It does. It's a key part in forging my new self, separate from the Morrigan. That's what I've been working on since the dating is on hold. I have little doubt you'll hear more soon, but my investments in it are already paying dividends."

[Investments in red?]

"Investments in my new persona, of which red is a part."

Apparently, she preferred to be cryptic for the moment. [I look forward to hearing more. How do you like your new residence?]

"Quite satisfactory. I have some improvements to make, but I can feel already that it is home and I am settling into it, though I expect to be traveling more and more in the weeks and months ahead. Shall we partake of some whisky and cheese?"

She flicked an idle finger at the congregation clustered around the table, all of them chatting amiably and smiling at one another, which was not ideal. A silent, brooding group of bored people would have been far more to my liking. But I nodded and we rose together to join everyone.

Nadia was mixing in, laughing at jokes and thanking people for their compliments and generally ensuring that people would not only return next week but they'd bring some friends along.

The table boasted an impressive spread of cheese boards, each intermixed with fruit—often grapes or dried apricots or figs—plus cracker breads and assorted compotes and jams. And the cheeses were all labeled with tiny signs in calligraphy that I noted because it wasn't in Nadia's hand, and it was also an interesting orange-red ink with a gold-flecked shimmer to it. Was that Diamine Blood Orange, perhaps? I must have murmured that aloud, because a young man at my elbow answered me.

"Close," he said. "It's Diamine Pink Champagne." He was a youngish ginger fellow with a red beard tinged with fine blond hairs here and there, dressed in blue jeans and Doc Martens, a grey vest buttoned over a blue striped shirt rolled up to the elbows, anchored with a worn leather belt. Odds were even that his jacket was leather too, or else a smart woolen number, but it was currently draped over a chair somewhere. Since it was a first meeting and there might not be another, I thought it would be safe to converse a tiny bit with him without using my phone.

"Ah, is this yer work?"

"It is." He flashed a proud grin.

"Fantastic job."

"Thanks. It's nice tae have someone notice."

"Stub nib?"

"No, just a medium. On this pen, actually." He pulled a black carbon-fiber pen with a rose gold–plated clip and trim out of his vest pocket.

"Oh, a Monteverde Invincia?"

"Indeed! Ye know yer pens!"

"Bit of an obsession," I admitted.

"For me as well. I'm Duncan Ettrick. Pleasure tae meet ye, sir."

"Al MacBharrais. How did ye come tae be here today, Duncan?"

"Friend of a friend of Nadia's partner. Ye must be Nadia's employer, then? I've heard yer name before."

"Aye. What do ye do tae pay the bills?"

"Currently in law school, so I'll eventually pay bills by splitting fine moral hairs and writing dicey legal arguments."

"Excellent. And yer opinion of Lhurnog?"

He shrugged noncommittally. "I don't know either way about him—I need tae read the text—but as far as religious services go, this is the best I've ever attended. Friendly, welcoming people and cheese, no hatred spewed from the pulpit, so what's no tae love? Plus, I just met someone who likes ma handwriting. I cannae find fault with it so far. What do ye think?"

"I think gods and religions are dangerous," I said, "but as far as services go, I have tae admit it was pleasant. Mostly for its brevity."

"Aye. Have ye tried the goat cheese there with rosemary? It's sublime, especially if ye pair it with the quince jam and one of the date walnut crackers."

I grabbed a plate and loaded up as he suggested, and he was right—the flavor combination was bloody good. I scooted down the table to get a shot of whisky, and Duncan joined.

"Shall we toast tae fountain pens and ink?" I asked, and he agreeably shared a dram with me and we surveyed the scene to assess our own place in it.

Roxanne was holding court nearby with several young men who were either smitten or simply awed by her. Nadia was at Dhanya's side now, chatting with a couple who looked to be in their forties. And there were clusters of people all around the hall, enjoying themselves. Few, if any, had left at the conclusion of the service.

"This is great," Duncan observed. "Everyone's happy. Making

friends. I know it's early and it's unfair tae judge, but the feeling I'm having is . . . this is what I always hoped religion would feel like but never did."

"Aye, cults can feel that way."

He scoffed. "Sure. It's why people join. Except that there's no coercion here. No harm being done."

"Well—heh!—give it time."

"Ah. Does yer cynicism come from a bad experience?"

"I think ye'll find very few people on the planet who *havenae* had a bad experience with religion. If not theirs, someone else's."

"True enough. An atheist, then?"

"Oh, I believe in gods. I simply have no faith in them."

Duncan's expression dimpled in confusion. "I'm no sure I understand the distinction."

"It makes perfect sense, but I cannae explain it, unfortunately. I must go now, but will I see ye next week?"

"Absolutely."

"With new cheese signs?"

"If there are new cheeses, certainly."

"Excellent. It's been a pleasure."

We shook hands and I took my leave. I was almost in the clear and out the door when Buck Foi staggered in.

"Aw, did I miss it? Looks like the service is over."

I nodded as I got out my phone and typed, [You're in trouble.]

"For what? I found yer cheesedick from Manchester. I did what ye told me tae do."

[Is his name Chase Digges?]

"How did ye know? Oi—did ye know that the whole time and still ye sent me off tae danger?"

[I found out shortly after you left.]

"Then why am I in trouble?"

[You have a certain candle. Return it now.] I held out my hand, and Buck flinched in surprise.

"Who told ye?"

I didn't answer but instead motioned for him to hurry it up.

Grumbling, he pulled the candle out of his vest and placed it in my hand. I noticed that it looked significantly shorter than the last time I'd seen it.

[Your father told me. He said you used it on him and claimed I was responsible. He's demanding the candle as compensation.]

"Wot? Ye're no gonnay gie it tae him, are ye?"

[No. You can stay to say hello to Nadia, but you need to be home before I get there. We have much to discuss.]

He groaned in frustration. "Choads an' chocolate, I cannae get a break."

[You can get some whisky and cheese, at least.]

"Aye. I wouldnae pass that up."

[There are nonalcoholic drinks available as well.] He pointedly ignored that as he moved past me to join the congregation, and I turned to take one last look. There were clusters of people in conversation throughout the hall, bubbling gushes of it amid rosy-cheeked grins and the occasional bark of laughter. It was a festive time at the Church of Lhurnog's Table, and I had little doubt that the congregation would grow.

Lizzie MacLeish and Gladys Who Has Seen Some Shite had joined Roxanne and her group of adoring men, and Gladys caught me watching and winked at me. For some reason, that sent an ice-cold chill of fear squirreling through my guts. What *was* she hoping to see?

CHAPTER 21

Red Roxanne

Buck was waiting for me when I got home, just as I demanded, though he looked impatient.

"Go on, then," he said. "Debrief me. Lecture me. Whatever unpleasant bollocks ye have on yer crabby agenda." He belched and followed up with a fart, then placed a hand over his belly. "Hoo. Powerful cheese at Lhurnog's Table. Has anyone done science on how much it contributes tae greenhouse gases? I've read some shite about what the cows contribute, but nothing about the smelly secondary effects from cheese eaters."

[Tell me what you learned about Chase Digges.]

"Awright. He's an industrialist being monitored by the Thunderpoots. Ye remember ma story about Holga Thunderpoot?"

[Aye.]

"Well, she has a granddaughter named Elegiac. She's beautiful, by the way. Strong yet soft, smoldering eyes, perky parts ye cannae miss, and she has the most adorable—" He stopped as I gestured energetically that he should skip past that part. "Right. Sorry. In my defense, I'm still horny. She said she liked ma whisky and said I could call on her sometime, so I'm smitten."

[Why is he being monitored?]

"Normally he wouldnae be, but the Thunderpoots realized that the politicians they were watching were being given their marching orders from him. He basically owns a dozen MPs. He's intae shipping, mining, real estate—plenty of things that give him lots of capital and the ability tae move it around, enterprises that allow him tae pollute the planet and make people miserable by jacking up rents and such. But that's just the semi-legal stuff, yeah? He's intae trafficking too, as we suspected, and he's got dirt on those MPs because of it. But that's no all, of course. By hook or crook, he's got law enforcement in his pocket too."

That confirmed the difficulties to which Percy Tempest Vane alluded in confronting him.

[To what end? Does Elegiac know what he hopes to accomplish?]

"Naw. But that may no be the right question tae ask, ol' man."

[What's the right one?]

"Ye have tae ask how he's able tae find Nancy so reliably year after year."

[Consider it asked.]

"The Thunderpoots believe—and I'm no making this up—that he's made a deal with the devil. Or *a* devil, anyway. Some dark power that's giving him this information and maybe guiding his actions."

[Surely not in exchange for his soul? He must have forfeited that long ago. He's getting benefits that far outweigh it.]

"Right. It's more likely that he's serving up a lot of other souls. They havenae confirmed that, tae be clear. But they know he's a shadowy force behind the government, and they think someone or something has a hand all the way up his arse too. That's what the Thunderpoots are worried about. Elegiac said they were actually gonnay approach ye about him if they could find out what's going on."

[Buck, that is excellent intelligence. Well done.]

"Thank ye."

[Now explain why you stole the candle from me.]

"I wanted ma family tae know that Da instructed me tae steal the Fullbritches' paragon years ago. Got him tae admit it in front of witnesses. He's been casting me as the villain for so long, and I wanted the Badhumps tae know he tried tae start a clan war."

[He thinks you want to replace him as the family head.]

"I don't want that at all. Truth is, ol' man, much as ye dae ma heid in sometimes, I'd rather be here than squabbling among the hobs in Tír na nÓg. There's so much tae steal and so many cops tae throw powdered donuts at. Recreational donut chucking is an unsung joy, ye know."

[I can't let it slide. You stole from me when I was incapacitated.]

"I know."

He required a punishment, but I couldn't think of one right away. The flat was already clean, because I'd taken care of that while he was away. But perhaps wearing him out doing good instead of making mischief would suffice.

[Do you know where Chase Digges lives?]

Buck shrugged. "Somewhere in Manchester."

[Find out. Go there and scout its defenses and layout, and be careful—if he's made some supernatural deal with dark powers, he may have magical wards. Discover what the Thunderpoots haven't.]

"This sounds like an assignment, no a punishment."

[Here's the punishment: Since Digges has made plenty of money off the backs of renters and no doubt evicted many of them, creating scores of unhoused, I want you to steal all his food and bring it back to Glasgow, where you will distribute it to the unhoused in the city center tonight. If you had a paragon, this would give you mojo. Instead, you'll be serving me, and I expect you to be thoroughly exhausted before you sleep. I'll want a full report of his estate tomorrow. Get to it.]

"Mangoes and merkins, ol' man, can ye no just make me watch

reality television or sumhin dire like that? Melt ma brain with human idiocy?"

I shook my head and pointed at the door. He sighed dramatically and exited.

That gave me a mostly peaceful evening—the one item of note being an email arriving from Percy Tempest Vane, who must be under serious pressure if he was working on the weekend. He had finally given me a number for the Blue Men of the Minch to call and expressed his expectation that there would be no further yacht disasters.

In the morning, Buck was snoring loudly and I snuck out with my laptop to see the Blue Men. I took the ferry, since I could use the sea air and there was no need to bother Heather or Coriander about it on a Sunday.

I got there in the early afternoon, bringing another bottle of fine single malt with me, and Mudgeon MacGill welcomed me to his hidden grotto. This time he invited me to sit at the exquisite bar of the Shark's Tooth, where I could admire the glass-tiled mosaic of the mermaid a bit better. A blue barmaid made us dry martinis with Isle of Bute Oyster Gin, a perfect pairing with the plates of beautifully sliced sashimi, cold and fresh.

We gave each other gifts with no expectation of favors owed or earned. He appreciated his new single malt, and he gave me a small hand-illustrated book written in the language of the Blue Men. I couldn't read it, but the artistry was what mattered: waterproof shimmering inks on waterproof material—preserved sharkskin—intended to be read underwater. It told the story of an octopus that befriended a shark.

"It's a story of hope. Reminds me of Blue Men befriending men," he gurgled, and I told him I would treasure it.

Once I filled him in on what we knew of Chase Digges and that the UK was willing to act on tips from the Blue Men, he assured me that they would give men a chance to prove they wished to work together.

"If they're not simply chumming us to make us rise, we'll work with you to update the treaty," he said. "But it will require their good faith and effort."

Using my text-to-speech app on my laptop, I said, [That's excellent news. I assure you that I am also working to bring him some justice on land.]

I spent the ferry ride home paging through that wondrous book, in awe of how beautiful other people can be when they wish to. When I got home, Buck found it as startling a work of art as I did.

"Oi, MacBharrais. Do ye think this might be some shite Gladys hasnae seen?"

[I don't know. I'll take it with me tomorrow and ask.]

"Things like that are why ye want tae get out of the house every so often. I cannae read even a single word, but I want tae make friends with an octopus now. That's powerful."

[I agree.]

He assured me that he'd cleared out the pantry and refrigerators of Chase Digges and fed a lot of people the previous night, but then Buck delivered the true intelligence I needed: "He's definitely involved in some naughty shite. He's got a secret door and a secret room, and in that room is an altar and some things painted on the floor and some bloodstains that won't ever come clean. Lookit."

Buck handed over his phone, showing me a series of photos he'd taken. The stains were real, and the arcane circle around the altar—with sigils very different from the kind I drew—shone reflectively in the camera's light.

[He's a warlock. Or knows someone who is.]

"Aye."

[He's made sacrifices.]

"Aye."

[Were there no defenses? How did you get these?]

"The defenses werenae designed with hobs in mind. I teleported past them, triggered nothing. And it helped that he wasnae home. Probably in some other home, or on one of his yachts."

Digges became even more dangerous in my mind. It wasn't that he was rich enough to have multiple residences; it was that he was clever enough to operate as a warlock under the radar for so long without me hearing of him until now.

I visited the Caffè Nero located close to my flat on Monday morning, since I was going to the shop early, before Lizzie and Gladys Who Has Seen Some Shite got there, and nothing would be out in the break room. I'd just finished ordering my usual with the barista when a voice behind me said, "May I get yer coffee this morning?" I turned and it was D.I. Munro. My shoulders sagged.

"Please, Mr. MacBharrais. I come in peace. I was hoping ye might be able tae help us with sumhin strange."

[Every time I try to help, you wind up accusing me of something.]

"Ye're in no trouble, I promise."

[Fine. Have ye planted another listening device on me like ye did last time?]

"Naw."

I wouldn't take her word for it, of course. I'd thoroughly inspect my coat after we parted ways, and I took the opportunity to delete all chats and messages from my phone. If she wanted to search it quickly, she'd find she couldn't. If she took it without a warrant, then my lawyer would have a lawsuit filed by the end of the day.

We took our lattes to a table and chairs and I sat, legs crossed, cane leaning against my side, and waited for her to speak.

"The past few days have yielded sumhin unheard of anywhere, so far as I know. It has tae do with sex workers in Glasgow, and since ye have expressed an interest in helping the trafficked ones, I wondered if ye might have heard a word or two about it, or if no, maybe ye can keep an ear open. Have any of yer contacts been talking about someone named Red Roxanne?"

She was watching me closely as she said the name, and I hoped I didn't twitch or give any sign that I recognized it. I shook my head.

[Who is Red Roxanne?]

"We dunno. That's why I was hopin' ye had heard of her."

[Context, please?]

"Right." She paused, took a sip of her latte, then continued. "A rash of men have been walking into our stations and confessing tae crimes they've committed against sex workers. They're absolutely terrified, begging us tae take them intae custody. And it's because of this Red Roxanne."

[What is she doing?]

"We don't know. They won't talk specifics. But they are scared tae death and very eager tae be punished for their sins. Couple of them even confessed tae murders, cleared some cold cases off the books."

[Well, that's good, isn't it?]

"Partially so, yes. But these confessions are clearly coerced. They're no coming in out of a sense of guilt; they're coming in because they fear this Red Roxanne. These are men who have means and security and access tae excellent lawyers. They were no even on our radar. So, on the one hand, I'm thrilled they're facing justice. But on the other, I'm worried about why and what happens tae any men who refuse tae be coerced. If ye hear anything about her, I'd appreciate a call."

[Very well. How are you progressing on the file I gave you?]

"We're moving on it," Munro said. "It's no ma department, ye understand. I'm mostly homicides and heists. But I can tag along here and there, and I sat in on an interview with one alleged trafficker that was very interesting. A bit disturbing too—might be the ugliest man I've ever seen, definitely looks the part of an evil bastard. Name of Ratimir Kovalenko, originally from Belarus. Know him?"

I shook my head, but I knew who she meant. The Silk Man.

"Thought ye would say that. But the interesting part was when he said someone fitting yer description sucker punched him in a public restaurant. Or rather struck him with a walking stick." She nodded significantly at my cane. "It was at The Bier Halle, tae be specific. Says he has five witnesses who can testify."

I sighed in frustration. The expected accusation had arrived.

[Naw, he doesn't,] I replied. [You'd be arresting me if he did.]

"I showed him a picture of ye and he said, 'Yeah, that's the guy.' Doesnae want tae press charges, though."

[Right, because he'd be revealed as a criminal if he did. Some of his witnesses are probably his victims. I hope you've arrested him for trafficking and freed them?]

"Again, that's no my department. But Mr. Kovalenko knows who ye are now and that ye set us on his trail."

[How?]

"He asked who ye were and I told him."

Unbelievable. [That puts me in harm's way. It's endangerment.]

"I'm tired of dancing on yer strings, Mr. MacBharrais. Long past time for ye tae be doin' some dancin' of yer own."

She'd crossed a line there—she knew it and didn't care. I'd obviously underestimated her personal animosity for me. Without intending it, I'd somehow become the dirtiest dug she wanted to collar. There were several things I could do in response. One: Run to my lawyer, file a complaint, all that. Two: Pull out my sigils and tell her to leave me the hell alone forever, which would risk doing some serious damage to her mind. Three: Cease to cooperate in any way. I typed out what I considered to be the last substantive thing I'd ever say to her.

[Until this moment, I respected you. You're being unkind and I'm disappointed. Good day.]

"I'm no paid tae be kind tae criminals. If I was, ma boss would be disappointed."

[Good day,] I repeated, silently congratulating myself for not typing *I hope yer next shite's a hedgehog,* which is what I genuinely felt at the moment. But I refused to be baited by her calling me a criminal. I *was* a criminal, of course, according to human laws. But I was protecting the humans from beings who were—often in a literal sense—above the law, as they were above everything.

The inspector maintained eye contact, willing me to break it, I supposed. Perhaps she wanted a staring contest. I was no longer interested in giving her anything she wanted, so I grunted contemptuously and looked down at my phone, idly tapping at it with a thumb and ignoring her, absently sipping my latte. She watched me for an uncomfortable minute, and I was just about ready to put my phone away and leave when she grunted herself and said, "Good luck out there."

By which, of course, she meant that I would meet with bad luck, and very soon. Clearly I could no longer count on the police to do the right thing. They should have moved on the traffickers by now, given the evidence that Norman put in that folder. Unless . . . they were after bigger fish? Ratimir was only one person in that folder, which Norman said represented half of Glasgow's illicit trade. What about the other half? They may have looked at what they had and decided to expand the investigation rather than be satisfied.

I Signaled Buck, who might or might not be awake yet.

Soon as you get the chance, nick a Polaroid camera and some powdered donuts. Let me know when it's done, and I'll give you a legendary assignment.

If D.I. Munro thought I was some criminal mastermind—a Moriarty to her Holmes—perhaps it was time I tried to be half so clever.

CHAPTER 22

The Golden Frame

On the way to the shop, I fired off a Signal to Norman Pøøts. It was far too early to expect him to be awake, but hopefully he'd see it late in the morning or early afternoon and get back to me.

Any gold from the heist left? I need a bar.

It was a fairly big ask, especially since a bar could run close to a million pounds depending on the market price, so I added an explanation: *It will put a nail in the coffin of those traffickers you gave me and maybe catch a really big fish in England.*

Once in the shop, I went straight to my ink-and-sigil room, pulled down a couple of bottles of ink I hadn't used in a while, and inked up a pair of pens with their contents. After I got the flow going, I used them to draw some sigils that might come in handy against Chase Digges: a Sigil of Dampened Magic and a Sigil of Disenchantment. I wouldn't be able to teleport across his defenses, but now that I knew he had them, they could hopefully be neutralized before they did me any harm. I drew several on my foldable cards and sealed them for later use.

Buck got back to me first, at around ten, after I'd taken a meeting with a paper salesman.

Got the Polaroid and donuts. Assignment?

Bring them to the office, but don't be seen. Use my hat with the Sigil of Swallowed Light on it.

Be there in ten.

And five minutes later, Norman let me know he had a bar left and I could stop by the bookstore to pick it up. I told him Buck would be doing it, and he gave me a thumbs-up emoji.

When Buck arrived, I told him Norman was expecting him at Gud Dug Books and what he needed to do with the camera.

"Wot are the donuts for, then?"

[Those are for later, which will be the fun part. This part has to be done first, though.]

He took off, and I wondered if it would be satisfying to rub my hands together greedily and chuckle like a supervillain anticipating the successful completion of his evil schemes. I tried it, and it really was remarkably satisfying. I felt like I understood characters who did that a bit better.

Buck returned at around eleven, and I tossed him the donuts before laying out the endgame. He grinned widely, said it was the best assignment I'd ever given him, and teleported away.

I broke out a new burner phone and set it to charging.

Alas, I had rubbed my hands too early—which was, I reflected, in keeping with what happened to supervillains who did that. During lunch break, Nadia delivered an unwelcome surprise by bursting into my office with a mouthful of sandwich.

"We god a pod when."

[What?]

She swallowed and said, "We got a problem. Sumhin bad's comin' here. I saw guns."

I stabbed the button for my sigil room and went in to fetch us Sigils of Kinetic Denial. They were wards that would save us from most gunfire and were fantastic so long as we knew the gunfire was coming and we timed it right. The sigil required a lot of energy and drained quickly. [Any idea who?]

"Naw. Just saw a flash of a face. Epically ugly man in a silk shirt."

[Ratimir Kovalenko. I half-expected something like this, just not so soon.]

"Who the hell is he?"

[Sex trafficker I knocked out a while back. Don't kill him. And let's go down to the lobby, where there's cameras. Let them make the first move so we can claim self-defense.]

"I'd do that anyway, Boss. I can't very well preach nonviolence as a priestess of Lhurnog and throw the first punch."

[Of course.]

Grabbing my cane, I followed Nadia downstairs to the lobby, gave myself Agile Grace, then readied the Kinetic Denial. We strode through the shop door, and something in our body language alerted Lizzie and Gladys Who Has Seen Some Shite that all was not well.

"Is something wrong?" Lizzie asked, when Ratimir Kovalenko and his two steroidal bodyguards yanked open the shop door and strode in, filling the lobby with muscle and malevolence. When they were so focused on doing harm, my official ID would have little effect on their minds.

"Ah, there he is," Kovalenko sneered, pulling out an extremely illegal gun. I would provide details of its shape and manufacture for those who like such things if I cared, but suffice to say it was something modern and not a six-shooter. Instead of focusing on that, I flicked open the Sigil of Kinetic Denial and stared at it, cloaking myself in the ward. Peripherally, I saw the barrel of Kovalenko's gun waggle in my direction. "You remember me, you shit cunt? Bet you—"

"How could he forget yer hackit face? Ye're the fuck-ugliest lump in the UK," Nadia interrupted. "Yer coupon looks like the chunks of sick I spewed last week after too many shots of vodka."

Ratimir wasn't used to women speaking to him that way. He reddened and shouted, "Fuck *you*, bitch!" as the gun shifted to point at her and his finger convulsed on the trigger. Nadia was already moving as he did so, sidestepping, ducking under the second shot, lunging, and slicing her straight razor down the knuckles of his right hand, forcing him to cry out and drop his gun.

The bodyguards, again, were a little slow on the uptake, probably thinking that there would be some dramatic attempt to talk their boss out of doing something rash, plenty of time to casually arm themselves while he enjoyed his power trip. Instead, Kovalenko had already shot twice and been disarmed. They were both reaching hands into their jackets, grasping at firearms in shoulder holsters, as I lunged forward.

I stabbed the head of my cane, a sculpted eagle in brass, directly into the left one's sternum, then flicked it up to catch him underneath his jaw. That staggered him and he withdrew his gun, and I brought the cane down hard on his wrist to deaden the nerves and make him drop it. I was pulling it back to prepare a cross to his jaw when something punched me hard in the ribs on my right side, underneath my raised arm.

The other one had shot me while Nadia sent Kovalenko screaming to the floor with a swipe of her razor at the back of his knee.

I did a fair tumble into the chairs that represented our waiting area while Nadia dropped both bodyguards with some grunts and cries.

"Boss! You okay?" Nadia said, idly kicking Kovalenko in the head to render him unconscious.

I nodded weakly. The kinetic ward had held, functioning much like a bulletproof vest. It absorbed most of the energy and prevented penetration, but I still felt it, and I had no idea where the bullet went. It must have ricocheted somewhere.

"Good. Let's get them settled." She produced some zip ties from her back pocket, which she'd picked up from our packaging operation on the floor, and used them to bind the men's hands. I got up and kicked their guns over to the other side of the room, never touching them with my hands.

"Might this business be from one of those unsavory pies you said Mr. MacBharrais had his fingers in?" Lizzie asked Gladys Who Has Seen Some Shite, in a tiny voice. The older woman smiled fondly at her.

"Indeed it is. But you see that the boss takes care of what needs taking care of. When the polis get here, don't mention the pies. Just say these men came in and started shooting and the bosses disarmed and immobilized them."

"But that's what happened."

"Exactly. Say that and nothing else. Anything outside of what happened, you don't know."

"Ah, right ye are. Is this just how Mondays are around here?"

"Oh, no, hosers can and will show up any day of the week they feel like it. Fact of life."

"Sounds true."

"Please call the polis, Gladys, and let them know we've had an incident involving guns," Nadia said.

I wondered if D.I. Munro would be disappointed that I survived this encounter. If I hadn't been uniquely prepared for it, I probably wouldn't have. And it was all due to her telling Kovalenko my identity.

I needed to give my lawyer a shout. And I had to make a very important call plus another text, so I excused myself and left the intruders in Nadia's more-than-capable hands.

The burner phone wasn't fully charged, but it was good enough for my purposes. I had a single call to make on it, and then it would be destroyed, including the SIM card. The call, however, couldn't be in my voice. It would be recorded, and I couldn't take a chance that they'd be able to analyze it and match my voiceprint. So I called my print foreman up to the office and gave him an envelope of cash, the burner phone, and a script.

[You are leaving an anonymous tip,] I explained. [You'll read the script, take the money, and tell no one this ever happened. We will never speak of it again.]

He peeked into the envelope and appeared impressed with its contents. "Yes, Mr. MacBharrais." He dialed the emergency number and started reading. "Yes, I need tae report gunfire and screaming at the residence of Ratimir Kovalenko in Glasgow. Somebody needs help. And I'm pretty sure you'll find that he was involved in that huge bank heist a couple weeks ago. He has a stamped gold bar in his study, swear tae God, and he's been laundering all that money. Please hurry, he's been a plague in the neighborhood and now it sounds like he's killing someone."

He hung up and handed over the phone, and I smiled and clapped him on the back.

The gunfire was a lie, but it was a necessary one to give the police legal authority to enter the premises and look around. I had no doubt they'd find all manner of terrible things, but I wanted them to find the gold bar and a few Polaroids of Buck Foi holding it with a huge grin on his face. That would connect Kovalenko to the heist. He was already going to face charges for assaulting us and firing weapons, and the police also had the evidence that Norman assembled, which indicated that Kovalenko was quite adept at money laundering as a human trafficker. So he'd take the blame for the heist, and they'd never believe his denials when they had such evidence. Who would frame somebody, after all, by sacrificing a million-pound gold bar?

Up next was a Signal to Iris MacCowan from my own phone letting her know I'd been attacked and would like her to run interference against the likely theory the police would put forward, which was that I must have done something to deserve it.

And then I sent a Signal to Buck to let the real fun begin: *Deploy the donuts.*

Aye, came the response, and I grinned. I dismantled both phones and removed the SIM cards and batteries. My phone got hidden in my ink-and-sigil room, and I'd maintain that it was lost until it was safe to use it again. I took the burner down to the printshop floor and fed it into our industrial shredder, snapping the SIM card in half and lobbing the battery into a bin.

That allowed me to return to the lobby and find D.I. Munro telling Gladys Who Has Seen Some Shite that she needed to see me right away.

"I can do that," Gladys said, and pointed at me.

"Oh." Munro was accompanied by four constables. "What happened here, MacBharrais?"

Lacking an app to communicate, all I could do was shrug and gesture that I needed a piece of notepaper and a pen from Lizzie. Once I began writing, Munro got impatient. "Where's yer phone?"

I shrugged again, then showed her what I'd written.

What happened is, Kovalenko came after me, thanks to you. It's all on our security camera.

She didn't like that answer, but she directed the constables to get statements from everyone and to call an ambulance to see to the restrained and bleeding men on the floor. Nadia helpfully pointed out that the men's guns were on the floor against the wall and we hadn't touched them. D.I. Munro was about to say something else when her phone buzzed and she checked on the caller, frowning, before answering.

"Yeah?" Her expression changed to surprise. "You're sure?" Then it was determined. "Where, exactly? Got it." When she hung up, she said we'd talk later, and she dashed out with two constables, leaving two behind. I toyed with the idea of rubbing my hands together again, because I knew what was happening, but didn't want to jinx it.

Buck had called in an anonymous report of "the wee pink man D.I. Munro was seeking in connection with the heist." He'd been spotted on foot near one of the pedestrian bridges spanning the Clyde River. I'd been counting on that phrasing and the mention of her name to get a call from dispatch, and it worked. There was a good chance that she wouldn't even hear about the supposed ruckus at Kovalenko's house for hours, since she was already on a call with Kovalenko himself, and the "emergency" would be assigned to some random constables anyway. She *would* find out about it, however, and I wanted her to, because I needed her to close the heist case and connect Buck with Kovalenko instead of with me.

Buck would wait for her to show up—it wouldn't take long—and then he'd throw donuts at her and possibly at her constables as well. The chase would be on after that, with the police having no chance of catching him. But Buck was supposed to keep them close, let them think they had a shot at bringing a notorious criminal to justice, as he led them to the pedestrian bridge. In the middle of it, he'd pretend to be tired and desperate and climb up to the railing, threatening to jump. I'd given him broad leeway there to be dramatic and to freely insult D.I. Munro with his most creative profanity. But at some point, he needed to jump and be seen plunging into the cold waters of the Clyde. And he could never surface. He'd teleport to shore from underwater while they were staring at where he'd disappeared in the murk. They would assume he drowned. Kovalenko would take the fall for everything—including his trafficking, of course—and the D.I. would have little reason to pester me anymore.

I couldn't do anything to dismiss the strange murder of Gary Carmichael at the stadium, but there would be no new evidence forthcoming on that either, so I'd have to be satisfied with this.

And I was.

Kovalenko's arrest made the news. The heist was "solved" as far as the public was concerned. D.I. Munro appeared on the telly and admitted they'd acted on an anonymous tip.

But the story I got from Buck when I eventually got home was immensely entertaining, and I felt like the occasion was worth celebrating, so we opened a bottle of very good single malt and he obliterated himself while I just sipped at a single dram.

"I tell ye, ol' man, I dunno if there's a much more satisfying sound than a powdered donut thwacking against a copper's trench coat and blooming in a cloud of sugar, followed by their howls of anger and maybe some clandestine rage-shitting going on in their drawers."

[I wish I could have seen it.]

"I should have live streamed it. I had reloads, ye know. I cached packages of donuts along the route I was gonnay run tae the bridge. I must have hit each of them a dozen times."

But Munro caught up with me a couple of days later at Caffè Nero again, when the police had had time to process everything.

"I know ye arranged the whole thing, MacBharrais," she said without preamble from behind me. "Ye love yer anonymous tips, and it was all too tidy. Our tech guys say that Kovalenko was absolutely laundering money, but they cannae find where the gold went. I know it's because he wasnae really involved. But the department doesnae care, because we have enough tae lay it on him and close a big case, and a very bad man is going tae prison. His victims are free and getting services, by the way."

I gave her a quick nod and thumbs-up for that.

"I'd thank ye for yer help, except I know ye didnae do it for me. I'm pretty sure yer pink accomplice is still out there somewhere. But ye'll screw up eventually, and I'll be waiting when ye do."

I had the good sense not to gloat, but I sorely wished to. And I was glad she'd figured it out—still incensed that she put me in danger, but otherwise I admired a worthy opponent. Moriarty always appreciated Holmes. So long as we didn't tumble down Reichenbach Falls together, I could live with that.

CHAPTER 23

Barhopping in California

I'd more or less assumed that Eli must have solved his problems on his own when he sent me a Signal.

Hey, Al. Remember when I said I might need your help?

Aye.

I tried to take care of it myself, but it's too big. Need a fresh pair of eyes on it and a cool head.

What's up?

Murders in a certain population committed with a silver knife. The population is getting very upset. Could boil over to the clueless population, who we don't want to get a clue.

Someone was killing werewolves. And the werewolves would certainly not be passively waiting for human law enforcement to nab the killer. They'd be actively looking for the perpetrator, and they would be prone to shifting around witnesses if they got agitated enough. That would be a difficult situation to contain.

Where do you need me?

Sacramento, as soon as you can manage. Coriander knows an Old Way that will dump you in the Sacramento Historic City Cemetery.

Any special sigils or inks I should bring?

Standard kit should be fine until we find out more. Maybe bring your monocle.

All right. Will this take a while? I need to plan my absence if so.

Yeah. I've already been working on it for a couple of weeks. Patrice is displeased.

Hmm. Suboptimal. I will pitch in as long as I can.

Thanks.

I first took the time to pack a set of sigils for action, drawing some new ones and sealing them with a Sigil of Postponed Puissance for later use. Then I had to inform Nadia, Buck, and Gladys Who Has Seen Some Shite that I'd be in California for a stay of unknown duration.

"Should I be comin' with ye?" Buck asked at home as I put together a bag for a week's stay. I hoped it wouldn't take that long, but it was best to be prepared.

[Naw. I will text if I need you. Coriander will bring you to me if necessary. Stay out of sight and work on your list of things.]

"Eh? Wot list?"

[Preparing to make a paragon for the Foi family. Reconciling with your father. Becoming a legend instead of a drunk.]

"Oh! Yeah. I never made a list. Ye told me tae craft a Machiavellian plot."

[Did you?]

"Naw. I havenae finished reading Machiavelli yet. I'm on the bit where he asks if it's better tae be loved than feared."

I typed a reply, then squatted on my creaky haunches to confront him eye to eye as I played it back. [This is a test of your mettle, Buck. What can you accomplish while unsupervised and given only the vaguest direction? Can you make progress and remain sober?]

"Why can I no make progress *and* enjoy a dram or five?"

[Maybe you can. But it has to be slowing you down. Every time you drink or get high on capsaicin, you waste part of the next day recovering. Which sends a signal that you believe you have nothing important to accomplish, when you absolutely do. If someone claims to have ambitions but exhibits no urgency to achieve them, what would you conclude?]

"Knobs an' cobs, ol' man. Can I no just run errands and enjoy ma self? Why do I have tae be introspective?"

[Because I want you to be a legendary hob. Be about it, please.]

He maintained eye contact while ripping a long, stuttering fart.

"Was that legendary?" he whispered. "Sounded like, maybe."

I rose, spun on my heel, and returned to packing, folding trousers and shirts into my suitcase and making trips in and out of my closet, while Buck complained loudly from the kitchen and made a sporadic ruckus as he searched for a pen and paper to make this Machiavellian plot he was supposed to have made.

"Goals, MacBharrais! Ye've got tae have goals!" he called. "What would I even choose as a paragon for the family name of Foi? Sumhin big that cannae be easily moved? Or sumhin wee that would be easy tae steal but also easy tae hide? I really should have thought more about what the hell a Foi is. But at the time I wasnae thinking of creating some grand family legacy."

He lapsed into occasional silence as he thought it through and maybe even wrote down something, but I heard the whir of the coffee grinder after a while and the assorted sounds he made while making a couple of mugs' worth of coffee in the moka pot.

Once he had it going, he called, "Hey, maybe I can go ahead and choose a proper hobgoblin surname and make Buck Foi ma first and second name, and then I'd be able tae craft a working paragon. Would ye help me do the official documents for that?"

I quickly texted him, *Aye*, and continued my packing, choosing several pinstriped shirts and some rather flamboyant vests but leaving all but one tie in my closet, since I figured California would not require such formality.

With everything packed and a new burner phone to activate once I arrived, I bid Buck farewell and rolled my suitcase to Gin71, where Heather hooked me up with Coriander, and I eventually traded the grey gloom of a Glasgow winter for the mildly brisk but clear skies of California.

The cemetery in Sacramento was surrounded by a tall wrought-iron fence; perhaps someone had been worried about goths draping themselves dramatically over tombstones for Instagram portraits. Or maybe there had been drug deals going down, or people going down on each other, and families had been scandalized by the thought of people boning atop Grandma's bones. Whatever the reason, the fence did not contribute to the idea that this was a place to rest in peace.

I texted Eli that I'd arrived and would be waiting outside the gate, and he said he'd pick me up in ten.

Eli rolled up to the cemetery in a white Cadillac Escalade with deeply tinted windows and winced when he saw me. He was dressed in something that looked like a very expensive tracksuit, bright pink and what I can only describe as diamond-hard powder blue, a color combination I could never dream of pulling off. There was a colorful baseball cap as well, though it did not display the logo of any team but rather some fashion brand.

Eli sniffed, looking me up and down. "I shoulda told you to dress casual."

[This is casual. I'm not wearing a tie.]

"No, I mean, American casual. You look like you walked out of a tweed catalog or some shit. You know how many people wear wool in California? I think it might be just you, man. Out of, like, forty million people."

I felt that had to be an exaggeration. Wool topcoats of many cuts were always in fashion, and the political crowd in Sacramento would be wearing them for sure. [Why does it matter?]

"We are going to be prowling downtown. I look like someone no one wants to fuck with. You look like a mark with a fat wallet to lift."

[Anyone who tries to pick my pocket will have an extraordinarily bad day.]

"I'm just saying we'll be one hell of an odd couple. People will stare, and that's not good when we're trying to blend in."

[Could I simply wear a hat with a Sigil of Seeming Absence?]

"No, because then it'll look like I'm talking to myself whenever I talk to you, and people will think I'm on drugs. And before you say I should wear one too, I don't like that one. I like to be seen."

[Fine. Take me someplace to purchase clothing you feel would be more appropriate. Though I beg you not to dress me in a tracksuit. Leave me some dignity.]

"Ha haaa! I'm gonna hook you up, Al. Wait and see."

I did not relish this hookup but resigned myself to the necessity.

[How are Patrice, Camille, and Pierre?] I asked. His family was his rock, and I envied him that.

"Aw, they're good, yeah, aside from being mad that I've been gone so long. How's that hobgoblin of yours? Still getting high on salsa?"

I snorted in amusement and nodded.

"He's doing right by you, though?"

[Yes. His service has overall been a boon, despite its numerous drawbacks.]

"Yeah? You think I should get me one?"

[I wouldn't recommend bringing one into a family situation. Perhaps if you arranged for them to be housed separately.]

"You know any looking for work?"

[I do. You can take your pick of Maladroit, Unforgettable, and Squidgy Badhump.]

"Squidgy? Are you for real?"

Another nod got him chuckling. "I might just do it so I can say the name every day."

I privately thought Patrice would never allow him to work with someone named Squidgy.

[So what is the situation here?]

Eli's amusement faded. "Werewolf pack lives about forty minutes northeast of the city, near Folsom Lake in a town called Granite Bay. The two forks of the American River form this peninsula jutting into the lake and it's state land, and that's where the pack roams during the full moon. That part's all good, no damage up there. The problem is, some of their pack members started getting knifed when they came into the big city. Now, you know, if you knife a werewolf with a regular-ass knife, unless you're very skilled or very lucky, chances are he's gonna heal up and shred you into confetti. These werewolves got stabbed just once while they were walking around as humans, and they bled out. So the pack knows it was silver poisoning, or else they would have healed."

[The werewolves were alone?]

"Yes. But they don't do that anymore. They travel in pairs at the minimum."

[How many lost?]

"Three now."

[I'm assuming they've tried picking up scents from the bodies?]

"Yeah, see, that's the part that's *really* pissing them off. The killer is spraying their bodies with ammonia, and it destroys scent clues. But that means someone is actively stalking them when they come to the city."

[All three murders were in Sacramento?]

"Uh-huh. Downtown."

[Maybe something is staking out a territory.]

"I was thinking maybe so."

[Does the Granite Bay pack have a feud going on with any other packs?]

"Asked them that already. They said no."

[You have a theory?]

"Solitary warlock who's up to some shit."

That sounded like Chase Digges, but obviously it couldn't be him. [Why here?]

"Sacramento is the capital of a state that has a larger economy than most countries. It's crawling with corruptible politicians and lobbyists throwing around cheddar."

[Okay, but why would he care about werewolves?]

"The first pack member to get stabbed happened to be a state representative. Might have been on a committee or something the warlock wanted to influence, and the werewolf was immune to his spells and whatnot, so, blam, he had to go."

I looked at him.

"What? Don't look at me. You asked for a theory and I gave you one. I never said it was any good."

[Where are we going?]

"Clothes first. Then we get you to the hotel and you can chill until it's time to go looking for trouble."

He drove us to a place on the east side of Sacramento called WEAVEWorks Recycled Fashion, an organization that donated all of its proceeds to victims of domestic abuse and sex trafficking. They had clothing for men and women, often name-brand items. It was in a strip mall on Arden Way, with a plain beige façade and a no-frills interior full of clothes racks and some stands dripping with old necklaces and bracelets.

"We'll get you some shoes somewhere else. But this is where you'll get most of your stuff," Eli said. "Distressed jeans, a T-shirt—well, maybe a polo shirt for your dignity—and can we leave out the cane? That's going to be noticeable."

[I'd have no weapon.]

"That mustache is a weapon. Plus you have sigils. We're going to be weird enough as it is with monocles. Speaking of which, we need to get you a baseball cap to give people a place to look besides your eye. The mustache will draw their gaze down, the hat will draw it up. Dodgers or Giants, nothing from the American League."

[Why does it matter?]

"I can't stand the designated hitter and it should be against the law. It's universal now but the National League didn't used to have the designated hitter until a few years ago. I'm with Crash Davis on this."

[Who?]

"Character from a baseball movie you'll probably never see."

That recalled a conversation with Buck. [Does this movie have ghosts in a cornfield?]

"What? Nah, that's a different baseball movie. Same actor in both, though. But you know what? Crash Davis had a bomber jacket. That would complete your look. People will think you're into wine and cheese."

[I honestly don't understand this preoccupation with how I'll be judged by the local citizens.]

"One of the locals is efficiently murdering werewolves. We don't want to tip them off that we're hunting them. It's okay that you look a bit unusual. Just can't have you look alien."

It was disorienting to be told that my everyday, perfectly taste-ful fashion would make me appear alien in this place. I took some time to try things on, and we had to stop at two more places to get me a cap and a pair of chunky brown work boots that no one would ever believe I'd actually worked in, but Eli said that was perfect. He claimed I looked like a well-off American who was attempting to dress down to appear working class and avoid re-sentment. This was more thought put into fashion in one after-noon than I'd spent in decades; I put my old clothes and shoes in the shopping bags and wore the new ensemble out of the store for Eli's peace of mind. I transferred the sigils I'd had in my topcoat to the bomber jacket we'd found.

We stayed at a place called Vizcaya, a bed and breakfast in central Sacramento that was essentially a big old house with a cream exterior, reddish-brown shingles on the roof, and one of those pillared front porches. Once in my room, I scooted my suit-case into a corner, since I wouldn't need it until bedtime. It was technically already past my bedtime thanks to the time-zone change, but I'd need to struggle on and stay awake.

I splashed some water on my face and Signaled Eli that I was ready to go out again, since I had nothing else to do; I'd neglected to bring a book. Perhaps we could remedy the situation?

We met in the lobby and Eli drove me to Capital Books on K Street, a lovely shop that was broadly appealing on the ground floor but possessed an absolutely stonking genre basement for science fiction and fantasy, plus a charming shop dog named Fern. Since I'd enjoyed *The Saint of Bright Doors* so much, I thought it would be grand to read another fantasy book, and on the advice of the bookseller—which I almost always took—I picked up *A Stranger in Olondria* by Sofia Samatar.

Across the street there was a place called Dive Bar, which turned out to be an appropriate name. There was a mermaid as part of the logo, and it wasn't an idle image. Upon entering, we were greeted by jellyfish light fixtures floating near the ceiling; they were made of iridescent glass in shades of magenta and neon green. Above the bar was a huge aquarium in which mermaids swam during prescribed hours—by which I mean humans slipped into fishtail costumes, because real mermaids would have been terrifying. The featured drinks were largely festively colored fruit explosions, but I ordered a black walnut old-fashioned since they had the bitters on hand, and Eli opted for a local craft beer on tap. We were just going to kill time until the sun went down.

"All three of the murders happened at night, and I've been conducting my searches in quadrants," Eli said, idly twisting his pint glass on the table as he spoke. "This particular area I've only been to once before—it's in between two other quadrants where killings occurred. And thanks to the pack, we have a brave volunteer to trail."

[Not a pair?]

"He's taking the risk of being alone in hopes of luring the killer out. But he's going to be wearing a stab vest underneath his clothes. He's going to meet us here—really just long enough for one drink so we can ID him—then he'll move on and we'll trail, watching who watches him."

[And perhaps being watched in return.]

"Maybe so," Eli said, nodding in agreement.

We were about to change the subject when a pair of women came over to flirt with us, and Eli sent them away by pointing to his wedding band. "It ain't for show, ladies, I'm sorry. I'm super married." One of them decided to grab a rebound and addressed me.

"What about you, Zaddy?"

Confused, I turned to Eli. "What the hell is a zaddy?"

He chuckled and shook his head. "Ain't you. You're more of a Stern Brunch Daddy."

"*Yeah* he is," the young woman said. "He's got an accent too. You want to hang out, Daddy?"

"Naw, please don't call me that. I'm no interested in whatever role ye want me tae play, sorry."

When they left, disappointed that we hadn't even offered to buy them a drink, Eli chucked his chin at me. "You just spoke aloud. How you doing on those curses?"

Back to typing, I said, [I recently learned who did it. I just have to figure out how to confront them.]

"You mean something short of killing them? Because curses like that deserve a killing."

[The problem is they're true immortals. Olympians. If I manage to kill them, they'll just come back and kill me.]

"Shit, I'm sorry. I'm glad I don't have to deal with them. I got nothing that nasty in my territory. I mean, Coyote keeps coming back from the dead and he can be a pain, but he's not actively malevolent like that."

[Cleverness is required. And I have been short on that, because I got severely concussed finding out who was responsible and I'm still recovering. But I'm working on it.]

"Damn, I'm sorry to hear about the concussion. And if you get free of the curse?"

[I'll be on my way to retirement.]

"Whoo! That'll be something, won't it? Just . . . not worrying about the next apocalypse. Letting someone else handle it, because you have a tee time at the country club."

[Is that what retirement is?]

"If you believe the billboards for retirement communities. They always have old white people smiling on golf courses."

[I've never played a single round.]

"Me neither."

We chatted until after the sun set, getting refills and largely ignoring the patrons of the bar and being ignored in turn. I told him about Brighid's new map sigil that acted like a navigation app on linen, and he told me how his apprentice was having trouble making the ink for the Sigil of Lethe River. The ink was notoriously difficult to get right, requiring a delicate balance of bases and acids on top of a silver shimmer.

"Last week he actually nailed it but didn't expect it to work. So he drew the sigil and stared at it long enough for it to activate on him, and he immediately forgot what he did right. Had to teach him the whole thing over again."

I chuckled. [That happened to me too. My mentor never let me forget afterward that, once upon a time, I made myself forget.]

A fit Latino man who appeared to be in his thirties entered the establishment alone and spotted us sitting along the wall. He gave us a bare nod of recognition and proceeded to the bar.

"That's him," Eli confirmed. "Our job is to watch his six all night as he barhops."

[Isn't barhopping alone strange behavior?] I put my monocle in place and peered at the man through it. His aura became clear, with the telltale silver glow of lycanthropy shimmering about him. I'm not sure if it was widely known among werewolves that their auras contained silver; it would most likely horrify them.

"If you're watching him from the start, it is. But the assumption is that he's going to be spotted by the killer, if at all, at some point along the way; then there'll be a quick strike. We don't know if the others were singled out on the street or in a bar, but the victims all visited a bar before they were murdered."

[We should both be able to text him.]

"For sure. Let's get that done now." He texted me the number of the man, along with his name: Pedro Arellano. I texted Pedro with a hello, letting him know I was with Eli and watching him. He replied with a simple *thanks*.

He got a beer, smiled at a couple of women who were smiling at him. Broad shoulders and thick hair and neatly trimmed beard, a cream-colored suit that was clearly tailored rather than off the rack, gold gleaming at the base of his neck—he was an attractive man. But he quickly chugged his beer and left. We were on.

It's different, walking city streets at night in America. Fewer smokers but more vapers. A bit less vomit and piss, perhaps, but the cars were loud and bloody dangerous, and it felt like a third of them probably had guns in the glove box, even if it wasn't true. Nobody gave a thin throttled shite about proper football, or indeed about anything beyond their immediate locale; all conversations were focused inward, a shared cultural narcissism that told them they were living in the only place that mattered.

We visited a bar or two on every block that had one, with Pedro ordering a drink, circulating throughout the bar simply to be seen, and often leaving before he'd finished. Every stop was like casting a lure into a lake and slowly reeling it in before moving on to another spot. Eli and I kept a wary eye out and got some stares of our own, but the auras we saw were uniformly human, until we had walked for miles downtown, visited a half dozen bars and pubs, and the clock ticked near to midnight.

The spot of bother—or, rather, the yawning abyss of doom—revealed itself on 15th Street as we were walking north from B-Side, a retro bar that spun vinyl records, to a bar called The Snug, a couple of blocks away. A raven-haired figure in a black leather jacket and vinyl trousers had taken up a position behind Pedro but in front of us as we exited B-Side to follow him. And that figure, viewed through our enchanted monocles, had a uniformly grey aura with two red glowing embers, one in the head and one in the heart. That meant it was a vampire, not a warlock, and we were wholly unprepared to confront one.

"Oh, shit," Eli breathed, and I reached out a hand and touched his arm, shaking my head vigorously and putting a finger to my lips. We didn't want to say a single other word, because the vampire would absolutely hear it if we said, *That's a vampire*. The violent reaction to that would be swift and we'd be dead.

I quickly typed a text to Pedro: *Keep going until we call out, then turn and greet us, giving a wide berth to the person in black behind you.*

Eli broke the seals on Sigils of Muscular Brawn and Agile Grace, but I didn't bother. If the vampire wanted me dead, I would die. I saw Pedro check his text, put the phone back in his pocket, and continue on. That's when I spoke up in just slightly elevated volume to Eli. "Hey, is that Pedro up ahead of us?" Then I shouted, "Hey, Pedro! Pedro, ya jammy bastard!"

Pedro and the vampire turned simultaneously to see who was shouting. The vampire's face was like the chalky cliffside of Dover, implacable and cold, with eyes hidden in shadowed sockets.

"Eyyy, you pinche culos, what's up?" Pedro called back, smiling. The vampire paused, reconsidering the situation. He could easily kill all three of us and probably knew that very well, but the likelihood that it would be witnessed or that he'd leave behind some trace evidence was greatly increased with three murders instead of one, and multiple stabbings at a single scene would draw far more attention than isolated killings days or weeks apart. He saw that Pedro was closing the gap with us and he'd be caught between if he didn't keep going. I expected him to press on and pass Pedro as if nothing was amiss, but he chose instead to cross the street, jogging unhurriedly in front of oncoming traffic.

Eli kept the charade going. "Good to see you, man! Where you headed?"

"Gonna get a drink at The Snug. You wanna join?"

"Hell yeah, let's catch up!"

I texted them both: *Use text. Do not say "vampire" aloud. He can hear us.*

Eli checked his phone and nodded, but Pedro texted back: *A FUCKING VAMPIRE?!*

I am sure you would have smelled him if he gave you the chance.

Aloud we said meaningless happy things about how lucky it was to meet up, let's make a night of it, and so on; we continued a much more intense conversation on our phones as we walked the remainder of the distance to The Snug.

Can you kill it? Pedro asked.

Eli replied, *Not now. We don't have the Sigil of Mycelial Bloom.*

No way to kill it tonight, I agreed. *We must survive the evening first. Then kill it.*

We turned onto R Street and there was The Snug, an Irish pub with a large hand-painted sign on the brick wall above the bar that read *Welcome Home.* We seated ourselves against a wall with a view of the door and thumbed through the menu, which was practically journal thickness; the bar proclaimed to have *a drink for every thirst.* I ordered a Spruce Goose, which turned out to be a pale-green potion made with cucumber-infused gin, house-made orgeat, amontillado sherry, absinthe, and lemon, with a cucumber garnish.

Pedro asked via text, *How long before you can get one of these sigils?*

I don't actually have one. Do you, Eli?

"Uh-uh," he said aloud, then texted, *Let me check with Diego,* referring to our colleague who made his home in Chattanooga but was responsible for the southeastern United States and everything south of that. He switched apps to contact him while Pedro inquired further.

Can't you just make one?

I don't have the ink. Haven't for years.

Why not? Don't you have vampires in Europe?

Plenty. But the sigil is almost useless in practical terms. If a vampire wants to kill me, I won't have time to reach into my coat and open a sigil in front of his eyes.

Should I call the pack down?

For extraction? Sure. That would be wise. But if they think they're going to get the drop on a vampire armed with a silver

*knife, you're going to lose a lot of friends. We need to regroup
and strategize.*

Eli looked up from his phone. "Diego doesn't have what we
need. And he's pissed at me for waking him up. Asking our friends
on the other side of the world," which meant Mei-ling in Taipei
and Shu-hua in Melbourne, but that part probably sailed over
Pedro's head.

It occurred to me that I might have someone to call as well, but
before I could, my Signal pinged with a message from Nadia. It
was just after eight A.M. in Glasgow.

*Al, I just had a vision. Wherever you are, find or make a wooden
stake right now. Incoming vampire.*

"Fuck," I said.

INTERLUDE: MUSHROOM JUICE

To make the Sigil of Mycelial Bloom, one must cook down a lot of mushrooms. You make a mushroom soup, essentially, using one fruiting body each of numerous species. It will not, at any point, be edible and will in fact be highly toxic, owing to the inclusion of a few deadly species, but as it is intended for ink rather than ingestion, it's one of my favorite recipes. It looks beautiful in the pot, smells earthy and robust as it reduces and concentrates, and if the ink is a bit of a gooey sludge, well, who cares? The sigil is supposed to be painted with a brush instead of a pen.

Since it's so easy to make, it's one of the first inks we teach apprentices. The difficulty lies in collecting all the proper mushrooms, which bloom at different times of the year in different climes, and then of course there's the difficulty of tricking a vampire into staring at its own unmaking.

While we live—and unfortunately while vampires and zombies exist in their state of undeath—the fungi within us all remain quiescent. When the sigil activates, it calls to those dormant fungi in the undead and urges them to bloom rapidly. Mycelium spreads throughout the flesh at a rapid pace, consuming as it goes, decomposing and devouring, and a vampire becomes quite the attractive display of mushrooms as the earth's recycling system reclaims the minerals and nutrients it was owed and denied for so long.

It is a simultaneously beautiful and horrifying end, though I have always been mildly annoyed that vampires might get even a smidgeon of beauty in their final doom.

My only experience using the Sigil of Mycelial Bloom occurred decades ago, near the end of the twentieth century, and it was in a very real sense a sanctioned assassination.

The leader of the world's vampires at the time, an ancient being known as Theophilus, had become incensed at one particular vampire, who was encroaching on the territory of another in Denmark. Normally this was allowed and even encouraged behavior, except that the vampire on the receiving end of the hostile takeover was personally beloved by Theophilus.

Theophilus could not move against the hostile party without causing an uproar among vampires as a whole, so he came to an arrangement with me: He'd convince a couple of vampires to leave Scotland and prey on England instead if I found an excuse under the current treaty with vampires to get rid of the offender, a man (or former man) named Søren Østergaard.

I didn't really care about moving vampires around the UK, but I wanted to see if the sigil worked, and being given a free hand to use it without fear of reprisal was too good an opportunity to pass up.

Vampires are, by their natures, immensely selfish creatures, draining the lives of others so that they may continue to exist. Killing the undead was, to me, merely restoring the natural order and inspired no more guilt than slapping a mosquito—another bloodsucking creature.

So I traveled to Denmark and presented myself at the castle of Søren Østergaard—he had moved into an actual castle—with two sealed Sigils of Mycelial Bloom: one hidden underneath a folded

card, as I typically used them, and one folded into a sealed envelope as a backup. I announced myself as a messenger from
Theophilus traveling under his aegis. Østergaard was pretentious
enough to have a thrall acting as a butler take my calling card on
a silver plate—and that is where I placed the folded card.

The thrall was dressed in livery, like he was employed by
sixteenth-century royalty, and he departed to deliver my card
after telling me to wait in the foyer. Marble floors, tapestries on
the walls, and ancient suits of armor displayed against them suggested I had stepped into a museum. The butler's footsteps echoed
in the hall until he disappeared into what must have been a car-
peted room, as I could no longer hear him walking. Approxi-
mately thirty to forty seconds later he emerged, screaming, and I
rushed forward in alarm, asking what happened. He gibbered un-
intelligibly and kept running, while others, like me, appeared
from elsewhere in the castle to investigate.

I burst into the library—for that is the room where it happened—
and beheld a burgeoning mass of mushrooms squirming atop a
writhing tangle of mycelia fed by the undead tissue of Søren
Østergaard. He'd been sitting in an antique upholstered chair,
and now the chair served as a sort of fungal diorama displaying
his unmaking. My sigil card had been opened and dropped to one
side, and I quickly picked it up before three other people entered
the room, demanding to know what was going on.

"Some unknown calamity," I said, gesturing helplessly. "Hor-
rific."

"Who are you?" one of the people demanded, and from his
imperious tone and overwrought fashion, I quickly deduced it
was another vampire, some lieutenant or spawn of Østergaard's.
The other two people were liveried servants.

"A contracted courier sent to deliver correspondence from
Theophilus. But it appears I arrived too late."

"What correspondence?"

"Well, it was intended for Mr. Østergaard."

"I am his designated successor, Torben Nordskov."

"If I give it to you, will you attest to Theophilus that you requested it?"

"Yes, yes, of course." He stepped forward with his hand outstretched. "Give it here."

I reached into my topcoat and offered him the backup sigil in an envelope. Nordskov snatched it away, broke the seal, and unfolded the paper.

"What is this nonsense? It's just a strange symbol painted in brown ink." He glared at me briefly, then turned the sheet over to see if there was anything on the other side. Finding nothing, he looked at me again. "Nothing more?"

Then it hit him and he gasped, his eyes going wide.

"Nothing more," I said, as the mycelium sprouted in his body, disrupting whatever enchantment governed his undead nervous system, and he toppled backward, convulsing, while the two liveried servants gasped and said some panicked things in Danish.

"You'd best leave while you still can," I told them, and they thought that was outstanding life coaching and took me up on it immediately. I watched Nordskov's eyeballs dissolve and two different mushrooms sprout in their place. More emerged from his nostrils, ears, and mouth. Others struggled out between the buttons of his shirt, and eventually the mycelium dissolved the natural fibers of his clothing as well, allowing more caps and toadstools to bloom. It was a remarkable sigil and an interesting solution to the problem of vampires.

Druids can simply unbind vampires. They're dead, so the unbinding is of as little consequence to Gaia as unbinding a lump of coal or separating ore from quartz, and Druids have the ability to target them and nothing else. But it was impossible to translate that to sigils, since there was no way to make an unbinding that targeted only the undead. Brighid came up with this solution that would work on the undead but not the living, since the living have excellent defenses against most fungi.

I took pictures of both Østergaard and Nordskov with a small camera I'd brought along—phone cameras were not really decent back then—and the finished prints would be sent not only to Theophilus but to the other sigil agents so they could see the results.

Fascinating but ultimately of limited practical value. After that episode, vampires had their thralls open all their mail and stopped accepting those little name cards, which they should have done long ago anyway, and they gave sigil agents a wide berth. The mushroom-juice sigil became little more than an exercise for apprentices.

But I never stopped thinking of it as a memento mori, how death lurks within us all, waiting to take us and recycle our bodies to serve some other life.

CHAPTER 24

Bears and Brass Knuckles

Honestly, gods bless the Irish. They liked their real wood furniture, and after soaking up a Sigil of Muscular Brawn, I had no trouble breaking some up to serve as a makeshift stake. I mean, the employees did not admire my efficient dismantling of a chair leg and especially did not like it when Eli joined me and Pedro chipped in, because then they had three men armed with sharp wooden stakes radiating their willingness to use them.

The stakes weren't for them, though. They were for the vampire that walked in the door moments later.

I'm not sure why he thought it was a good idea to approach us in the bar—perhaps he intended to do a little recon and maybe sneak in a quick stab to Pedro's kidney if conditions allowed. But thanks to Nadia, what he discovered was the three of us standing near the entrance with weapons designed specifically to end him, which he did not like at all—especially since it meant that we knew exactly what he was and that we'd somehow anticipated his arrival.

"You ain't welcome here," Eli said.

"Does Leif Helgarson know where you are?" I asked, referring to the current leader of all vampires in Rome. The vampire's jaw unhinged, agog at the name drop.

"We're going to hunt you," Pedro added, to which the vampire scoffed and sneered.

"Wolves don't worry me," he said, his accent old and Slavic. A silver knife—doubtless the murder weapon—appeared in his right hand, dropping from his jacket sleeve. "But who are you?" He pointed the knife at me, his fingernails long enough to count as claws.

"Are you old enough to know who Søren Østergaard and Torben Nordskov were?" When he nodded, I pointed at my chest. "That was me."

"Hmmph," the vampire said, and he backed away, exiting without another word—though I did hear Eli's phone camera shutter-click before he was out the door. Quick thinking.

I held back Pedro, who'd begun to pursue.

"No, we've got this. Call in the pack to get us out of here, in case he wants to ambush us on the street. I'm going to make some calls of my own."

"You have a vampire hunter on speed dial?" he said, his voice practically a growl. Pedro was fighting off a shape-shift, barely in control. His skin rippled and bones creaked. His wolf wanted revenge.

"Something like that, yes."

Eli and I had to pause, however, to deal with management, who were understandably upset about how we'd ruined not only the vibe but a good chair.

We deployed our official IDs and also bought a round for everyone, plus we gave generous tips to the servers and some extra to buy some new furniture. There was no need to kick us out or call the police after that.

Once seated, I called Gladys Who Has Seen Some Shite in Scotland and asked for two numbers: Granuaile's and Leif Helgarson's. Once I got them, I called Leif first.

"Mr. MacBharrais," his silky yet stilted voice said. "To what do I owe this pleasure?"

"There's a vampire in Sacramento, California, who's killed three werewolves. Might you know who it is and why he's here?"

"I know neither. This is a surprise."

"I'm gonnay send ye a photo." I forwarded the snap that Eli took and said, "Slavic accent of some kind."

After a pause, Leif said, "Ah, yes. That is Zbigniew Szczygiel, a Polish vampire who has been incensed for some time that he can no longer dwell in Poland owing to a treaty I signed with a coven there."

"Is he aware of the treaty you signed with the Druids a while back?"

"Very aware. All vampires are."

"So you would have no objections to enforcement of that treaty, which would end his existence?"

"None whatsoever. He made his choice. He thinks this rebellion against my rule will weaken me in the eyes of other vampires. We can replace him with a new vampire who will be much more cooperative."

"Thank you."

"I appreciate your courtesy, as always. If you are able to confirm his unmaking, I will broadcast it as an example to others and remind all vampires that consequences for violating the treaty are final."

Granuaile was next. I simply asked her for the number of the nearest Druid—the one who had asked for the treaty to keep the western United States free of vampires. He went by the name Owen Kennedy, and he did not appreciate being called so late—or, rather, so early—in the morning. As he was in Flagstaff, Arizona, it was a similarly late hour there.

"Who the fuck is this?" he demanded in a querulous Irish baritone, half asleep and half furious.

"Al MacBharrais, a sigil agent currently in California confronting a vampire who's here in violation of the treaty you signed in Rome. I got your number from Granuaile."

A quick explanation had him promising to meet us at the bar as soon as he could by traveling the planes. And once he did get there, I had to say I was impressed. He was like a short lumberjack, a hairy and muscled man with a full dark beard, blue jeans, red flannel shirt, and work boots. But one absorbed these details later, because the first thing that caught my eye was the brass knuckles. Even in the low light of The Snug, they gleamed, bindings carved into their surface.

Three additional members of Pedro's pack also arrived, and one of them, a brown-haired man called only Abe in my hearing, used an alley to transform. Howls of pain and snapping bones heralded the shape-shifting of a man into a powerful wolf. Abe picked up the scent of the vampire near the entrance of The Snug, and we followed him to begin our hunt.

Eli and I quickly learned that we'd need Sigils of Agile Grace just to keep up. Werewolves and Druids move fast. And people got out of our way: A pack of people running at speed at night—chasing a large wolf—is fairly alarming. Much to our surprise, the trail led us to the fenced cemetery where I'd first arrived. The scent trail indicated that the vampire Szczygiel had vaulted the fence, but most in our party weren't capable of that at the moment. We circled around to the gate, now locked, but Owen made quick work of it, and we returned to the spot along the fence where the vampire had entered, picking up the trail on the inside. We lost it somewhere in the middle, and Abe's wolf form growled in frustration. With a sinking feeling, I realized what had happened.

[He used the Old Way. He learned it somehow and now he's in Tír na nÓg.]

"There's an Old Way here?" Owen said.

"Yeah," Eli answered. "It's how Al and I came to town."

"Well, let's get after him, then."

"I don't know the steps, and I don't think Al does either. Coriander escorted me and I just followed."

"Gods below. Can we get him here to help us, then? This is worse than parasites on your privates. Vampires traveling the planes is the last thing we need."

"Yeah, I can make a call," Eli replied, getting out his phone. "Wouldn't the vampire burn up, though?" he asked while he punched a number. "The eternal sunshine in Tír na nÓg has to be a drawback."

"If he's prepared for it, he could last a little while. And if he's very old, that would help him too. Theophilus—the last bastard in charge—was something like three thousand years old, and he could walk in the daylight."

Eli spoke quickly to someone on the other end of his call, telling them that we needed Coriander immediately at the Old Way in Sacramento and that a vampire had used it to get to Tír na nÓg. When he ended the call, he said, "Ten minutes on the bright side, could be as much as a half hour, depending on how long it takes my contact to find Coriander."

"Bollocks. He could be almost anywhere if he knows how to get out. And he has to, right? There might be a world where he only knows one Old Way, but this isn't it. I'll tell ye one thing, though: I won't rest until he's ashes," Owen said.

I leaned against a tombstone, catching my breath as the sigil faded and my old bones and muscles complained.

[Thanks for coming so quickly,] I typed.

"Ah, think nothing of it. I'm grateful ye called. This needs to be handled. That treaty with the vampires—that provision where they're not supposed to settle west of the Mississippi—was for me. I have six apprentices, and if I can get them to be full Druids, I think they have a shot at saving the world. But beyond that, they're adorable and like family to me, and I'm going to protect that with everything I've got."

"Pleasure to finally meet you," Eli said.

"Likewise. I heard about sigil agents from the other Druids. Thanks for doing what ye do. It sure takes a load off my plate."

"Six apprentices is a hell of a plate. I just have one and it's plenty."

Owen chuckled. "I understand. I had just a single apprentice once. Turned out to be an important one, because he saved Druidry by surviving two-thousand-plus years. But I wasn't kind to him, and I think that was a cock-up."

"You were Connor Molloy's archdruid?"

"Aye. Though he was Siodhachan Ó Suileabháin back then. I got myself trapped on a time island in Tír na nÓg and he retrieved me from it, dropping me into this new age, with all its wonders and horrors. And it was a chance to try again, see? He gave me that brew of his he calls Immortali-Tea, reversed my aging, and took me from a decrepit seventy-something to a healthy forty-something. I was given this opportunity for a new life. I'd already tried being a cynical, cantankerous arse, and it had brought me nothing but bitterness. So I'm trying to be gentler to myself and others, and ye know what? I really like it. I have a girlfriend and a werewolf pack who loves me. I have these brilliant apprentices who are going to be incredible champions of the earth. And there's a sloth in the Amazon rainforest who likes to see the world with me. I have hope, finally, and it's the sweetest honey after so many years of sourness. Vampires are one of the few things that can cock it up for everyone, though, so I am all in."

I thought he was right—vampires had the potential to ruin everything, should they become motivated to do so. Narcissists who had no trouble letting others perish to extend their own life were predisposed to ruination.

Owen asked around about everyone else and told them that should they get stabbed with a silver knife, he could remove the poisoning if he had time. The plan was that Eli and I should use our healing sigils as a sort of holding action until Owen could detoxify their systems, at which point the werewolves would heal quickly on their own. And then he pulled out two wooden stakes that he had tucked in the back of his jeans and gave them to Eli and me, telling us to ditch our improvised ones from the Snug.

"These were crafted by Creidhne of the Tuatha Dé Danann. Stab a vampire anywhere with it—thigh, big toe, it doesn't matter—and he'll be unbound."

"Thanks," I said, but took it with some trepidation. I hoped this wasn't Chekhov's wooden stake—the sort of situation where if you saw a weapon in a story, it had to be used—because if I got close enough to a vampire to use it, I'd probably not be surviving the evening. As if to underline my danger, I got a Signal from Nadia.

Al, be careful. I see multiple vampires in your immediate future. And they really don't like you.

Wait, multiple? We're chasing one.

You're going to catch more than one. He's got friends. Can't see what happens beyond that.

Thanks for the heads-up.

I informed everyone that a seer in my employ warned me of multiple vampires ahead.

"They might all have silver blades," Owen pointed out. "And, look, there's no need for ye all to come. I can handle it, and the last thing I want is for more wolves to get hurt."

I was about to ask why he thought werewolves would ever consider for a moment that discretion might be the better part of valor, but he was told roundly and loudly to fuck off with that idea—the pack was all in too.

Coriander appeared and greeted Owen cordially, then wondered aloud if everyone would be coming along. He appeared concerned when the answer was yes.

"Have you all been to Tír na nÓg before, or is this your first trip?"

He had to give a quick primer: Don't say *thank you*, do not beg anyone's pardon, accept no gifts or food, and in general be safe by not talking to or interacting with the Fae in any way. Then he led us through: a Druid, two sigil agents, and four werewolves—Pedro, Abe, and two named Nick and Dirk, names so monosyllabically manly that they probably spent most of their time shaving with Bowie knives and hauling firewood around in large diesel trucks.

It was disorienting to step out of a dark Sacramento night into a bright sunny day in Tír na nÓg—I couldn't fathom how a vampire could stand it for even five seconds. Zbigniew Szczygiel had discovered a workaround, however, since Abe picked up his scent right away from the exit point and led us toward a stand of trees with a dense canopy providing plenty of shade. It was easy to see how he'd be able to abide there.

Owen stopped us for a quick word. "Let's go quietly now and beware an ambush. Every trunk, every branch, could hide an attack, so keep your eyes moving."

Coriander left us at that point to go report to Brighid that at least one vampire had learned of an Old Way and was running around Tír na nÓg. That would prompt some serious action from her—I foresaw a trip to Rome in my future. She'd not only be investigating how that knowledge got leaked; she'd want assurances from Leif Helgarson that there weren't any more like Szczygiel.

Eli and I both popped another Sigil of Agile Grace before we followed along, stakes at the ready and eyes scanning for movement around the trees.

There was something odd about our trek through that forest, and it took me maybe a hundred paces to figure it out: It was eternal summer in Tír na nÓg. That meant that there weren't any leaves on the ground, no detritus from past seasons to crunch through. Our booted feet were fairly quiet, though of course vampires would be able to hear them just fine. It was simply disconcerting to me until I identified what was off. Then it became unnatural: This really wasn't earth.

Abe became more and more agitated, the scent getting stronger, as we ran for perhaps four hundred meters into the forest. Then a hillside rose before us, and the mouth of a cave yawned with stone teeth and an abyss for a throat.

"Whoa, hold up, don't go in there, Abe," Owen said, and we all slowed to gather in front of the cave. The Druid turned and said, "That's a feckin' trap, and we'd have to be madder than a yoga mom who got served the wrong kombucha to go in there." His eyes flicked up to the trees and abruptly started. "Al, duck and roll!"

I did what he said and felt something whiff over my head—the blade of a silver knife. Simultaneously, everyone else was shouting and moving. The anticipated ambush had literally fallen on us from above.

Pensioners who fall down do not normally spring back up—at least not quickly, and with a profound lack of springing when they do. But the sigil that granted me increased agility was still in effect, and I used it to keep rolling out of reach of whatever vampire was trying to stab me—there were more than two of them, because more than two of us were fighting something, but I didn't exactly have time to conduct a proper head count. Perhaps that was the reason Nadia couldn't see anything else in my future?

She hadn't mentioned anything about me getting stabbed, but that definitely happened. Ice cold slicing into my flesh and searing pain in its wake when it was withdrawn, multiple times, as I rolled. The only "fortunate" thing was that the strikes didn't fall where intended or sink as deeply, thanks to my constant movement and perhaps my bomber jacket hiding the true contours of my torso somewhat.

Tired of being a pincushion, I took a risk and stopped rolling when next my torso was face up, and I made a thrust of my own at my assailant, using the stake Owen had given me. He was an anonymous snarling vampire in a grey hoodie with *Szczebrzeszyn* emblazoned on it, and since he was surprised by my sudden halt, he basically ran onto the stake, groin first.

It was not the way I'd want to go.

He screamed, yanked out the stake with his left hand because the silver dagger was in his right, and then he fairly exploded, showering me in gore and assorted undead chunks. Both the stake and the knife were propelled some distance, and that left me unarmed and wounded, facing the charge of Zbigniew Szczygiel, who had just disarmed and stabbed Eli. My colleague was still falling when the vampire lunged at me.

He wasn't after the werewolves now; I was the intended target. My first clue was the murderous eye contact. The second was him shouting, "For Søren!"

I thought that was it for me, but a black bear leapt over my head to intercept him and bore him to the ground. The vampire stabbed repeatedly, blade flashing and then disappearing into the beast's mass of muscle and fat, but the bear just struck once with its claws, which appeared to be coated in gold or brass. They swept through his flesh and bone like it was cottage cheese, and Szczygiel's head sailed in a rainbow's arc until it bonked against a tree trunk and fell to the ground.

Both the bear and I looked around for more foes and discovered that we were the only two even mildly able to stand. In addition to Eli, the four werewolves were all down and wounded somehow. Pedro seemed the least affected, as he'd been wearing a stab vest, but he was groaning and clutching a wound in his thigh. Abe, who'd been in wolf form, was sprawled out in front of the cave mouth, either unconscious or dead. Dirk was gurgling from a punctured lung, struggling to get adequate oxygen, and Nick was clutching his abdomen, blood spilling between his fingers as he tried to keep his guts in place.

Around and among them were vampire parts, torn limbs and heads scattered about like dolls that some furious child had decided to dismantle. That wasn't the way werewolves worked, though. That black bear must have done it all—or rather, Owen Kennedy, as I realized somewhat belatedly that he must have shifted to one of his animal forms.

Even as I pieced that together, the bear's shape wobbled and collapsed and re-formed into the Druid, a much faster and apparently painless shift compared to that of werewolves, its gleaming claws turning back into brass knuckles. He was nude and had some bleeding wounds that were closing before my eyes.

That reminded me of my own problems. A puncture in my right side had glanced off a rib; my left scapula had prevented a hole in my upper back from being any deeper; and a defensive wound on my left forearm might have caught me in the throat or head if I hadn't been covering up. Fumbling in my jacket pockets, I found a Sigil of Knit Flesh and a Sigil of Healing and opened them to get me started. Eli, much to my relief, was doing the same thing. He had been stabbed in the side too, but it looked deeper and might have hit an organ. He would be okay but feel mighty poorly for a while.

Owen grimly began speaking what I assumed was Old Irish, his eyes focused on the vampire remains, and they began to dissolve into sludge, bit by bit, as he unbound them. They would get no opportunity to heal.

But the werewolves needed help. They all had silver poisoning from the daggers, and though Pedro's wound didn't look to be life-threatening, the others would shuffle off their mortal coil without help. I could do nothing about the poisoning, but I followed the plan and used healing sigils on Nick, Dirk, and Pedro to help them stabilize until Owen could render aid. Werewolves are immune to most magics, but some sigils can sneak past their defenses since they're taken in through the eyes.

Abe was beyond my help. His fur was matted with blood, his teeth bared in a snarl, and his eyes were closed and he remained unresponsive. I couldn't use a sigil on him.

Owen came over and knelt next to me, placing his right hand on Abe's side.

"He's alive but just barely. I'll get him fixed. Saw that ye got one of the vampires. Well done."

Searching for my phone, I eventually found it and typed, [Thanks. I saw that you got all the rest. That's not bad.] Owen snorted. [How many were there?]

"Six. Told the wolves I could handle it, but no, they just had to come and get stabbed. Good thing is that the vampires really overstepped here. Brighid is going to shit a live badger when she hears that six vampires got into Tír na nÓg without her knowing about it. She'll be impossible to please until she finds out how it happened. She might demand reparations from Rome. I know this pack will, and they should."

We didn't move from that spot until all the werewolves had their systems cleansed of silver and their natural regenerative abilities could take hold. Eli and I didn't feel particularly well, but we could at least manage a weary stagger out of the woods and back to the Old Way that would dump us in Sacramento. Owen shook our hands and made his own way back to Flagstaff, where he had a change of clothes waiting for him and some apprentices who'd need their morning lessons soon.

The werewolves parted with us at the cemetery gates, thanking us for our help before walking gingerly back to their vehicles, parked near The Snug.

Eli and I eventually made it to his Cadillac and he drove us back to our hotel—I had never been so glad to see my suitcase. I couldn't wait to strip off my bloody clothes, shower, and slip into something comfortable.

When I unzipped the case, an unholy stench assailed my nostrils. It was rot—terrible rot of some kind.

"Uggh! What the hell?"

I pawed through my clothes and discovered the source of the smell near the bottom: raw chicken and fish fillets that had gone bad and permeated my clothes with their foul perfume. Buck must have slipped them in there while I was packing, making noises in the kitchen about coming up with a surname worthy of a paragon and then sneaking in to take the piss out of his employer with a time-delayed prank.

Technically I shouldn't get mad. I could wash the clothes. They weren't permanently damaged, which is exactly the kind of thing he was allowed to do. But the timing couldn't be worse. I needed to feel comfortable, and now I couldn't.

"Gods damn it, Buck!" I said.

I scooped the offending flesh out and threw it in the bathroom bin, which had a bag I could tie off and take out of the room. I had to do that in the bathrobe provided by the hotel. That done, I sealed my suitcase again and cleaned up as best as I could, deciding in the shower that I'd stay in California for the rest of the week to cool off and heal. But I did send a Signal to Eli.

Do not, under any circumstances, contract a hobgoblin to your service.

The time off did me good. Not only did I regain my equanimity, but I finally figured out how I'd confront Ares. I even had Plans A, B, and C.

CHAPTER 25

The Whisk(e)y Kiss

I made it back to Glasgow in time for the second service of the Church of Lhurnog's Table, taking a long and masked airplane flight since it was a return from vacation and not the sort of thing Coriander would appreciate being called for. I got some sleep on the flight and felt fine, so I went straight to the event rather than home, taking my suitcase with me, which now had clothes in it that didn't smell like death. Accurately anticipating the need, Nadia had rented the next largest hall in the community center, and it was packed—three times the attendance of the first meeting. A good number of people were masked like me, which pointed to a congregation that believed in science but was also willing to entertain belief in a man-eating god. I could only conclude that free whisky and cheese were powerful lures, and my hopes that this nascent cult would fizzle were dashed upon the rocks of reality. It could still go wrong: Nadia might come to the podium and say something unhinged or unwelcoming and turn people off. But I thought the odds of that were slim, and in truth I didn't have the heart to wish for it.

As before, I took a seat in the back, and soon enough Roxanne entered the hall and joined me, once again dressed head to toe in vibrant red.

"Hello, Al. It's good to see a friend here."

[Roxanne. Likewise. Feel like you're settled in now?]

"Fantastically well, yes. I'm very pleased. Tremendous progress made."

[Glad to hear it. But I've been approached by the police about someone known as Red Roxanne. Might that be you?]

"Oh, that's my Nancy."

[Beg your pardon?]

"I'm going to be known as Red Roxanne now, scourge of the patriarchy. I dispense justice for women. Prayers and evocations from women who need me will sustain my power and allow me to leave the Morrigan behind. That is how Nanshe did it—a name change and a specific purpose, but no chains of theology to cage my character and prevent me from loving."

[So you are responsible for this rash of men turning themselves in for crimes against sex workers?]

"It seems you've heard. Yes. I pay them a friendly visit, which they just so happen to perceive as terrifying, and then I offer them a choice: Face human justice or mine. Most of them choose human."

[And those who don't? What happens to them?]

"For them, the visits cease to be friendly. I would not want to be indiscreet or burden your conscience with details. People may, however, eventually notice an uptick in missing persons."

I sighed. This already had the makings of an enormous headache. [This is who you want to be?]

"Absolutely. I love it already. Unlike my previous incarnation, the slain in this case are practically choosing themselves. And I'm just getting started. Edinburgh is next. I'll work my way south from there, and by the time I clean up London, I expect word of Red Roxanne will have spread internationally. And that's when the real power will begin to flow my way."

[Aren't you worried that the human authorities will catch up with you?]

"What is there to worry about? I have the right to face my accuser. Any who accuse me will die. It's a perfect plan, you see? Justice or death for a very specific kind of criminal. And death will also be justice."

I did not have the time or energy to argue that last point. Wading into the morality of her actions would be a project with no guarantee of success, even if she were receptive to such arguments. As it was, a short burst of music and a brief dimming of the lights signaled that it was time for the service to begin. People quickly got seated and applause broke out as a figure emerged onstage to take her place at the podium.

Nadia looked resplendent in some black material with a two-tone pinstripe—matte black contrasted with a somehow shinier black, which gave a sense of depth rather than an endless void. She beamed at the swollen congregation and said, "Welcome, all, tae Lhurnog's Table. We are so happy ye came tae join us, and let me assure all of ye newcomers that ma messages are brief. Our purpose is tae live in peace together and know one another, not tae listen to me prattle on for an hour.

"So let me speak tae ye about what awaits at Lhurnog's Table in the world after this one. It is not heaven or Shangri-La or any other afterlife ye wish tae name. It is called Celethon, spelled with that hard Celtic C, and there, my friends, ye will be able tae experience delights ye never knew while living. And many delights that ye do know but don't have the time or money tae enjoy now.

"All the books ye never got around tae reading will be there, and ye will finally have time tae read them all, in a rocking chair in front of a crackling hearth with a good dug at yer feet, or in a café with pleasant conversation burbling around ye, or on the front porch with a glass of lemonade, or in the endless library of Lhurnog himself.

"And there are forests and coastlines and jungles and deserts tae walk in, and good dugs ready tae go with ye, their happiness and yours compounding, and if ye feel like singing, birds will add their thrilling descant, and ye will see all the animals that inspired ye tae awe and wonder as a child.

"And at Lhurnog's Table there will always be plenty. There are omelet chefs and pastry chefs, sushi chefs and culinary artists of all kinds, craft brewers and sommeliers, and accompanying this smorgasbord of excellent food from around the world there will always be the glorious company of others who lived their lives in peace, like you.

"I would stress that these others will not all look the same. Yer acquaintance with peoples of the world will grow, and language shall be no barrier tae yer conversation. In Celethon there is growth rather than stagnation, stimulation rather than tedium—an eternity ye will be excited tae experience rather than an endless boredom.

"All this is detailed in *The Gob of Lhurnog,* of course, a copy of which ye should have received by now. I urge ye tae read it so that ye may know more. For now, we should practice what will come in the hereafter: convivial fellowship with our neighbors. Please join me in hallowing the Unhallowed if ye feel moved tae do so."

And she led the congregation in her ritual prayers to Lhurnog, hundreds of people worshipping him in concert, then released everyone to the table to partake of the whisky and cheese.

I remained seated with Roxanne at first while there was a general shift toward the banquet tables on one side of the hall. Before everyone rose and blocked my view, I could see that there were many small signs posted above the offerings, so Duncan Ettrick must have been busy with his Monteverde pen. I wondered if he stuck with Pink Champagne or used a different ink this time—that would draw me over more quickly than the food. In fact, I had little intention of remaining long, since Nadia had managed to make the fellowship a part of the worship of Lhurnog. I'd be contributing to that if I lingered and participated.

"I absolutely adore how upset you are with these delightful services," Roxanne said softly.

I didn't get a chance to answer as several young men that I thought I recognized from last week came over to say hello to her. She had a fan club. Or, as it appeared to me, a rather amorous collection of suitors. She could not fail to realize they were smitten with her.

"Gentlemen," she said to them after quick hellos, "this is my friend Al." She pointed to each in turn as she continued, "Al, this is Fergus, Stu, and Robert."

I gave them all courteous nods and noticed that Roxanne appeared amused by my unease.

"Stu and Robert, I wonder if you might give me a moment to speak with Fergus alone? I'll catch up with you later."

Brief flashes of disappointment crossed their faces, but they politely excused themselves and Fergus was left wondering why he'd been singled out. He was smartly dressed for a young fellow, a tall and ropy sort with a squared face and dark hair. Roxanne briefly leaned closer to me to whisper, "Watch this," before turning her complete attention to Fergus.

"Forgive me for being blunt, Fergus, especially if I am misreading some body language, but might you be somewhat attracted to me?"

"More than somewhat," he said. "Very much so, if ye don't mind me saying."

"I do not mind. I enjoyed meeting you last week and have been thinking of you. I appreciate your restraint and manners." She rose from her chair, standing close to him, and continued, "Tell me truly: Did you have an agenda in coming here today, some hope you've been harboring in your heart?"

Fergus gulped, suddenly terrified, but had enough grit and confidence to plow forward. "I was hoping ye liked me too."

"I do. It's not so obvious, perhaps, as the signals you're send-ing," she said, looking pointedly down below his belt, at which he blushed and I did too. The point of asking me to *watch this* was abundantly clear. She enjoyed my discomfort.

But I was curious about what she intended. Was this a seduc-tion in keeping with her powers as the Morrigan? Was she exert-ing some influence over Fergus at the moment, or was he truly that incapable of controlling his arousal? I dimly remembered that lack of control as a teenager, decades past now. Testosterone is a hell of a drug.

"Forgive me," Fergus said. "I've never met anyone like ye. You're a bit intoxicating."

"Aw, I'm not intoxicating. But this is," she said, reaching into that red coat of hers and pulling out a slim bottle of Tullamore Dew, a fairly inexpensive but flavorful Irish whiskey. She cracked the seal on it and took a pull, then offered it to Fergus. "What do you say, Fergus? Are you opposed to sharing an Irish spirit with an Irish woman?"

"Not at all. Thanks." He accepted the bottle and took a good swallow, containing the burn and managing not to cough or splut-ter at all.

"Attaboy," Roxanne said.

Fergus flashed a grin. "I wonder if . . . well: Would you mind if I kissed you?"

"You may, since you asked. That's the proper way to approach me. Always get consent."

They went to it, gentle at first, which I hoped would be the end, but unfortunately it was just the beginning. They got more heated and were soon practically gnawing on each other, and I felt it was time for me to be elsewhere. I discreetly vacated my seat and made my way over to the banquet table, hoping to say hello to Duncan if I could find him but wondering in the meantime what I was supposed to conclude about that display. I supposed it meant that Roxanne was settled now, and we didn't need to worry about her anymore. She'd found her way and become something other—

without my help, apart from securing her legal bona fides in the human world—and she was happy. I felt certain she would eventually bring more trouble to my door, but for now, at least, I could let her dwell in the background, along with any number of gods and monsters that I left alone until they forced me to pay attention. Just thinking that eased my mind a good deal; it was like moving a giant file from the inbox to the outbox.

I banished her from my thoughts completely as I neared the banquet table. The new signs labeling the cheese used a teal ink with a red metallic sheen in addition to a golden shimmer.

"Would you care to guess the ink again?" Duncan's voice said behind me as I was admiring his work for a sign labeling the Cabécou, a petite round French goat cheese.

"It looks like Emerald of Chivor by J. Herbin?"

"Correct! Outstanding eye."

"Well done once again, Duncan," I said, and we shook hands. "I cannae stay this week, but perhaps next week we'll have a chance at a proper blether."

"I'll look forward to it."

Buck Foi was notably absent from the service. I'd sent him a Signal letting him know I was returning and when. He'd responded with a curt *Aye,* but nothing more. What horrors, I wondered, awaited me at home?

CHAPTER 26

The Unbearable Hardness of Softwood

Never have I so cautiously unlocked the door to my flat. It absolutely had to be rigged with a bucket of custard or fish guts or something to dump on my head, because Buck knew I was coming and had ample time to arrange an ambush. Maybe a spring-loaded boxing glove would punch me in the groin when I entered. Perhaps a piquant spritz of fart spray would hiss into my face. Surely he would not pass up this opportunity to surprise me.

With the lock disengaged and the doorknob turned, I shifted over to one side and then used my cane to push the door all the way open, followed by some spirited waggling of the cane to trigger a wire or whatever he had set up.

Nothing exploded, splashed, fell, or launched. I did, however, get some giggles—one that was recognizably Buck's and one that was not. It sounded like a woman's voice.

"Did I no tell ye?" Buck said.

"Oh, aye," the woman agreed. "Ye told me true. He's that paranoid. Ye put the fear of hobs in him for sure."

"Come on in, ol' man, it's safe. I swear by the Crack of Dawn no harm of any kind awaits ye."

"I swear it too," the woman added.

Peeking around the corner, I saw two pink-skinned hobgoblins grinning at me from over the back of the couch. Buck was on the left, and his guest was on the right. She had her hair tied up in little drumsticks that started out at all angles from her scalp; it was dyed a bright cyan, and the ties at the base of each stalk of hair were a very loud yellow. There was probably a name for the style, but I decided it was all hers.

"This is Elegiac Thunderpoot. Remember I told ye about her?"

I stood at the threshold and got out my phone. [Yes. Why is she in my flat?]

"She's ma guest."

[In violation of the Fae treaty. She's not supposed to be here.]

"Hold on, now. She's here because of the assignment ye gave me."

[I gave you no assignment.]

"Ye absolutely did, ya bitter bowl of leached lima beans! Ye said tae stay sober and craft a Machiavellian plot tae become legendary!"

[Oh. That was more of a challenge than an assignment.]

"I accepted the challenge! Elegiac here is part of the plot. Will ye come in now and hear it?"

No. This had to be a trick. I extended my hand with my cane over the threshold again and waved the cane above the door, trying to trigger anything that might be waiting above, because I hadn't probed that space earlier. I even tapped against the wall and prodded the ceiling. Nothing. Buck and Elegiac shook their heads in disbelief, but I didn't care. It was all a trick. It had to be. I pushed my suitcase in on its wheels. It scooted across to the back of the couch unmolested.

"There? Ye see?"

Suddenly the ruse was clear. [I want both of you to raise your hands where I can see them, and they'd better be empty.]

They blinked and exchanged a glance of amusement, but complied.

[Now teleport to the kitchen island with your hands up.]

Elegiac started laughing. "He's got you figured out, Buck."

"Damn, I guess he does."

They teleported to the island, chuckling, and I entered the flat and approached the couch. Peering over the back at the cushion, I saw two bowls full of powdered donuts, ready to throw at me. They had been planning to treat me like a cop.

Shaking my head, I typed, [Tell me the plot. It had better include a good reason why she's here.]

"I found out how ye start a clan and craft a paragon. Ye have tae have a patriarch and matriarch who freely consent tae leave their old clans and start a new one, and they swear this in front of Brighid and get married. But that's just the beginning, aye? Because then ye have tae make yer paragon and go tae other clans and convince more hobs tae join ye and contribute tae its strength. Otherwise ye're just a married couple with a weird talisman."

[Again: Why is she here?]

"Because I'm contracted to yer service, MacBharrais. We cannae proceed without yer consent first. If we get married, then we have tae live here or in Tír na nÓg. And I cannae live in Tír na nÓg if I'm gonnay serve ye."

He stopped, and silence fell. Was he really asking this?

[You just met her a couple of weeks ago, and now you're going to get married and want me to give Elegiac permission to live here?]

"Yes," they both said in concert.

I looked down at the bowls of powdered donuts.

[I can't take that. I just spent most of a week away from here because your last piss-taking taxed my patience.]

"Wot, the chicken in yer suitcase?"

[Yes. Eli even asked me about contracting a hob, and after that I told him not to ever consider it. And now you want me to double that misery? No.]

"She doesnae have tae be in yer service."

[She has to be contracted to someone. Without a human employer or a contracted mission from Brighid, hobgoblins cannot stay on earth. We looked the other way when that troll was terrorizing hobs, but not now.]

"So let her be contracted tae another sigil agent or one of the Druids, or . . . whatever."

[I'm not stopping her. She's free to contract service with anyone who's authorized to do so. I'm just saying it won't be me. And you can't live here as a married couple. You'll have to find other accommodations.]

Their faces fell. "I cannae believe ye're pissing all over the plot before it's even begun."

[Fine. Pretend that Elegiac has been contracted and the two of you are able to remain on earth as a wedded couple to start a new clan. What's the clan name, by the way?]

"Erotica."

[So your name would be Buck Foi Erotica? And hers Elegiac Erotica?]

"That's right."

I sensed that they wanted me to ask what their paragon would be and felt sure that the answer would give me nightmares, so I made sure to ask something else.

[Okay, so if the Erotica clan is established, what then?]

"First, I stay sober, like I have been all week. I'm off the bevvy and solving problems, MacBharrais—and it's no because I met her, it's because ye were right: I couldnae craft a proper plot with ma heid all fuzzy, and I couldnae confront the real problem without crafting a plot. And the problem is—and always has been—ma faither, and it has been for most of ma life. Running from that problem is no gonnay solve it. I need ma own family tae break his hold on me. Fortunately, Elegiac also wants a family and doesnae mind that I'm currently without a family name. She actually *likes* me, ol' man."

"I love ye, Buck," she said, gently correcting him. "I'm no shy about sayin' that."

He looked at her, his expression luminous, and squeezed her

hand. "That's a gift, that is. I love ye back. But!" He raised a finger. "We cannae get sidetracked. MacBharrais wants tae know the plot." He turned back to me. "Once we establish the Erotica clan with our marriage, then we recruit some other hobs tae join us, and ye authorize them tae visit earth for one specific mission: taking down that cheesedick warlock from Manchester. Because ye have tae, right?"

[Take him down? No, warlocks are allowed to exist and follow their own agendas.]

"Except when their agenda threatens another group under treaty, right? If ye don't handle him, the situation with the Blue Men is just gonnay get worse."

[He's not threatening the Blue Men. They're threatening his trafficking business.]

"Oi, ye can object tae the fine hairs on ma arse all ye want, but ye know it's the right thing tae do and ye can find a justification for it if ye want."

[Do you mean splitting hairs?]

"Apples and armpits, ol' man, focus! Taking down that cheesedick warlock would be a check on an evil douchelord abusing his power, which is what hobgoblins were born tae do, and it would be a huge initial boost for the Erotica clan. No tae mention it would benefit you."

It would certainly fulfill my promise to Nancy that I'd make sure Digges didn't find her again. And resolving things with the Blue Men would get Percy Tempest Vane—and, by extension, the UK government—off my case. But, most important, a victory and a claim to legendary status would get Buck in the proper frame of mind to help me confront Ares. Because he would normally never agree to confront a god of war.

"What's happening? He just froze," Elegiac said.

"He's thinking. It's rare, but it happens. Watch. He's gonnay say yes, but there will be conditions."

To make him look good, I typed, [I have conditions.]

"See?"

[Elegiac has to find contracted work first. Then the two of you will need to find a place to live that isn't here.] I had gone my entire life without overhearing a single second of hobgoblin sex, and I wanted that to continue.

"Got it. We'll find unoccupied flats that some bastard land-lords are keeping off the market."

[The number of people who can offer her work is very limited, and they're in different time zones. So you need to understand that you might not have very compatible schedules.]

"Oh." They looked at each other uncertainly. "Okay."

[You know that gold bar that Norman gave us to frame Kova-lenko?]

"Aye."

[Elegiac has to steal it back from the polis and return it to Nor-man without getting caught on camera. That will prove to pro-spective employers that she's up to contract work.]

"Sounds like that needs tae be first. Okay. Anything else?"

[Finding a flat somewhere else is first. Give me some peace here tonight and report back tomorrow morning. Sunday's a good day for a heist. I'll talk to the other sigil agents on Monday.]

We ticked boxes after that: I got the hobgoblins out of my flat. Elegiac nicked the gold, returned it to Norman, and no doubt ruined the Monday of any number of police when it was discov-ered missing. Diego, the sigil agent based in Chattanooga, sur-prised the ever-loving shite out of me by offering to contract Elegiac for service, which meant she'd be spending a lot of time in Central and South America. Once that was inked and sealed, Diego joined me in Tír na nÓg to witness the union of Elegiac and Buck Foi. They became Mr. and Mrs. Erotica in a ceremony at the Fae Court, and their paragon was, as I feared, a hot-pink dildo.

It was a moment where their cups of joy runneth over. The Snothouses and Fullbritches attended, reconciled, and returned their paragons to each other, acknowledging Buck for his role in maintaining the balance of power and declaring that his good mojo should accrue to the Erotica paragon. The Thunderpoots also attended to support Elegiac, and several upstanding members volunteered to join the Eroticas. The dildo fairly glowed with power.

And while I was of course very happy for Buck's connubial bliss, I was more relieved that he'd managed to correct his self-destruction. I would be watching to see if he resumed, because binge drinking was a different form of the same disease, but I allowed myself to hope that while I was away, he had finally conducted that internal inventory, found the key to his problem, and unlocked his own recovery.

The obvious fly in the soup—the maggot in the haggis—was Softwood Badhump. He attended the ceremony with perhaps a dozen others of the clan, scowling all the while. One would think that he'd be satisfied, for how could his son take over the Badhumps, as he feared, when Buck was starting his own clan? One might even think he'd be happy for his son for falling in love—because Buck and Elegiac did seem genuinely thrilled with each other's company, though I'd missed the entirety of their whirlwind courtship. But Softwood had a hard heart.

He said nothing during the ceremony, but after Buck and Elegiac kissed and held their pink paragon over their heads in tandem, they announced that they would accept applications from other hobs to join their clan. They got a decent dozen before the first Badhump volunteered—it was the tattooed one I'd met before, Maladroit—and that's when Softwood stamped his foot and balled his fists.

"Naw, none of that! There'll be no Badhumps joining these upstarts."

"It's no yer decision tae make, Softwood. It's mine. Away and dip yer sack in tuna water and let a cat lick it clean. That's how ye can get off, not by tellin' me what I can and cannae do."

"That boy's done nothing tae deserve yer loyalty."

"Away and shite! He's no a boy. And he's done more than you have. All ye do is complain and hurl abuse. Buck Foi stopped a war ye tried tae start with the Fullbritches and then stopped another between them and the Snothouses. Plus he gave us two bottlings of his Best Boosted—"

Maladroit didn't get to finish, because Softwood teleported and sucker punched him with a right cross, knocking him out. An outraged chorus of "Oi!" swelled in the Court, and Buck delivered full care of the Erotica paragon to Elegiac.

"I'll take care of this," he said, and his new bride urged him to think about it.

"Ye shouldnae confront him in public, Buck."

"He made it public. It needs tae be finished that way or he'll control the talk while we're no here."

"Can ye honestly fight yer own faither?"

"If he behaved like one, then no, love, I couldnae. But he's a fire that needs tae be put out. Hold on tightly tae that paragon, now. He'll most likely try tae steal it." Buck raised his voice at that point so none could fail to hear.

"I heard the application of Maladroit Badhump tae join ma clan and accept him as Maladroit Erotica. Softwood Badhump, ye attacked a member of ma clan. I demand reparations."

"Ha! Fuck off with that. He's no part of your wee clan."

"The wee clan of a wee man is the Badhumps. All those wonderful people languishing under yer shortsightedness. Somehow ye found a way tae grow smaller."

"Shut it, Gag."

Now that was a dick move, as the Americans say. Calling someone by a name they no longer use is simply rude and disrespectful. And, in this case, intentionally hurtful.

"Make me, Softwood. Or I call ye coward in front of everyone here, as Brighid is ma witness."

Brighid *was* a witness, like Diego and myself, but we were keeping our mouths shut, because it was none of our business.

Of more importance to Softwood was that pretty much every clan had at least one representative there. If he didn't respond to

Buck's challenge, then he'd indeed suffer far more than if he'd just let Maladroit leave the clan without protest. He'd had a chance to be gracious and proud—or, if not that, to make a minimal parental effort and be quiet—but now, because of his pettiness and insecurity, he was trapped into fighting his own son. The only way out was through. So he leapt unto the breach with a roar.

Hobgoblin duels, for the record, are exhausting to watch, because the main objective of each fighter is to exhaust their opponent to the point where they are unable to mount an adequate defense. There's a rapid series of teleportations where each tries to surprise the other and land a blow, because any that land will decrease stamina and position them well for the endgame. But eventually they get tired, the teleportations slow, and whoever's got any juice left is usually able to land a good kick or punch from behind—a boot to the bollocks from the rear, called a "hindnut," is a favorite move—and then they slug it out like normal folks, except they're already gasping and reciting recipes they're going to use for their opponent's haunches, and so on.

The two of them popped in and out of our vision at different places, remaining confined to an area about a hundred square meters, but Buck was a tiny bit cleverer, opting on a couple of occasions to port high above the field and fall, locate Softwood, then port down for a quick hit.

Despite this, Softwood got in a beauty of a kidney punch before they slowed down.

Buck scored an almost perfect hindnut. It sounded like a thunderclap. But that was because Softwood was wearing protection—an admission that he'd come spoiling for a fight—so it did not drop him as it should have, but he felt it, and everyone saw how he'd been outmaneuvered.

Once they were toe to toe, Buck took a couple of hearty jabs, then deployed some moves that Nadia had taught him from her pit-fighting days. He ended it with a spin that brought his left elbow around to connect with Softwood's left cheek, which

sprayed a good number of teeth and laid him out on the mani-
cured grass of the Court.

Buck did not throw up his hands in a barbaric yawp of tri-
umph. He spat to the side, mostly blood, and wiped more blood
from his face before turning to regard the silent faces around him.

Seeing that it was an opportunity to speak, Buck pointed at his
father and said, "This is what happens when ye stop trying tae be
better. When ye see the world changing—as it does—and instead
of changing with it, ye get mad. I'm tryin' tae be a better hob, and
I think whatever success I've had is because people have been
helping me. MacBharrais has been at it awhile, and in the wee
time I've known her, Elegiac has helped more than I can say.

"And what I'm trying tae say now is, if any of the Badhumps
or other fine hobs here want tae join the Eroticas, we'd be honored tae have ye, so long as ye want tae be better too.

"Elegiac and I are gonnay lead from the human plane, because
we're both contracted now, and that's a difficulty tae be sure, but
it's also an opportunity. We'd like tae see a hob with every sigil
agent, because they're positioned tae let hobs do what we're supposed tae: curb the abuse of power.

"And I should mention before ye throw yer lot in with us that
we're gonnay confront a warlock soon: the cheesedick from Manchester. Aye, he's a warlock. Turns out he's made himself intae a
power behind the government of the UK—an unelected one,
who's done his best tae make himself untouchable. Well, we're
gonnay touch him."

The hobgoblins all sniggered.

"No like that! But listen: It'll be dangerous. Sure, there's glory
and honor tae be had in taking down one such as him. But he
cares nothing for the lives of others. He's devoid of empathy. So I
have tae emphasize the risk that, in pursuit of this glory and
honor, ye might wind up deid. Knowing that, are there any more
here who would like tae join the Erotica clan?"

Unforgettable and Squidgy Badhump volunteered, coming

along with Maladroit, and perhaps another dozen also asked to join from other clans. I may have lost a precise accounting, but at least two dozen hobgoblins—maybe closer to thirty—committed to humbling Chase Digges. And that fact did not go unnoticed.

"Al MacBharrais," Brighid said, crooking a finger at me. "I believe I am overdue for a briefing on this warlock situation."

CHAPTER 27

————— • —————

The Key to a Warlock

Some people labor under the misunderstanding that warlocks and witches are essentially the same thing, just different genders. It's easily excused, except that the gender bit turns out to be incredibly important, since it's inextricably tied up with the problem of patriarchy.

Witches pursue magic because they want power outside the patriarchy—enough to counteract it, if not defeat it. They want to protect themselves and their loved ones from a population of bastards.

Warlocks already have the power and privilege that patriarchy gives them, so they pursue magic because they want to be the King Shit Arsehole in Charge.

History would have you believe that witches were a huge problem, but again: That was patriarchy and misogyny, not reality. The big problems always came from warlocks, and history erased that because: patriarchy.

Indeed, the entire reason we have Druids—and therefore sigil agents—is a response to what a warlock did millennia ago in North Africa. He wanted all the power he could grab, so he possessed an elemental, which was similar to (and about as wise as) sticking a firehose up your anus and turning it on. Thrilling for maybe a fraction of a second, but then it's way too much and you pop. The elemental died too, unfortunately, creating the Sahara Desert in the process. Gaia didn't want a repeat. Druids were supposed to fight warlocks—or anything else that threatened the earth's elementals. That did include the occasional witch, but in practice a demon or something summoned by the magic user often provided the true threat.

Chase Digges was unusual for a warlock in that he'd managed to keep a low profile for so many years. Normally the power-hungry aren't willing to wait and ramp up slowly. They want to sprint at a buffet table of spoils and attempt to eat them all. But he was clever enough not to draw attention—and had the Blue Men of the Minch not been so offended by his trafficking, I still probably wouldn't know he existed.

Once I shared everything I knew about him with Brighid—the human trafficking, the polluting industries he owned, and his mysterious ability to find Nancy every year—she agreed that he needed to be neutralized and I could authorize a trip or two of the Erotica clan to earth to make sure it got done.

"And that's not a euphemism for assassination," she said, pointedly including Buck and Elegiac by making eye contact. "His ability to perform magic—his access to it—needs to be neutralized. I'll tell Coriander to assist you with travel as needed for this project."

We were highly motivated after that. I wanted this over so I could lift my curses, and Buck wanted the mojo. He and Elegiac had a single night of honeymoon somewhere—I didn't want to know—and then Buck and I got to planning the next day, while Elegiac began her duties with Diego.

Norman Pøøts, we decided, could help us conceptualize the enormity of the task. We went to visit him beneath Gud Dug Books.

"Here's the problem," Buck explained over an Irn-Bru at the bar. "Even if we find all the dirt on him, it won't do us any good if the police won't arrest him or his lawyers spring him the next day and he fucks off somewhere tae be rich and obnoxious."

"Don't use the police, then," Norman said. "Use the press."

"He probably owns them too."

[He does. When his yacht went down recently, not a word of it made it to the newspapers.]

"He doesnae control the whole world, though," Norman pointed out. "No yet, anyway. Get all your evidence, send it everywhere, and upload it tae the Internet. He might have paid off everyone in the UK, but if everyone sees what he's done and the UK does nothing, well, the pressure builds."

[How do we get all our evidence?]

"Through highly illegal means, of course. Is that no why ye came tae see me?"

"Aye," Buck admitted.

"I can see what I can find out from the periphery, but he's gonnay have excellent defenses. It would be more effective if we had passwords and the like. Roll in a Trojan horse through his rich walled compound. Can ye get near him personally while he's using his phone?"

Buck nodded. "Aye. I should be able to."

"I can do several things once he unlocks it. Clone it first, then install spyware. It compromises his end-tae-end encryption, so we're on one end and everything's unlocked. That should give me plenty tae start with. Then, when we're ready, ye just nick it and I start going after his accounts. The two-factor authentication comes tae the clone and he doesnae know what we're up to. Is there sumhin ye want me tae find in particular?"

[His human-trafficking networks using his yachts. You tug at that thread and you'll find a huge network of criminals. If you can make that plain, it would get multiple countries involved besides the UK, because he's smuggling foreign nationals.]

"Okay. Find the yachts first."

"And his hidey-holes, wherever they may be," Buck added. "We have tae check them all for evil shite."

"Right. Well, let's see what we can find from publicly available information."

Norman led us to his workspace behind the vault door, logged in to his console, and did the most basic search to find an image of the guy—we hadn't seen him yet. Several pictures from business articles showed up: groundbreaking ceremonies with him wearing a hardhat, ribbon-cutting ceremonies with oversized scissors, and photos with some MPs at one event or another, which told us exactly who was in his pocket.

Chase Digges had the salt-and-pepper hair of a man in his mid-fifties: grey at the temples, with a few streaks shot through a virile pompadour. There was a dimple on his right cheek when he smiled with cosmetically perfect teeth. Clean-shaven, lean, wearing tailored suits from London with matching ties and pocket squares. He didn't immediately look like a practitioner of the dark arts, which meant he was doing it right.

"Huh. I was kind of hoping for robes and a wizard hat," Norman said. "Awright, gie me a few hours and I'll see what I can pull together."

[His current whereabouts would be good too,] I said.

"Gotcha."

Buck went scouting for a flat that he and Elegiac could occupy for a time without anyone noticing, because the one they'd used previously was now occupied. I returned to the shop to draw some sigils for the coming infiltration of Chase Digges's properties and arrange to buy some cheap digital cameras and cheaper black hats. I wanted the small horde of hobgoblins to visit the sites wearing the hats with sigils on them and snap pics while they explored. The problem with using phones for that would be activating so many and then leaving a trail of tower pings behind. I presumed the hobs would need to travel to multiple sites around the world—Digges couldn't be entirely loyal to Manchester—and it wouldn't do to have the phones ping towers everywhere and then all return to Glasgow.

I had to whip up a fresh bottle of the ink required for the Sigil of Seeming Absence, but I was out of cuttlefish chromatophores. Luckily, Shu-hua in Melbourne had some and was willing to trade for it; she sent her apprentice, Chen Ya-ping, through the planes to visit me, and that was entirely pleasant. She had all but completed her training and would be a full sigil agent soon, and we would have the excellent problem of deciding where best to deploy her talents and set up her home base.

[You may be interested to know that my hobgoblin has started his own clan and has taken steps toward sobriety,] I said. Her parents had exited the world via their own drunk driving, and she had expressed concern about Buck before.

"That's good news. I'm happy for him and hope it sticks."

[I do too. But should you be interested in contracting a hobgoblin to your service, we will shortly have a stable of proven performers to choose from.]

"Yeah? Is it worth it?"

[Vexing at times. But his aid has allowed me to avoid some direct confrontations that would have been highly dangerous. Think of a hobgoblin as a hammer. Helps you drive nails and get things done, but every so often, you accidentally smash a fingertip.]

"Thanks. I'll keep that in mind."

Norman got back to me with a list of properties that Chase Digges owned, many of them large buildings full of flats to be leased, but a few were flagged as personal residences. His summary read: *He's acquired lots of properties in Southeast Asia recently and has a big place in the Bukit Tunku neighborhood of Kuala Lumpur. Can't say with 100 percent certainty, but that's my best guess at where he is now. He's got a metric buttload of shell companies that I'm still working through, which points to the idea that he's hiding additional properties—pretty sure he has something in Dubai, since he has so many other properties in the region. As far as yachts go, he may have them, but I haven't found any yet. Get me into his phone and I can find out a lot more.*

The address in Kuala Lumpur was included, along with some pictures of the place. It was walled and gated, luxurious by any measure, and had mundane security in evidence but no doubt magical security as well.

I shared this with Buck and said we should take a small squad in to scout. [Who do you think we should bring?]

"Maladroit, Unforgettable, and Squidgy for sure," he said. "And maybe two more from other clans that joined us. Let's see, how about Aromatic Erotica? She was a Vadgewater, goes by Ro for short. And Splat's a good guy tae have at yer back. Glad he joined us. He was a Shitesquirt."

[Okay, I'll write up the travel pass for them and get the hats ready. You make sure they're armed, in case we run into trouble, but emphasize that we are there to document and scout, not start a fight. And they all need gloves—can you take care of that?]

"Aye. When are we doing this?"

I wanted it done sooner rather than later, and there were time zones to consider. Malaysia was eight hours ahead of us.

[I want to do it in daylight, when we won't need to use flashes on the cameras, and hopefully while he's at work. That means we leave at two A.M. to get there just after ten.]

"Ah, so we're going tonight? Excellent!"

There was still plenty to do. I informed the other sigil agents that if I disappeared, it was because of a warlock named Chase Digges in Kuala Lumpur. Normally that would be Shu-hua's territory, but I felt responsible for pursuing him as he was originally from my territory.

I consulted Nadia just before the end of the workday: [Any forebodings about my future?]

"Naw, I havenae seen anything."

That was reassuring. But I loaded up for a worst-case scenario, bringing most every sigil that could possibly be useful or lifesaving against a warlock of unknown power. I took some zip ties with me too, since they had come in handy against Kovalenko. There might be security guards we needed to immobilize.

Dinner with Buck and Elegiac was enjoyable, because Elegiac was so excited about working for Diego on the other side of the planet. For her it was lunch, because she had to get used to a different schedule now, but her ability to travel the planes via the Old Ways meant that she could spend at least some part of her day with Buck.

"I didnae know it was gonnay be like this! There's some Mayan gods he wanted tae make happy for some reason—don't ask me which, because I know fuck-all about how tae say their names right, much less what their powers are—and the way tae do that was tae return some idols and artifacts tae their worshippers that had been stolen by colonizers long ago. It was a heist, Buck! First day on the job and I'm robbin' a museum! If that's no a belter of a way tae start a contract, I dunno what is."

After that, Buck and I gathered our gear and went to Tír na nÓg to organize the scouting mission and brief the team.

"We are no there tae steal," Buck said to them. "Strictly reconnaissance. We take pictures of everything and maybe we'll go back tae steal sumhin later. We wannay find secret rooms, any safes he might have, artifacts he shouldnae have, and any evidence that links him tae human trafficking or other super-evil shite. Maybe his safe is full of passports, for example. But listen: Touch nothing, ye understand? It could be booby-trapped, because this is a warlock we're talking about. If ye find a safe, take a picture and then report it tae MacBharrais. Let him check things out first with his monocle that lets him see in the magical spectrum. This is all about assessing the lay of the land; our attack will come later."

Coriander came by for a brief consultation on where we would emerge in Kuala Lumpur and how far we'd have to travel to get from there to Digges's estate. We'd be north of the city, near Batu Caves, a Hindu temple and tourist destination. The preserved jungle mountains nearby would provide our entry point, and from there it would be easy to pick up a cab outside the gate to the temple entrance. I would need to exchange pounds for ringgits when we got to Kuala Lumpur. I had enough in my wallet, I thought, for cab fare there and back; Coriander was not going to join us but rather wait at the Old Way for extraction.

The bowler hats the hobgoblins wore all matched mine: They had both Sigils of Swallowed Light and Seeming Absence on them, so that they would be invisible to cameras and undetectable to humans.

[You can still be heard and you can still trip motion and infrared sensors,] I cautioned them. [But visually we'll be cloaked. When you want to take a picture of something, make sure no other hobs are in your line of sight, or your camera won't work.]

"Also," Buck said, "I have tae warn ye: It's near the equator and full of rainforest, so walking around is gonnay be hot and wet, like soup."

That proved to be more accurate than I would have wished, but I'm glad he mentioned it, because we thought to bring along umbrellas and had some protection from the downpour in progress when we arrived.

A five-minute walk brought us to the Batu Caves gate, where I took off my hat to hail a cab. When one pulled over, I opened the rear door and the hobgoblins piled in, making some grunting noises as they did so. Since the Sigil of Seeming Absence made them invisible, the driver could not assign the sounds to anyone but me, and a tinge of fear entered his eyes. But this was replaced with joy when I gave him a hundred-pound note and said he could keep it.

It was a twenty-minute drive to a corner about a block away from Digges's estate. We got out there, again with much more noise than a single Scottish man should make, but the driver was willing to overlook it, because I gave him a fifty to pick us up in an hour on that corner and showed him the other hundred that he'd get for taking us back to Batu Caves. Very expensive cab rides, but worth it when you needed quick and reliable transport in a foreign country.

We strolled through the rain until we got to the gated entrance to Digges's estate. There were cameras and an intercom system but no visible guards in the immediate vicinity. I did see one near the front door, however, wearing sunglasses and a little curly wire, which trailed from his ear down the back of his neck. That meant he had someone to talk to, and I typed, [Guards on the grounds.] I distributed Sigils of Restful Sleep and zip ties to all the hobs.

"Sleepytime," Buck said. "Find all guards on the perimeter, put them tae sleep, zip-tie them, and remove the earpiece. Meet back at the front entrance."

Five hobgoblins popped away, while Buck and I ported to the front entrance and delivered the guard there into peaceful slumber. Three minutes and we were all assembled, with reports of three more guards dreaming of . . . union wages, I supposed.

I gave them more sigils and zip ties. There might be guards inside, but more likely they'd find household staff.

Digges's place was a contemporary minimalist monstrosity with lots of glass—so much that the entrance and foyer were made entirely of it, and we could see inside. The walls and interior showed us clues of what lay beyond, but it was to create the illusion of intimacy and transparency without actually providing any.

Trying the door, I was pleased to discover it opened. We would not need to worry about setting off conventional alarms. Checking the time, I saw that it was 10:45 A.M. locally.

Buck told the others, "Stay quiet. Touch nothing. Find the naughty shite. Take pics."

Splat, Ro, and Maladroit went left. Unforgettable, Squidgy, Buck, and I turned right. I put on my monocle, because anything that gave off the telltale glow of magic in this place was probably the sort of thing we wanted to document.

Splat found a maid; Maladroit found the head of security, who was loudly demanding that someone, anyone, report, so that gave us some peace of mind, since he obviously hadn't made an outside call yet. Ro found a chef and a sous chef in the kitchen and came back to get an extra sigil from me before subduing them, and she also had the presence of mind to turn off the stove and oven. It was going really well. I was thinking, *Ha! Who needs guns and special forces when ye have sigils and six hobgoblins? No one can match such nonlethal efficiency!*

I surfed on that feel-good wave for about five or six delicious seconds before I realized, *Holy shite, I'm on a mission alone with six hobgoblins. I'm gonnay fuckin'* die. And the reason Nadia didn't foresee any trouble was that she'd been long asleep. Usually her premonitions came much closer to actual danger. It was true she'd had dreams of trouble when I went to Australia, but only because she'd had time enough to have them. I'd decided on this course of action and embarked upon it all in the same day. There was still plenty of opportunity for something to go wrong.

Such as a very large and boring house—so clean and uncluttered that it appeared as if no one lived there and it was simply waiting to be photographed for *Shite Architecture Today* or *Bland as Fuck Interiors*. There was some vague art on the walls, the kind where they get a big canvas and then splatter or spill paint on it with a mop and think they've done something clever. I checked each for magic and, when I found none, checked behind the canvases. No safe. Parlors and drawing rooms and billiards rooms dominated the main floor, along with the gigantic kitchen, a dining room intended for large parties, and a room full of televisions to watch all the sports at once, plus five bathrooms to accommodate an outbreak of food poisoning among the guests, I supposed. Off in the left wing, Splat reported that there was an old-time arcade room full of vintage machines, beeping and booping with classics like *Dig Dug, Centipede,* and *Street Fighter II.* My phone had more computing power than they did. He also found the security room, its banks of monitors doing absolutely nothing to keep us out.

What we didn't find was a library or study or any stairway to the basement. That was odd. There had to be a room full of tomes and grimoires, right? Perhaps it was on the second floor.

I went upstairs with Buck to reconnoiter and asked the other hobs to keep looking for basement access. So far we'd netted a whole bunch of nothing.

The bedrooms were all lavishly appointed, and there was indeed a study or office up there as well, located above the kitchen, with a dumbwaiter to send covered dishes up and dirty dishes down. The shelves had plenty of books and knickknacks and gewgaws to investigate, and there were probably documents to photograph, and there was definitely a laptop I was tempted to order Buck to steal. But it didn't feel real.

[This is bullshit,] I told Buck. [A veil drawn before our eyes. There's nothing truly important here. There's no magic in the room. It's too easy to reach.]

"Well, wot about all of those guards? Getting past them wouldnae be easy for most folks."

[Aye, but a warlock has secrets to protect from people like us. And none of that is here.]

"So . . . we just go?"

Checking the time, I saw that it was 11:30. Fifteen minutes until our cab ride showed. Frustrating as it was, we should think about leaving.

[Let's have a closer look at the master suite first.]

There had to be something here. The bloodstains in those pictures of the altar in Manchester that Buck had shown me were old. He hadn't practiced his dark arts there in many months, if not years.

No books on the bedside table. The art piece above the bed was a stunning oil painting of tentacles. No head; just tentacles. I was not interested in knowing why he made that choice.

No safe behind the tentacles.

The bathroom had one of those showers with digital temperature control and multiple water jets and steam settings and a bank of dispensers full of oils and foams and shampoos.

The walk-in closet was an apartment unto itself. So many suits and drawers of neatly folded ties and cuff links. Racks of polished shoes. Shelves of folded shirts. Several different topcoats. Four tuxes. A floor-length mirror in which he could admire his pompadour—wait. A flash of something in the monocle. By the mirror? Yes. But not the mirror itself—the gilt frame.

[Buck, I might have something here.]

"And I have an idea," he replied. "How about I just steal all the left shoes? That'll drive him mad."

[Yes, but he'd take it out on the staff.]

"Oh. Right. Never mind. Wot was that ye were saying?"

[There's magic around the edge of the mirror. I think it's a door.]

"Brilliant! How does it open?"

[Give me a second.]

I fished out a Sigil of Disenchantment and pointed it at the mirror's edge. After ten seconds, the coruscating light that limned the edge pulsed and fizzled away to nothing. And once it did, a mechanism clicked and the mirror—definitely a door—inched open just a skosh.

"Whoa. He's got a secret room behind that mirror?"

[Maybe. Let's step to either side to get out of the way of any booby traps and open it.]

We did. The mirror creaked open on hidden hinges. No crossbow bolt launched itself from there. No spray of acid or huge spiders jumping out to eat our faces. I counted to ten and then peeked into the space behind the mirror and beheld . . . a fireman's pole. I looked down and it descended into unfathomable black.

[This is it. This shaft must be hidden behind a wall on the main floor. It goes to the basement. Get everybody up here now.]

"Right." Buck popped away, and in less than a minute the closet was full of six hobgoblins. They'd had no luck finding a basement entrance.

[Volunteer needed to go down and then teleport back here. I

need to know that it's not warded against that. We have to have a way out.]

Maladroit volunteered. As he slid down the pole, the shaft lit up with motion sensors. I worried that there might be more sensors—if Digges *didn't* have some sort of alarm rigged to signal him when someone was accessing his secret lair, it would be unforgivable negligence on his part. But Maladroit made it to the bottom, had a quick look around, then teleported back up to report.

"It's full of wicked shite down there," he said.

[Okay. Clock is ticking. We need to find the goods. If there's a laptop down there, steal it.]

One by one, the hobgoblins descended, and I made sure they were out of the way before I went down. The motion-activated lights were on, and they revealed all the wicked shite Chase Digges didn't want his polite rich guests to see.

There was an altar with much fresher bloodstains. Grimoires on the voluminous shelves, covered in leather that might not be cowhide. A very clear and effective summoning circle. Candles and daggers and drains in the floor for convenient cleanup of sacrifices. Artifacts in glass cases and on the bookshelves as well that were absolutely stolen from other cultures and magical traditions.

There was an extremely unsettling bifurcated penis in a jar full of embalming fluid. I'm not sure it ever belonged to something from this plane. The hobs were taking pictures like mad for later reference, documenting everything on the shelves, everything contained in the glass cases. I noticed that many of these things glowed in the magical spectrum.

The room stretched for some distance away from the pole but clearly continued around the corner, and I went that way, passing several hobs, as Buck Foi called to me from there.

"Oi! MacBharrais! There's stairs here! And I found a safe."

Turning the corner, I was greeted with an even larger space, lined with bookshelves and curiosity cabinets, an antique mahogany desk, and a laptop we absolutely would steal. The staircase led up to a closed trapdoor, and there was a very clear button to press that probably opened it automatically.

"Shall I press it?" Buck asked, his finger hovering over it.

I shook my hand and waved off the idea. [Wait. Let me examine it through my monocle first.]

Once satisfied that it was a perfectly mundane button, I nodded and he pressed it. The ceiling or floor shifted heavily, and some familiar beeps and boops floated down the staircase.

"It's the arcade," Buck said.

[Go up and see where he hid this trapdoor, please.]

Buck hurried up, looked around, and came back down to report. "It was hidden under the *Dig Dug* machine. Whole thing slides intae the room on rails."

[He hid the entrance to his subterranean lair under *Dig Dug*? Bastard thinks he's funny.]

"Ye want in the safe?"

[I don't think we have time to crack it.]

"We might no get another chance. Once he knows we've been here, he'll probably move whatever's inside."

[Who's good at safecracking?]

"I am," Ro piped up from a nearby shelf. Almost all of the hobs were on this side of the room now, methodically taking inventory pictures.

[Okay, go for it,] I typed, and was just about to hit SEND when Unforgettable gasped from across the room. She was clinging to some higher shelves and pointing at a gorgeous blue glass bottle with some gold flecks in it—that's what I saw out of my unaided left eye. Through the monocle over my right eye, that bottle seethed and churned with oily black clouds.

"Lookit this fancy bottle," Unforgettable said, and she put down her camera and reached for it.

"No, don't touch it!" I shouted, but I was too late. As soon as her fingertips connected with the bottle, Unforgettable screamed, seized up, convulsed a couple of times as if she were held there by an electric current, then fell away, dead before she hit the floor. Digges had laid a death curse on that bottle.

The hobs all rushed to see if there was anything they could do to help Unforgettable, but I was worried about what came next. And curious about what Digges had thought worthy of such a dire curse.

Striding over to get a closer look, I saw some words in golden Arabic script around the bottle's lip and realized I could cross one thing off my massive to-do list from the review of my files.

"This is the djinn that's been missing for twenty-odd years," I said, speaking aloud because I felt we were on emergency footing now and didn't have time for typing. The hobs needed to know why Unforgettable died over that bottle. "Probably the basis of all he's built. He stole it from the Middle East. I bet one of his wishes was asking how tae find Nancy every year. Almost like wishing for more wishes, getting access tae knowledge like that."

The bottle looked the same in both eyes now, the oily black cloud dispersed as the curse was spent. I still didn't think it safe to touch—not without more inspection—but I would have to come back for it later, because my phone pinged. It was Nadia.

Boss. Wherever you are, get the fuck out now!

She must have had one hell of a nightmare.

"Everyone stop. Someone grab Unforgettable and her camera, someone grab that laptop, and then let's all port up to the foyer and look out for trouble."

Maladroit took care of Unforgettable, and Splat grabbed the laptop. The lot of us ported up to the foyer—thereby avoiding the growling thing that was waiting for us at the top of the stairs in the arcade room.

Unfortunately, Chase Digges was also occupying the foyer. He sensed that something odd had just happened and was looking around, trying to locate the source of numerous small noises and strange pops in air pressure. Since his eyes didn't focus on anyone, the Sigil of Seeming Absence must be working on him. That was good to know.

Dressed in a grey suit with an orange tie and pocket square, he looked perfectly put together and only mildly vexed. He had a tan now and, if anything, looked better than in the photos we had of him from years before. He was uncertain perhaps, owing to a lack of information, but not fearful. Confident that he could handle whatever intruders had called him home from the hard work of exploiting others for profit. But he took a few steps back to the right, toward that first living area with couches and splatter paintings, and spoke some words in a language I didn't know—which meant he was casting and manifesting verbally. His eyes focused on us after that: He'd either neutralized my sigils or counteracted their effects. His eyes widened in surprise, and I supposed it would be surprising to have me and a cadre of pink hobgoblins materialize in your foyer, all wearing black bowler hats like cosplayers from a René Magritte painting.

"Who the hell are you?" he asked.

"Justice," I replied. "For your human trafficking, your dark arts, and the djinn you stole from Saudi Arabia a couple of decades ago." That was enough. He knew what he did. To the hobs I said, "Knock him out now."

Five hobgoblins who can teleport into your face *and* deliver a wicked nut punch inside of a second are impossible to deal with, unless you are surrounded by kinetic wards, like Coriander, and Chase Digges wasn't. They teleported in a synchronous assault so deft that he had zero chance of remaining upright. Maladroit delivered the sack hammer, Splat got him in the throat, Ro actually kicked him in the teeth, while Buck and Squidgy hit him on either side of his heid, treating his skull like an accordion. He went down, and we were all just fine with letting his noggin bounce off the hardwood floor.

"Use his pocket square and tie to gag him first, then get him zipped," I said. "But keep an eye out. There's something else here."

"That's for sure, ol' man," Buck said, pointing behind me. "On yer six."

Whirling around, I discovered the source of the growling. Back down the passageway that led to the house's left wing, where the arcade was, a creature of unusual size hissed and steamed and looked upon us with flaming eyes.

"Wot's that?" Ro asked from behind me. "Is that, like, a balrog or sumhin?"

She was close. It was a foe beyond most of us, for sure: an ifrit, which Digges must have summoned to take care of us when he got here. I hadn't had to face one before, and without even learning what else it could do, I knew it could cook us down to bacon, and I had no defenses against fire. That's what Nadia must have been worried about. I had a single sigil as a last resort, but against a certain class of opponents there *was* no other resort. So I pulled out a Sigil of Unchained Destruction and showed it to the ifrit. It inhaled a breath and flexed its shoulders and pecs, drawing back its hands a bit prior to unleashing a gout of flame in our direction, but a cone of blistering force engulfed it instead and tore it to shreds. Then the force kept going and took that side of the house with it. Gone was the kitchen and most of the dining room, and gone was a good portion of the landscaping, all the resulting material blown into the neighboring backyard and swimming pool. There were pipes spewing water into the air, but a fire had also started somewhere. I hoped the basement was still intact.

"MacBharrais, what the *fuck*?" Buck said.

"This is no longer a scouting mission. It's containment. Get the fire put out if you can, please. I'm calling in reinforcements. Oh, and put my hat on the cheesedick so no one sees him." I tossed my hat to Buck, and he caught it neatly.

"Who's gonnay see him?"

"Hopefully no one. But we will have emergency services here soon if the neighbors are home. We need to keep this buttoned up."

After that I switched back to using my speech app. I'd spoken aloud more than was probably advisable, and battlefield orders weren't necessary.

I sent a Signal to Shu-hua and Ya-ping in Melbourne, since this was their territory: *Emergency containment needed in Kuala Lumpur. Warlock neutralized but situation critical. Many magic items need removal before authorities get access to damaged site. Get here soonest.* And then I appended the address.

I checked the time—11:45. [Buck, port me to the corner where the taxi is.]

The taxi driver smiled when he saw me, the man who overpaid for fares. He smiled even wider when I gave him another hundred and asked him to wait one more hour, maybe two, before we were ready to ride.

"Okay, I do that," he said.

Back to Digges's mansion, where we had a very brief time of calm before emergency services arrived. I commiserated with the hobgoblins.

[I'm very sorry about Unforgettable,] I said. [But what you did here today is truly good for the world. Now that I know how dangerous he is, I will not be delivering him to human authorities. They couldn't hold him anyway.]

"Wot's the plan, then?" Buck asked.

[We abduct him. We take his phone and that laptop and give them to Norman. He will unravel the cheesedick's empire and make it public. Plenty of corruption will be exposed, and we'll liberate his trafficking victims when we find them. The Blue Men will be satisfied, and that djinn he has bottled up in his basement will be freed.]

"Hold on—freed?"

[The djinni are a tribe of beings that just want to be left alone. Do you notice that they're not doing anything to hurt anyone right now? The problem is the sorcerers who bind them and use them for wishes, and that's torture and enslavement. Whenever I find a bound djinn, it's my duty to free it.]

"Oh, well, yeah, of course." Buck pointed at the unconscious warlock. "Where we gonnay keep him, exactly?"

[The Blue Men would probably be delighted to watch over him in the short term. We'll worry about the long term later.]

Fire and police arrived and were sent away with the liberal use of my official ID and the assertion that there was absolutely nothing wrong here. Once Shu-hua and Ya-ping arrived, I went back down to the basement and took off the cold iron amulet that the Iron Druid had let me borrow, draping it over the head of my cane. I used that to touch the bottle and the shelf all around its base, allowing the cold iron to destroy any remaining magical booby traps. When I was sure it was safely defused, I removed it and returned upstairs to show it to my colleagues, only to find Ya-ping in a discussion with Buck about how hobgoblins viewed contracted service.

"For us it's both prestigious and fun, because we get tae steal a lot of shite. And even when we don't, it beats doing next tae nothing in Tír na nÓg."

"I'm glad to hear it. You should be proud, taking down a warlock who's done so much harm."

"Oh, aye, I'm proud as fuck. Far as I'm concerned, these are the best hobs in the universe. Plus ma bonny bride, who's in America somewhere now with that Diego bloke."

Ya-ping made a point of meeting them all, and I would bet she'd ask Ro to serve soon.

Handing Shu-hua the bottle, I typed, [Been looking for this forever. I bet there's plenty more naughty shite like this down there. May I leave this situation in your hands and abscond with the warlock?]

Shu-hua nodded and gave me back the bottle. "We'll take care of it and let you know what we find."

I gave myself some Muscular Brawn, which allowed me to carry the unconscious deadweight of Chase Digges fairly easily to the cab. It had finally stopped raining, so that was a mercy. The driver was puzzled by the very heavy invisible something I put in his trunk, and he tried not to seem concerned by the noises the hobgoblins made. He liked making more easy money for a ride back to Batu Caves.

Our walk from the cab back to the Old Way where Coriander was waiting to escort us home was laden with a warlock and the means to undo all his malevolent work—except, of course, for the death of Unforgettable. Buck said in low tones, "Remind me never tae scoff at a scouting mission in the future, aye? I don't know how ye can plan anything bigger than this."

[I've already planned it.]

"Ye have?"

[We're finally going to Olympus to lift my curses. You are the key to Plan B.]

"I am?"

[Aye. It requires your unique talents and some vanilla yogurt.]

CHAPTER 28

⸻ • ⸻

The God of War

The contracts governing the behavior of the Olympians were among the first crafted by the inaugural sigil agent for Europe back in the early nineteenth century. They had been in effect, with few amendments, ever since then. It was time for an update, I thought; the paper was brittle and the ink was fading. But taking those contracts with me to Olympus would be instrumental to achieving my goal. That visit had to be arranged in advance through Coriander: He had to contact the Greek herald, Hermes, and arrange a formal meeting—all the gods in general synod to discuss and mete out punishments for a major contract breach. I gave no further details than that; let them consult oracles and seers if they wished.

I was accompanied by Buck and Nadia and Gladys Who Has Seen Some Shite, who chose to appear younger, slimmer, and sheathed in a suite of green diaphanous layers that sparkled with glittering diamonds and emeralds worked into the fabric. Her hair was unloosed and full, every inch of her vibrant and buoyant, finally looking very much like an avatar of Gaia instead of her wonted disguise as a matronly Canadian woman.

Nadia brought no weapons with her but did possess a black shield of exquisite yet ancient design and a suit of armor that I'd never seen before. When she showed up for our escort to Olympus in that kit, I quirked an eyebrow and flicked a finger at it by way of query.

"Roxanne gave all this tae me," she explained. "Fetched it from her old place in the Fae planes. Said she wouldnae be needing it anymore anyway and it should protect against most things short of a thunderbolt."

I felt underdressed by comparison. I had not, in fact, done anything to dress up for the occasion beyond my usual clothing and topcoat, though I had excavated a pair of socks from my wardrobe that my wife had given me for Christmas long ago, so that I would be wearing a small token of her love if this was to be my end.

Buck was all in black too, his typical outfit of dark jeans, leather belt with a brass buckle, and a vest with no shirt on. He was armed with two menacing tubes of vanilla yogurt, the kind that schoolchildren sometimes get in their lunch pails.

Together we were ushered into a misty miniature amphitheater carved from the peak of Olympus. The gods filled the seats, looking down upon us as we stood as supplicants on the stage. Zeus sat front and center, and there was, no doubt, some sort of hierarchy at play in the seating from there. Poseidon sat on his right, Hades on his left. I'd been hoping for something more modern, but they were all doing the toga thing.

Hera and Athena were directly behind Zeus in the next row. Hephaestus and Aphrodite sat to their right, and to their left were Apollo and Ares. Artemis was another row back, and I didn't recognize many others—there were innumerable lesser gods, nymphs, and the like filling the seats. Hermes introduced us, and most of the expressions were bored until he announced Gladys Who Has Seen Some Shite. We were mere mortals and would be dead soon and were therefore not worthy of notice, but Gladys was different. The Olympians visibly stirred and Zeus directed a question to her, even though I had called for the synod.

"Have we done anything to draw your ire?" he asked.

"I'm here merely to observe, in a purely passive role," she replied in perfect Greek. "Please ignore me."

And then they proceeded to do just that.

"Tell us, Aloysius MacBharrais, what grievance you have against Olympus," Zeus said.

I decided to go ahead and speak aloud, even though Nadia and Buck were in my hearing and either or both could be close to the edge of triggering my curse. I figured that I'd either have it dispelled or be dead in short order, so it didn't matter much. And I decided to use my Greek, though it would suffer in comparison to Gladys's.

"Ares—" I began, but got no further.

"What!" he shouted, and stood from his seat. "You dare accuse me?" The god of war, I noted, wore more than a toga. He had a leather strap slung across his chest and the handle of a sword peeking up over his shoulder.

"Not yet," I said. "But I would like to inquire if Phobos and Deimos are here?" He ignored this and stabbed a finger at me.

"You never come but to complain about treaty violations. Enough!"

"I would stop complaining if you would stop violating the treaty. It's very simple."

"The insolence of this mortal!" he bellowed, looking around to see if any of his fellows would back him up.

"I'm only doing my job. All the pantheons have an interest in keeping the gods walled off from humanity."

Zeus raised a hand to stifle Ares before he could retort. "Hold, Ares. Mr. MacBharrais, I ask again and hope you will not be interrupted this time: What is your grievance?"

"I have been doubly cursed for many years now. Ares is responsible."

"Ridiculous!" Ares spat. "A pernicious slander! Where is your proof?"

"I asked the sirens, and that was their assessment."

A murmur went through the assembly, and as that indicated I had made a powerful indictment against him, Ares turned red-faced. "So what? Some bird women shrieking on a rock in the Mediterranean is no proof."

"It is, in fact. It is well known among the personages here that the sirens see the truth of things. And these curses were crafted to hide their origins as much as possible."

"Lies! I did not curse you."

"True. But you ordered it done."

"I will not abide these insults to my integrity!" Ares crouched and then launched himself up over the gods in front of him, drawing his sword in midair, landing dramatically across from us on the amphitheater stage.

This was not going at all the way I'd hoped. I hadn't even got to the candle or the contract yet, both of which were key to my plan. Or key to Plan A, anyway. This was rapidly deteriorating to Plan B, and Plan C was the Monty Python gambit: Run away. Which would do us little good, as many of the Olympians could fly.

Switching to English, I told Buck and Nadia, "Better sigil up," and I did the same, popping open a Sigil of Agile Grace and a Sigil of Muscular Brawn. The strength and speed they gave me would certainly not allow me to defeat a god of war, but maybe I could dodge or parry a blow if I could get my cane in front of his sword. Though considering how poorly I'd fared against the sirens, I didn't think I had much chance of doing better against Ares.

It's often been noted by military figures that few (if any) plans survive contact with the enemy. Mine were ably proving the axiom. There was still some time left to salvage things, but it was ticking away rapidly, and with every step in my direction Ares shrank my odds of victory—and it was always going to be victory or death. Death approached me now in a toga.

"You cannot accuse me without proof in front of the gods! Withdraw your baseless accusation or face me."

"I can present proof if you will allow me," I said, over some muttering that may have been coming from either Buck or Nadia—or both. They were standing in front of me, while Gladys Who Has Seen Some Shite was a bit behind me and to the right, making no sound. "You're too quick to anger. Give me a moment to get to the truth."

"More time for more lies? No, I think not. Prepare what meager defense you can."

Ares continued to advance, twirling his sword, and Buck and Nadia shifted back defensively to get a little bit closer to me so that Ares couldn't simply leap over them. He could doubtless leap behind me, but that would put him at the edge of the stage, which had no backing, just a sheer drop off a cliff to the crags of Olympus.

Athena abruptly startled everyone by laughing and speaking in English. "Ha ha ha. He's going to die."

The pronoun didn't have an antecedent, so it was discomfiting to everyone, not least of all me, since she'd chosen to speak in English.

"Now, Buck," I said, and the hobgoblin muttered as he brought the tubes of yogurt to his teeth and tore off the ends.

"Cocks an' candy, ol' man. I cannae believe my legend is gonnay end like this." Buck teleported into midair in front of Ares and just above his head, squeezing both tubes as he dropped, ejaculating them into the god's face, saying, "Hnnngh!" before teleporting back to us as Ares's sword swished through the space the hob had just occupied.

"Arrgh! What is this?" the god demanded, halting his advance and using his left hand to clear the mess from his eyes and cheeks.

"Aw, quit yer whining," Buck called, and then taunted the god of war: "It's just gooey and delicious, like yer maw."

There was a collective gasp from all assembled, because Hera, the mother of Ares—not to mention his father, Zeus—was *right there*. And they plainly all heard it and understood English very well.

Ares was not prone to solving problems with logic or quick-witted repartee. He approached problems with weapons and rage, and Buck's legendary taunt had dialed up the latter to eleven.

"I'll kill you!" he roared, and charged.

This was the tricky part of Plan B: We had to survive long enough for me to get the contract's provisions to trigger. The co-operation of Zeus, however, was required, and he was currently on the other side of Ares and more than a little offended by the insult Buck had just given to Hera. Buck's role had been to goad Ares into an attack, and he'd done that spectacularly well, but as with most tasks performed by hobgoblins, there was a price to pay for it.

Nadia sidestepped into Ares's path to intercept, and he threw a dismissive slash at her shield to knock her out of the way, only to discover that she slipped underneath it and tripped him with an extended leg. He sprawled ungracefully, faceplanting on the tiled stage floor, unused to being outmaneuvered.

"How'd ye even get yer job?" Buck piled on. "Because ye kind of suck at this, ya petty, execrable shitbox of a god."

That drew another roar from Ares and he scrambled up to stab at Buck, who remained still as I darted to the left to circle around Nadia and put her between the angry god and me. Buck simply teleported out of the way at the last moment, a talent that Ares had apparently forgotten he possessed. He reappeared in Ares's line of sight but well out of reach. The hobgoblin shrugged, hands splayed out helplessly at the god's unbearable thickness, attacking a teleporter like that. Frustrated, Ares turned on Nadia, to whom he hadn't paid enough respect.

"Who are you again? An accountant?"

She was far more than that, but she didn't bother to answer him. She was still muttering something unintelligible as I passed her and dug the contract out of my coat, waving it at Zeus. He wasn't even looking at me. He was staring open-mouthed at the god of war confronting a human accountant and looking over-matched.

"I wasn't paying attention before," Ares growled, setting himself in a fighting stance, for once exhibiting some discipline. "But I am now."

"Zeus, this attack itself is a violation of the treaty," I said. "You must stop it."

The All-Father never looked my way, his eyes riveted to the tableau before him, but he flicked his fingers dismissively at me, so I turned to watch too. Gladys Who Has Seen Some Shite was circling the perimeter in my direction, her eyes wide and glued to Ares vs. Nadia, her expression rapt and tremendously entertained—all she lacked was popcorn. Buck teleported to her side and kept pace, likewise watching the two combatants—or, rather, the one combatant and the one playing defense. For that is what Nadia did: She dipped, ducked, stepped back, lunged forward to take a strike on the shield, and Ares paused, clearly surprised. He probably thought his sword was supposed to cut through anything, but Roxanne wouldn't have given Nadia just any old armor. It was likely every bit as magical as Ares's steel.

"You may not be an accountant," he said, "but you can die, mortal. You will tire. I will not. Those sigils will wear off soon, and you'll be weak and unable to keep up. That shield will grow heavy and you have no weapon. Eventually you will feel this blade enter your body, and it will end. If you surrender now, I will spare you."

Nadia did not answer; her mutterings continued, but they were no more discernible to Ares than they were to me. Eventually his expression hardened.

"So be it. You will die here now."

He renewed his attack, his blade clanging off the steel of Roxanne's shield and once against Nadia's bracer, but after five or six of these blocked strikes something changed: Nadia shouted something at a volume I could hear, and it was in English, and Buck Foi joined in.

"Lhurnog, hear my prayer!" they said in concert, and shortly thereafter everyone clapped their hands to their ears for two reasons: The air pressure in the amphitheater abruptly changed, causing eardrums to pop painfully, and then a Godzilla-like roar erupted from behind Ares. The source was a grey-green glistening hulk, twelve feet tall, with slavering fangs and a mouth wide enough to accommodate a pickup truck. An eye-watering funk of alcohol and cheese wafted throughout the amphitheater on the strength of that roar. Ares whirled around in time to see a large, clawed hand reach out for him, and he struck at it, but his blade bounced off that skin like a plastic straw against a boulder. The fingers, thick as aspen trunks, wrapped completely around Ares's body and immobilized him, and he cried out in actual fear as his feet left the ground and he was fed into that gaping maw, whereupon the jaws closed, the teeth scissored into his flesh, and golden ichor squirted out from between rubbery lips. Lhurnog the Unhallowed had manifested and claimed his first meal.

"Ah ha ha ha! Told you so!" Athena said into the brief shocked silence before the amphitheater erupted. This was an attack on Olympus, some strange new titan that had to be put down, and they did not understand that this adversary was invincible. Apollo and Poseidon leapt down to the stage as Ares had. Poseidon punched the floor, setting off a quake underneath Lhurnog's feet, and Apollo somehow produced a strung bow and shot a series of fire arrows at the hulk, which bounced off him with all the military effectiveness of Nerf projectiles. Lhurnog found Poseidon more annoying—or perhaps he just looked tastier—and went after him first, a long arm plucking the god of the sea from the stage and chucking him into his gob to be crunched like Ares. Once Poseidon had been swallowed, a long, pink, froglike tongue zapped out and plastered itself to Apollo with an audibly juicy slap, then retracted with the flailing Olympian attached, helpless to avoid becoming the third course.

Athena and I urged everyone else to make no moves, assuring them that Lhurnog would not respond unless attacked. There was some doubt about this and rather a lot of shouting, but as Lhurnog remained still, exhibiting no signs of his intent to kill everyone, the Greeks stayed in place at the command of Zeus, who told them to hold fast for the moment, and someone had better fetch his thunderbolts this instant, and why weren't they here to begin with, and by the hairy tripled testicles of Cerberus, Athena, how did you know that Ares was going to die? His rant allowed me the time to check on my companions.

Nadia stood before Lhurnog, shield discarded, her hands clasped in front of her as she spoke in hallowed tones to the Un-hallowed, and though I could not make out her words over the cacophony of outraged Olympians, her shining eyes and expression of awe told me she was overcome that she had, in her own way, given birth to a god. His golden eyes, half-closed now in postprandial bliss, swiveled down to regard her. What she had been muttering, no doubt, was similar to my ritual evocations for Nancy on the subway; she'd been praying to him and willing him to manifest, and it had obviously worked. A few hundred in-person worshippers, then, with a sacred text and ritual service, were enough to summon something out of nothing—or, rather, out of nothing more than faith. And I supposed that made sense, since it was tribes of people, after all, who manifested the oldest gods in ancient times.

Buck Foi, meanwhile, was barely upright, leaning heavily against the leg of Gladys Who Has Seen Some Shite, in the throes of raucous laughter. And the avatar of Gaia was faring little better, bent over with hands braced against her knees, tears streaming down her face as she wheezed, so convulsed by merriment that she was unable to breathe properly. She did catch my eye, however, and waved weakly and tried to move toward me, which toppled Buck to the tile. He didn't mind; he simply curled into the fetal position and kept giggling.

Gladys Who Has Seen Some Shite clutched her middle as she continued to laugh all the way over to me. When she arrived, she folded me into her arms, squeezed tight for a few seconds, her body still shaking, and then she pounded me on the back a couple of times before letting go, wiping tears from her cheeks.

"Thank you, Boss, hee hee!" she said when she could gulp enough breath to speak. "That shite was absolutely worth the wait. Witnessing a god manifest for the first time to eat another god? Or, no, wait—*three* gods? When will I ever see that again, eh? Never! You Scots sure are some wild. You're fuckin' beauties, that's what you are. Hee hee!" She turned to the Olympians and waved a finger at them. "And, you guys, whoa dang, I tell ya what. You guys are just a legendary bunch of hosers."

CHAPTER 29

Fear and Dread

Zeus was not entirely sure what a hoser was, but he understood that it wasn't a compliment and further that he really couldn't do anything about it. Squaring off against Gladys Who Has Seen Some Shite would not work out well for him. But he could be incensed with me.

"What just happened?" he demanded in English. "What is that creature you summoned?"

"I didnae summon him, tae be clear," I replied, "but that is Lhurnog the Unhallowed, a god who eats the violent. Ye may speak as ye wish, but so long as ye offer no violence, ye're safe. If we can continue with my audience, we'll be able tae resolve matters quickly and order shall be restored."

Zeus glared at me, folded his arms, and told everyone to be seated. He remained standing, dividing his attention between Lhurnog and me. The newborn god was grunting softly in response to something Nadia was saying in hushed tones. She was probably giving him a list of tasty warmongers to eat on earth, autocrats and dictators and the like. It might sound fine for them and their bodyguards to become Lhurnog's next meal, but it could quickly spiral and destabilize the world. That would be my next problem to solve. First things first.

"I must speak with Phobos and Deimos. Bring them before me, please."

Zeus bellowed for Phobos and Deimos to present themselves on the amphitheater stage. It took a minute, but two shady figures stood from the crowd and made their way down to face their accuser. Like Zeus, they crossed their arms and glared at me, but they were not nearly so confident. They knew what they had done, and while they may not have felt any particular guilt, they certainly did not relish being held accountable for their actions.

Phobos, like most of the Greek gods, was extremely pale and thin; blue capillaries showed underneath the skin of his cheeks, making him look either undead or extremely cold. His eyes were mostly in shadow from a prominent brow, his jaw a hatchet blade, and his teeth filed to carnivorous points. He'd be nightmarish in low light for sure, and he probably had a forbidding set of armor stashed somewhere to inspire fear, but in the sunlight and dressed in a toga, he looked unhealthy and unvaccinated.

Deimos was far beefier, a corn-fed brute you'd never want to meet on the battlefield, with the sort of jacked steroidal body that inspired thoughts of retreat and a squirming urgency in the bowels. He too was milk-white, giving his musculature the appearance of marble, a stony implacability that spelled doom for any who dared stand before him.

Now that Lhurnog had made it possible, it was back to Plan A. I tucked the contract away for just a moment and instead withdrew Nancy's candle. I sparked it up with a lighter and held it in my right hand, facing the god of fear.

"Phobos, did ye lay a curse on ma heid at the behest of Ares?"

He sneered at first, scoffed, then the candle worked its magic upon him and he said, "Yes," much to his surprise and everyone else's.

"Deimos, did ye lay a curse on ma heid at the behest of Ares?"

"Ha!" he barked. "What do you think? Of course I . . . did."

"So now ye all know that the sirens were correct, as always. Phobos and Deimos: Did ye both attempt tae craft these curses in such a way as tae conceal their origin?"

"Yes," they admitted in concert.

"Excuse me, but are you compelling their testimony somehow?" Zeus asked.

"This candle compels truthful answers tae questions. Surely ye have no objection tae the truth?"

"I . . . normally do not, but in this case I'd rather my grandsons remain inculpable for their actions." Zeus's eyes flared in anger. "Put out that candle now!"

"In a moment. Yer answer requires its own investigation: Were ye involved or complicit in these curses being laid upon me?"

"No. I knew you had been cursed but not by whom."

"That's a relief tae hear. But now that ye have heard these confessions and we have established that Ares was responsible, we must confront their effects and face consequences." I retrieved the treaty from my jacket and held it aloft. "According tae the treaty ye signed in the nineteenth century, sigil agents are tae remain untouched and no retaliation is tae be levied against them for the performance of their duties or the enforcement of the treaty. Should anyone have a problem with a sigil agent's behavior, there are remedies spelled out. But what we have just proven by the testimony of the sirens and their own lips is that Phobos and Deimos cursed me at the direction of Ares. The punishment spelled out for attacking a sigil agent is disintegration. Ares has already received that punishment, thanks to Lhurnog. But Phobos and Deimos have not."

"Hold on, now," Phobos said. "A curse is not an attack."

"It absolutely is. Your curse has robbed me of ma most cherished relationships. I have been estranged from friends and family for years and forced tae use a speech device so that I don't alienate others."

"Oh, shut up, Al, just *shut up*!" Nadia exploded from behind me. "Can ye be any more of a fancy pompous roaster? I'm so sick of ye, ya clatty, howlin' lavvy heid!"

Turning to face her, I saw from her expression that she was in earnest. Anything I said now would only make it worse. If she were moved to violence against me, it might even get her killed, since Lhurnog was present.

Sighing, I blew out the candle and put it back in my coat, along with the treaty, and withdrew my phone, which I used to type a response with my thumbs.

[And now that curse has been triggered with my accountant, despite my many careful years of trying to minimize my speech in her presence. This has done me irreparable harm and continues to plague me. It is absolutely an attack.]

"Agreed," Zeus said, unprompted.

"What?" Phobos cried.

"Mine was not an attack upon him," Deimos protested, and I began composing a reply even as he continued. "He suffered nothing."

[A curse is an attack, period. But I absolutely suffered. I suffered the loss of seven apprentices, which is an attack on the very existence of sigil agents. I should be retired already, but I can't do so until I have my replacement. Those were innocent people you killed with your curse. And you have no remorse.]

"I agree that Deimos's curse was also an attack," Zeus said, and those massive shoulders on Deimos slumped. "But why did Ares do this?"

[The sirens said it was because he was annoyed with me for preventing his involvement in the Syrian civil war.]

Athena snorted. "He's been annoyed that he can't jump into every war around the globe. He hates that treaty more than any of us."

"True enough," Zeus said.

[Will you administer the prescribed punishment in accordance with the treaty?] I asked.

The thunder god's eyes flicked behind me to the looming bulk of Lhurnog. "I would," he said, "except that doing such violence may turn me into dessert."

[Good point. A moment.] Turning to Buck, I typed, [Would you please ask Lhurnog to allow this violent administration of justice, explaining that Phobos and Deimos will not be permanently harmed? They will respawn.]

"Why don't—oh," Buck said, realizing that since Nadia hated me now, she would take unkindly to me approaching her baby god. Then he shrugged and said, "Sure, why not? It wouldnae be the first impossible thing I've done today."

Everyone watched as the hobgoblin crossed the stage back to Lhurnog, a tiny pink figure looking up at a twelve-foot-tall behemoth.

"Oi! Lhurnog! It's me, Buck Foi. I been feedin' whisky and cheese tae yer gob, remember?"

The faceted yellow eyes focused on him, and the head tilted minutely in acknowledgment. Nadia scowled but said nothing.

"Great tae meet ye in person; love how ye ate three gods like they were gumdrops. Listen, that pair of bastards over there did some super-naughty shite and have tae be disintegrated according to a treaty. It's a legal procedure, and since they're Greek gods, they're gonnay respawn in a little while, no real harm done. Will ye let Zeus do that bit of violence in the name of the law without eating him for it?"

Lhurnog shifted his bulk to regard Zeus, and the eyes drifted down for a moment, clearly noting the gilded quiver that contained Zeus's thunderbolts, forged for him by Hephaestus. When Lhurnog finally spoke, it was in a deep bass that shook the air, and I felt my mustache flatten from the force of it.

"I will allow it," he said.

"No, no, no," Phobos pleaded. "All-Father, I beg you, reject this mortal's usurpation of your power and judgment! Why should we be beholden to that treaty?"

"I signed the treaty," Zeus said. "Enforcing it does not usurp my power. It reaffirms it. Let all here witness and understand: The treaty that we have—similar to the treaties every pantheon has with humanity—allows us to coexist. It is fundamental to our continued survival. Do not violate it, and look that you do nothing to sigil agents going forward."

And with that, he pulled two thunderbolts out of the quiver and threw them simultaneously at his grandsons, obliterating them in an explosion of flesh and ichor. Witnessing that, I had to admit, was tremendously satisfying.

"Will that be all?" Zeus said.

Instead of answering, I turned to Gladys Who Has Seen Some Shite, who was clapping and whooping as chunks of Phobos and Deimos fell about the amphitheater.

"Are the curses gone?" I asked her.

"Ooh, let me see now." She squinted and peered at my head from several angles before smiling. "Yep, that did it, Boss. Their deaths did the job. You're a beauty, eh? And now I'm going to resign and go find something else remarkable to witness. It's been some hoot, I tell ya right now, but Lizzie can take over from here. Thanks for being a kind and decent man. We could use a lot more of you on the planet and far fewer of the other sort."

"It has been ma great honor and privilege tae know ye," I said. "I hope ye see some truly amazing shite."

She giggled. "It's sure going to be tough to top what I saw today. You know, Gaia's going to be in such a brilliant mood when I tell her. The whole planet will feel good when she laughs." She waved goodbye to me and blew a kiss at Nadia and Buck. Once they waved back, Gladys Who Has Seen Some Shite laughed throatily, faded into transparency, and thus exited our lives.

"You are all dismissed," Zeus announced, and to me he said, "Please remove your god from Olympus, and never return with that candle again."

He wasn't my god, I nearly said, but it was pointless to argue. He was certainly my responsibility. Though Nadia might beg to differ.

I approached her and she was blinking a lot.

"Al, did I just blow up at ye for no reason?"

"Ye did."

"I was raging at ye for sumhin, but I cannae remember what. I'm sorry about that."

"The curse finally triggered on ye, because I'd been talking so freely here. But it's gone now. I can talk as much as I want. A mighty weight lifted." I'm not typically one for wide smiles, but I felt one spread across my face with the sheer joy of being able to talk to Nadia without fear.

"It's really gone?"

"Aye. I'm speaking tae ye now and ye're no getting any angrier. It's gone."

"Then that means ye can talk tae yer son again!"

"It does. And I can get a new apprentice without worrying they'll die before they complete their training."

Nadia's face mirrored mine, with the widest unrestrained grin I'd ever seen from her. "This is amazing! I feel like we should hug. Shall we do a hug?"

"Sure."

Neither of us was really the hugging sort, but on such a special occasion, it was good to hug a friend.

Nadia was vibrating with excitement afterward and let loose with a squee. "And Lhurnog's here!" She threw a thumb in his direction. "Is he no just the greatest?"

"Well. Let's hope so. We need tae talk."

"Aw, naw, Al, we cannae confine him yet! Think of all the good he can do. We can just feed him autocrats."

"It's a conversation—a very polite, friendly conversation—that we should take elsewhere."

Someone made a throat-clearing noise, and I turned to see Hermes hovering nearby, his little ankle wings blurring like a hummingbird as they kept him a few feet off the ground.

"Zeus has asked me to escort you to a different plane of your choosing."

"I suggest Tír na nÓg, Nadia. We can perhaps arrange transport there to and from Lhurnog's plane."

Her eyes started in surprise. "His plane?"

"Yes. The one that you and Buck imagined, in fact. Celethon, I believe ye called it? Something about lots of food, lots of books, lots of good dugs, and luxury toilets?"

"Whoa! And that's a place we can go now?"

"It should have manifested at the same time he did. Not sure how occupied it will be, but he needs tae get there. His absolute reality will be certified once he does."

"Why can we no go there now?"

"Lhurnog may not possess the ability tae escort us out. We need someone like Hermes or Coriander tae take us there."

"Ah, good point; I didnae think of that. Awright, Hermes, take us tae Tír na nÓg, please."

CHAPTER 30

———— ◆ ————

At Lhurnog's Table

The appearance of Lhurnog at the Fae Court—for that is where Hermes took us—caused something of a ruckus and no little embarrassment. We arrived on the edge of the meadow opposite Brighid's throne, and for some reason Lhurnog thought it was an ideal place to drop a jobby. It was loud, disgusting, and . . . golden.

Molten gold, in fact. A lot of it. Squirting from his backside and steaming on the grass.

"Oh, my! Sorry," he said in his rumbly bass voice. "Ichor is spicy."

"What is happening?" I whispered at Nadia, who was madly applauding the mess. "How is he no potty-trained?"

"Ye really need tae read *The Gob of Lhurnog*, Al," she said. "This is exactly how we wrote it."

"This? Ye wrote it like this? This seemed ideal tae ye?"

"Look, the idea was that consuming the violent would make him shit gold as a method of reparations tae the victims of the deceased. When he eats whisky and cheese or anything else, ye get nice polite pellets that make outstanding fertilizer for the fields.

When he eats someone violent, it's no mere digestion that occurs but a mystical alchemy that causes him tae drop golden jobbies. We're gonnay use this tae help the church grow. Maybe make a little golden idol or sumhin, because we need some bloody ecclesiastical artifacts, yeah?"

"But why did he have tae do it here and now? That was an incredibly fast process."

"Well, if ye had molten gold in yer guts, I think ye'd want tae get it out as soon as possible."

Coriander appeared next to us. "Hello, Al, Buck, and Nadia. Brighid is curious about your friend and would like an introduction."

"Of course." Turning to Buck, I said, "Here's a challenge for ye: Instead of stealing that gold, protect it from all the Fae who will try tae steal it once we walk away."

"Auggh! Ye cannae ask me tae be the polis, ol' man!"

"More of a security guard. And not for long. Think of it as personal growth! We'll be as quick as we can."

Nadia beckoned and Lhurnog lumbered behind us as we crossed the meadow to what used to be the Iron Throne—a hulk of a chair signifying Brighid's absolute power over the Fae—but now was an exquisitely carved wooden piece crafted by the Fae to signify a newer, fairer relationship. It probably had a fancy name, but I hadn't heard it yet. The Fae wisely made room and stared, agog at the spectacle of Lhurnog.

Brighid sat robed in white and green, red hair falling in waves about her head, undisguised delight on her features. She was a very old being for whom novelty was prized above all, and she'd never seen a newborn god before, so she was smiling like a child who'd just been given an ice cream cone.

Coriander presented us, and Brighid said, "Welcome, all. Lhurnog, do you have a preferred language?"

"I speak all languages," he rumbled.

"Excellent. We are pleased to have you visit. I understand you have just come from Olympus?"

"Yes."

"And do you have your own plane?"

"Yes. It is called Celethon, though I have not been there yet."

"Might you agree to us establishing a connection between your plane and this one, to allow for embassage and commerce and social calls?"

"Yes. That would be ideal. You are the resident deity here?"

"One of many, yes. But my title is First among the Fae, and outside of that I am an Irish goddess of poetry, fire, and the forge. What about you?"

"I am a god of fellowship, scholarship, and gustatory bliss. I welcome all and love all, except for the violent. I eat the violent."

"He just had a snack, in fact," Nadia broke in. "He ate Ares, Apollo, and Poseidon."

"He . . . You did?"

"I did. They did not seem like quick learners, however. I may have to eat them several more times before they understand that there are better ways to solve problems."

Brighid laughed musically. "Changing their behavior would be truly remarkable. But we should probably discuss putting you under treaty."

"Treaty with whom?"

"With humanity." Brighid gestured to me. "Al MacBharrais there is a sigil agent, empowered by me to draft a treaty governing your interaction with the planes, but especially the mortal plane of earth. Every single pantheon has a treaty with humanity, because it keeps us all from ruining someone else's day. Direct intervention on earth upsets faith and should be minimized. That ensures that we get to coexist, so long as there are people around to worship us."

"What if I do not wish to be governed?"

"Details can be negotiated. But the pantheons of the world will not allow you to operate without a treaty."

"Do you mean they would attempt to force me to sign?"

"Not physically. They would employ other pressures. Consider that several deities are omnipotent. They would have the ability to isolate you—render you powerless without harming you. That would be tremendously vexing and frustrating, and wholly unnecessary. We want you to thrive. But we also want everyone else to thrive. I know that you are new to the world and have much to learn. Al can explain and work through the details with you, but for now, the key thing is that you do not visit earth and eat violent people. They won't respawn like Olympians, and your intervention would create problems among other pantheons too numerous to count."

"It sounds like I would be prevented from serving my purpose."

"Not at all. Your purpose will be served—it will simply be regulated."

After a pause, Lhurnog said, "I look forward to learning more."

The two of them issued invitations to each other for feasting at a later date, and then we were bid farewell and allowed to move on to Lhurnog's plane—but not before Brighid asked that a wheelbarrow and shovel be brought to scoop up Lhurnog's golden dung, which had cooled enough at least to solidify.

"Aye, this is glamorous," Buck said, his voice dripping with sarcasm.

Coriander then accompanied us to Celethon, and he too looked excited to experience something new. It would be a plane he'd never visited before—indeed, no one had—and he relished the opportunity to reacquaint himself with wonder.

We arrived in a sunny garden with grassy paths through familiar vegetation, all the plants native to Scotland so far as I could tell, with fat bumblebees buzzing among blossoms and songbirds chirping their joy at a sky streaked with attractive, unthreatening clouds. Hills in the distance climbed up into mist, grasses wrapped around them like shawls, and sheep grazed on their slopes in bucolic contentment.

Lhurnog led us through the garden to a heath with red-and-white-striped pavilions, and underneath these were dining tables and an open-air kitchen. Dozens of good dugs played and yapped around the pavilions, from tiny terriers to deerhounds. Some of them stopped to regard us, their tails wagging, but none approached to jump on us or anything like that. Brewing and distilling tanks could be seen off to one side, and off to the other, lurking behind the pavilions, a gothic architectural wonder awaited.

"What's that building?" I asked.

"That's the library," Lhurnog said. "You are welcome to anything, of course. But perhaps we should slake our thirsts and take our ease for a moment after the excitement of the morning."

"It'll take a lake tae slake ma thirst," Buck said.

"We have one of those. Great fishing. And this looks like Scotland because it is currently the Scottish who worship me. As more people feed me whisky and cheese, Celethon will grow and contain the landscapes of the mortal world."

Near the edge of the pavilion, on a base that could rotate to face either the heath or the dining area, sat a throne made entirely of hard cheese. Or maybe it was semi-soft, to simulate the padding of upholstery? Regardless, Lhurnog climbed onto it and sighed in satisfaction. And once he did, some . . . beings appeared, streaming out of the kitchen, much to Nadia's delight.

"They're here!" she said. "The connoisseurs exist!"

"What?"

"They're professional servers who are experts in food and drink. But don't worry, they're well compensated and ye don't have tae tip. Or even pay."

"That's all a relief, though one might wonder what compensation would be necessary in an afterlife. But it's no what I was worried about. I'm wondering why they bear an uncanny resemblance tae me." Each connoisseur was a uniform five feet tall—a fair bit shorter than me—but otherwise looked exactly like me, in a white shirt with a black tie and black paisley waistcoat. They had impeccable mustaches but also . . . mascara. They were goth Mini-Me's.

"I associate you with connoisseurship, Boss. That's it."

One came over and greeted us in my own voice. It was strange and unsettling. "May I get ye anything tae eat or drink?"

"What do ye have on the menu?" Buck asked.

"Anything. Everything. Ask for it and it shall be summoned forth. Or, if ye prefer, I can make suggestions based on yer general preferences."

Curious about how Lhurnog's kitchen would handle traditional Scottish fare, I ordered haggis, neeps and tatties, and some breakfast tea. The eventual result, delicately slid in front of me by one of my short doppelgängers, was fragrant, delicious, and artfully plated. Nadia had a bacon mushroom omelet and an Ardbeg Caesar, a Scottish variant on the classic Canadian cocktail, and Buck eschewed breakfast and ordered a bowl of cullen skink paired with a ginger beer and lime, while Coriander asked for a salad of edible flowers.

Lhurnog, for his part, was served platters of cheese and charcuterie and a half barrel of whisky, and we watched as an artillery team of connoisseurs rolled out a small catapult and then launched alternating payloads of fried chicken fillets and buttered waffles into his open gob with unerring accuracy. Buck and Nadia whooped and clapped and looked at me.

"Eh? Come on, Al!" Nadia said.

I smiled and chuckled. "Okay, I admit it: That was immensely entertaining. Especially since it was a squadron of Aloysiuses delivering the deliciousness."

Our plates were cleared away, and a connoisseur asked if we would like to take a walk and, if so, might we be interested in animal companionship?

Why, yes, to both. We decided to walk across the heath to the library. Butterflies flitted among flowers. Two blue-grey Scottish deerhounds accompanied me and let me pet them; Buck was amused by a capybara with a squirrel monkey sitting atop it; and Nadia was escorted by a small but chattering waddle of king penguins. Lhurnog followed behind, a gyre of singing songbirds over his head and a bounding mob of kangaroos all around him. Coriander kept pace but did not ask for companionship, content to enjoy our entourage instead.

The library was a monument to the written word, with very tall doors and wide throughways inside to allow for the passage of Lhurnog. It smelled of leather and paper, ink and glue, and sounded like the pregnant silence before a secret is revealed. There were two main floors to the square building, including a central reading garden with topiaries and fountains and plenty of benches, rocking chairs, and hammocks in which to read. And the librarians were like the connoisseurs in the sense that they were all the same, but instead of looking like me, they looked like the actress Minnie Driver.

I lifted an eyebrow at Nadia over this, and she knew exactly what I was thinking.

"Look, Dhanya and I have a thing for her, awright? Happens all the time. Ye watch a movie and ye wind up fancying a movie star. Perfectly normal. Who would you have made the librarian?"

I did not need to think. "Emma Thompson, of course."

"See? There ye go."

"If we check out a book here, can we leave the plane with it? Will it exist on earth?"

"One way tae find out. Check out something."

"Excellent. Excuse me, Miss?"

"Yes. What can I help you find?"

"Might you have a copy of Kurt Vonnegut's *Breakfast of Champions*?"

"Certainly. And for you?" she asked Buck.

"Have ye got one that explains why murder rates are so high in small English towns?"

"I believe so. *Your Guide to Not Getting Murdered in a Quaint English Village*, by Maureen Johnson and Jay Cooper."

"Sounds good."

"And for you?" she asked Nadia.

"Sumhin epistolary and very sweetly gay," Nadia said.

"I know the perfect book: *This Is How You Lose the Time War,* by Amal El-Mohtar and Max Gladstone. Anything for you, Lhurnog?"

The Unhallowed considered for a moment before replying, "I'd like to know more about who I ate today. Do you have anything about the Greek gods?"

"We have quite a lot, actually. Perhaps *The Iliad* by Homer?"

"The Emily Wilson translation is fabulous," I volunteered, and Lhurnog requested that. Minnie Driver—I mean, the librarian—promised she wouldn't be a minute and walked into the stacks. Almost as soon as she disappeared from view, she reappeared again, holding the requested books. Something magical had obviously happened there. As she distributed them, she invited us to enjoy reading on the second floor, where there were many excellent places to sit, blankets to drape over our legs, natural light streaming in through stained-glass windows, and endless cups of gourmet hot chocolate and slices of warm banana bread if we wanted them.

Nadia sighed happily. "That sounds perfect. But we must be going, unfortunately. Another time. Thank you so much."

Our favorite animals were waiting for us outside and walked us back across the heath. Over the noises of the penguins, Nadia said, "Boss?"

"Yes?"

She gestured to the paradise before her. "Can ye believe I did this?"

"Absolutely."

"I mean, who knew it worked like this?"

"Plenty of people. Me. You. A nice long list of others."

"Right, but most of humanity's clueless."

"An evergreen statement if I've ever heard one."

"They don't know their own power."

"True. And ye're just now appreciating yer own."

"Aye. It's like those allergy-medicine adverts, where they clear away some filters and ye see everything better. Revelation, but no in the Book of John sense. Ma uncertainty and insecurity about who I am is gone, and I need tae chew yer ear about it a bit. Ye're gonnay retire soon, right? Train up an apprentice who won't die and then, ye know, fuck off happily somewhere?"

"That's the plan."

"Then let me inform ye now I'll be retiring with ye."

"With me?"

"I mean at the same time. Because I think I've finally figured it out."

"What, exactly?"

"What the hell I'm supposed tae be doing. It's this. I'm no supposed tae be a battle seer who stands up against gods of war. I'm no supposed tae be an accountant or a printshop manager. I'm definitely no supposed tae take some preordained place in the Hindu pantheon, despite ma mysterious parentage. I'm supposed tae let people know that they can leave humanity's history of violence behind. And those who don't, well—Lhurnog will take care of them eventually."

"Literally or metaphorically?"

"Both. I know ye have tae do yer thing, because if ye don't, the other gods will shite their drawers and cause all kinds of headaches. But let it go for just a bit, yeah? Some negotiating time where Lhurnog can do some good?"

"I am all for doing good, of course," I said. "But overt action in the world without a treaty will inspire some howling and ill will, especially if he eats someone who is favored by another pantheon. Ye will have limited room tae work before I am forced tae act, so I advise ye tae be discreet and quick."

"Thank ye, Al. Not only for this, but for . . . everything, ye know? I don't think I would have made it here if ye hadnae found me in that pit fight years ago. Shown me shite I never would have seen."

"Ye're welcome, of course. And I thank ye for the many times ye saved ma old bones from the meat grinder. Like today, for example. And I'm eternally grateful for the accounting and management too."

"It's been ma pleasure. And will continue tae be until ye're done."

"I appreciate that." I petted the Scottish deerhound walking by my side and smiled. "This is a good place, Nadia. Maybe the best place. I think I'll give *The Gob of Lhurnog* a read before I revisit Vonnegut."

"Really? Oh, Al, that means a lot tae me! I feel . . . no, I cannae feel that twice in one day! Well? Ye know what? I do. I feel like we should hug again."

"It *has* been a rather extraordinary day."

We hugged once more, bade farewell to Lhurnog, the animals, and the connoisseurs, with a promise to visit again soon, and discovered upon our return to Glasgow, courtesy of Coriander's escort, that our books had survived the journey home.

- - · - -

CHAPTER 31

The Eighth Apprentice

Lizzie MacLeish was disappointed to hear the next morning that Gladys Who Has Seen Some Shite had resigned and would not be returning. The corners of her mouth drooped and her shoulders slumped as she said, "I'm sorry tae hear that."

"You're getting a pay rise, however, starting today," I said. "And some other benefits as well. Were ye informed that ma business can be a bit unusual at times?"

"Oh, yes, Mr. MacBharrais. And I've seen the truth of it, what with criminals coming intae the lobby and discharging firearms."

"Right. Honestly amazed ye stayed on after that. Simply dismissing it as unusual, though—it's a bit vague, in't it? Do ye know anything beyond the fact that it's unusual?"

"Just that I shouldnae be surprised if ye have some more strange visitors uninterested in printing and binding."

"True. We can leave it there, or if ye want tae know more, I can share that with ye, with the caveat that I cannae predict how ye'll take it."

"Well, I also know that ye're into contracts. Gladys Who Has

Seen Some Shite said these filing cabinets I cannae open are full of them. But I don't know what the contracts are for."

"That's the meat and potatoes of it. The truth is, printing is ma side hustle. Ma real business is in those locked filing cabinets. And that's a secret ye may be fine with keeping, or ye may no. And ye may prefer tae operate in blissful ignorance. I cannae know which is best for ye, so ye have tae tell me how much ye want tae know."

"Is it illegal?"

"Technically no. More like extralegal. There are no laws against it, since Parliament doesnae know there's anything tae outlaw."

"I see. Well, can I go on in blissful ignorance for now and then ask for a full disclosure later? Because I like being employed and do no want tae risk losing that."

"Perfectly acceptable. Ma door is always open."

"So ye can talk just fine without apps now?" she asked.

"Yes. That simplifies matters, does it no?"

"It does, Mr. MacBharrais."

"Thank ye, Lizzie. Make sure ye talk tae Nadia about yer raise when she gets in."

When I got up to my office, I stood just inside the door and wondered what in fifteen hells and five oubliettes I was doing. Why was I not running to my son's house and knocking on the door? Ringing numbers I hadn't called in years owing to the curse shearing my friends away? It deserved some reflection.

I supposed it must be a raft of fears. Fear that, despite the curse being lifted, they might all still wish to have nothing to do with me—that they would look back at the years without me in their life and decide that had been just fine, no reason to change that. Or—perhaps worse?—they'd let me back in their lives out of indifference. The relationship wouldn't be the same—how could it?—and I'd have to contend with a tepid tolerance rather than true affection. Or perhaps they'd construct a story in their head to assign the blame for the relationship souring to me.

I had a blissful week of work, drafting a starter treaty for

Lhurnog and an addendum for the Blue Men of the Minch that would protect yachts and cruise ships while also creating a mechanism for them to police their waters in conjunction with human authorities—essentially holding ships suspected of trafficking rather than sinking them. I got quick approval for the language from Percy Tempest Vane, and D.I. Munro was nowhere to be seen, even though the rash of men turning themselves in for assaults kept growing throughout the UK and the newspapers had finally noticed. She would surely come after me again if given the slightest reason, but for now, at least, she apparently had better things to do than harass me. Law enforcement in general was occupied with bigger fish, as Norman had released a fair mountain of evidence implicating MPs and other officials in shady doings connected with Chase Digges. The whereabouts of the now-notorious billionaire were still unknown, but his network was being exposed and scandals were running rampant as a result.

So I was in a good mood on Saturday when I attended the next service at the Church of Lhurnog's Table. Nadia was understandably fired up but could not exactly share that Lhurnog had manifested and eaten a trio of spicy gods. People would want receipts, for one thing, and all she had was a wheelbarrow of gold. Lhurnog had turned Ares, Apollo, and Poseidon into about twenty-five troy pounds of it, which would allow the church to buy property and begin building a large space for services. They would definitely need that space, since she was already filling up the largest hall available to rent in Glasgow.

Roxanne was there with her arm entwined with Fergus, who looked deliriously happy with what he perceived to be his good fortune. I worried about what might happen to him when they had their first quarrel but firmly told myself that interfering in Roxanne's relationships would spell my doom in large HOLLYWOOD-size letters. Best to let them be happy while they could.

Lizzie was there too, with a friend or perhaps a romantic interest sitting by her side. Or maybe it was a cousin or a brother—

I don't know. He was spare and baby-faced, one of those men who never had to shave. But they smiled at each other with a fondness that spoke of a deep relationship, not the tight-and-polite grins of the newly acquainted. It was just the tiniest hint of a life outside work, but it gladdened me to know she had one and was happy living it.

But I had come to see Duncan Ettrick and invite him to the printshop to *ooh* and *ahh* about fountain pens and inks. He agreed to join me after the service, and on the walk over I asked him how law school was going and if he had a particular field he was interested in.

"Oh, aye. The field where the wee guy takes on the big guy. Representing Davids against corporate Goliaths, if ye don't mind me alluding tae another faith."

"Nae bother, that's fine. It's perfect, in fact. I'm gonnay make ye an offer along those lines."

"I'm no licensed tae practice yet, but if ye have a legal problem, I can refer ye tae someone good."

"Ach, naw, it's nothing like that. It will take some explaining, and ye can take some time tae think about it. We'll get tae that soon enough. Why don't ye tell me about where ye get yer inks?"

"No place fancy. I buy them online."

"Ever make yer own?"

"Naw. I figured I'd spend far more money in ma attempts and wind up making an inferior product, so why go tae the expense and trouble?"

"It's a valid point. It can be expensive and time-consuming. However, the rewards are myriad and manifold. I hope you'll agree."

"You've been making yer own inks?"

"Aye, for decades now. It's no so hard once ye get the hang of it. Ye get yerself a pigment and a binding agent and ye're in business. But the real fun comes with adding bonus ingredients. Seashells ground down tae fine powder. Moth-wing dust. Shite like that."

"Moth-wing dust? Why on earth would ye even want that?"

"Special effects."

I opened the door to the office, dark and empty now, but the clack and roar of the printers, always running, could be heard behind the shop door. I took him through there, waved grandly at the presses and binding machines, and led him upstairs to my office. He was relieved once I closed the door and silence fell.

"Whew. The shop is loud."

"It sure is." I pointed to the whisky table. "Drink?"

"Why not?"

I poured us each a finger from the bottle and then moved over to my desk to press the hidden button to access my ink-and-sigil room. Duncan's eyes widened as he saw the bookcase begin to move and reveal my true workspace.

"Oh, my God, ye're living the dream," he said. "Everyone wants a secret room behind a bookcase, and ye have one."

"I highly recommend them. Please, after you."

Duncan shuffled in, mouth open in awe as he took in my stoppered bottles of inks and ingredients, my dozens of pens, the stacked cards and papers, and the framed prints of warding sigils that were both functional and aesthetic.

"Whoa. When ye said ye were a bit obsessed with pens, I didnae appreciate the understatement. This is a metric fuckton of gear."

"I've had a long time tae accumulate it. Ye're still young."

"What are these . . . symbols?" he asked, pointing to my framed wards from the Chinese tradition.

"Sigils. They serve different purposes. Draw a specific sigil with the matching ink, ye get a magical effect."

"How d'ye mean?"

"I'll show ye. Get out yer phone and turn on the video camera, but don't actually record, awright?"

He pulled his phone out of his pocket and pointed it at me as I selected a Conklin matte-black-and-gunmetal pen containing the ink that would allow me to craft the Sigil of Swallowed Light. I talked as I drew it on a card. "I'm gonnay hold this up tae yer camera, and I want ye tae watch carefully. When the ink fully dries, the sigil will activate and black out yer camera."

"What?"

"Just watch. Ye have tae wait ten tae twenty seconds for it tae dry. Are ye watching the camera now?" I held up the finished sigil and pointed it at the phone.

"Aye. So far it's working."

"Give it a few more and let me know when it blacks out."

"Awright, I will. So far it's—whoa. It's totally black. What happened?"

"This sigil happened. The ink contains moth-wing dust because moths are attracted tae light. It disables cameras while line of sight is maintained and tells the surveillance state tae fuck off."

"So ma phone is broken?"

"Naw, disabled. Keep looking. I'm gonnay flip the card around and the camera should work again."

I flipped the card in my fingers to face me, and Duncan visibly reacted. "It's back!"

"See? The sigil disables devices but doesnae damage them. Watch." I flipped the card back and forth, causing his camera to switch off and on as I did so.

"I cannae fuckin' believe it. This sigil is doing that?"

"The sigil plus the proper magical ink. Draw the sigil with any store-bought ink and it's just a pattern. Ye have tae make the ink yerself. And I do most of ma work here. That setup behind ye is no for food prep. It's ink prep."

Duncan turned and registered the sink, cutting board, knives, and assorted beakers, decanters, and pipettes, along with a proper cookpot and hot plate.

"Whoa. I thought ye were just intae calligraphy. This is . . . another level."

"The top level, aye. I'm a sigil agent, Duncan. There are five in the world, though it will be eight soon enough, because some of the others have apprentices. And that's the offer I wished tae make: Be my apprentice."

"What? I don't even know what a sigil agent is. And I'm gonnay be a lawyer."

"Ye can still be lawyer, and ye should. It's perfect. Ye need a legit business tae hide yer real business."

"What is a sigil agent's business?"

"The enforcement of magical contracts and treaties with gods and monsters. That's the David-and-Goliath bit I promised ye: Humanity is David, and there's any number of Goliaths. So it's in keeping with yer values."

He snorted. "Are ye having a laugh right now?"

"Naw. I'm serious. I know it sounds mad. But so does the morning's newspaper. And I'm willing tae show ye proof."

"Proof of what?"

"Whatever needs proving. But the sigils help ye keep the peace so that if humanity's gonnay shite the bed, we'll do it ourselves and no get pumped by the wrath of some god."

"You can make a living as a sigil agent?"

"There's no actual salary, but revenue tends tae be plentiful if unpredictable. The sigils can get ye access tae money at any time, depending on yer scruples. Best tae keep the day job, though."

"What do these sigils do, besides disable cameras?"

"Increase yer natural speed and strength. Dispense pain tae gods who violate treaties. Convince authorities tae leave ye alone. Healing, protection. And it comes with perks, like traveling the planes. I'll have tae show ye that one—has tae be seen tae be believed. But it beats the hell out of flying. Last week I got from here tae California in thirty minutes."

"Huh." Duncan threw up his hands. "I have tae admit, I don't know what tae do with this. Are ye unwell?"

"Naw, just old. Need tae retire. You'd be taking over ma territory."

"Which is?"

"Europe, the Middle East, and North Africa. I assume ye have a little bit of Latin from yer law schoolin', and that's very good, but I'd recommend ye pick up Arabic and maybe Icelandic too, since that's close tae Old Norse."

"And the rest of the world is . . . ?"

"The responsibility of other sigil agents. Look, I know it's a lot, but let me give ye the full pitch, and if ye don't think it sounds good by the end, well, ye can just forget it."

"I don't think I'll ever forget this conversation."

"Oh, ye will if I want ye to. There's a Sigil of Lethe River that makes ye forget the past hour. Tremendously helpful for things like this."

"Are ye serious? You'd do that tae me?"

"Only if necessary. This is some secret magic shite, man. I have tae tell ye everything so ye can make an informed decision. But I have tae protect the secret too. It's among the rarest jobs on the planet, and I think ye can hack it. And if not, well, ye won't even know what ye're missing."

So I showed him how the Sigils of Muscular Brawn and Agile Grace could help him in a scrap. I took him to Gin71 and let him wear the monocle enchanted with magical sight so he could see that the beautiful bartender, Heather MacEwan, was really a faery named Harrowbean. She escorted us to Tír na nÓg, where he saw all manner of winged and differently appendaged creatures, and I explained that it was a plane tied to most every other, a sort of Grand Central Terminal that also allowed one to hop around the world quickly. He took it all in with the air of one who suspects he's hallucinating or dreaming and he'll wake up soon.

"Where in the world," I asked, "have ye always wanted tae go?"

"Hmm. I've always wanted tae see the Alhambra in Granada, Spain."

Taking him there from Tír na nÓg sealed the deal. The privilege of not queueing up for an airline or a train is a mighty inducement to the life. I had to outline a good deal of the job and what an apprenticeship would entail, and that took us well into the night, but once I had his agreement to begin on Monday, a curious freedom relaxed the tension in my shoulders and back. A new apprentice—one that wouldn't die because of a curse—meant an exit ramp ahead for me. Just a short while to go, and I could lay my burdens down.

And that left very little on my to-do list except an attempt at reconciliation with my long-estranged son. He tended bar at The Citizen on St. Vincent Place, and I went there at four on Sunday, fairly confident that he'd be working.

He was indeed there, dressed in the white shirt and black braces that served as a staff uniform. Business was prospering, but it wasn't a crowded rush that would mean he was slammed. There were three open seats at the bar, and I took one that I hoped would be served by Dougal. My guess proved correct, because he came over and put one of those custom little coasters in front of me before saying good afternoon and then looking up to meet my gaze, startled.

"Dad?"

"Hi, son."

"I . . . what are ye doing here?"

"I came tae see ye. It's been a long time."

"Yeah, it has. It really has." Suddenly remembering he was at work, he said, "What can I get ye?"

"Old-fashioned, made with the Highland Park 12."

"Excellent. I'm on it."

He got out a rocks glass and dropped in a demerara sugar cube with a pair of tongs, then dashed some bitters onto it, added a small squirt of water, and muddled it with a muddler. Then he poured in a double shot of the Highland Park 12, dropped in a huge cube of ice and a dehydrated orange wheel, and gave it a quick stir to let the sugar dissolve and the ice dilute the whisky a wee bit. He placed it in front of me with a smile.

"Thank ye, it's lovely. Dougal, I want tae apologize."

"For what?"

"For whatever I did tae get ye so angry with me."

His smile faded. "I really was angry with you, aye?"

"Aye."

He said nothing for a while, dunking some glasses in a soapy sink and rinsing them. His body was running on something close to autopilot as he performed accustomed tasks while his mind wrestled with his thoughts. "I cannae remember why. What did ye do?"

"I was never too clear on the matter ma self. But I'm more sorry than I can say. I've missed ye sumhin awful."

"Well, I . . . I've missed ye too. I don't know why I cannae mind what made me so mad, but I know that I was. Maybe I owe ye an apology ma self."

"Naw. But even if ye did: All is forgiven, son. I don't have room for a milligram of anger in ma heart for ye. Because it's all love, ye see."

Duncan bowed his head for a few seconds, leaning against his prep area with elbows locked, and then he sniffled and wiped at his eyes quickly. "It's the same here, Dad. I'm just upset because I don't know what happened. We lost so much time, and the fact that I cannae account for it is driving me a bit mad."

"We cannae do anything about the past, so let's gie it a shove out of our way. Let's focus on moving forward. Would that be all right? Can I maybe visit ye again?"

"That would be wonderful," Dougal said. "Truly. I know the kids would love tae see ye. Listen, I have tae keep working, but do ye have tae go? Can ye stay a bit and we can talk as I have the time?"

"I can think of nothing I'd rather do."

"Great." He reached across the bar and squeezed my hand briefly. "Thanks, Dad. I'm so glad you've come."

I wasn't able to reply, but not from any curse—no, it was simply a throat constricted with emotion. So I nodded with a tight smile as he moved away to fix a series of drinks that had been ordered for a table of four.

I slowly let out a long sigh that had been building behind a decade of accumulated anguish. It was, at the end, all going to be okay.

The Librarian

The hot juice and joy of youth cools as one ages, hopefully not to the degree where there's a thin layer of gelatin on top—and, bollocks, I had better think of a better metaphor than that. This is going to be a nightmare if I cannot summon a thought that doesn't immediately repulse everyone.

The terrors of youth, like a great-aunt's mustache . . . Naw, that's rubbish. Come at it a different way, Aloysius.

How about this: The peaks and valleys of one's life are not so intensely affecting as one ages because the advantage of perspective allows one to appreciate the ride as a whole. There is a quiet confidence that darkness cannot persist, coupled with an awareness of entropy that downshifts euphoric mania to a soft glow of contentment. When I felt twitchy and nervous in the lift to the special-collections floor of the Mitchell Library, therefore, it was notable for me. I have faced down gods that could destroy me and maintained my equanimity, but I was a seething cauldron of anxiety over so simple a thing as issuing an invitation. Sheer terror that I would make a bloody shambles of it, leavened by hope that

I wouldn't and a cold acceptance of the fact that what I felt may very well not be reciprocated.

Mrs. MacRae smiled at my approach when I exited the lift, and I returned it as I doffed my hat and got out my phone. She was dressed in black with a vibrant scarf of purple and gold.

"Mr. MacBharrais, what a surprise! It's no yer usual day. Ye must have an excellent question for me."

[I do. At least I hope you'll agree that it's excellent, but you shouldn't feel any pressure to.]

"Oh?"

[My recent travels have been to seek out treatments for my condition, and I'm pleased to say that they have been entirely successful.] I placed my phone on her desk as that played back to her, and when it finished, she looked a little confused.

"What does that mean, exactly?"

"It means I can finally speak tae ye with my own voice. Hello, Mrs. MacRae."

Her eyes widened and her mouth formed a tiny o of surprise. "Ach! Ye can talk!"

"Aye. And it's a pleasure."

"I imagine so! Congratulations—it's lovely tae hear yer voice!"

"Thank you. What I wished tae ask is no something ye need tae answer now, as it might require a bit of a think, but if ye ever have the time and inclination, might I take ye tae tea? I imagine we'd have much tae discuss."

She blinked rapidly as she tried to adjust to this new situation and abrupt proposal, and I feared I'd bungled it.

"Much tae discuss, eh?" she finally said, and then her mouth curved up at one corner. She glanced at her watch, a thing so few people did anymore because watches had gone out of fashion. "Well, I can put ye on the spot and see what that might be. It's near enough lunchtime tae call it so. Why don't we go downstairs tae the café and ye can regale me with all sorts of interesting whatnot?"

It was my turn to blink. I had not prepared any topics for discussion, so I would have to improvise. A challenge.

"I would be delighted."

Together we went down to the second floor and purchased some premade sandwiches and tea. I could barely taste the food, leached as it was of nearly all nutritional value and freshness, but at least the tea was hot and flavorful.

"Where did ye get these treatments, then?" Mrs. MacRae asked once we were seated. It was a large open space with a high ceiling, and sound bounced off its tiles and marble—murmurs of conversation and the clink of silverware on porcelain.

"I sought out advice in Italy at first—fabulous and unique vocal specialists there—but ma treatments were conducted in Greece."

"It wasnae surgical, though?"

"Naw, I'm no sure I can explain the procedure medically, tae be honest. Seemed like divine intervention. But at the end it felt as though a curse had been lifted."

"Wonderful. Do ye feel as if yer life has changed significantly?"

"I do. Just being able tae sit and have a conversation without typing is a blessing. Soon I'll be able tae retire and sell ma business, and that will be another blessing."

"Ah, do ye have grand plans for retirement, then?"

"Large portions of it are flexible, but I am certain it will include good dugs and good books."

"A solid foundation for happiness, tae be sure. That reminds me—have ye heard there's a new bookstore on Bath Street now called Gud Dug Books?"

"I have. It is a place of many hidden treasures. We might be able tae find something properly rare and wonderful if ye would like tae visit together sometime."

"That sounds very fine. Do ye have a good dug now?"

"Naw, ma business requires me tae be away for too long at unpredictable times. No fair tae the dug that way. I'll wait until I'm free of the grind of commerce, and then I might buy a place doon the water somewhere, walk in the mornings with ma dug, listen tae the cry of seabirds as they circle around their meals in the ocean, and in the afternoons I'll write letters tae the editor like a proper pensioner, followed by some experimental cooking for dinner and a chapter or five of a book tae get me tae sleep. And that's only if I cannae think of something better between now and then, but it feels like a good place tae start."

"It does. I have a dug, a Scottie named Pippin. I named him after Peregrin Took, but Americans keep thinking I'm talking about some retired basketball player. Now, I ask ye: Why would I name a wee dug after an athlete instead of a hobbit who likes tae eat?"

"Americans," I said, shaking my head.

"Anyway, he likes when I read tae him at night. I think yer retirement sounds ideal. It doesnae sound too far off what Frank would have wanted."

Her voice trailed off and up at the same time, seized by mournful memories.

"Remind me: How long ago did he pass?" I asked.

"Seven years ago now."

"I can tell he was good tae ye."

"Aye, he was. He tried tae love me the way I'd always hoped I'd be. Didnae always succeed, but his effort was unflagging, and I adored him for it. I still miss him something terrible." She sniffled, her voice breaking at the end, and took a sip of tea to hide the trembling in her lip and chin.

"I understand completely."

"Ye miss yer wife, then?"

"Aye. Every day, of course. Together we were a sum greater than ourselves. It's been thirteen years, and I havenae felt I've added up tae much since. Plenty of work tae keep me busy, but the accomplishments are simply a distraction, are they no?"

"Aye."

"I have a decent time ahead of me yet, and Josephine will always have her space in it. But perhaps something soft and fine can grow in the space between her and the time I have left." I cleared my throat nervously. "Someone could share that space, I mean. The part that isnae set aside tae be hers forever."

"A space for her. I never thought of it like that. Why, I should have a space for ma Frank. Something like—I don't know, a metaphorical chapel of sorts. A holy place ye visit and it's sacred, inviolable."

"Sacrosanct, yes. But outside it there can be blessings too, and they in no way diminish the beauty of the chapel."

"Oh, that's lovely. That . . . that actually helps me." Her eyes welled again and tears spilled down her cheeks, which she furiously dabbed at with a napkin.

"Good. I'm glad I could help."

She laughed, partly in embarrassment, and I gave her a tight-lipped grin, which I hoped communicated that it was perfectly fine to feel emotional over her late husband and I empathized completely and did not mind at all. The gods knew I'd spilled many a tear over Josephine and would do so again.

Mrs. MacRae sniffed and lifted her chin, her face flipping through emotions like a thumb fanning through pages of a book. "Ha ha. Well. It appears we do have plenty to talk about, Mr. MacBharrais."

"Excellent."

"In fact, I've been wanting tae ask ye something recently. Ye know an awful lot about mythology and the occult, because ye actually read all those books I help ye find. In all yer reading, have ye ever come across a mention of someone called Red Roxanne?"

"No, nothing that I've read," I said, hoping that my voice didn't sound too surprised. "What do ye know about Red Roxanne?"

"Well, I'm no sure. She gets talked about like she's either a goddess or a demon, I'm no too clear about which, so I thought maybe ye might recognize the name."

"When ye say goddess, do ye mean a benevolent one or a sinister one?"

"Oh, benevolent, definitely."

"So there are people talking of her as a benevolent deity but others who speak of her as a demon?"

"Yes, exactly. I've had several ask about her in the library recently, inquiring if there might be something written about her in the occult section."

"Interesting. Do these two camps of people share anything else in common?"

"Oh! Well." Her eyes traveled up to the domed ceiling as she thought about it. "I suppose they do. The people saying good things about her are women, and the people who are afraid of her are men. How extraordinary. I hadnae noticed until ye made me think about it."

"Well, I happen tae know her—she's no in any books yet, but she's real."

"She is? Ye mean a real woman?"

"Aye."

"So which is she: benevolent or demonic?"

"Both. Everyone is telling the truth. She is capable of anything. And that is what I find so inspiring about her."

"Oh? Ye're no afraid of her?"

"Naw. Only a certain type of man need worry about Red Roxanne. Once upon a time, she was uniformly terrifying. But she has, late in life, grown intae a fully realized person. The darkness is still there, but it's leavened by a good bit of light now. And it gives me hope."

"Why is that?"

"I'm coming up on a change ma self. We both are, aye? Retirement is an undiscovered country, with customs and a culture foreign tae us now, and we must adapt and learn tae navigate it, tae grow instead of decline. If we must ride intae the sunset, let it be one tae savor instead of fear."

Mrs. MacRae's eyes slid off me as she took a sip of tea, thinking it over. "There are many kinds of sunsets, it's true. Only thing they have in common is that we each get our own. The orange and gold, the storm-tossed grey, the soothing lavenders, or those ribbons of pink. Do ye have a preference?"

I blinked, trying to think of my favorites, and then settled on one that usually gave me peace.

"The kind where ye have piles of clouds in the sky that have accumulated all day and they look ominous and forbidding, but the sun kisses them with orange underneath as it sets, looking back on them in a way, and showing us that even storm clouds can be blessings."

"Ah. Lovely. I wouldnae mind a bright daisy yellow at first, and then it fades slowly intae a soft cobalt goodbye."

"Mmm. Sublime. You have such an excellent eye for colors, Mrs. MacRae," I said.

"Thank ye." She looked pleased and set her teacup down in the saucer, then took a breath, evidently having decided upon something. She kept her eyes on her cup, but her voice was confident as she said, "You can call me Millie, Mr. MacBharrais, if ye like."

I placed a hand over my heart. "I'm deeply honored, Millie. Thank ye. You can call me Al."

ACKNOWLEDGMENTS

————— •❖• —————

A gigantic thank-you to readers of both this series and the Iron Druid Chronicles: You're the bestest. Thank you so much for coming along on this journey, and please let me pile some more thanks on you for telling your friends and family about it.

I'm grateful to Tom Hoehler and his Unnamed Cousin for finding the ideal spot for Nancy to manifest in Brooklyn.

Stu West has, throughout the series, been a delightful expert in the Weegie dialect of Scots, giving me just enough to keep things authentic without overwhelming English readers with new words. Any errors, of course, are mine and not his.

Thanks to Emily Wilson for giving the English-speaking world such fantastic translations of *The Odyssey* and *The Iliad*. The introductions to both works are revelations in themselves.

Props to the late great artist, John William Waterhouse, for his painting of *Ulysses and the Sirens*. That work, together with many classical sources that inspired it, was the basis of interpreting the sirens the way they're depicted here.

Much love to the real-life locations in Sacramento that Al visits, used here fictitiously: Capital Books on K, The Snug, B-Side, Dive Bar, WEAVEWorks Recycled Fashion, and Vizcaya.

Love also to the real-world Weegie locations used fictitiously: Gin71, The Buttery, the Glasgow Necropolis, and Ibrox Stadium. Bath Street does have a bookshop, but Gud Dug Books is entirely fictional, alas: It does reflect my wish that my local bookstore had a secret underground lair.

The castle near Stornoway is likewise a real place you can visit, but I don't recommend looking too hard for the Blue Men of the Minch, because you just might find them.

Shoutout to the amazing cover artist, Sarah J. Coleman, who penned not only this series' artwork by hand but also the gorgeous reissues of the Iron Druid Chronicles.

Grateful for the phenomenal Del Rey team: Metal Editor Tricia Narwani, Ayesha Shibli, copy editor Kathy Lord, David Moench (the G.O.A.T.), Sabrina Shen, Julie Leung, Ashleigh Heaton, Tori Henson, Alex Larned, Ted Allen, Dave Stevenson, Ada Maduka, Keith Clayton, and Scott Shannon. Major props also to the PRH Audio folks: Rob Guzman, Abby Oladipo, and Brittanie Black.

A special thank-you to narrator Luke Daniels for his outstanding years of work on these series and his readiness to take on the sometimes absurdly difficult names I throw at him.

While writing is a solitary endeavor, encouragement and support come from a wide community of folks. Thanks to Amal El-Mohtar, Stu West, and Kate Heartfield for cheese boards, coffee, and writerly companionship in Ottawa. High five as well to Brandon Crilly and Marco Cultrera for many café writing sessions; more high fives to Evan May, Marie Bilodeau, Erin Rockfort, Nathan Smith, Suyi Davies Okungbowa, and Derek Kunsken. Long-distance fist bumps to Kace Alexander and Jason Hough on the West Coast, where it is so very moist, and love to my homies Chuck Wendig and Delilah S. Dawson, who frequently share bird pics and other sanity-saving stuff with me.

Kimberly, Levi, and Mom are of course eternal fonts of love and support without which I could not exist.

To keep up with me and my future projects, please subscribe to my newsletter at wordsandbirds.ink, since social media has become an unreliable method of getting the word out.

I hope you all have enough whisky and cheese for both your gob and Lhurnog's; may you, like Gladys, see all the shite you want to see, and enjoy the bounteous wonders of Celethon in the hereafter, with good dugs and good books and plenty of that drink you like along with a comfy chair and a warm blanket. Thank you again for reading.

About the Type

This book was set in Sabon, a typeface designed by the well-known German typographer Jan Tschichold (1902–74). Sabon's design is based upon the original letter forms of sixteenth-century French type designer Claude Garamond and was created specifically to be used for three sources: foundry type for hand composition, Linotype, and Monotype. Tschichold named his typeface for the famous Frankfurt typefounder Jacques Sabon (c. 1520–80).

extras

orbit-books.co.uk

about the author

Kevin Hearne is into nature photography, heavy metal, and beard maintenance. He likes to plan road trips and sometimes even takes them. He is the *New York Times* bestselling author of the Iron Druid Chronicles, the Ink & Sigil series, and the Seven Kennings series, and is the co-author of the Tales of Pell with Delilah S. Dawson.

kevinhearne.com
Bluesky: @kevinhearne.bsky.social
Instagram: @kevinhearne

Find out more about Kevin Hearne and other Orbit authors by registering for the free monthly newslettter at orbit-books.co.uk.

if you enjoyed
CANDLE & CROW

look out for

THE MONSTERS WE DEFY

by

Leslye Penelope

Clara Johnson can talk to spirits — a gift that saved her during her darkest moments, now a curse that's left her indebted to the cunning spirit world.

So when a powerful spirit offers her an opportunity to gain her freedom, Clara seizes the chance. The task: steal a magical ring from the wealthiest woman in the District.

Clara can't pull off this daring heist alone. She'll need the help of an unlikely team: from a handsome jazz musician able to hypnotise with a melody, to an aging actor who can change his face.

But as conflict in the spirit world begins to leak into the human one — an insidious mystery is unfolding, one that could cost Clara her life.

1

THE CROSSROADS

Some folks say it wasn't just being born with a caul that made Clara Johnson ornery as a red hornet, it was being born at the crossroads. Her spirit, unlike most, had a choice to make right there at the beginning. Cold or hot, salty or sweet, lion or lamb. She came into this world through one of the forks in the road, and Clara being Clara, she chose the rockier way.

See, her mama and daddy was migrating up North from Gastonia, North Carolina, riding in the back of a wagon with her grandmother and two other distant kinfolk from down that way, when her mama's water broke. They was about to cross the Virginia state line, just outside a place called Whitetown, which didn't give nobody in that vehicle a good feeling, when they had to pull over to the side of the road—one of those roads that no Colored person wanted to be on at night—just so that gal could push that baby out.

Her mama was hollering up a storm and her daddy was holding a shotgun in one hand and his woman's hand in the other when he first caught sight of his baby girl—a slippery little thing covered head to toe with the birthing sac. Mama Octavia pushed her son aside and did what needed to be done, freeing the child so she could breathe and making sure to wrap that caul up in a sheet of newspaper and put it in her satchel.

Everybody was breathing a sigh of relief that mother and child were healthy—for a first baby she came out smooth and quick without too much bleeding or tearing or anything like that. And then that baby got to screaming. It was like to wake the dead. In fact, it did shake loose a few spirits who'd been hovering over yonder, waiting on someone like Clara to come round. And they're more than likely to do their hovering closer to a crossroads than not.

Mama Octavia sat back as her son's common-law wife tried to hush the child, and the menfolk watched the darkened road for signs of trouble. She scanned what little she could see by the moonlight and the lantern-light and caught sight of a pile of ashes and wax someone had left in the center of the crossroads. A shiver went down her spine like someone walking over her grave.

She realized her mistake, that precautions should have been taken when a child was born this close to a fork, but it was too late to do anything about it, and she didn't have the working of things the way her own grandmother had back there at Old Man Johnson's plantation, so she said a prayer for the soul of her grandbaby, hoping the child's little spirit had chosen well.

It wasn't long before she, and everyone else, found out exactly what Clara Johnson was made of. Or just what else her birth had awakened.

Clara Johnson paced the sidewalk in tight, agitated circles, trying in vain to release some of the pent-up anger welling within. "That pompous, arrogant sonofabitch," she muttered under her breath.

Her fingers coiled, pressing almost painfully against her palms, taut as the head of a drum with a tempting rhythm of rage beating against it. Like the *thump, thump* of fists meeting flesh.

Her grandmother's voice chided in her head, *You know you ain't about to fight no grown man.* Which might have been true, but that didn't mean she couldn't fantasize about kicking him in his family jewels and bruising up the face that the other girls in the office seemed to think was so handsome.

Footsteps sounded behind her, but wisely kept their distance. "Miss Clara?" a cautious voice called. She took a breath and turned slowly, grabbing hold of the trickle of calm that accompanied this distraction.

Young Samuel Foster stood watching her, more worry than wariness in his gaze. "Thought you'd left without me," he said, breaking into a grin. Tall since his recent growth spurt, with an ebony complexion, the boy would be a heartbreaker in a few years.

Clara smiled back and shook out her clenched fists. "And deprive you of the pleasure of my company?" She let out an unladylike snort. "Let's get going. Happy to leave this place behind for the weekend."

Samuel chuckled and fell into step beside her, heading toward Rhode Island Avenue. "Dr. Harley nearly made you blow your top back there. I thought for sure you was gonna let loose on him."

"Nearly did." Thoughts of the man in question and his smug, punchable face almost made her turn back. "Still might." Though higher on the food chain in the office than she, Harley wasn't really her boss, but he took great pleasure in ordering her around with his nasally whine and treating her like warmed-over trash. And while he had a good foot of height on her and probably one hundred pounds, he didn't know how to fight dirty like she did. "I'm sure I could take him. He'd probably be afraid to scuff up his shiny brogans."

Samuel shook his head, watching her carefully until the light changed, as if anxious she might really go back and start a fight. "Can't let folks like that get to you none, the ones always trying to tear you down. Nothing gets built up that way."

Clara turned sharply to look at him. From the mouths of babes.

That boy has more sense at fourteen than you do, her grandmother's voice lamented.

Blinking under the force of her scrutiny, Samuel changed the subject. "Big plans for the weekend, Miss Clara?"

She exhaled slowly, her fit of pique now almost completely dissolved, replaced with a welling sadness she refused to show. "A stack of library books is waiting on me. What about you?"

"Shifts at Mr. Davis's drugstore and making deliveries over at the print shop." His chest puffed up with pride.

"Didn't you hear, weekends are for resting?" She bumped him on the shoulder.

"Dead men can rest, until then I got to work. Got me some big dreams, Miss Clara." And a handful of younger brothers and sisters all relying on the paychecks from his various jobs, but he didn't mention that so neither did she.

"I ain't forgot," she said instead. "You gonna own one of these businesses on U Street. You figure out which one yet?"

He scratched his chin, considering. "Not quite yet. But I will."

"You keep going the way you are and you'll be working at each and every one of them."

That infectious grin returned. "I'll have one heck of a résumé, then."

Clara admired the boy's drive and determination—she wished she could borrow a little of it for herself. She was happy enough to have the one job. The big dreams she'd leave to him.

They chatted as they walked through the edge of the Washington, DC, neighborhood once known as Hell's Bottom. The intense poverty and crime had faded to the edges. Now the streets were well maintained and safe, filled with a wide range of Negroes battling the August heat.

Here were folks coming home from a long day of work whether in an office or labor yard, going to change, eat, and rest a bit before heading over to U Street for the evening. Maybe they'd take in a picture at the Lincoln or a band at Café De Luxe or maybe go dancing at the Palace. None of which Clara had ever done.

As usual, Samuel insisted on walking her to her door, though it took him several blocks out of his way. But he was resolute since it was the gentlemanly thing to do. After they said their goodbyes, he turned and ambled off, while Clara dug her key out from her purse.

The billiard parlor she lived above was still shuttered until later that evening. Miles, the owner, took Fridays off to "sleep in"—probably a good idea seeing as the place wouldn't close again until Monday morning.

Miles was a friend of her daddy's, and before he'd gone back down to North Carolina a few years ago, he'd asked the man to keep an eye on her. Miles owned the whole building and charged her a fair price for two rooms with heat and hot water, and though living here was often noisy, Clara had long ago been forced to learn to sleep through just about anything. The workweek was over and she wanted nothing more than a bath and her lumpy mattress. The heat and her receding anger had left her bone-tired. She turned the key in the door, ready to shut out the world for the weekend.

"Miss Johnson? Miss Clara Johnson?" Her shoulders tensed at the lilting voice calling her name. All she had to do was twist the doorknob and slip inside, pretend she hadn't heard.

It could just be one of her neighbors—the voice was unfamiliar, but she had more of a "nod as you pass by" relationship with them than a speaking one. Ruth Anne, the woman who ran the beauty parlor next door, often looked like she wanted to start a conversation. And it wouldn't be too unusual for folks to know her name—every Negro in the city knew her name at one time.

But the questioning, halting tone to the voice made her almost certain this was no neighbor. The urge to slide inside the narrow vestibule and slam the door in the face of her would-be questioner was strong. However, the husky voice whispering in her mind minced no words. *Gal, you better turn your narrow tail around and see what that young woman wants!*

Clara sighed deeply, and pressed her forehead against the wood of the door.

I know you hear me talking to you, Clara Mae. Best not ignore me.

"Yes, ma'am," she uttered under her breath and turned around.

The girl standing on the curb behind her looked like she'd been cut from the pages of a magazine. Her chestnut hair was smartly pressed and curled—immune, it seemed, to Washington's formidable humidity—with a fashionable cloche hat perfectly positioned on her head.

Her face was somewhat plain, but you'd never know it from the way she carried herself. She looked several years younger than Clara, maybe eighteen or so, wearing a green silk dress and shiny patent leather oxfords.

"Miss Johnson," she said, holding her hand out. "I'm Louise Wyatt, and I need your help."

A stinging sensation nettled Clara, uncomfortable and insistent, locking her into action. It wasn't due to the heat or the traffic; this was pure magic. She could not deny someone who came to her for help, that was the deal she'd made when she was about Louise's age—and one she could never ignore. Guilt for something that hadn't even happened yet attached itself to her like a suit of armor.

"Come inside, then," she grumbled and pushed the door open.